Gadiantons
and the
Silver Sword

By
Chris Heimerdinger

For Jim Brogan,
who inspired it.

And for Jorge Riveros and Edgar Corral,
who shared in it.

Covenant Communications, Inc.
Library of Congress Catalog Number 90–086122
Gadiantons and the Silver Sword
First Printing February 1991
Second Printing April 1991
Third Printing February 1992
Fourth Printing November 1992
ISBN 1–55503–315–6

Acknowledgments

I feel compelled to recognize the efforts and encouragements of several persons without whom this work would not have been pursued with as much vigor and dedication. I thank Daniel Schlyter, whose critique of the first draft saved me immense embarrassment, Joseph Allen, whose Spanish translations were offered freely and cheerfully, Lee Simons of *Deseret Book* in the University Mall in Orem, Utah, whose bubbling enthusiasm toward my first book gave me the confidence I needed to write another, and finally, my wife, Beth, my first and foremost critic, and the one whose comments make me the most angry—though I've discovered it's the criticisms which make you the most angry, which are usually the most correct.

PROLOGUE

I remember the fog, twisting just below the summit like icy white fingers around a helpless victim's throat. The hill was very high, almost too high to be called a hill, and it was blanketed by an Eden-kissed jungle, rife with every life-sound that God ever saw fit to give a single patch of earth. But the summit itself appeared barren, only a tiny cluster of trees, cushioned in a nest of billowing grasses, and silhouetted against an angering sky. In the center of it all was the blackened trunk of a lightning-scarred tree, the fire having long since consumed its branches. This trunk marked the very pinnacle of the hill, nature's totem, jutting skyward to remind us in which direction we might find heaven.

Blinking my eyes, I saw a man standing there as well, a product of the mist. His head was hoary, his features were olive and aquiline, and his garments were reminiscent of an ancient and idyllic age. He stretched out his arm and earnestly beckoned me toward him, as if nothing else mattered, as if my communion was his last vestige of hope. So I began walking, but he never drew nearer. In spite of my determination, and the quickening of my pace, I couldn't seem to reach him.

This was my dream, the only dream of the night, Saturday, August 8th, three weeks before I returned to BYU to face my Junior year.

The same night as the accident.

CHAPTER 1

You know what frustrates me about girls? They're like a pound cake in a hot oven. If you don't let 'em cook for just the right amount of time—if you open the oven too soon by letting 'em know you *like* them or some terrible thing like that—then you've got yourself a tortilla instead of a cake. My problem is, I ain't much of a cook.

This girl had been hittin' on me for weeks. Every morning I'd pass by her window on the way to my nine o'clock class and she'd be patiently perched behind a bowl of *Honey Nut Cheerios*, waiting for me to pop into view. Then she would wink—a perfect, methodical wink, like she was in a play in the De Jong Concert Hall and had to communicate the gesture to the balcony's back row. I would smile the 'kool smile' and send her a coy, two-fingered wave, walking by with my pectorals pumped higher than was natural. How I looked forward to this game every morning as I left my apartment.

This girl rivaled the most beautiful creatures I'd ever seen. There was something about long hair, black as ebony, and stormy eyes with a shine in them like a distant lighthouse, that had always melted my heart, as far back as I can remember. I lay awake a night or two wondering how I might influence fate and meet this girl. Fate was good to me one Friday after my American Heritage class.

I was passing through the Wilkinson Center enroute to my car which was parked next to the Law Building when—

lo and behold!—she was seated on the bench beside the courtesy phones. After dousing myself in an unction of charm, I moved in for the kill.

"Well, hi!" I called over to her.

She looked up at me with a blank, confused expression, as if she'd never seen me before.

Awkwardly, I identified myself, "I live in the other ward at King's Court Arms."

No response. "I, uh, pass by your window in the mornings."

"Oh, you do?"

This moment should have been my first clue. She didn't fool me. This chick knew darn well who I was. A little red "trouble" light when off inside, but all my God-given instincts about life and women were clouded by those eyes of hers. I introduced myself as the notorious Jim Hawkins.

Her name was Renae Fenimore and she was free that night.

I might have overdone it a little: New wardrobe at *Jean's West*, a splash of my roommate's *Polo*, flowers from *Gary's Floral*, dinner at *Magelby's*, sundaes at *Carousel*, topped off by a starry night drive that took us to Utah Lake and around the Provo Temple.

For all that, a guy might feel he deserves a goodnight kiss. But see, being a returned missionary, and being the 2nd Counselor in my Elder's Quorum, and being an all-around upstanding kind of guy . . . .

Okay, so I was a little disappointed when she didn't grant me a goodnight kiss. Instead, she slipped inside her apartment without so much as a handshake. I'd have gone to sleep that night sulking if I hadn't heard her sultry voice beckon me back. Renae leaned out the door, her hair dancing in rhythm with the soft October breeze, and blew me a kiss. The kiss hit me hard. In fact, I think it knocked me unconscious, because I don't remember driving home that night.

Maybe I got a bit impetuous. By the second date I was already imagining which temple we'd be married in. She must have seen the 'Moroni spire' in my eyes because her attitude grew real chilly. On our third date she sat me down in a booth at the *Cougareat* and flogged me with a speech about moving too fast and feeling overwhelmed and dating other people and . . . .

She went on, but I was too busy sweeping pieces of my heart off the floor to listen.

Afterwards I punched myself in the mirror. I knew better! I'd only played this dating game for six years! (Well, four if you subtract my years in the mission field—but still!) Anybody knows you don't call a girl every night after making her acquaintance. They think you've got no taste, like you could fall in love with anybody. Can I help it if I recognize a good thing when I see it?

As the weeks slipped by, I'd pretty much consigned myself to the fact that if Renae and I had signed a marriage contract in the pre-existence, the angels had torn it in half. I was just getting ready to cut loose my heart strings and let it brave the elements again when I learned that my roommate, Andrew, had asked Renae to Homecoming—and Renae had had the nerve to accept!

Andrew! Of all people! Andrew Southwick was the most obnoxious of my BYU roommates—past, present, and future; a California money Mormon who lets you smell his family's wealth in everything he wears, everything he says, how he acts, and what he drives. All the apartment's amenities were his: the VCR, the TV, the microwave, the stereo. Of course, we could use his stuff anytime we wanted—as long as there wasn't something *he* wanted to watch, listen to, or cook. In such cases he'd toss someone else's sandwich out of the microwave with thirty seconds left and replace it with his own.

Our apartment was one of those privacy models with four single bedrooms and two bathrooms. Two people shared one bathroom and two shared the other. I was the unfortunate sap who got the quarters opposite Andrew. Having carefully timed the available hot water, he insisted I be out of the shower in precisely seven minutes and twenty seconds or the thump, thump of his fist would echo on the bathroom door. On occasion I'd endure some scorching showers to try disrupting Andrew's timing system and give him a nice chill.

In one respect Andrew reminded me of an old childhood friend of mine named Garth Plimpton. Both Garth and Andrew were voracious readers. They'd practically committed to memory every Church book and commentary ever printed—though their conclusions about such material seemed diametrically opposed.

The only time I found Andrew even remotely entertaining was when our apartment engaged in intellectual conversations about the gospel—which was almost nightly. Andrew always took on the role of 'Devil's Advocate'—a role in which he seemed quite at home. When I got off my mission I'd have sworn I knew *everything* about the gospel. But Andrew trumpeted controversies even the most flagrant anti-Mormons never knew existed. He was a genius in getting Benny and I so twisted in our words, we had to throw up our hands and parrot, "All I know is, the Church is true," which, of course, only sated Andrew's ego.

I used to wish Garth were around at these moments. Certainly he'd consumed much the same books and pondered all the same issues, seeking answers through a completely different spirit. Mr. California seriously needed a slice of humble pie, but Garth Plimpton was far across the country, a busy undergrad in Archeology at Harvard.

Now my next roommate, Lars Packard, was a different egg altogether. Though he and I never 'bucked heads' so to speak, I'd still put him in the category of the 'weirdest' roommate I ever had. Lars was a UFO nut. All over his room were posters and newspaper clippings of flying saucers, aliens, documented sightings, Easter Island—you name it. If it had to do with close encounters between humans and little green men, Lars was the resident expert. He belonged to UFO clubs all over the country. During our apartment's gospel discussions he'd often chime in with a view that was more off-the-wall than all of ours put together. Lars was always trying to tie extra-terrestrial phenomenon and Mormonism together. The guy was bizarre, but at least he was docile. Lars didn't have much of a social life. He spent most of the time secluded in his room reading or playing with his computer. He never served a mission—at least not yet—and if he went to church, it wasn't at our student ward. With his family living as close as Sandy, Utah, he zipped home every weekend.

My obituary would have read "Jim Hawkins died of insanity his Junior Year at BYU," if it hadn't been for Benny. Benny Burns and I had become friends the previous winter semester as sophomore residents in the on-campus housing establishment of Heritage Halls. Come the conclusion of winter semester, we both committed to finding an apartment with single rooms. Thus, when we discovered King's Court Arms, we'd nailed two birds with one stone—a single room, and at least *one* roommate we could get along with.

Benny had only one character flaw. He was *too much* like me. I suffered from the same ailment Joseph Smith once tagged onto himself during those obscure days before translating the Book of Mormon. He diagnosed it as levity. What I had was a worse case of the same disease. That is, the tendency to take nothing in life seriously—not even church. Unfortunately, Benny had the same problem. During the first few months of my Junior year, being around Benny, my attitude became more and more cynical, my sense of humor got more and more 'off-color,' and my convictions grew more and more lax.

In spite of all this, would you believe they called me to the Elder's Quorum Presidency? I was the worst second counselor in Latter-day history. Though it was my duty to set the example, I probably went home teaching once all semester—and that was only because I heard she was cute. Part of the problem was assigning Benny as my companion. He spent all his extra hours cultivating a year-old romance with a brunette named Allison, so we let the months slip by and justified the whole thing by saying students don't really want to be home taught anyway.

Every better habit I thought had frozen solid in my psyche during my two-year mission in Oregon appeared to be crumbling away. In Oregon the spirit had seemed as bold and readable as a *New York Times* headline. Coming home, I was so frustrated with the lack of fire in my ward, I considered putting them all on report with the First Presidency.

Only a short year later, I found it a real struggle to get through a single chapter of scripture. I was lucky if I prayed once every other night—or maybe it was once every third night. Three hours in church was like an eternity of watching paint dry. Sometimes I'd just take the sacrament and go home.

I knew my attitude was wrong. I knew it was *really* wrong, but I couldn't seem to muster the energy to turn things around. I guess I thought I needed to get married. That would be the perfect excuse to end my gospel vacation.

Thanksgiving was looming on the horizon only four days away. A big reunion was scheduled in my home town, Cody, Wyoming. My oldest brother, Mitch, and his family were flying out from Virginia. My second oldest brother, Steven, and his family were driving over from the nearby town of Lovell. And the newlyweds!—my third oldest brother, Judd, and his new wife, Krystal, would be driving down from Billings, Montana. My Uncle Spence and Aunt Louise would be there. Even my little sister, Jenny, the BYU Sophomore, was adding to the crowd by bringing home a new boyfriend. Including my parents, our house would face an awesome army of sixteen people!

The timing for me was all too perfect. I desperately needed to breath the ole' homestead air again and reorient my bearings. That's why I was so taken back, so dumbfounded, when I called home and got such an unexpected reaction.

My mother picked up the receiver.

"Hey! How's my favorite mom!"

"Jamie?" Mom confirmed. She was the only person on earth allowed to address me by my true given name.

I continued, "Just calling to let you know we'll be leaving here about ten o'clock Wednesday morning, so don't expect us till around six. Unless, of course, *I* drive the whole way, in which case, we should be there for lunch—"

"*Jamie,*" my mother repeated, cutting me off. Her voice was unusually tense. "Maybe you shouldn't come home right now."

My jaw dropped.

"Excuse me?" I said, hoping my mother had developed a

sense of humor similar to mine, and was thus giving me a taste of my own medicine.

"I don't think it would be safe. There are people looking for you. Were you 'into something' last summer?"

My mother was truly shaken up.

"What are you talking about?" I insisted.

"Like drugs or . . . I know you wouldn't be involved in anything like that—but maybe you made some people angry?"

I couldn't believe I was hearing this.

"Mom, you're sounding crazy. I don't have the foggi-est—"

My dad came on the line. "Jim?"

"Dad, what's going on?"

"We need *you* to tell *us*. Some men came to the house. One on Friday and three others less than an hour ago. They were looking for you."

"What for?"

"Jim, please don't hold out on us. Your mother is very frightened."

"Dad, I promise, I have *absolutely* no idea."

"The one on Friday acted friendly enough in the beginning. He asked where you were. We told him you were off at school and that you'd be home for Thanksgiving. He asked when Thanksgiving was—which we found odd enough—but when we asked for his name so we could pass on any messages, the man walked off, refusing to answer!"

"Did he say what he wanted?"

"No, he never did. Jim, *think*. For your mother's sake—who *are* these people?"

"I couldn't even begin to guess, Dad."

"The men tonight wanted to know the same thing—where you were and when you'd be home. This time, your mother wouldn't tell them. The one who knocked asked us another question as well. It was very unusual. He asked if you owned a sword."

"A what?!"

"A metal sword," Dad repeated. "Then he gave us a warning. It almost sounded like a threat. He said if the first man returned, we should *kill* him. Not send him away. Not have him arrested. He said 'kill' and he *meant* it. That's what's got us so upset."

"Dad, this is *insane!*"

"We've called the police. The first man has been back since. We saw him standing under the streetlight in front of Molhollend's yard when we came home last night. He was watching the house."

"This is nuts," I proclaimed. "What am I supposed to do?"

"Don't misunderstand us, son. We want you to come home. We've been looking forward to it. But I'm not sure it would be safe. If only you could give us some idea—"

"Dad, I *need* to come home."

There was silence on the line. It seemed like forever.

My dad finally spoke, "I'm not going to tell you *not* to come home, Jim. I just wish we could get to the bottom of this beforehand."

"It seems to me the only way we can do that is if I come home. What did they look like? Can you describe them to me?"

"Indian," my dad answered, "They all looked sort of Indian. Not quite like the ones around here but—the first one was even dressed like one."

CHAPTER 2

I thought I'd felt every range of emotion in my twenty-two years on earth, but paranoia was new to me, and I wasn't quite sure how to deal with it.

Though I'd convinced my dad I had no explanation for the mysterious visitors, I racked my brain to think of who they could be. What might have happened this summer to inspire anyone to seek me out? For the most part my summer vacation had been dreadfully dull—six days a week of digging irrigation ditches up the North Fork. There wasn't much opportunity for making peculiar acquaintances.

One thing my dad mentioned in our phone conversation did strike a chord. It was the business about the sword.

One Saturday in August, I worked an unusually long day in the trenches, unable to break away until shortly before dark. Driving back into town, I came upon the aftermath of a terrible accident.

There's a stretch of highway west of Cody locals call "Colter's Hell,"—so named for a deep chasm of the Shoshoni River Canyon running parallel to the road. That night the name was most appropriate for a new reason.

Some guy had been wandering in the middle of the road at twilight, perhaps a little tipsy from an evening's merriment at the nearby Bronze Boot Nightclub. An oncoming car killed him instantly, then skidded out of control, smashing through the guard rail.

Arriving seconds after impact, I found the '85 Buick Skyhawk teetering on the cliff edge—a seventy-five foot plummet into the shallow, swift river. The lady inside the Buick was frozen with fear, knowing the slightest move would topple her vehicle. My efforts to talk her out were futile—and every few seconds I heard rocks grinding under the chassis as her car continued to slide. If I didn't act immediately, I'd spend the rest of my life wondering if my hesitation had cost this lady her life.

Tossing open the door, I got a firm grip on her wrist just as the car began to drop away. This lady was not under-weight, so I have to credit a little help from both heaven and my adrenal glands. As the Buick fell, flipping end-over-end and smashing on the river rocks below, we were both safely lying in the stickery weeds near the edge of the road.

Within five minutes, two patrol cars had arrived, and soon after that, an ambulance. Because of the other motorists that had gathered, I never got close enough to see the pedestrian before they took him away, but I overheard the police saying the victim had no identification. Nobody seemed to know who he was or where he'd come from. Someone also mentioned he'd been oddly dressed.

Wandering over to the edge one last time, I gazed down at the hulk of overturned automobile. There was barely enough light to see the river swirling around its tires. I shuddered at how close that lady had come to going down with the ship. Maybe I'd been delayed at work that day for good reason. It didn't occur to me at the time that Providence may have had more motives than one.

Lifting my eyes from the accident, I noticed something flicker on a cliff shelf just below where the pedestrian's body had landed. In spite of the dim light, I was drawn toward it, and found myself carefully climbing down to see what it was. Upon reaching the shelf, my fist wrapped around the hilt of a shiny silver sword. It was quite heavy, with polished stones inlayed into the metal base. The blade was razor-sharp on both edges, stretching all the way from my hip to my ankle, and topped by a triangular tip. The surface appeared to be a plating of silver, and there were tiny places where the surface had been chipped away, and a rusty, copper-looking metal was visible underneath.

My first feelings, as I lifted the sword, were strangely diametric. First I was repulsed, as if touching something dead. Then I felt exhilarated, as if I drew a kind of energy from this object. I envisioned myself a dauntless knight in King Arthur's court, looking across 'Colter's Hell' for dragons and damsels. The voice of Officer Finlay broke my spell. Todd Finlay was a thin man with sandy blonde hair, a drooping face and gold-rimmed glasses. Unfortunately, he wasn't one of the more respected members of Cody's police force. Locals put him in a category much more akin to Barney Fife than Joe Friday.

With his thumbs in the loops of his belt, Finlay watched me climb back up the cliff, the sword dragging at my heel. Intrigued, he took my discovery in both hands, touching his index finger to the edge. The metal sliced into his flesh like butter, and a drop of blood trickled down the blade. Cursing, Finlay dropped the sword and wrapped his bleeding appendage in a Kleenex.

The lady who'd driven the Buick said the sword wasn't hers. Whether it had been knocked out of the pedestrian's arms on impact, or whether it had been there on that ledge all along, I had no way of knowing. Officer Finlay said he'd have to put it on file at the police station. If it was still unclaimed in ninety days, I could have it back. Those ninety days had expired the first week in November. Dad's statement reminded me of my intention to see if it was still there when I got home for Thanksgiving.

It was hard to focus on school those last two days before vacation. There was an exam in my Doctrine and Covenants class on Tuesday, and I greatly feared I would bomb it. Benny planted me down at the kitchen table on Monday evening to review the test questions.

"Which section discusses eternal marriage? Quick! No time to think!" he cried.

"Section one-hundred and thirty," I answered.

Benny made a sound like a penalty buzzer. "Wrong! One hundred and thirty-*two*."

Heaving a sigh, I mourned, "I'm gonna need a miracle tomorrow."

"Don't sweat it," offered Andrew, slicing tomatoes for a BLT. "No career recruiter is gonna care what your religion grades were."

"They will if it takes my GPA below 3.0," I responded.

"I'm tempted to say," started Andrew, pulling his bacon strips out of the microwave and carefully unraveling them from the grease-soaked paper towel, "our required religion credits are a sore waste of time. I'm glad I got them out of the way as a sophomore."

"I think the idea," Benny replied, "was to take one religion class every semester so we could—"

"—keep a balanced curriculum," finished Andrew. "Yes, I know. I suppose that's good for the proletariat, but the fact is, I could teach circles around most of the religion professors *I've* had at BYU."

I wanted to believe Andrew's overbearing manner was simply the result of deeply sown insecurities, but I picked up no such hints. Andrew seemed convinced of his intellectual superiority and he made no apologies for it.

"Maybe in details," I defended, "but not in doctrine."

Now I'd done it. Study time was over. Them was fightin' words and Andrew wasn't about to let them slide.

"I don't understand your distinction," he challenged. "Details *are* doctrine."

"With you it's facts without spirit," I asserted.

I wish I'd sounded righteously indignant instead of desperate. Until I'd forgotten Homecoming and his shanghai of Renae, I couldn't claim to be neutral about anything Andrew said or did. The bottom line was, I was in no spiritual condition to pass judgement on anyone.

"Well, I'm not an apologist, if that's what you mean."

I didn't quite get what he meant, but I wasn't about to ask. It didn't matter. He assessed our ignorance quite readily and proceeded with an explanation.

"In other words, I don't expend vast amounts of energy,

like most Latter-day Saints, justifying contradictions in LDS history and doctrine."

"What contradictions are you talking about?" Benny countered. Then, as if acknowledging human weakness, which prophets and church leaders were always free to admit, he clarified by adding, "You're not gonna find any contradictions in the scriptures." Then, as if remembering Joseph Smith's proclamation that the Bible was only true so far as it was translated correctly, he further added, "at least not in the Book of Mormon or the Doctrine and Covenants."

Andrew gracefully spread a layer of mayonnaise on his toast, "Oh, don't be so sure. The D&C section you just mentioned contains one of the most glaring contradictions in all Mormonism."

"What do you mean?" Benny asked hesitantly.

"Section One-thirty-two," Andrew reminded him. "That's where Joseph Smith declared polygamy a principle of God, in spite of the fiery sermon denouncing such practices in the second chapter of Jacob."

"Now hold on," Benny said, grabbing his 'three-in-one' like it was a Colt 45. He turned to the book of Jacob.

Andrew balanced his sandwich in both hands, devouring it as confidently as he felt he was devouring our egos.

"Let me save you some time," he offered between chomps. "Read Jacob 2:24."

Benny read, "'Behold, David and Solomon truly had many wives and concubines, which thing was abominable before me saith the Lord.'"

"Now read D&C 132:38"

Benny read, "'David also received many wives and concubines, and also Solomon and Moses my servants, as also many others of my servants, from the beginning of creation until this time; and in nothing did they sin save in those things which they received not of me.'"

Andrew swallowed his last bite of sandwich and sat back in his chair, swabbing a spot of mayonnaise off the corner of his mouth with a napkin, "So in one scripture it's all 'abominable' and in the next, it's divinely sanctioned, save in those things which they received not of the Lord. Even the concubines were approved!" He mocked our supposed western drawls. "Now if'n you don't think that there's a contradiction, I suggest you take a course in basic logic."

"You're pulling it out of context," Benny accused.

Andrew shrugged, "So read it in context. You'll come to the same conclusion. In fact verse 39 of Section 132 solidifies the problem even further. There are several other errors I could point out, but I've got homework."

Andrew arose and started for his bedroom. Benny interrupted him for one last question.

"If you're so sure of all these errors, how come you're still a member of the Church? Do you have a testimony?"

Andrew grinned, "Of course. I'm at BYU, aren't I?"

Andrew disappeared into his room and closed the door, leaving Benny and I to wallow in the spirit of contention left behind.

"Well?" asked Benny.

"Well, what?" I responded.

"What's the solution?"

"I don't know," I answered.

"Then is he right? Is it a contradiction?"

I shrugged.

Some General Authority once said that an anti-Christ was anyone who tried to destroy another person's testimony. It seemed to me that Andrew, in spite of taking the sacrament every Sunday, was guilty of that objective on more than one occasion. Still, I couldn't put the blame on Andrew. We'd asked for it as certainly as ordering a hamburger. Andrew was the calm, reserved one. It was the two of us—and particularly Benny—who got genuinely upset.

"Benny," I said, "You can bet Andrew's not the first one to discover such things."

Benny nodded slowly, staring off into space.

"Hey," I told him, "the Church *is* still true."

Benny crinkled his face and huffed, feigning insult that I would think his testimony could be so easily shaken.

"I know that!"

Benny went to grab his coat off the couch. "I gotta meet Allison."

As was typical these days, when Benny got upset, he retreated to the arms of his girlfriend.

Lars, the UFO freak, had been on the couch with his nose buried in an engineering textbook during the whole conversation. When there was a lull, he looked up to ask me if I'd like to attend a Wednesday night meeting of the newest UFO sensation in Utah. This club was the best, he said, and it was even based in Salt Lake.

"They're called the Bernardians, because they believe in advanced alien life on the second planet of Bernard's Star—eight light years from Earth," he explained. "If I bring someone else, I don't have to pay dues."

"I'll be on the road to Cody," I apologized.

"I'll go with you, Lars" offered Benny, zipping his coat, "*If* you drop me off at the Salt Lake airport afterwards. My flight leaves at 11:10."

"Deal," agreed Lars. "I think you'll like it. Don't let what Andrew says get you down. Remember, ours is the only religion on earth that clearly teaches there's life on other planets. If you need your testimony re-confirmed, one of those meetings is the best way I know."

Looking away, I rolled my eyes. If it took a UFO club to confirm man's testimony of truth, humanity had sunk to a sorry state indeed.

For all I knew, a mafia assassin could have been waiting in the back seat of my Mazda 626—or rather, Jenny's Mazda 626—when I went down to the parking lot on Wednesday morning. To my relief, there was no shootout. I was starting to think there was a completely rational explanation for what had happened in Cody and that my parents had over-reacted.

Since Jenny lived in campus housing, she let me use her car most of the semester. At times she griped that I should buy my own wheels, but to be honest, I think Jen was suffering from a kind of driving phobia. Even when we were together, she insisted that I sit behind the wheel. While I was gone on my mission Jenny had a close scrape with two oncoming trucks on a two-lane road. Ever since then, she seemed more content to be a passenger.

I filled up with gas at the *Quick Stop*, bought some tortilla chips and other assorted munchies to make us all as ill as possible before arriving, then headed up to Heritage Halls to pick up my sister and her new boyfriend.

I think Jenny and I were about as close as a brother and sister could ever get. I'm not saying there weren't times we didn't want to pull each other's hair out—it wouldn't be a true brother/sister relationship if there weren't such moments. But there was a unique bond between us—I can't quite explain it—but it tended to make me over-protective. Ever since Jen had blossomed into a Cover-Girl caliber blonde in high school, there was a lot to be over-protective about.

Jenny would have intimidated most guys into oblivion if not for her special talent: she was an expert flirt—the kind about whom legends are told. She knew how to get the shy types to make the first move; how to get the 'God's gift' types to think she was the only girl on earth; and how to get the "no-time-for-social-life" types to flunk their classes. Her problem was, she was *so* good at flirting, she never acquired an instinct for selectivity. That's why she respected *my* opinion so much.

I felt my future brother-in-law should be . . . well, like me!—handsome, amiable, and street-smart. However, he must rise above me in spiritual areas—be the most turbo-stalwart priesthood holder ever to grace the gospel. Not a wishy-washy, 'question-everything' wimp like myself.

Her latest catch had the name of Parley, which I suppose is forgivable—certainly not his sin, but his parents'. The guy was built like a tank, towering about 6'4"—and that was *without* the cowboy boots. My 5'3" sister needed an elevator just to get a goodnight kiss.

Parley must have been briefed about the importance of my opinion. Thus he thought it best that I be cowed into complacency. As he approached me to offer greetings he took three gargantuan strides, causing me to wonder if it were possible for him to stop before I'd be trampled into the pavement. But stop he did, and at just the right distance to be sure our 'look up to' and 'look down upon' relationship was established from the beginning. Then the cowboy stuck his tongue in his right cheek and exhaled the words, "How ya doin'?"

"Real good," I replied with a squeak.

He then took my fingers into the vise-grip otherwise known as his right palm and proceeded to crush them together while hiding behind the pretense that we were shaking hands.

"Jenny's told me a lot abou'cha."

"And you believed her?" I said.

Parley raised an eyebrow in confusion.

My sister giggled and slapped my arm. "Oh, come on," she teased. "There's only great things to tell."

Just then it hit Parley that I was joking. He pretended a belated laugh, which sounded worse than if he hadn't laughed at all.

Only eight hours to go, I thought.

Jennifer opted to take the front seat, which didn't set too well with Parley. I think he was expecting to cuddle with her in the back the whole trip with me as chauffeur.

"So how long you two been datin'?" I asked along the interstate between Park City and Evanston, Wyoming.

"A little less than a month," Jenny answered. "Par and I met on the fifth floor of the library."

"And the rest is history," added Parley, reaching his hands around to give Jenny a shoulder massage.

"Things must be going well," I concluded, "if she's already inviting you to Thanksgiving dinner."

"Oh, that was Par's idea," Jen corrected.

"Oh, yeah?" I said.

"Yep," Parley confirmed. "You got an awfully special sister here, Jim. I had to see what kind of parents would raise such a girl."

The fog was rising off this scenario. My sister had woven her web a little tighter than she'd realized and now this poor lug was under the impression he couldn't live without her. Stopping for fuel in Rock Springs, Jenny followed me to the cashier to ask me what I thought of him.

"Well, he's the *biggest* one I think you've ever caught."

"But do you like him?"

"What do *you* think of him?" I hedged.

"I think he's sweet. Not as sweet as Bryan, but sweet."

"Bryan? I must have missed that boyfriend. When did you break *his* heart?"

"I didn't break his heart. We had a mutual agreement to start dating other people."

Renae taught me the true definition of that line. "In other words, you dropped him like lead balloon."

"He was getting too attached."

"So what's the story with *this* one? Are you in love with him?"

"Do you think I should be?"

I paused in writing out the check to the cashier. I don't think he minded. He seemed to be enjoying the conversation. "Jenny, if you're not sure of your feelings, don't you think you might be misleading the guy by inviting him home to meet your parents?"

"He said he had no place to go for Thanksgiving. I couldn't feel good about leaving him in Provo. Besides, with all the strange people coming up to the house, you could use a bodyguard, right?"

"Jenny, you can't play with guys' heads like this!"

The male cashier looked at Jenny and nodded in agreement.

"I'm not!" she defended. "I mean . . . I don't know what I want. Parley seems to have all the right characteristics. He's loyal. He's responsible. He's 'teddy-bear' cute! He's also got a job lined up in sports medicine after he graduates. I need my family to help me decide who I should fall in love with."

"Why can't you just trust your feelings?"

"For the same reason I need to rent videos from *7-11* instead of *Blockbuster*."

"Huh?"

"There's too much to choose from at *Blockbuster*. They all look so good. I have no objectivity. I sometimes spend as much time deciding on a video as it would have taken to watch it. Then I choose something lousy. I need a *7-11* social life. I can't handle *Blockbuster*."

The cashier looked as perplexed by Jen's analogy as I was. If only Jenny knew how grateful some of us would have been with as many options as *7-11*.

Four hours later I could see the peaks of Cedar and Rattlesnake Mountains rising in the foreground. And not a moment too soon before Parley could begin another Pollack joke. The climate was at least ten degrees colder up here than it was in Provo. Though the ground was free of snow, which was a bit unusual for this time of year, Beck Lake had a thin sheet of ice kissing the surface. As we rounded the turn in the highway that brought us into Cody's city limits, I couldn't help but feel my hometown was rather quiet for 6:00 p.m. There were only a few cars on the road and only a handful of customers in the parking lot at K-Mart.

I might've thought it was "High Noon." The train had just come to town and I was on it. In anticipation of a showdown, the townsfolk were clearing the streets.

Ah, don't be ridiculous, I thought. There were no villains in black hats waiting at the corner next to McDonalds as we turned off the main strip and headed into the residential neighborhood. Again I decided it was all some big misunderstanding.

But if that were true, why was I biting my fingernails at the same time I was turning the steering wheel. Why did I feel unwelcome in my own hometown, as if there were a voice in the icy wind urging me to turn around?

CHAPTER 3

Pulling into our old familiar driveway gave me a rush of relief. This was home base; nobody could tag me 'it.' I parked behind my Dad's Ford Taurus and beside my brother Steven's Toyota Celica. Looking down the street, I saw an old lady making her way along the sidewalk in front of the Watkin's house, enjoying an evening stroll through the crisp, holiday season air. Looking the other way, I found the streets were empty. Whoever my parents thought was prowling the neighborhood must have taken a few days off to spend Thanksgiving with relatives.

My mother greeted us all with her usual warmth, even offering Parley a hug, saying, "Since you're here for Thanksgiving you might as well consider yourself one of the family."

Everyone had arrived except Mitch and Judd and their respective clans. My Uncle Spencer waved to us enthusiastically from the couch, sandwiched between two throw pillows, watching the opening kick-off of one of the various football games. My older brother Steven was beside him chewing chunks of ice from a tall glass, as was his trademark. My two-year-old nephew, Cory, was busy pulling pots and pans out of the cupboard. When he saw Jenny and me, he dashed over for a hug from his favorite uncle and aunt.

I got my fair share of "How are ya?"s and "How's

school?"s but it wasn't long before Dad brought up the subject on everyone's mind.

"Have you figured out who these people are yet?" he asked.

"No, Dad," I replied.

"That man—the first one who came to the door—was waiting on the corner in front of Molhollend's driveway when I came home from work," Dad reported.

Dad got home from his job as superintendent of Cody Public Schools at five p.m. That meant someone had been there only an hour before we'd pulled up.

Dad added, "The police are starting to think I've lost a few nuts and bolts. I've asked them to drive by the house six times in the last four days. Each time they come, the man is gone. I don't want you going out of the house this weekend, Jim."

"Dad, I can't live that way," I protested. "If they want to talk, I'll talk. I've got nothing to hide."

Parley stepped over to us at that moment and promised, "I'll stay with him every minute, Mr. H. If anybody tries anything, they'll have to deal with me."

"Thanks, I can take care of myself," I said.

Parley sniggered at that concept and walked away. Nevertheless, my dad was somewhat comforted by Parley's proposal of help, so I agreed to let Parley tag along whenever I left the house. That opportunity first presented itself shortly after eight o'clock. Tonight was pie-making night for my mother and my Aunt Louise. In bygone years I remembered Mom waiting until Thanksgiving Day to bake such confections, but the convenience of warm pie via the microwave had shattered such traditions. The house was smothering in the aromas of cherry, blueberry, pumpkin, pecan, and lemon meringue. The anticipation was too torturous for a household already infested by five ravenous males. It was mutually agreed upon by Dad, Steven, Parley, Uncle Spencer, and I that the blueberry pie would not live to see Thanksgiving Day. But the grief we felt upon discovering there was no vanilla ice cream to accompany it was too tragic for words. I found myself volunteering my services for the arduous task of going to *Steck's IGA* in quest of ice cream and a few other crucial items that mother realized were missing for tomorrow's feast. My father objected at first, offering to go himself, but I knew the game on television was one he'd anxiously awaited, so I sat him back down in his Lazy Boy and whistled for Parley.

Stepping out onto our front porch, a shrill wind had crept out of the canyon, making the chill factor much worse than the temperature. The streetlights were blazing and the stars were shrouded by a thin sheet of cumulus. Exhaling, my vision was blurred by my own vapors, but when it cleared, I could see a figure standing under the light post on the corner across the street, in front of Molhollend's yard. Parley saw him as well and leapt from the porch, taking several threatening strides across the lawn.

"Hey!" he yelled, surely awakening anybody who might be asleep in this neighborhood or the neighboring neighborhood. "You got somethin' to say? Come here and say it!"

But the man had already scampered around the high wood fence on the northern edge of the Molhollend's lawn and disappeared.

Parley looked as though he might take off to catch the man. I jumped after him to grab his arm.

"Parley," I cried, "If you scare him away for good, I might *never* know what's going on!"

"Just lettin' him know we can't be intimidated," said Parley.

The parking lot at *Steck's IGA* was not well lit, and it hosted only four or five cars, which seemed kind of unusual for the night before a major holiday. There was a video store situated right in the entranceway at *Steck's*. As the sliding glass door closed out the cold behind us, Parley delegated me to find the groceries while he selected a couple of movies.

"You like Chuck Norris?" he asked.

"Make a stack and I'll tell you which ones Mom might allow beyond the front door." With that, I went through the second set of doors into the main part of the store.

There was only one cashier working. She had a line three

persons deep and a conveyor belt loaded down with Butterball turkeys. Otherwise the store was remarkably quiet. I yanked a shopping cart out from under another and proceeded to make my way toward the dairy section along the back wall to fill my mother's request for eggs and eggnog.

I stood beside the egg rack, deciding between large or extra-large. The place was so still I could hear the phosphorescent lights buzzing overhead. I happened to glance toward the frozen foods aisle and saw a man standing there, watching me through a Western Family Macaroni display—failing miserably if he had any intention of appearing discreet. The man was old and wizened as if he suffered from a kind of cancer, or as if some creature which made a habit out of sucking life from the human soul had latched onto his face. He was dressed almost comically—like a duck hunter—a bright red vest, khaki pants, hiking boots and a visor cap which read "Wyoming, Love it or Leave it." What made my heart swell and rise into my throat were his Indian features. I couldn't have told you what kind of Indian—the Navaho or Crow I'd seen in Fourth of July parades seemed to have a different look—more rounded. Maybe he wasn't Indian at all, but I was limited in my comparisons.

I sent him a good-day-to-ya smile and shifted my attention back to my shopping, playing casual, hoping he'd wonder if he had the wrong guy. He remained steadfast, refusing to move a single inch toward me or away. To get to the ice cream I had to stroll past all the aisles in the store. In each aisle, another man was waiting, watching, most of them similarly dressed, though the vests were randomly colored and the slogans varied on each visor cap.

They must have followed me inside, though I didn't remember seeing any other cars pull in when we were crossing the parking lot. Surely Parley had noticed them. Where was my faithful guard dog when I needed him?

Reaching the frozen foods aisle, I tossed a half-gallon of ice cream into the cart. I doubt it was the brand I wanted, or even the flavor, but it didn't matter, if only I'd be awarded the blessing of tasting it. There were other things my mother had wanted me to get, but I couldn't recall what they were. Making my way to the checkout counter, I was grateful to see the line had subsided.

The cashier cheerfully proceeded to ring up my items. I said nothing to her, which I'm sure she took as rude. Instead, I kept track of each man's position at all times.

There were five of them. As I pulled out my wallet and handed the lady a ten dollar bill, they closed in, stepping over the chains of unattended check-out counters. I took my change and waited for the lady to prop the plastic bag over the metal holder and slip my eggs, eggnog and ice cream inside. The cashier seemed oblivious to any peril, thinking perhaps these other men were friends of mine. She forced a smile despite my rudeness and handed me my groceries with a charge to have a happy Thanksgiving.

I made a beeline for the door. The five men instantly pursued. I hurried to the video store where I had left Parley. My only hope was that he would see my dilemma and come to my rescue with his mouth a-foaming. But Parley was gone! The only person in the video store was a teenage girl at the counter, glued to the promotional screen on the wall playing the *The Little Mermaid*. I prayed to myself that Parley was in the car. I turned back to verify that I was still being followed. The older, decrepit man was leading the way. He seemed amused by my determination to escape and when he smiled I could see wide gaps between many of his teeth.

The outer door slid open and I launched into the darkened parking lot, making a mad dash for my car. The men bounded after me. I yelled Parley's name and dropped my groceries onto the asphalt. It was a three-way tie to the door of the Mazda, and as I tried to open it and climb inside, four powerful arms slammed it shut again and stood over me like vultures.

"What do you want!" I finally blurted spinning to face the wizened wraith with gaps between his teeth. Though the nearest streetlight was at the other end of the parking lot, the light seemed to collect preternaturally on his face.

He stood before me basking in the satisfaction of finally having me in his grasp.

"Hello, Jimawkins." He ran it together as if my name were only one word. "It's been a long time."

I was panting and shaking but I managed to answer, "What do you want from me? Why are you chasing me?"

Another man came forward. This one was younger, though no less ominous. The corners of his eyes were long and sharp, making them appear dagger-thin without squinting. Somewhat annoyed at the older man, he reassumed his rightful position of leadership, a position which the older man seemed naturally to usurp.

"We've come to protect you," said the second man. "To warn you. That way, when the time comes, you may be willing to do us a similar favor."

"Who are you?" I demanded.

The older character removed his cap, revealing a rosy scalp, and a thin grey patch of hair. I thought the gesture was an awkward attempt to be polite at first, but then he grinned wryly, stuck out his chin and asked, "Don't you recognize me?"

"Of course not," I answered. "I've never seen any of you before in my life."

But even as I was proclaiming my ignorance there was something about this wizened wraith which was mystically familiar. Was he a character from a childhood fairy tale? Perhaps a phantom from a recent nightmare? I couldn't decide. Whatever the connection was between us, I was certain it wasn't a good one.

The old man pretended to be hurt. "Has it been so long? Soooo, you're memory has been excised!" He mused, "Very interesting."

"There's nothing interesting about it," I insisted. "You've simply got the wrong guy."

A third man let out a guffaw. The slogan on his cap read, "I'd rather be fishing." I doubted that very much. This man's neck was nearly as big around as his head. The thin-eyed man stayed his cackling by the firm placement of his palm on the man's breast.

Then the thin-eyed man stated, "We only wish to ask you one question. If you answer it, we will present you with information which will save your life. If you do not answer . . . we will not help you."

I shook my head, "I can't imagine what I could tell you. I'm afraid you're going to be disappointed."

He got right into his question, "You saw a man killed three moons ago. You were there when they took his body away. Were you not?"

I thought a moment, "The accident at Colter's Hell? Yes, I was there. But I have no idea where they took him. The police can tell you—"

The older man interrupted, "We are not interested in his body. We are interested to know if he was carrying a weapon. Perhaps a sword?"

I considered not answering, but these men appeared quite determined. I was so anxious to get away, I decided my best course was full cooperation.

"There *was* a sword found," I admitted.

The older man replied quickly, "Ah! Yes! A sword. Very good. Can you tell us where we might find this sword?"

"I gave it to the police."

"The police? And where might we find the police?"

"Where? You keep crowding me like this, holding me against my will, they'll likely come to you."

A fourth man came forward at that moment and motioned to the older man that finding the police was not a problem. This man, and the one standing beside him, looked to be typical white caucasians, but no less exuding of moral darkness than their companions.

The thin-eyed man motioned his men to back away, "Forgive us. We mean you no danger. We are only soldiers in the cause of . . . righteousness."

The others laughed at his word choice.

He continued, "You've helped us immensely. Now I'll give you a warning."

Reaching into his inner vest pocket, he pulled out a hand gun—a powerful one—.357 Magnum. I felt like the warning I was about to receive was the same one my mother gave me when I was four years old: 'Never talk to strangers.' But to my relief, the cannon was not aimed between my eyes. The thin-eyed man held it by the barrel and placed it in my hand.

"There is a man who wishes to kill you," he began. "He will do so without the least hesitation—unless you act swiftly and kill him first. This weapon should be quite adequate for the job."

"Why does he want to kill me?" I asked.

"That would be a foolish question to ask him," he replied. "He will not take the time to answer."

The thin-eyed man waved his companions to follow him into the alleyway. They reacted swiftly and headed toward the darkness—all but the old wizened gentleman, lingering behind to study me a moment longer.

Pointing at my right hand, he commented, "That's a nice ring."

He was referring to my ring with the shiny blue stone which I'd worn for . . . I don't remember how many years.

"Thanks," I said curtly.

"I knew a craftsman in my city who made such rings. He was a very talented man."

The wizened character looked back into my eyes, grinned once more for the road, then slunk off into the night behind his comrades, leaving me alone beside the door of the Mazda holding a loaded pistol in my palm. After the last of them had faded out of sight, I opened my door and dropped the pistol onto the back seat, as if it were something poisonous.

I began to fear for Parley. Where had he gone? Had they knocked him unconscious—or worse? Maybe he was lying in the alley or in the back seat of any one of these cars. I stepped over to the only pickup in the lot and glanced in the bed. It seemed the most logical place to dump somebody in so brief a time frame, but inside the bed I only saw some old twine and bundled newspapers.

About then Parley came rushing out of the store.

"There you are! I've been lookin' all over for ya! You had me all freaked out!"

Parley noticed my sack of groceries on the pavement and picked them up. Egg yolks came oozing out from a hole in the bottom of the plastic. Parley, looking back at me with a confused gape on his mug, could only bring himself to ask the obvious, "Is everything okay?"

As it turned out, Parley had decided to take a quick trip to the rest room about the time I was accosted. Had he been a real guard dog, another owner might have shot the worthless mutt. I told Parley something had spooked me and I overreacted. I didn't want to tell him what happened. I wasn't sure I knew myself. The best way I could think to collect my thoughts and slow my heartbeat was to go back into the store and replace Mom's fractured eggs.

We skipped the video idea. Though the decision somewhat rankled Parley, I was too uptight to wait around while he decided between "Firewalkers" or "Missing In Action II." On the way home he noticed the .357 Magnum lying on the back seat and picked it up.

"How long's this been here?" he wondered.

Parley rolled the weapon over and over in his hands.

"I, uh, keep it under the seat for extra protection," I said.

"Nice." Parley looked down the barrel. "Almost too much gun for one man."

Passing Molhollend's yard, I was relieved to see no one standing under the light post. We pulled into the driveway and parked in the usual spot behind Dad's Ford Taurus. I wanted to grab the pistol from Parley and keep it at my side, but I decided carrying a firearm into the house would only further stress out my family. I opened the car door and proceeded toward the porch when a voice whispered from the other side of my brother's Celica.

"Jimawkins?" it asked, making the word one, just like the wizened character at Steck's.

The voice almost made me leap right out of my socks. I'd been warned of an assassin. I'd been warned he would strike mercilessly and with lightning speed. The next thing I knew, the pistol discharged. Parley, as startled by the voice as I was, had responded like a shell-shocked marine and fired a haphazard bullet through the window of my brother's car. Ducking down to shield my face, I glimpsed a shadow dart out from behind the Celica and move around the Mazda to make a rear attack on Parley. Before I could call out a warning, Parley squawked in pain and the pistol fired again.

By now my family was stepping over each other to see out the front door. As I cautiously arose and gazed across the hood of my car, into the flower bed by the fence, Parley was lying face down in the brittle remains of Mom's summer chrysanthemums. Standing over him, and currently wielding the gun, was the same mysterious man who we'd seen under the light post as we left the house, his features still half-shrouded by shadow. Upon seeing me arise, he threw his hands over his head.

"Please—!" he cried.

Stepping forward, the man set the pistol onto the hood of the Mazda. Raising his arms again, he continued to plead.

"I mean no harm to either you or your family!"

His face was now better illuminated by the porch light. He was young. Early twenties. Perhaps my age. He wore an old coat with many greasy stains and huge rips in the lining. I couldn't help but wonder if he'd obtained it from somebody's garbage. Underneath the coat were the clothes my father had described—a kind of pullover tunic which exposed the legs to the cold and sandals with leather straps crisscrossing up the calf. His jaw was square, hair was black and thick, and his skin was unusually tan for November. All in all, his features were very similar to the men I'd already encountered tonight, though his countenance seemed less . . . desperate?

Nevertheless, I snatched up the pistol and pretended to command the grit of a gunslinger, though I'm sure the reality of the scene wasn't quite so dramatic since my arms were shaking and felt like Jello.

"Don't move!" I cried. It seemed an appropriate injunction, though my surrenderee was already as still as an oak. I looked over at Parley, still unmoving. "What have you done to him?"

Just then Parley started to stir and groan.

The man glanced over at Parley, who was now rising drunkenly to his feet, and then back at me. With a look of apology, the man declared, "I didn't want to be shot."

Parley's daze, now subsiding, was replaced with fury. He'd been humiliated by this stranger, though the man was at least five inches and fifty pounds his inferior. All the cowboy remembered from the grapple which left him unconscious was that a powerful hand had seized him from behind, pinching off his jugular. The cowboy's fists were in full gear, but my family had since surrounded us and my father and brother held him at bay while the drone of a police siren drew nearer.

"Why have you been prowling around my house?" I demanded. "Terrorizing my family?"

"I haven't been prowling," he explained. "I've been waiting for you. I've come to seek your help. For the sake of my people and yours, *please*, listen to me."

"What do you want from me?!" I ranted, "I've never met you—*or* your friends at the store!"

"Trust me," he said, "if you've met others like me, they are not my friends—or yours."

I lowered my voice and uttered one final question as the police car screeched to a halt in the gutter in front of my house. My voice was imploring—begging for something I could understand, something I could believe, "*Who are you?*"

"My name is Muleki," he answered. "You knew my father, Captain Teancum."

CHAPTER 4

The veil seemed gossamer thin this night before Thanksgiving, but the phenomenon wasn't consoling. Every time I closed my eyes to sleep, I kept seeing his face—the man who called himself Muleki—pleading with me silently while the police clamped him in handcuffs and stuffed him in the back seat of their patrol car. Even as they pulled away, Muleki wouldn't take his eyes off me. It didn't matter how tight I shut my lids or how hard I pressed my nose in my pillow, his features only became more fixed in my mind.

I did fall asleep eventually, but never deeper than dreaming—and my dreams were all messed up, like the dreams one has when running a fever—plots don't make sense; people don't talk right; events are out of sequence—yet my brain was unwilling to acknowledge a problem.

Worst of all, that hill kept appearing—the one with the tiny cluster of trees, and the man in the mist, still beckoning me onward, still driving me crazy.

At a quarter past one, I bolted up, disgruntled and utterly exhausted. Propping my shoulders against the headboard, I buried my face in the sweat of my palms and heaved a dreary sigh. Then I said a prayer, brief and ungrateful, pleading to be granted the sleep I deserved. My thoughts drifted off before I'd properly closed the prayer, and I found myself drawn in by the blue-stone ring on my right hand. The room was pitch black except for a single beam of illumination through a sliver in the curtains, emitting from the light post in front of the Molhollend's yard. As I sat up in my bed, the beam fell directly across the ring.

I stared at the shiny blue stone. It seemed funny to have persistently worn it all these years. The last time I took it off was shortly after my mission. Normally I'd worn it on my pinky, but fooling around one day, I got it stuck on my ring finger. A nurse told me not to worry unless I felt it was cutting off the circulation, so I made up a corny game. Like Arthur's sword-in-the-stone, I decided the girl who could remove that ring would be the girl I would marry.

"Menochin," I said out loud.

Now why did I say that? The name popped into my head like the "ting" of a bell. Suddenly, I began to see other things, like memories from another life, entrenched enough to make a Mormon consider reincarnation. I saw an ancient city with a towering wall. A bustling marketplace and lazy green river. I saw a mighty warrior, invincible in the fury of battle. And finally, I saw a little boy of four years, leaping into the arms of this mighty warrior and calling him Father while the warrior called him Muleki.

Muleki.

I'd have sworn I was dreaming had I not hit my skull against the headboard and glanced at the clock to verify the hour. Escaping to the kitchen, I guzzled a rim-filled cup of the coldest water in the tap. Then I wandered into the living room and slouched in my dad's easy chair. Soon I'd resolved to learn every mystery this man whom the police had hauled off to jail might possess. If my mother would have it, there'd be another place setting tomorrow for Thanksgiving dinner.

"The holiday spirit come over you, eh?" commented the officer on duty at the Cody Jail.

I informed him I was completely willing to drop the charges of trespassing and harassment and allow the prisoner, who'd maintained the singular name of Muleki, to go free. When he was brought out to me, still wearing the moth-eaten coat and ancient-style tunic, it was apparent he hadn't enjoyed much sleep the night before either.

"He said some awfully crazy things during the night," the officer reported. "I was gonna turn him over to someone at the State Hospital tomorrow. I'm still not sure that wouldn't be the best course of action."

"I'll take care of him," I promised, and Muleki was placed in my custody.

"Thank you for coming, Jimawkins," Muleki said.

"Jim. Just call me Jim. And here—" I peeled off his greasy jacket and dropped it in the waste can beside the door. "You won't need it. My car is heated."

Exiting through the station doorway, he followed me out to the parking lot, folding one arm over the other to keep warm. Overhead, the courthouse clock sounded the half-hour dong. Muleki jumped, almost defensively, and stared up at the clock's green-glass face.

"Hop in," I instructed. Muleki approached the Mazda, and looked down at the door handle, hesitating.

"It's all right," I said. "I didn't lock it. Just pull up." I felt silly explaining to him how to open a car door. After all, he wasn't a two-year-old. Yet only after demonstrating by opening my side, was he was willing to give his a try. The task a success, he carefully scooted onto the seat and placed his feet firmly in the center of the mat.

Although we remained parked, I started the engine and got the heat flowing to cure Muleki's goosebumps. Then I pulled up the emergency brake and turned to glare at my bewildering passenger. He continued to sit in perfect discipline with his arms at his side.

"I can't believe I bailed you out. I'm goin' on nothing but instinct right now, partner, so don't let me down. I had a long, lonely night, and I saw a lot of weird things. I'm countin' on you to explain them to me."

Muleki was silent.

"Have you had breakfast?" I asked.

"They gave me a meal in the prison. Eggs—I don't know from what kind of bird—and bread. Orange juice, very sweet, and strips of meat. I did not eat the meat. I feared the animal it came from was unclean."

"You mean bacon? I doubt there was anything wrong with—" Then it hit me what he meant. "Are you a Jew?"

"My kinship is Jershonite, from the lineage of Mulek," he responded, "though my blood is no longer pure."

I took that as meaning yes. "So you've eaten then?"

"Not really. You came before I could finish. I've eaten little since coming to this land. My food ran out two days ago."

"Are you a foreigner?"

"I'm a citizen of Zarahemla," he replied.

"*Please!* No more of that!" I threw my hands over my face. My hopes of avoiding a headache this early in the day were waning. Lowering my hands I said, "Let's start from the beginning. Tell me again who you are?"

"I've told you. I am Muleki, son of Teancum. Captain of the Guard in the Palace of Helaman, Chief Judge of Zarahemla."

I seriously considered handing this guy back over to the police, admitting the State Hospital thing wasn't such a bad idea. He must have seen my disbelief, because his face suddenly blossomed with understanding.

"Ah, it's true what I suspected. You don't remember. Helaman said this would be possible."

"You guessed it, buddy!" I exclaimed. "I don't remember anything! And it's driving me nuts! Did I have amnesia for a year of my life or what?"

"You were not with us that long."

Attempting to slacken the tension, I vigorously shook my jowls and blew all the air out of my lungs. Then I closed my eyes, and inhaled, long and slow.

Opening them again, I stared straight ahead at the emptiness of space and admitted, "Sometimes I see faces. I hear voices at night. I'm not sure what's real anymore. I don't even know why I've come here today except that there's something nagging inside me—telling me *you* know the answers. I'm begging you to help me. *Please*, if you have any answers . . . tell me what you know."

"There were two of you," Muleki began. "I saw you with my father when I was a little boy. You were both so pale, like so many of the people in this land. The other one had many spots on his skin and his hair was like amber."

"Garth?" I wondered. "Was Garth there too?"

"They say his full name was Garthplimpton," Muleki confirmed.

My body stiffened. This wasn't happening. Oh, how I'd hoped this guy was only a nut case, and I could just go forward with my life as it had been before, but that was impossible now. In spite of every whit of logic within me which said his words were ludicrous, I had to consider them to be true.

We went to the *Irma Grill Restaurant* since it was about the only place open on Thanksgiving Day. There, I ordered him a full-course breakfast, with more eggs and a stack of pancakes.

When the meal came, he dug into it with both hands. As several other patrons began wincing at the yolk and syrup dripping down his palm, I prevailed upon him to use a spoon. He downed the breakfast as though it were his last meal. I considered telling him to slow down—there'd be a lot more eating before the day was over. But I didn't think any amount of food would have intimidated that appetite.

I listened intently as Muleki told me about a cavern at the base of a volcano in a land he called Melek. He also told me about a secret passage at the top of Cody's own Cedar Mountain which served as a bridge between his time and mine. But having one question answered only brought up dozens more. Unlike I had hoped, my frustration wasn't subsiding.

"How old was I?" I demanded.

"You were much younger. About thirteen."

"How long did I stay in this . . . time warp?"

"They say it was only two moons, but in that time you saved my father's life and helped defeat Amalickiah, the Lamanite king."

"If you're a Nephite, how come we understand each

other?" I challenged. "Shouldn't we be speaking different languages?"

"I don't know," replied Muleki. "I've spoken to only a few people since coming, yet I understand every word they say. It's a powerful gift that anyone who makes the journey seems to possess."

I needed a fast drive on a long stretch of road with the cold wind blowing in my face. His words were like peroxide, offering a potential cure to my distress, but inducing a greater anguish by so doing. As he spoke, I felt memories slowly filling in the darkened gaps of my mind. The images remained quite blurry—but I could see them. Why had they been taken from me in the first place? Why had I been so tortured? Was it so wrong to remember such an adventure?

"There was a girl," I recollected, "with black hair and brown eyes. I'm almost certain she gave me this ring. Her name was Menochin."

"Yes!" Muleki exclaimed, grateful that my memory seemed to be returning. "She is my cousin."

Shyly, I wondered, "Is she still around?—I mean . . . "

"Of course. She is a great woman," Muleki proudly replied. "She is the wife of Judge Helaman, son of Prophet Helaman."

"You mean she's married? Already?"

"She has been for fifteen years. She has seven children. Two boys—Nephi and Lehi—and five girls."

My shoulders dropped and I sat across the booth in consternation. I couldn't believe it! My heart was telling me Menochin had been my first love. How could she betray me like this? I didn't even get a Dear John! Then it occurred to me, if I'd met Muleki when he was four years old, that would make Menochin over thirty by now.

As if reading my thoughts Muleki explained, "The bridge between our worlds is not entirely stable. You've not aged as much as I have. When I return, I hope it is to the same day I left, but I knew there was a possibility it would not be."

"Why *have* you come?" it was time to ask.

Muleki placed his spoon beside his plate. "Like my father, I am a soldier," he began. "I have come to prevent a great evil from being unleashed upon your land. And I have come to insure that this evil cannot return to mine—at least not in the wrong hands. I am searching for a sword— silver-plated—with precious stones in its hilt."

"That sword again!" I blurted. "What is it with you people? You come all the way to another dimension of time and space with the sole intent of retrieving a measly sword? The men last night asked me for the same thing."

Fear swept over Muleki's face, "Did you give it to them?"

"No. I didn't have it to give."

"But you *have* seen it?"

"Yeah, a man was carrying it with him along the highway west of town. A lady ran over him with her Buick."

"I know this man," Muleki declared. "His name was Rerenak. He was one of the most foolish people ever born."

"No doubt," I agreed. "What kind of idiot would wander in the middle of the highway at dusk?"

"One who was unfamiliar with the workings of this world," answered Muleki. "One who was a member of the secret band of Gadianton."

My heart skipped a beat. "You mean a Gadianton *robber*?"

"He was not an important member. Yet he was very ambitious. He stole from his band the most precious article they possessed and thought to use it in this world as a means of gaining great power. Only, he forgot the oath he swore when he was initiated—that his life belonged to the Evil One if ever he betrayed his clan. There was nowhere he could hide. Thus, he died for his crime."

"Let me get this straight," I said. "He died because he took a sword? This thing must be pretty valuable."

"Only to those whose works are done in darkness. The Sword of Coriantumr was forged by Akish from the ore of Ephraim Hill when the Jaredite peoples covered the face of the land. It was passed down through the generations of wicked kings."

"What could be so terrible about a sword?" I asked.

"You know much more than is necessary already," said Muleki. "It isn't wise for me to tell you more."

"How did you know *I* had seen it?"

"We found the woman who killed Rerenak."

"*We*?" I felt myself swallow. "Are you a Gadianton?"

"I am not," Muleki promised. "But I've been in false league with them for nearly a year now—though I've never taken any oaths. I've learned many of their dark ways. This enabled me to save Helaman's life and to end the wicked days of Kishkumen."

My head was spinning. "*You* killed Kishkumen? *The* Kishkumen? The same one as in the Book of Mormon?"

"I wouldn't know. I've never read this book." Muleki went on, "When Gadianton fled Zarahemla, I followed his band into the wilderness. My mission was to find Coriantumr's Sword and take possession of it. It was a quest for which I was willing to give my life. When Rerenak stole it from Gadianton's tent, I volunteered to be part of the company which would retrieve it. They let me come because I knew a way to the volcano which would not pass through populated regions."

"And the men I saw last night—?"

Muleki finished, "They were the other members of the company."

"They wanted me to kill you," I reported. "They claimed you would kill *me* if I failed to strike first."

"I'm not surprised. They always prefer others to do their dirty work," said Muleki.

"One of them knew who I was. But I can't seem to place him. He was an older guy—really withered-looking."

"That would be Mehrukenah," said Muleki. "Since Kishkumen's death, Mehrukenah is Gadianton's personal assassin—the most powerful member of the band besides Gadianton himself. Though he is older and seems quite feeble, don't be fooled. A viper would never bite him for fear his poison would be worse than its own. If you betrayed Mehrukenah during those days when you knew him, beware. It is said he has no personal enemies. None of them are still alive."

I tried again to reach inside my memory, but I just couldn't recall him.

I continued, "Another one had really shifty eyes, with sharp corners."

"That man is Shurr. He is Gadianton's brother, and though he is guilty of many savage crimes, I consider him weak and reckless. Gadianton made Shurr the leader of the company only because of Shurr's loyalty. He is to be the sword-bearer, and only he may touch it when it is found. Gadianton fears what Mehrukenah may do if he gets hold of it first."

Muleki concluded, "The last one is Boaz. He is also a member of Gadianton's inner circle. Each of these men are as dangerous as any man which has ever walked the earth. Never try to defeat them with craft or wit. They would chew you to pieces. The only way to crush them is with the righteousness of God."

Wouldn't you know it? Just the thing I was running a bit shy of.

"But I saw *five* men," I stated.

"The others were recruited the first few days after we arrived. One is named Clarke. The other is Bridenbough. They were already well indoctrinated in the ways of the band. Apparently your world is not free of Gadianton's stain. I don't know much about them, except that it was with their help that we found the woman who killed Rerenak. She was the one who told us you had the sword. I knew it was no accident that you found it first. My Uncle Moriancum spoke often of your courage. I broke away from the others and tried to warn you, but, regrettably, I was five days too early. I'm sorry your family has suffered. I'm even more sorry that *you* have been troubled. If I can have the sword, I will depart immediately and you will be no more disrupted by this business."

"But I gave it to the police," I confessed.

"The police?"

"When I was bailing you out, I asked the desk officer where it was. He told me nobody would be in to dig up something like that until tomorrow."

"Then I will leave as soon as I can tomorrow," promised Muleki.

"What are you gonna do with the sword after you return?" I wondered.

"I will destroy it," he proclaimed.

"How? Melt it down? Break it in half?"

"No," said Muleki, smiling painfully at my naiveté. "There is no fire that could melt it and no stone that could break it."

This was getting a bit melodramatic. "You're kidding me, right?"

Muleki did not look amused. He treated this subject with a discomforting amount of seriousness.

"Then how do you intend to destroy it?" I asked.

"By laying it to rest in Ether's coffer."

"Ether's what?"

"It's a stone box in the earth."

"Where's it located?"

"At the highest summit point of the Hill Ramah in the land of Desolation."

"What's putting it in a box supposed to accomplish?"

"Please don't force me to tell you anymore," Muleki begged. "If I thought it could help you—if I thought it could save your life, believe me, I would tell you."

Muleki might have read the cynicism on my face and decided not to cast any more pearls before swine. It just didn't make sense to see such stress stirred up over an inanimate object.

Staring at Muleki across the table, I felt sorry for him. The beleaguered Nephite seemed to be terribly lonely. For the last year he'd endured the company of the most evil men of his time, pretending to be one with them. Such an existence could take the wind right out of the human soul. I'd been taught to avoid anything involving the occult like the plague. They said the scars caused by such tampering might never heal. The discipline it must have taken Muleki to come away from this experience with his salvation intact was no less than superhuman. Even so, I saw a certain misery in his eyes—the misery of a soldier who'd survived a hundred wars only to be tortured the rest of his days by the haunting memories.

When I asked Muleki his plans after his mission was accomplished, he shrugged his shoulders and finished his meal. Perhaps he didn't feel himself worthy to raise a family and lead a normal life anymore.

In spite of my skepticism, I decided to help Muleki in any way I could to obtain the sword and return safely to his people through the caverns of Frost Cave in the heart of Cedar mountain. The primary question which burned in my breast as we drove back home to join the Thanksgiving festivities was what Muleki had meant when he recited his fear of this sword being unleashed on the people of my day. Just what did he suppose would be the result of such an occurrence? I couldn't help but conclude that the ancient Nephites, though they may have had the true religion, still couldn't escape the primeval grip of superstition.

Good thing modern Saints aren't so gullible.

CHAPTER 5

I informed Muleki that I'd explained the situation to my parents before driving down to the police station to get him. I told them it had occurred to me during the night that the strange prowler who'd been stalking their neighborhood over the last week was none other than Muleki Jones—one of the more colorful converts I'd had the privilege of baptizing on my mission in Oregon.

"I laid it on pretty thick," I admitted to Muleki. "They think you were raised by Oregon hillbillies and that those other fellows are brothers and uncles that aren't too happy about your conversion to the gospel. I don't much enjoy fabricating to my parents, but it accomplished what I'd hoped. Their hearts melted, and they insisted I bring you home for Thanksgiving dinner."

I could smell the turkey roasting even as we climbed out of the car. We parked in the street since Mitch and Judd and their families had arrived. There was a square of cardboard fastened by strips of duct tape over the bullet hole in the window of Steven's Celica. As we walked through the front door, the Nephite was greeted by a host of forgiving arms. My mother hugged him breathless and apologized profusely. My dad scolded him for not explaining who he was from the very beginning and my Uncle Spencer took him around the shoulder and proceeded to tell him all about one summer he'd spent on the Oregon coast, not too concerned when I told him Muleki was not from that particular part of Oregon. I think the Nephite was quite touched by the reception. It had probably been some time since he'd enjoyed the company of friendly faces.

Muleki was fairly close to my size, so the first thing I did was have him climb into a pair of jeans and throw on my Cougar sweatshirt. Socks were a new concept for the Nephite, one he accepted with visible apprehension, but he found my old tennis shoes quite comfortable.

I thought my brother Steven would spoil the atmosphere of compassion we'd created when he approached Muleki with an estimate of forty dollars to replace his window. Muleki reached into a pouch he'd stuffed into his pocket and pulled out a nugget of pure gold.

"Will this correct the damage?" Muleki asked sincerely.

My brother stuttered, feeling a sting of shame for bringing up such subjects on Thanksgiving. He tried to return the nugget, but Muleki was insistent, so Steve salved his conscience by promising to return the change.

Of course, I didn't expect Parley to own up to any blame, though he'd been the trigger-happy cowboy who caused the problem in the first place. In fact, Parley was the only one in the household that didn't approach the Nephite with remorse. I think his pride still smarted from being knocked unconscious in front of everybody.

But a worse blow to his ego was yet to come. It was inflicted when I introduced Muleki to my sister, Jennifer. The Nephite's tender handling of Jenny's hand befitted the suitors of royalty. For the briefest moment, when her eyes met his, the Queen of the Flirts went immodestly flush.

The rest of the day, and all through Thanksgiving dinner, as we stuffed our faces with the finest spread of my mother's celebrated career, and despite the screaming kids and the volume blast on the football games, it was difficult to overlook the mesmerized silence which took hold of my sister. Jenny utilized some of her more sophisticated predator skills, even going to the trouble of placing name tags on everyone's place at the table. Of course, her plate was just to the right of Muleki's. Parley, unfortunately, ended up with a torturous position on the opposite side of the table where he could watch the display in living color.

Parley masticated his food particularly well that meal, and I can't say as I blame him for fuming. Muleki didn't coax Jenny on at all. In fact, he was entirely oblivious to her advances—or at least he pretended to be. It was about the time Jenny was plopping whipped cream on Muleki's third piece of pie that the cowboy finally grabbed my sister by the arm and insisted that the two of them go for a walk.

I thought I was the only one aware of what was going on until my Uncle Spence leaned over to me and uttered, "Look's like a certain little girl's about to get some comeuppance."

"Don't count on it," I replied.

I could imagine how my sister was burying this guy in ten feet of snow job, explaining how her actions were strictly the result of feeling sorry for the stranger, and how foolish Parley was acting, and how he shouldn't carry on so when there was nothing to be jealous about. Sure enough, when they came back through the front door, hand in hand, Parley's temper had suitably quelled—though it threatened further inflammation only thirty seconds later when she dropped his hand before the Nephite could see it.

There were a couple of times during the day when I thought Muleki would blow his cover and make it apparent he was some kind of alien. He watched the hands on the grandfather clock for a full half-hour, waiting for the cuckoo bird to make its second appearance. He leaned behind the television, straining to understand where the moving people were coming from. It was obvious he was having a little too much fun with the ice maker on the refrigerator, and that he was frightened by the doorbell when the Watkins came by to borrow a bread pan. But when he began unrolling the toilet paper and inquiring for what purpose it was intended, I think everybody raised an eyebrow. Certainly even a hillbilly wasn't *that* backwards.

The evening floated on: the children were put to bed, the adults suffered through a game of *Uno*, and, finally, the party started to break up. My parents' home became a hotel. Mom and Dad had threatened many times, while watching their children move away, that they would sell the big house and move into a condo. I couldn't believe they'd ever go through with it. Reunions like this were too important to them—and, I might add, to the rest of us as well.

I slept in my old room again. One of the mattresses was hoisted off the frame and laid on the floor for Muleki. My sister, of course, had to peek through the door after we'd turned out the light to wish Muleki goodnight. Then the ancient Nephite and I maneuvered ourselves comfortable for a long winter's sleep.

"Jim?" Muleki said just before I dropped off.

"Mmmmm?" I responded.

"It was a wonderful day. The greatest day I've had in a very long time—like the feasts we used to hold in the Jershonite neighborhood when I was a boy, before my father died. I will always be grateful to you and to your family."

His words again reminded me of the terrible loneliness he must have borne in recent months. Perhaps it was a loneliness which had gripped his heart for years, ever since the day the little boy was told his father had been killed by the servants of the Lamanite king. Being told his father died a hero would not have softened the choking lump which swelled in a little boy's throat. Contemplating his pain caused a tear to soak into my pillow.

"Go to sleep," I said. "Tomorrow could be a very eventful day for you, too."

At three minutes to nine a.m., Muleki and I stood before the claims clerk at the Cody Municipal Police Department. I was quite anxious to retrieve the sword and escort Muleki back to the entrance of Frost Cave. If the lady sensed our agitation, she deliberately ignored it. Not until the digital clock displayed nine exactly was she willing to address us.

"Can I help you?" she finally asked.

"I've come to reclaim a lost article," I replied. "I was told I could have it back if it were unspoken for at the end of ninety days."

"Do you have a claim number?"

"A what?"

"Do you have a claim number?" She repeated the intonation exactly, like a recording. When the confusion didn't leave my face, she went on to explain, "You should have been given a claim number when it was filed. It would be hard for me to find your article if you don't have a claim number."

"I was never given one," I said. "I handed it over to the police at the scene of an accident last August."

The clerk sighed, "What is the article, sir."

"A sword, about yea long, with jewels in the hilt."

"We don't have anything like that."

Muleki's brow furrowed.

"Are you sure?" I demanded.

The clerk was growing impatient. "I walk back there every day. I'd surely remember something that unusual. Who was the officer you gave the sword to?"

I thought a moment, "Finlay. Todd Finlay."

"Well, there's your problem," responded the clerk. "Todd Finlay was suspended around the middle of August. He skipped town shortly thereafter. His wife and daughter haven't seen or heard from him since. If he's arrested, there's a good case to convict him for abandonment—as well as other things."

"Why was he suspended?"

I'm sure it wasn't entirely proper for her to answer my questions. Nevertheless, the lady seemed to take on a different air. Perhaps her true disposition as the station gossip was starting to emerge.

She explained, "The paperwork says insubordination, but I heard it through a reliable source that Todd Finlay was a drug dealer. Some say he even sold the stuff while he was on duty."

How terrible, I thought—even if such rumors were false. Still, you had to wonder what would lead a guy to skip town on his family.

The clerk summed it all up by saying, "If you want to find your sword, you'd better find Todd Finlay, 'cause as far as I know, he never registered it."

Exiting the police station, there was a cloud of depression over Muleki.

"I knew it couldn't be this easy," he sighed.

"Why would Todd Finlay have stolen such a thing?" I wondered.

"If a disposition for evil was already entrenched in his soul," Muleki revealed, "the sword would inspire the rest."

We found Finlay's address in the phone book and drove down Alger Avenue in search of the corresponding numbers. On the last block, we found a tiny frame house with a peeling white fence and dead leaves smothering the lawn.

As we tried to unbolt the hasp on the front gate, a miniature mongrel dashed out from under a bush and alerted the occupants. A small hand pulled back the curtain on the front room window, and the frame of a haggard-looking, middle-aged woman stepped onto the porch, pinching a cigarette between her fingers.

"What do you want?" she threatened.

"We just wanted to talk to you for a minute," I replied. "It concerns your husband."

She sucked a long drag of tobacco and stood there on the porch a moment longer, considering our request. Finally she responded, "I don't have a husband anymore."

"Please, Mrs. Finlay," I pleaded. "I promise we won't take very long."

The dog was running in circles, its barking having grown more frenzied and insane.

"Vera, get your dog!" the lady yelled.

A little girl of seven trotted out the door and across the porch. Her clothes were plain and her bright yellow hair, unkempt. Despite the cold ground she wasn't wearing any shoes, though I supposed her fear of what might happen if she didn't jump to her mother's command outweighed a need for warm feet.

As she lifted the dog into her arms, she sent us an awkward smile and explained, "He really doesn't bite."

She retreated to the house, passing her mother who had followed her down the front walk. The woman had decided to talk to us, but clearly she wasn't too comfortable with the idea of letting us inside.

"What do you have to say?" she demanded, crossing her

arms, almost burning an elbow with the cigarette's dangling ash.

Muleki replied, "We wondered if you could tell us where Mr. Finlay might be."

Mrs. Finlay choked out a laugh, "I thought that's what you were here to tell *me*!—Or maybe to tell me he was dead. I haven't seen him since August 21st, and to be honest, I don't care if I ever see him again."

"Can you tell us where his kinship is settled?" asked Muleki.

"Pardon me?"

I clarified, "Do you know where any family members live?"

"The only relative I know of lives just across the street from the Methodist Church. That'd be his mother. But she doesn't know any more than I do."

"If there's anything you can tell us," Muleki urged, "we'd be very grateful. We fear he may be involved in something very dangerous. Something he doesn't understand."

"Well, that doesn't surprise me. Todd was always a little off center. He told me the only reason he became a cop was so's he could carry a loaded gun. If Todd's into something weird, I'd just call that par for the course."

"Before he left," asked Muleki, "did you see him with a sword—long and silver?"

Mrs. Finlay opened into a chorus of swear words. Somewhere in the midst of all the profanities she admitted she did indeed recall such a sword.

"Todd would've slept with that thing if I'd have let 'im. After he got suspended, he spent more time with that hunk of metal—polishing it, talking to it—than he ever did with Vera or me. I think the only thing he took with him the morning he left was his '68 Mustang and that (blankety-blank) sword. Oh, and fifteen hundred in savings. That was everything we had. Only time I've heard from him since then was at the end of October. I got a letter with twelve hundred dollars in money orders. I knew that was Todd's way of saying goodbye forever."

"The envelope," I interrupted. "Did it have a return address?"

"Nope. It was postmarked Salt Lake City, Utah, though."

"Utah? Did he know anybody in Utah?"

"Nobody I know of, and I doubt he'd have stayed in any one place for very long."

"Did the money orders have the name of any particular bank on them?" I wondered.

She took another long drag on her cigarette to give herself a moment to think. "There were four checks. Each one for three hundred dollars. They were from a grocery store—*Smith's*. That was it."

"Did you save the envelope, or maybe a stub off a money order?

"Sure didn't." Mrs. Finlay started back toward her house, "I gotta get back to things inside, boys. To be perfectly honest, Vera and I'd prefer not to think about him anymore. We never talk about him."

"I'm sorry if we've upset you," Muleki apologized.

"If you find him, don't bother to tell me," she said. Reaching the porch, she turned back and added, "But if you happen to find that sword, I wouldn't mind you bringing that by. Nothing would give me greater pleasure than to bust it up in a million pieces."

We didn't say much while we drove home. As Muleki looked up to watch a plane leave its white streak of exhaust across the sky, I think the awesome task of finding that sword was starting to dawn on him. He'd come from a much simpler world. A world where a man could never get farther away than what he could walk in a day—not a world where a jet could cart a person to the other side of the globe in a couple of hours. I know *I* was certainly discouraged. But my worst problem, I hated to admit, was that my heart wasn't entirely committed to this tenuous cause.

"So what's the plan now, Muleki?"

"*My* plan, at least, is to go to this place, Salt Lake City."

"And what a coincidence," I responded, only partially aware of the implication of my words. "Such a place happens to be only about forty miles from where I go to school."

CHAPTER 6

We first heard the news from the pet department manager at the *Pamida* discount store on Saturday afternoon. While Muleki was in the dressing room, trying on some additional clothes he could take to Utah, I wandered over to look at the colorful varieties of saltwater fish in the hexagonal tank next to the "Employees Only" corridor. The pet department manager was just inside, talking with another employee about how gutsy it was to stage a robbery at a police station.

"What was that?" I interrupted.

They looked at me like my intrusion was a terrible *faux pas*. "What did you say happened?" I repeated.

They responded, "The police department—some men held it up this morning."

They were anxious to continue their own conversation, but I persisted, "What time?"

"Don't know. Early."

Realizing I wouldn't get much more out of them, I pounded on Muleki's dressing room door and announced it was time to leave. Back in the Mazda, we switched on the radio, already tuned to the local station, *KODI*. After listening for about three minutes, a recap of the story was broadcast.

The reporter said five men, heavily armed with handguns and rifles and dressed in hunting attire, stormed the Cody Municipal Police Department this morning at 4:35 a.m.

". . . They were seeking what personnel on the scene described as a kind of ancient battle sword with silver plating which may have been filed as lost or missing evidence earlier in the year. Unable to provide them with the requested article, shooting broke out, injuring one officer and at least one of the gunmen. The five men, escaping the scene of the incident in a White Chevy Impala, are still at large, and are said to be extremely dangerous."

The newsman went on to discuss the condition of the injured police officer in a Billings, Montana hospital—a bullet in the right shoulder—and the initiation of road-blocks on all highways surrounding the town, and at different checkpoints throughout the states of Wyoming and Montana. The words 'terrorism' and 'baffling' were used several times throughout the report.

An incident as unique as this would certainly reach the major wire services, but the local station's approach offered a connection that an *Associated Press* or a *United Press International* might have ignored. They said that the clothing and weapons used by the gunmen may have been stolen merchandise from the after-hours robbery of a small sporting goods store on the West Cody Strip the previous week.

"They'll be looking for *us* now," Muleki warned. "They'll think you lied to them and that you still have the sword. Or that you at least know where it is."

How unfortunate that the Gadiantons had recruited modern minions to their cause. It gave them uncountable advantages. Without them, how would they have ever learned to use a gun, or escaped in a getaway car? I'd seen the gold nugget Muleki had in his possession. It wouldn't take too many of those to earn someone's loyalty. The frightening reality was, if they could solicit two men to their band, they could solicit others. Watching out for someone with swarthy skin or 'Indian-esque' features was not going to guarantee our safety. Just as I began to shake my head and wonder how I'd gotten into this mess, another concern crossed my mind.

"The police will be looking for us too," I concluded. "That gossipy clerk is certain to make a connection, considering we both requested the same unusual article."

Nearing my parent's home, I feared it might be surrounded by cops. Fortunately, there were no flashing red lights igniting the neighborhood. Thank goodness I hadn't given the claims clerk my name. Trying to explain why we had common ground with five terrorists might hinder Muleki's mission permanently—as well as put us both in a loony bin. But of more immediate concern were the Gadiantons themselves. If they were stuck in town, unable to bypass the roadblocks, they'd strike at the first possible opportunity. We agreed to leave for Provo within the hour.

My parents were a bit disappointed by the news. They were hoping everyone could be together for Sunday services in my home ward. I invented the explanation that Muleki had a bus leaving Provo for Oregon at 7:00 a.m. the next morning. It was the only one running on Sunday, and unfortunately, emergencies at home forced him to travel on the Sabbath.

Jenny actually seemed relieved to be heading back early. Or maybe it was just that anywhere Muleki was going, she was happy to be along. The only one truly annoyed by our change of plans was Parley. He knew his influence on my sister was waning. Our adjusted schedule dashed his hopes of taking her on a long country drive that evening to rekindle the flames.

Our last hugs and kisses with relatives were exchanged about 6:30 that evening. If we didn't stop for anything but gas, we'd reach Provo's city limits by about 2:30 the next morning. Parley complained about how cramped it would be in our tiny car with four people instead of three. Muleki sat in the back seat, thinking it to be the most unassuming position. Determined to keep the peace, he'd have probably insisted on riding in the trunk, if it hadn't already been packed with luggage.

Under the circumstances, it soon became clear he'd chosen the worst seat possible. Jennifer was quick to spot the opening and with a speed faster than Einstein had ever considered, she slipped into the back seat beside Muleki. Parley gave her a lethal glare, then reluctantly plopped into the front, restraining a temper which may have left burn marks on the cushions.

As we passed Beck Lake and turned onto the Meeteetse Highway, the night had already reached its darkest pitch, which in this sparsely populated basin, was about as dark as nighttime ever got. We were stopped by highway patrolmen about five miles out of town. They blinded us with a flashlight for a few seconds, then slapped the hood and sent us onward. Obviously, the five gunmen had not been captured. We kept the radio on, hoping to hear a positive update, but we lost our reception of all Cody stations just beyond Thermopolis as we entered the Wind River Canyon.

I felt certain the Gadiantons wouldn't be able to follow us to Utah. Even if they could, why would they go to the trouble? By now they may have uncovered much more specific information about Todd Finlay than we had, and were setting their sights on an entirely different part of the country. Between the police and common sense, the chances we would ever run into a Gadianton again seemed remote indeed. I felt like I could breathe much easier.

Just out of Lander, as we began the long stretch over South Pass and into Rock Springs, I happened to glance in the rearview mirror and notice Jenny leaning her head on Muleki's shoulder. Muleki's body became as stiff as a tombstone. Jenny appeared asleep, but I knew better. Does a black widow sleep when there's a male in her web? A few minutes later, Jenny pretended to have unconsciously slipped onto Muleki's lap. She purred a peaceful sigh and settled into place. Muleki looked at my face in the rearview mirror, begging for advice on his best course of action. I shrugged my shoulders.

A short time later, Parley looked back, though now Muleki and Jennifer were both asleep, or feigning such. Turning forward again, Parley let the air whistle through his gritted teeth. Poor Parley. You couldn't help but feel for the guy. He just didn't know what he was up against when he started dating my sister. It's not like he wasn't due for such abuse. Parley was a die-hard chauvinist, the kind used to having a subservient female clinging to his arm. I'm sure the thing about Jenny which attracted him the most was the challenge she presented—how soon it might take to put such a girl under his thumb. Clearly it was his ego, not his heart, which was bruised.

When we reached Rock Springs to fill up with gas, everyone climbed out to stretch. Just outside the station's restrooms, Parley commanded Muleki to sit in the front seat for the rest of the trip. Muleki wasn't about to object. He didn't want to create any more trouble than necessary during his sojourn in the twentieth century. It's not that he feared Parley. A king's principal bodyguard would have little reason to fear a lubberly cowboy.

Still, it might have been better if Muleki had objected, at least for show. Parley's kind was quick to take advantage when observing anything which might be construed as weakness. If Muleki had huffed and puffed a bit before he backed down, it might have been a little more sating to the cowboy's pride.

Instead Muleki said, "That would be fine. It must be very uncomfortable up front for you."

As Muleki turned away, Parley grabbed his shoulder. He hadn't interpreted Muleki's statement as referring to physical discomfort. He took it as meaning it must have been uncomfortable for him to watch the "goings on" in the back seat, which was doubly embarrassing for the cowboy.

"Are you trying to make a fool out of me?" he asked.

"Of course not."

"You sayin' I should be jealous of you?"

"I was trying to be polite."

"I think you were trying to make me out to look like the south end of a horse, that's what I think."

The two men faced each other. Muleki's stance became defensive.

"Please don't force me to subdue you," warned Muleki.

Jennifer ran to my side shrieking, "Jim, do something!" Parley was laughing. "I don't think you're gonna come up on me from behind this time, hillbilly."

"C'mon guys—" I pleaded.

But this was one confrontation Parley didn't want stopped. As I moved forward to come between them, the cowboy launched his fist toward the Nephite's face. Muleki twisted slightly—artfully—and dodged the swing without stepping one inch out of his stance. Then he grabbed Parley's shoulder with one hand, his neck with the other, and tripped the cowboy into the inertia of his own swing, causing him to roll into a full flip and land flat on his back in the gas station's gravel.

Parley shook his head a time or two, then pulled himself to his feet to continue the attack, this time outstretching his arms to utilize his full size and weight to simply crush the obnoxious little twerp. Three seconds later, Parley was once again horizontal, this time face down, close enough to the gravel to chew a few pebbles.

A couple of other motorists had gathered to see Parley's final lunge. It was even more embarrassing than the first two, and Muleki ended it with a sharp-quick blow at the base of the skull which rendered the cowboy unconscious at the Nephite's hands for the second time this week.

Muleki felt terrible about the fight and repeated his regret several times to Jenny and I while we hoisted the groggy cowboy into the back seat.

As I was bending his knees to get them in the car, I noticed something unusual about twenty yards away, at the end of the gravel. There was a car there, parked just off the highway near a tangled strip of barbed-wire fence which separated the gas station from an adjoining cow pasture. The headlights on this vehicle were off, but the motor was running, and if I squinted my eyes I could make out the silhouettes of four persons within. Suddenly, the headlights burst on, in bright position, and the car, a weathered green Mercury Cougar, pulled onto the road and skidded away.

Muleki was too busy trying to make Parley comfortable to notice. Could it have been who I feared it was? It just wasn't possible. Not only was the vehicle not a white Impala, there were only four persons inside. I knew the Gadiantons were *five* in number, and besides, the odds of finding us in the middle of the Wyoming desert were far too great.

The cowboy didn't regain full coherence until just beyond the Utah border. Parley wouldn't say a word the rest of the trip. Jenny at least had had the decency to sit in the back with him and tend his bruises, but you could tell by the smiles she sent to Muleki, her heart was elsewhere.

The night wore on and my passengers dropped off to sleep again, one by one. I took this time to contemplate how different Thanksgiving vacation had been from what I'd expected. As we emerged from Provo Canyon and the highway became University Avenue, the events of the past three days came tumbling down upon me like an avalanche.

Brigham Young University had come to represent reality for me over the past couple of years. My home in Cody was a fantasy—a place where the innocence of childhood could be re-lived, a place where I could retreat and gear up to face the real world while Mom cooked my meals. Somehow, it was okay if peculiar things happened to me in Cody. They were always temporary.

Provo was where I faced reality and set my goals. This was where the world was supposed to be normal and I could learn to conquer all of life's challenges by utilizing normal rules. In Provo I didn't want to face the renewed entry in my memory banks about an ancient land I'd visited when I was thirteen years old. I didn't want to believe I'd ever met Teancum or stared into the eyes of Captain Moroni. I didn't want to believe I'd ever walked the market streets of Zarahemla or carried an obsidian-edge sword in battle against the Lamanites.

I didn't want to know that a conduit into another time lay beyond the "Rainbow Room" in the deep recesses of Cedar Mountain. I didn't want a Nephite, a Captain of the Guard in the Palace of the Chief Judge of Zarahemla, to be sleeping on the floor in my bedroom at King's Court Arms. And mostly, I didn't want to believe that Gadianton robbers might be lurking in the shadows, harboring desperate motives of revenge.

I just wanted to go back to my boresome life. I wanted to study for the semester finals which would begin in two weeks. I wanted to argue politics and religion with my roommates. I wanted to take girls to the movies and out for sundaes at *Carousel*—even if they broke my heart like Renae had.

Muleki stirred in the seat beside me, seeking a better position to sleep. Glancing at him reconfirmed my loss of normalcy. He was real. The Gadiantons were real. My only hope was to help Muleki find his mysterious sword as quickly as possible. Then he could go home and the pieces of my world could fall back into place.

I dropped by Heritage Halls and helped my sister carry her luggage into her apartment. When Jenny and I got back to the car, Parley had tossed his duffle bag in the trunk of his own vehicle and was pulling away. Jen waved goodbye, as if nothing had happened between them, though I'm sure it was unlikely the two would ever speak again.

Then my sister took Muleki's hand and told him what a great pleasure it was to meet him and how she hoped he had a safe trip to Oregon and how she wished he would keep in touch. At that point I admitted to Jen that Muleki was not taking the 7:00 a.m bus to Portland, but that he would be staying with me, at least for a couple of days. She was quite pleased by the news and had a difficult time masking her enthusiasm.

During the short drive to King's Court Arms I decided to warn Muleki about the obvious.

"She really likes you," I said. "I've never seen her chase someone so aggressively."

"She is very beautiful," Muleki admitted. "But I'm afraid there is no place in my heart for a woman right now."

And that ended that.

My apartment was empty and silent. All around me were reminders that I was home. Lars had left a nice heap of molding dishes in the sink. Andrew's door was bolted shut with a padlock, and Benny's *Sports Illustrated*, "Swim Suit Issue," was lying open on the front room floor. I kicked it under the couch before Muleki could notice.

Then I turned up the heat and told Muleki he might as well sleep in Benny's bed tonight. Tomorrow my roommates would arrive, and he'd have to sleep on the floor in my sleeping bag. "Church starts at eleven," I told him, and retired to my bedroom.

Of course, during the night, my ancient man returned, still standing behind the lightning-scarred trunk in the midst of that tiny cluster of trees, and still beckoning me forward, ever forward.

CHAPTER 7

We were late for church, as might have been expected considering the dismal hour we got home. To allow for the number of students still on vacation, our meetings were combined with the other ward at King's Court Arms which held their services in the Pardoe Drama Theatre of the Harris Fine Arts Center.

Muleki wore my blue *Mr. Mac* suit—the one I'd contemplated tossing in the trash after my mission. It had battle-worn knees and a badly ripped inner-lining—nevertheless, the Nephite thought the raiment was beautiful and expressed much gratitude that I would allow him to wear it. I told him, 'no problem,' and felt ashamed that vanity prevented me from being caught dead in such a thing.

We sneaked in just after the sacrament hymn and found a place in the back. Even before they began blessing the bread, I noticed Renae Fenimore seated on the stage, behind the podium, radiating in a bright pink-lace dress. Just my luck. She'd come back from Pocatello a day early to give a talk. How was I supposed to concentrate during sacrament? Seeing her up there entangled my intestines into a snarl of painful knots. After all these weeks, I still wasn't free of her spell.

"What's going on?" Muleki whispered.

Caught up in my own troubles, I'd entirely failed to realize that Muleki's church experience did not include the

sacrament. Where he was from, the law of Moses still prevailed, as I should have remembered from the occasion
he'd refused to eat pork.

"Like the prayer stated, we eat the bread and drink the
water in remembrance of the great sacrifice of the
Messiah," I explained.

I wasn't sure if it was proper for Muleki to partake. The
sacrament was intended to help renew the covenants we
made at baptism. Although the ancient prophet, Alma,
may have baptized in the wilderness before Muleki was
born, I wasn't certain if the ordinance was universally insti-
tuted among the Nephites until after Christ's coming. I
almost advised him to let the plate pass him by, but as the
bread arrived, I felt an urge not to interfere.

"I believe in the Christ," Muleki whispered humbly,
"and I believe in his sacrifice for my sins. This is a good
thing."

As I watched Muleki reverently eat the bread and drink
the water, each time bowing his head in prayerful contrition, I felt like I'd learned an appropriate lesson on the spirit of the law.

Renae's talk was on gratitude, as should have been
expected considering the season. I found it trite and over-
long. Of course, if Renae and I had been on better terms,
I'm sure I'd have found it brilliantly insightful.

In the hallway outside our classroom for Sunday School,
I couldn't escape her approach.

"Jim!" she called. "How was your Thanksgiving?"

This had to be played just right. I couldn't make it obvious I was still pining, and yet I couldn't be rude. In these
few moments I had to sell the impression that I couldn't
remember ever having dated her at all. Yet she had to be
convinced I still thought of her as a "dear, dear" friend.

In spite of her resistance some weeks before, when I'd
come on so strongly, I was certain she hadn't shaken the
flattery such attention leaves behind. How would her ego
stand it to think she may have been wrong about my feelings? Oh, the subtle games that humans play. If only the
rules of love were more akin to tic-tac-toe than chess.

"Renae!" I responded enthusiastically. "You look great! I loved your talk! There's someone I'd like you to meet."

Perfect delivery! What a tiger I am. If I were taking the trouble to introduce her to other guys, she would certainly wonder if my affections were all in her imagination.

"This is Muleki Jones. Muleki, Renae Fenimore."

"Hello," said Muleki.

"Nice to meet you," she replied. "Muleki, eh? Almost sounds 'Book-of-Mormonish.' *¿Habla Español?*"

"I suppose I do," Muleki answered.

Renae kinked an eyebrow in confusion, "You *suppose?*"

"He does," I assured her. This gift of tongues thing was gonna get us in trouble yet.

"Your family doesn't happen to be from Mexico, do they?" Renae asked.

"No. Uh—Oregon," said Muleki.

"The reason I ask," Renae explained, "parents in this country don't often name their children after heroes in the Book of Mormon. In Mexico it's different. The family I lived with as an exchange student down there had kids named Moroni, Helaman, and Nephi."

I couldn't help but fear Renae had called my bluff and was modestly flirting with my Nephite friend. Then she turned the attention back to me.

"My assumptions on Jim's name were wrong too. I thought he might have been named after the main character in *Treasure Island*, but Jim says no."

"That's because my real name isn't Jim," I admitted. "It's Jamie."

"Really?" Renae said. "You never told me that."

Ah, my ploy was working. She was hurt that I'd kept secrets from her.

"If I'd known that," she continued, "I might have gotten into the habit of calling you Jamie. That's always been one of my favorite names."

Something about this conversation was sounding awfully familiar, as if another black-haired beauty, in some distant land, had also preferred I go by my given name. The coincidence annoyed me. I had a bad habit of looking for hidden meanings in life, especially when it came to women. I had this fairy-tale notion that a miracle would help me identify my eternal mate. During my Freshman year at BYU, I met a girl I swore I'd seen before in dream—except, she was already engaged to some Romeo back in Colorado whom she married that February. Since then, I'd tried to ignore '*de-je-vu*-type' coincidences.

Still, I couldn't deny the fact that Renae was acting unusually warm toward me. I had to be cautious though; she may have only been trying to solicit a sign which told her I was still on the string.

Then she pulled me aside and said, "I want you to know something. I've wanted to tell you this for quite some time. If I had known beforehand that you were Andrew's room-mate, I would have never accepted his invitation to the Homecoming dance."

"That would've been silly," I responded. "Why should our friendship change your dating habits? It just goes to prove it's a small world."

Never had another human being mastered the art of 'cool' as well as I. I could tell my response was not the one she expected. Disarmed, she could only repeat, "Well, I just wanted you to know that."

"Thanks, that was thoughtful. But I never felt you'd done it deliberately anyway. It's nothing to worry about. I promise."

I didn't even bat an eye. What I really wanted to do was shake both her shoulders and moan, "Why, why, why did you ruin my life you insensitive cavewoman?" But I held my tongue, and she, awed by the omnipotence of my sincerity, could only hang there for a moment with an open mouth, until, finally smiling, she announced that class was beginning and we ought to take our seats within.

That afternoon Muleki and I drove over the Point of the Mountain on I-15 and entered Salt Lake County. The awesomeness of the task Muleki insisted we undertake was mind-boggling. In all, I counted nineteen *Smith's* grocery stores in the Salt Lake phone directory. Having no photograph of Todd Finlay, we could only hope some *Smith's* employee in one of those nineteen stores remembered a thin man in glasses buying four three-hundred dollar money orders in late October. Who was to say we'd even catch this employee during the right shift, or that the person even worked for *Smith's* anymore?

Add to that the fact that neither Muleki or I had any authority to be asking such questions. If I worked in a grocery store and somebody came in requesting me to remember certain money orders I'd written up in October, I'd have probably called the police.

Upon reaching the first store on our list, just off 53rd South in Murray, we discovered today's efforts had been a waste of time anyway. The department which sold money orders wasn't even open on Sundays. Driving back to Utah County, I couldn't help but express my overall opinion of this campaign.

"It's hopeless!" I barked. "I can't begin to tell you how much I would rather search for a needle in a haystack."

"We'll come back tomorrow," declared Muleki.

"I can't," I insisted. "I've got classes."

"If you understood what I was seeking," he proclaimed, "you would not hesitate."

"Well, I *don't* understand!" I cried, "I don't understand *any* of this. What makes this rusty sword so doggone important?!"

Muleki sighed, "Jim, you do not understand the evil rites which were performed when it was forged. Nor do I, but I do know that Akish, the founder of secret combinations among the people of Jared, gave it to his followers and asked them to use it to behead his father-in-law, which allowed for him to take possession of the throne. It then inspired a wilderness battle which destroyed his kingdom and reduced the population to all but thirty souls. The last king to possess the sword was Coriantumr. With it, he pursued a war which wiped out every last man, woman and child that called themselves Jaredites. This was the same blade he used to smite off the head of Shiz atop the Hill Ramah. Don't you see? Each time a kingdom has destroyed itself in my land, the sword was there."

"Men are accountable for their own wickedness," I stated. "You can't blame a sword."

"What you say is true, but the sword entices a mind, already corrupted by the wants of this world, to perform greater evils than it could ever imagine on its own. It feeds on the human soul like a maggot, persuading men that they can rule the world, when in reality, it wrenches from them even the power to rule themselves."

If this sword was all Muleki said it was, why were we trying to find it? Wouldn't we want to be as far away from such a thing as possible? It was all so hard to swallow. Yet as I thought back on my readings of the Book of Ether, Muleki's statements seemed all the more intriguing. The final conflict of the Jaredites had a subtext of pure and simple insanity—a hatred so entrenched that even when they could see the slopes of Ramah littered with thousands of the slain, they continued to fight, until finally, Coriantumr was all that remained, left alone to wander in the wilderness with only the sword as his companion.

I had to consider the remote possibility that what Muleki was saying was true. What if my skepticism permitted the sword to get into the hands of some madman in the Middle East, or some despot in South America, or even some power-hungry general in the United States? Or maybe worst of all, into the hands of men already convinced of its potential—the Gadiantons.

"All right," I reluctantly agreed. "I get out of class early on Tuesdays. We'll try again then. But I gotta tell you, Muleki, the chances of that sword even being in Salt Lake are pretty slim."

"No," Muleki disagreed. Then he became pensive and softly uttered, "It is here."

When we got back to my apartment, Benny and Lars had arrived home from Thanksgiving vacation. I introduced them to Muleki and told them he would be staying with us for a week or so.

After making Muleki and me some dinner, I asked Lars and Benny how they'd enjoyed their Thanksgivings. It became evident they were much more excited about events occurring *before* Thanksgiving. Lars went on and on about the UFO meeting he and Benny had attended before Benny's plane left.

"The Bernardians are like no other UFO club," Lars insisted. "Their evidences are much more profound as to why aliens visit this planet."

"Interesting ideas," agreed Benny. "They made a lot of sense."

"Has he got *you* hooked on this stuff now?" I asked.

"Well, I'm not ready to sell the farm," Benny admitted. "But I *am* convinced there's a lot about this universe we don't understand. I was impressed. I have to admit."

As Muleki remained seated at the table, trying to master the art of coiling spaghetti on a fork, I joined my roommates on the front room couch and asked, "So why *are* aliens visiting planet earth? And why don't they visit the *New York Times* instead of some old bass fisherman in the middle of a swamp?"

"For the same reason that Moroni didn't visit the *New York Times*," said Lars. "The world isn't ready for it. You gotta start small and grow. The Bernardians—I'm referring now to the extra-terrestrials, not the club—are helping to prepare the world for the ushering in of the Millennium, or as they call it, the Fourth Period. I can't explain it like they do. You gotta go to one of the meetings in person. They're having a meeting here in Provo a week from tomorrow."

"If all this is true, why hasn't the Church come out on it?" I asked.

"I think they will," declared Lars. "I wouldn't be surprised to see the two organizations merge one day."

I laughed scornfully, "That'll be the day." Then I looked at Benny to see if my attitude was sobering him up a bit.

Instead he added, "Nothing I heard contradicted anything in the gospel, Jim. It almost *proves* the Church is true. None of the founders are Latter-day Saints, yet they talk about the pre-existence, the state of the soul after death—they even talk about the earth as a living being—"

"I could show you a scripture in the Doctrine and Covenants that purports the same thing," interrupted Lars.

Benny concluded, "If I'd heard anything I thought was contradictory, I'd have walked right out of there. They say they don't want to take anything away which we already have—just add new insights that will give us greater happiness. Seems like a worthwhile motive, doesn't it?"

Something didn't sit right with me about this whole thing. Maybe I was just responding to the natural recoil which everybody has for new ideas. What made me most upset was seeing such an overwhelming change in Benny. He was taking this stuff so seriously, I was afraid we no longer had anything in common.

I went on, "It also says in the Doctrine and Covenants that only the prophet can add new revelations and teachings to the church."

"Yet Harold B. Lee told us men like Confucius and Buddha were inspired to teach many truths," Lars defended. "Latter-day Saints are commanded to seek all knowledge which is worthy and of good report wherever they find it. There's no reason to close your mind until you've checked it out, Jim."

About then Andrew burst through the door, his arms loaded down with a suitcase, a duffel bag, and a newspaper.

"Hey, Hawkins," he blurted before even saying 'Hello,' "I read all about your home town today." He tossed the newspaper on the counter.

"Did it hit *your* newspaper?"

"Page A-3. Bottom," he said and continued an uninterrupted beeline into his bedroom.

Benny waited for Andrew to close his door, then he leaned over to me and whispered, "By the way, Renae Fenimore called for you."

"You sure she was calling for *me*?"

"Positive," and then Benny gave me a wink. It was relieving evidence that Benny was still the same old Benny.

So "Operation Recover Renae" may have been working. So much was on my mind tonight I wasn't sure if I *wanted* it to be working. Did I have time for a social life when I was busy helping Nephites find swords and roommates make reservations on the first flying saucer to Neptune?

Whatever the case, I wasn't going to call Renae back tonight. Let her stew for a while.

Returning to the counter, Muleki stood over me as I read the headline: *Police Station Held-up, Gunmen At Large.*

There was disturbing new information in the article. It reported that the white Chevy Impala the Gadiantons had used to make their getaway was found abandoned on an old dirt road near Farson, Wyoming. Farson happened to be within a couple hours of where we filled up with gas in Rock Springs. In the trunk of the Impala, a man's body was discovered. He was identified as Larry Bridenbough, a citizen of Missoula, Montana with a reputation for drug abuse and petty theft. Bridenbough had been shot in the abdomen, no doubt during the exchange of bullets at the police station. Nevertheless, it was said he died from other wounds—wounds which had been inflicted with a knife. No doubt Mehrukenah had concluded that dragging along a wounded man was cramping their style. So much for honor and loyalty among thieves.

The article went on to say the police were now looking for a green Mercury Cougar, reported missing from a ranch house only a half mile from the abandoned Impala. Apparently the other modern recruit, Mr. Clarke, had taught the Gadiantons well how to survive in modern times—including how to hot-wire an automobile. Later, as Muleki was laying out my sleeping bag on the floor of my room, I told him about the car I'd seen at the gas station in Rock Springs, how it had turned on it's brights and skidded away.

"As I feared, they're following us," Muleki concluded. "They've learned about this school—this Brigham Young University. They may be watching us every moment, waiting for the right opportunity to move in. Jim, I beg you, don't go anywhere without me at your side."

"But I have classes," I said. "I can't hardly drag you with me all over campus."

"You say your school is owned by the Church?" asked Muleki.

"Yes, that's right."

"Then it is God's land," the Nephite determined. "It is like a temple. I don't think they will go there. You should be safe as long as you don't wander out of its bounds alone. Still, I'll remain as close as I can."

It occurred to me what Muleki meant. The land upon which the university sat had been dedicated by prophets and apostles. But could that guarantee anything? I'm sure about every crime imaginable had occurred on BYU property at one time or another. Maybe it was a question of how far gone the Gadiantons were. Being so blatantly committed to evil, they might actually feel a sort of physical discomfort there, almost like a severe allergic reaction, making them unable to breathe or function.

After I'd agreed to Muleki's terms, he closed his eyes and drifted off to sleep. Unable to do the same, I climbed out of bed and flipped on the screen of my personal computer.

There was still one task to perform before I ended my day. I had a letter to write. It would be addressed to Cambridge, Massachusetts. Though I had no idea what to say, or even how to say it, my old comrade, Garth Plimpton, had to know about the harrowing events of the previous week. I'd have called him, but despite Garth's full-tuition scholarship, his beggarly budget had not allowed for a phone.

Maybe Garth, unlike myself, had succeeded in retaining his memories of the Nephite world. As close as Garth had always kept to the Spirit, I felt his insight on this escapade might be priceless. Besides, why should I have to bear this burden all by myself? After all, Muleki had accused him of being just as guilty of teenage time-tampering as I was.

CHAPTER 8

Arriving on campus Monday morning, Muleki carefully checked his artillery before climbing out of the car. He hid one knife in the inner pocket of his jacket and another under the pant leg on his right shin. Since I knew the Gadiantons had guns, I wasn't sure how protected I was supposed to feel.

"As long as the Gadiantons think you still have the sword, they will not kill you," Muleki explained.

"Oh, that's great news," I sarcastically raved. "So can I at least hope to be tortured? Muleki, how am I supposed to concentrate in my classes?"

"When I return to my land with the sword," Muleki said, "the Gadiantons will follow me back. Your part will be over."

I don't remember my professors' lectures that day. This was not a good state of mind for me to be in two weeks before finals. Each time I came out of class, Muleki was faithfully waiting. Since I had Racquetball in the Smith Fieldhouse before lunch on Mondays, I usually went across the street for Hawaiian fast food, but Muleki wouldn't allow it since the restaurant was off campus. Instead, we ate dessicated chicken burgers at the *Cougareat*.

The day ended without conflict. Hoping to close the day on a bright note, I dragged the phone into my bedroom, since Andrew was studying at the counter, and finally took the initiative to call Renae. She answered after only one ring. I revelled in the thought that she might have waited by the phone all night and all day.

Renae and I talked an hour, about the weather, old times, it really didn't matter. I made my demeanor warm and caring, but not *too* warm and caring. Actually, my immediate frame of mind helped convey the impression I sought. It was obvious to Renae that there was something I didn't feel comfortable discussing. Such only served to draw me further into her heart. Before the conversation closed, Renae and I had determined to try again, Friday night, with another all-out, honest-to-goodness date.

Hanging up the receiver, I could only contain myself for about a second. Then I did a Toyota jump and hollered, "YES!" Muleki rushed in from the living room, fearing my yell had been a plea for help.

Suddenly, I remembered my promise to let Muleki tag along wherever I went. My exhilaration started to deflate. Friday had to be an exception. I couldn't have a Nephite stalking ten paces behind me the whole night! Then I got an idea which would at least make things tolerable.

"Muleki, you and I are going on a double-date Friday."

"Double-date?" asked Muleki.

"Dating is the way we court women," I explained. "We take them to dinner or a movie or a ball game—whatever! Don't tell me you don't date in Zarahemla?"

Muleki shook his head, "I don't think we do it in the same fashion."

"Well, I hope a Twentieth-century date will be the best memory you take back with you. Now, it's just a question of who." The answer was obvious. I picked up the receiver again and dialed the number of my beloved sister, Jenny.

It started snowing heavily during the night. By Tuesday morning the stuff was coming down in flakes as big as silver dollars. Muleki had never seen snow before, except on the tips of distant mountains. His body had yet to climatize in this land—in fact he seemed to be endlessly shivering, even under the weight of my old ski parka. Yet, as we stepped out of my apartment surrounded by eight inches of heavenly whiteness, Muleki's eyes lit up, reminding me of the four-year-old boy I once saw greeting his father, Captain Teancum.

The Nephite dropped to his knees in the powdery cushion beyond the front walk and tossed an armful into the air. It floated down all around him, carpeting his hair, and dangling on the ends of his eyelashes.

"It's wonderful!" he cried. "I want to carry a sack of it back to my nephews!"

"You'll have to carry a refrigerator with it," I told him.

Muleki couldn't resist the temptation we'd all overcome as children to open his mouth and catch a flake on his tongue. Succeeding, he savored the taste of it like a drop of chocolate. I couldn't help but laugh with the Nephite. Anxious to introduce him to yet another great snow tradition, I scooped up a handful and packed it for launching. But when I lifted my head to scope my target, the expression on Muleki's face had changed.

He was standing as frozen as an icicle, looking at something between the buildings on the other side of the yard and pulling his stone blade out from within his parka. I turned to see what had drawn away his attention, but the thin walkway, forty yards ahead, was empty of all but the sound of water dripping off the roof.

"Is there a problem?" I wondered.

Muleki was slow to answer, as if he hadn't heard me.

"No," he finally confirmed. "I thought I saw someone. I may have been mistaken."

"Might have just been a student," I said. "After all, this is a school day."

Muleki requested that he not participate in scraping the snow off my car. Instead, I did all the labor, while he carefully watched the surroundings. During the drive to campus, Muleki remained overly wary and cautious. It was a grateful moment when we pulled into the Law Building's parking lot on campus. I think it was the first time I drew a breath since leaving King's Court Arms.

As soon as my last Tuesday class had let out, the Nephite and I braved the snowy interstate and returned to Salt Lake

County. The wind made conditions no less than a blizzard. Traffic jams kept us on the highway for two hours before we could again reach the first *Smith's* grocery off 53rd South.

At each stop the story was the same. First they asked if we were cops, then they'd sic their managers on us. The managers always spouted store policy that no one, except the police, or the individual who'd purchased the money order, could see the records. The whole thing was terribly embarrassing. Often there was a long line of people behind us, watching us argue and hoping we might drop dead so they could step over us. Every clerk we talked to stated she had no recollection of such an individual, and half of them added that even if they did, they couldn't tell us. We struck out in Murray, Sandy, and South Salt Lake—but then, in West Valley City, we struck gold.

It was all on account of my new approach. This time, when it became my turn at the booth, I claimed *I* had written the money orders and that I needed the totals for tax purposes. The deception worked like a charm. They opened up the books to me without hesitation, even providing a quiet corner for me to browse.

Muleki waited for me in the frozen food aisle, utterly fascinated by all the varieties and colors. He interrupted me once to show me a bag stuffed with frozen corn-on-the-cob, ecstatic to have found something he recognized.

Only a moment later, my finger landed on the bullseye. A man by the name of Todd West had purchased four three-hundred dollar money orders on October 21st. But my elation was short-lived. In the space beside his name, where a customer was asked to write his phone number, the words "no phone" had been scribbled.

I had no option but to come clean with the lady in the service booth and confess it wasn't me that had bought the money orders. I explained that the *real* Todd Finlay, (alias Todd West) had left his family and that we were trying to catch up with him before the authorities did.

The clerk, a heavy set lady with bouffant hair, was touched by my dramatization of abandoned wife and daughter, the plight igniting her motherly instincts. She admitted to remembering the man who'd purchased the money orders.

"A skinny man with glasses and a beaked nose, am I right?" she asked.

"Dead on," I replied.

"He buys money orders here regularly—always breaking them up to suit our three-hundred dollar limit on individual checks. I remember asking him why he didn't just get the whole thing from a bank. He said he didn't like banks."

"Did he tell you anything which might help us locate him?"

"No. He always writes 'no phone,' just like you see."

"The next time he comes in," I pleaded, "could you try and find out where he lives? Maybe you could tell him you've had a change of policy and if he doesn't have a phone, he needs to write down an address. *Anything* which might help, we'd greatly appreciate."

The lady squinted one eye, scrutinizing us closely.

I coiled my hands together on the counter. "Please. We're trying to keep him from getting into a lot of trouble."

She pursed her lips and shook her head from side to side. "Terrible thing, abandoning your family. I always wondered what drove a man to do something so awful."

"He's not well," I stressed. "We need to get him some help."

"Well, I think you boys have undertaken a worthwhile cause," she commended. Pointing at her name tag, she said, "My name is Katie. I'll keep an eye out for you. If I find out something, I'll let you know. You boys got a phone number?"

This lady was heaven-sent. I almost fell to my knees repeating, "Oh, thank you, thank you . . . "

Driving back over the Point of the Mountain, I allowed my spirits to peak. There was hope looming on the horizon that my life would soon return to normal.

By Friday afternoon, the lady at the store—Katie—had not yet called. Was it selfish of me to say I was glad? I'd been told that somewhere out there was a mystical sword endowed with the power to influence humanity to genocide. If it were true, I hoped my descendants would say I was intoxicated with the folly of youth instead of suffering from hopeless apathy, because this night my heart was giddy beyond words at the prospect of spending the next few hours with Renae.

"What is this?" asked Muleki.

"Cologne," I answered, arranging my hair in the mirror. "Put some on. Girls like the smell. It makes 'em crazy."

"I should want your sister to be made crazy?" he asked.

"It's the kind of crazy that *nobody* objects to," I winked. Muleki picked up the green *Polo* bottle and turned it over in his hands, eyeing it like an exotic weapon—which, in a way, wasn't too far off. I was going to have to teach this guy a thing or two about the subtleties of male vanity.

"If you insist on staying at my side tonight, you're going to have to look the part," I insisted. "Time, or no time for women, I'm not going to double-date with a dweeb."

I presented the Nephite with my second sharpest button up shirt and slacks and stood him in front of my bedroom mirror. Then I taught him the value of stick deodorant and how to apply it to the under arms without removing the shirt. He didn't like the feel of it much.

"It's slimy, like oil on a fish," he winced.

"But it smells a lot better, eh?"

"I'm not so sure."

We moussed his thick black hair—not too much, for it might dispel a girl's temptation to run her fingers through it, but enough to keep it in place. Pouring a little *Polo* into my hand, I pressed it into both palms and slapped it onto my cheeks. Muleki imitated me and after slapping it to his face, his eyes grew wide and he staggered back a step.

"It is *strong*," he said.

"You may have used a bit much. Don't worry, it fades."

Don't get the impression I felt comfortable doing this. Nephite or not, it just wasn't proper for guys to help other guys get ready for a date, and I wasn't about to make this a habit. I just wanted to say that.

We were ready. I should have known Muleki hadn't defocused his one-track mind when in my bedroom I watched him slip the knife into the sheath strapped to his calf. Still, I wouldn't have guessed that Muleki was two-thousand years old for anything. He was a twenty-first century man, right off the cover of *Gentlemen's Quarterly*, and all I could say as we left the apartment was "Look out world! Never has man nor Nephite looked so good."

"Jershonite," Muleki corrected.

It was a beautiful night, quite warm despite the snow. We drove down 9th East enroute to pick up Jenny at Heritage Halls. Nearing Maeser Hall, where she lived, Muleki turned to me and said, "I hope we're planning to stay on campus."

"Muleki," I pleaded, "This is not the attire of a campus date. This is the attire of a classy restaurant—*Magleby's* or *Sill's*. I promise we'll stay among people—*lots* of people."

"That may not matter anymore," the Nephite revealed. "They are getting more desperate every day."

"We haven't seen anyone or anything out of the ordinary all week!" I pointed out.

To state the obvious, Muleki charged, "Just because we haven't seen them, it doesn't mean they're not here."

My zeal for creating a memorable reunion with Renae was clouding my common sense. Of course Muleki was right. After all, the Gadiantons might have a dozen more men in their band by now.

But what was there to do on campus? A campus date was something only a freshman would force a girl to endure—and only because he was either lacking wheels or imagination. I hadn't seen a movie at the Varsity Theatre or gone bowling downstairs in the Wilkinson Center since before my mission. Then Muleki got profound.

"It's for the best. If this girl likes you, she won't care where she goes."

The Nephite was absolutely right. In fact he was a social genius! If Renae's feelings remained phony or uncertain, I'd find out early in the evening.

I urged Muleki to knock on the door of Jenny's apartment. He objected at first; I don't know if it was out of shyness or because of his desire to get through this evening without giving her the wrong impression. He was with me tonight strictly for my protection, he explained, and he couldn't allow himself to be distracted.

"We'll be on campus," I reminded him. "Feel free to give yourself a moment to be distracted."

From the car, I watched him step into the lobby of Jenny's building. He looked back at me for assurance before he knocked. After I nodded, he let his fist strike thrice on the door. I could tell Jenny had answered by the way he stood there gaping. She was wearing her ivory sweater with the glitter specks. Her blonde hair hung all the way down her back and her make-up had the perfect nuance of glamour. Jenny didn't need much anyway.

She put her arm out for Muleki to take it. Muleki was confused by the gesture. Instead of taking her arm, he took hold of her hand—a move slightly too personal for a first date at BYU, but Jenny didn't object. In fact she seemed to enjoy the strong grip of her Nephite warrior.

Renae told me to pick her up at her uncle's house in the "tree streets" east of campus. Along the one called Cherry Lane we found a mailbox emblazoned with the 'Fenimore' name.

Muleki's words to me before I departed the car were, "Don't leave my sight, or I'll be forced to come in after you."

Jenny gave him a queer look, laughing once, wondering if his warning was some sort of private joke.

"Right," I impatiently agreed, and strolled up the walk.

Meeting Muleki's specifications, I stood in the doorway while Mrs. Fenimore fetched her niece. I waited there for several minutes, giving me enough time to adequately defeat her twelve-year-old cousin in a staredown. Finally, Renae emerged from a second-floor room and gracefully glided down the stairs to greet me. She was more attractive tonight than I'd ever seen her—a stylish black suede jacket with a lavender skirt, tan nylons, black pumps, and just the right touch of *Chanel No. 5*.

"Shall we go?" she invited, her eyes bright with anticipation.

I told her aunt how nice it was to meet her and we were off. The news that we would be spending the evening on campus was either received quite well, or else both Renae and Jenny were excellent liars.

"They're showing *The Bicycle Thief* at International Cinema," Renae proclaimed. "Oh, *please*, let's go. It's one of my favorite movies."

Everyone agreed. There was an early showing at 6:10 which still left us plenty of time to grab a bite in the *Cougareat* when it let out. This was Muleki's first movie. If Jenny was hoping the Nephite's attention would be exclusively hers for the evening, she may have found the International Cinema idea somewhat disappointing. The warrior's eyes remained glued to the screen.

"The people are so *big*!" he exclaimed soon after the auditorium went dark. "Not like the house box where they're so small."

A few of the people around us looked at him like he was nuts. I think his date was reminded how deep in the Oregon mountains he may have been raised. It was equally disquieting when he laughed at lines spoken by the Italian characters before the subtitles had come up on the screen.

"How many languages does this guy know?" Renae whispered to me.

"All of them," I answered, then I turned to her and smiled wryly, as if to say, "Had you going there, didn't I?"

When the movie was over, we took the elevator to one of the upper floors on the Kimball Tower and found an unlocked classroom with a wide view. At first Muleki hesitated going near the window for fear he might fall, but after a moment, with his face pressed against the glass, we again watched the Captain of the Guard in the Palace of the Chief Judge of Zerahemla drop his jaw in awe of our modern world. The Christmas season had given the city twice as many sparkling lights as usual, and as always, the Provo Temple was the brightest beacon of them all.

"There is nothing so high where I'm from," he declared. "Nothing but mountains and great soaring birds."

As he said it, I noticed Jenny at his side, looking up at the Nephite with equal awe. It was his naiveté which she found so enchanting. There was nothing pretentious, nothing insincere, about a single bone in Muleki's body. He seemed to have mastered the art of being childlike while maintaining a masculine grip on everything around him. Jenny was convinced she'd found her own "Crocodile Dundee," and I could tell she wanted to stuff him in a closet somewhere before someone else could discover her secret. Muleki reciprocated her feelings only as much as was chivalrous and polite.

Perhaps my Uncle Spencer's prophesy would come true: Jenny would receive her comeuppance. I'd been around Muleki long enough to know that he was too much like his father. Duty came first—-nothing could stand in its way. Muleki was all too aware that he did not belong here. Seeing the wonders he saw now could only be enjoyed in light of the grave duty he'd been sent to perform.

I wanted to pull my sister aside and tell her who he was. After all, she had been with Garth and me among the Nephites. In fact, it was Jenny's folly which had led us into the time passageway in the first place. She'd known the ancient peoples, and it wouldn't have taken much for her to understand their commitments. If only her memory could be jogged in the same way mine had been. Yet it was clear to me it might be best if she *didn't* remember. For now, it appeared her life was not threatened. The less she knew, the better.

After the girls declared their hunger, we descended the elevator and made our way across campus to the Wilkinson Center. Inside the ice cream parlor on the bottom floor, I read the menu aloud, for Muleki's sake. He leaned toward the idea of getting himself a banana split since it actually had an ingredient he recognized. While Jenny was deciding what she wanted, Renae whispered in my ear a desire to go upstairs and get a pizza. I slipped Muleki enough money to cover the bill and told Jenny we'd meet later in the step-down lounge. I could tell as we walked away, Muleki was sorely tempted to follow, but Jenny had a viselike grip on his arm.

What a relief to finally have a moment alone with Renae, without Muleki breathing down my neck. Entering the *Cougareat*, we passed the booth where Renae and I had broken up earlier in the semester. Renae grabbed my arm and whisked us by. She may have been thinking there was no need to re-live unhappy mistakes. When we got to the counter, the guy behind it, whose name tag said 'Larry,' broke the sad news that they were out of pizza for the evening.

"What?" I cried, mocking anger. "No pizza? How could this have happened in an age of enlightened men?"

"Sorry," replied Larry.

"Ah, don't worry about it," Renae insisted. Then she told Larry, "I'll just have a cheeseburger."

"No!" I shrieked. "No lady of mine need settle for second best. If you want pizza, then you shall have pizza."

"You might try *Leonardo's*," hinted Larry.

Leonardo's was a pizza place just below campus.

"What do you think?" I asked my date.

"Sounds great. What about Muleki and Jennifer?"

"I sense they need to be alone for awhile. We'll bring a couple of pieces back for 'em."

Renae and I escaped out the back door of the Wilkinson Center and headed down the salt-strewn sidewalk under the power plant. We laughed another time or two, and then everything got quiet between us. Renae took my hand as we walked, staring down at the rock salt under our feet.

Without looking up, she said, "I'm glad you didn't give up on me." And then she turned to see my reaction.

I said nothing. Let her grovel a bit longer, I told myself. Then she added, "I never told you, but I was engaged last summer. It had only broken off a few months before we started dating. I must have still been a little gun-shy."

In spite of her confession, I wasn't going to slip into the same trap. I replied, "Let's just take it slow then. One day at a time. I'm in no hurry. Are you?"

A deep smile formed on her face—one so brimming with affection it made me want to kiss it. But the fear that such a move would ultimately be fatal kept me from executing the attempt. Instead, I put my arm around her shoulders and tightly drew her in.

Just then, I realized we'd reached the street which marked the boundary of BYU property. I hesitated, almost letting my shoe stop in mid-air over the curb. "What's the matter?" Renae asked.

The streets were nearly empty. A few cars skirted by, tossing up the slush. Up near the BYU Health Center another boy and his date were laughing, making their way home in the opposite direction. To the south, where *Kinko's Copies* and *Leonardo's* were located, we could hear the faint voices of cheerful people and see the glimmer of headlights as they turned down 700 East.

I thought about Muleki's statement—his theory really—that the dedicated land of Brigham Young University was a barrier against evil. It seemed absurd. The Gadiantons may have been evil, but they were evil *men*—not evil spirits or demons. This campus had certainly seen its share of evil men. It was only logical to conclude that the reason we hadn't been attacked on campus was simply because there was no one yet in Provo who wanted to attack us.

"Nothing," I replied to Renae.

The light of the streetlights was stark against the new fallen snow, making the night brighter and the shadows less foreboding. It was this light, finally, which gave me the confidence to step off the curb and lead Renae across the street.

It was only a block or so to *Leonardo's Pizza Parlor*. To get there we had to cross another parking lot—one belonging to a nearby condominium complex—and one other street.

The way was not as well salted as the walks on BYU campus, so Renae and I laughed each time we had to save each other from falling. Nearing *Leonardo's*, I was thinking how satisfying it would be to tell Muleki about where we had gone. I'd offer it as proof that we could end this silly practice of him staying near my side every minute.

Just then a voice called out to me from behind.

"Jimawkins."

CHAPTER 9

There were three of them, standing among the cars at our left, emerging from the night like sharks from murky waters, without warning and giving us no hope of escape. One of them was the modern recruit, Mr. Clarke. The other two were Gadiantons: the big-necked one called Boaz and the wizened old man called Mehrukenah.

They were wearing different clothing—shabby looking, as if from a thrift store. Mehrukenah appeared unarmed, as did Mr. Clarke, but Boaz wielded a handgun, a large one, the same kind as the one they'd given me. Draped around his massive neck was the mangy collar of an oversized grey parka. Though he'd hidden the pistol inside the coat's sleeve, I could still see the barrel, coal black and aimed at my heart.

Renae's grip on my arm was like a tourniquet.

"Who are they, Jim?" she whimpered.

"We are angels of vengeance," answered Mehrukenah. "Though we might have been envoys of friendship."

The three of them moved cautiously nearer, pleasantly surprised to find us entirely unarmed and helpless. I wanted to look around, see if there was anyone nearby, but as I began to turn my head, Mehrukenah's voice became tense.

"Don't move a single step," he warned. "If you do, Boaz will kill you both, and believe me, I won't lose a single night's sleep for it."

"Hand them your wallet, Jim," Renae suggested.

Mr. Clarke laughed. He and Boaz had stopped about ten feet away. Mehrukenah stepped closer and smiled.

"We don't want your wallet," he clarified. "We want the sword. And we *don't* want any more lies."

Mehrukenah quickly drew a knife from inside his coat. It was black and sleek, very similar to knives I had seen once before . . . where had it been? Mehrukenah noticed my reaction to the blade.

"Do you recognize me now?" he asked.

Skewing my eyes, I let his features sink into my mind, again searching for a corresponding memory. From the depths of my psyche, a suppressed image broke its chains and rose to the surface. I remembered him now. We'd first seen his face in the crowded throngs of an ancient market-place. In secret, Garth Plimpton and I had watched him purchase seven sleek obsidian knives—exactly the same type as the blade he now possessed. Like spies in a dime-store thriller, we'd followed him through the streets of Zarahemla until he entered a dark and abandoned building filled with conspiring kingmen whose ambitions were to use these knives as tools of assassination against seven of the Nephite's highest ranking leaders.

"I see you at least recognize this knife," Mehrukenah noted. "You should. You've seen it before. It was once meant to kill the notorious Captain Moroni. But, alas, it never tasted his blood."

Finally, I remembered him in prison, his jaw clenched in hatred. The conspiracy which he had espoused was all but crushed, due to a warning we had sounded. All this man awaited was someone to connect him with his crimes. Garth Plimpton and I had pointed the finger.

"I spat at you once," he claimed, "though, it seems to me I may have missed. Not that it matters. I don't spit upon people anymore. There are more satisfying ways to express displeasure." He was inches away now, close enough for me to count the gaps in his teeth. Abruptly, Mehrukenah shifted his attention to Renae and seized her around the neck. She shrieked as Mehrukenah dragged her between

Boaz and Mr. Clarke and spun again to face me. One hand was clasping Renae's chin and the other held the knife to her throat. I started to lunge forward, but Mehrukenah only pressed the blade tighter against her skin.

"Where is the sword?" he demanded.

Renae's eyes were full of terror. Her life had been one of peace and quiet ambition—nothing more dramatic than an exchange trip to Mexico or the collapse of an engagement to be married. Every shred of security in her innocent world had been stripped away in a fraction of a second. I was dying inside for her.

"You have until I count three to answer," he said, "or I will kill her. It's that simple. *One.*"

My girlfriend was about to be murdered before my eyes! There was no way to prevent it! Had I known where the sword was, I'd have turned it over in an instant—*but I didn't!* Was there nothing I could do to save her?!

"*Two.*"

I opened my mouth to speak, to admit that I couldn't help him—to beg for mercy—to say *anything* which might stay his hand! But the words choked in my throat, and all efforts to dislodge them were futile. I couldn't utter a single sound. Not even so much as a cough.

"*Three!*"

"All right!" I blurted. "I'll tell you what you want to know."

What kind of words were these? They just came to me—the inspiration of a malevolent muse, solving nothing.

"Start talking," commanded Mehrukenah, the blade still cold against Renae's throat.

"It's at my apartment!" I cried. "In my bedroom."

Pleased, Mehrukenah lowered the obsidian knife, but he did not relax his grip on Renae. He smiled at me proudly, and with a jerk of his head, indicated a white Honda Prelude parked about three spaces away. Obviously, the newspapers had convinced the Gadiantons to ditch the Mercury Cougar and steal a new set of wheels.

"Then let's go," he said, wasting no time. "We'll even let you drive, Jimawkins."

Mr. Clarke tossed me the keys, then he climbed into the Prelude's back seat, sliding all the way over. Boaz stepped around and gave me a shove toward the automobile with the barrel of his gun. Mehrukenah guided Renae toward Mr. Clarke's open door and stuffed her in to sit between them, never taking the knife far enough away from her flesh to leave any doubt whether his threat was still imminent.

Boaz, feigning kindness, opened my door on the driver's side. Climbing in, I looked back at Renae. She appeared surprisingly peaceful. So peaceful I thought she might be in shock.

"Are you all right?" I asked.

"Yes," she replied calmly.

Renae seemed to have mustered enough nerve to face whatever lay ahead. Mehrukenah struck me in the ear with the back of his hand.

"Drive!" he ordered. "She'll be fine as long as you continue to cooperate and as long as you're telling the truth."

Boaz climbed into the passenger's side, slamming the door behind him, keeping me in the sights of his gun.

I started the car and slowly rolled out of the parking space. Before we pulled onto the street, I glanced in the rearview mirror. Above the shadowed faces of Mehrukenah and Renae I could see the BYU campus. At this moment Muleki and Jennifer were just finishing their banana splits and beginning to wonder where we'd gotten off to. Even if they concluded we were missing, I had the keys to Jenny's Mazda in my pocket. Last summer, I'd made an extra set and hid them under the mat of the front seat, but I wasn't certain if I'd ever told Jenny—and even if I had, I couldn't imagine she would remember.

We were cooked.

As I stopped at the end of 820 North, preparing to turn onto 900 East, Boaz turned to Mehrukenah.

"What about Shurr and the others?" he asked.

"We'll come back and pick them up after we get the sword," Mehrukenah replied.

"But that wasn't the plan," informed Boaz.

Mehrukenah glowered at his ancient comrade, but suppressing his anger, he turned to Mr. Clarke.

"Get out and find the others," he ordered. "Tell them what's going on." His eyes widened into an odd, knowing look, as if communicating some sort of clandestine intention. "Do you understand me?"

"Yeah," Mr. Clarke replied, receiving his message, "I understand you."

Mr. Clarke climbed out of the car. As we drove away, he remained standing in the street, making no immediate attempt to begin looking for Shurr, but Boaz did not turn around to notice.

These men appeared to have been staking out the borders of campus all night—perhaps even since Monday—just waiting for us to make a wrong move. As I feared, more people had recognized their secret signs and had been proselyted to their cause. It was impossible to be sure how many were in league with them now.

"You don't know how satisfying it is to finally be this close to you," Mehrukenah said to me. "I've always thought of you as my quetzal feather, Jimawkins—my greatest prize. When the war with Ammoron's Lamanites was over and we were all released from prison, I searched for you and your friend for nearly a year. You see, I've always made it a habit to repay my enemies. But none deserved my consideration more than you, my quetzal feather. You should be grateful that I've given you a way to repent. When you give me the sword, I'll consider that your debt to me has been paid."

I knew better than to believe that. Even if I had the sword to give, I wouldn't have expected him to depart without cutting my throat. Not that it mattered, because when he learned there was nothing in my apartment even resembling a sword, I was subject to his lethal surgery anyway. Nevertheless, we continued our course toward King's Court Arms.

Mehrukenah continued, "After gaining the confidence of certain members of the Jershonite kinship, I learned you were no longer among us—that you and your friend had gone away to a secret place—a volcano in the land of

Melek with a tunnel leading upwards. Not until Rerenak had stolen the sword did I follow through with my ultimate intention of entering the tunnel to find you. Who would have thought such a land as this could exist? And who would have thought we would find *allies*?"

We turned onto the street of my apartment complex and drove past the neighboring buildings. I knew they'd learned where I lived. Muleki's sighting of one of them on Tuesday morning had not been a mistake. I couldn't postpone the moment of truth by dragging them around town. Pulling into my parking lot, I found an empty stall close to the first building.

"I'm very pleased," said Mehrukenah. "I expected you to try something stupid and force me to do something tragic in return. Thank you for not being foolish."

Mehrukenah moved closer to Renae and tightened his arm around her waist.

"Now here's the plan," he announced. "Boaz will follow you into your apartment. You will retrieve the sword, and Boaz will accompany you as you carry it back here. It's a simple plan because I don't want you to misunderstand. I'll remain here with your lovely lady friend in case you make an error."

I could see the reflection of the streetlights on the obsidian blade as he pressed it, once again, against Renae's throat.

"Get out of the car," Boaz instructed me.

I looked back at Renae, wondering if I would ever again see her alive.

"Hurry, Jim," she pleaded, unaware of my lie, faithfully believing that I could provide them with what they desired.

"Yes, do hurry," repeated Mehrukenah.

How could I leave her, knowing there was nothing in my apartment with which to gain her freedom? It suddenly seemed so foolish not to have told Mehrukenah the truth. Maybe he would have found some value in what we'd learned in Salt Lake. My instincts told me his anger at having been deceived a second time, no matter what I had to say, would have been interpreted as deserving of grave punishment. Did he know that if he killed Renae, I would become useless to him? Unable to live with the guilt, I'm sure I would consign myself to die with her. Boaz thrust the barrel of his .357 Magnum into my ribs.

"Go!" he commanded.

When I climbed out of the car, shutting the door, Boaz did the same.

"Let's move!" he repeated, again pulling the gun inside the arm of his parka so it couldn't be seen. I walked toward my apartment with Boaz at my heels.

Adding to Mehrukenah's threat, he said, "If you try anything, I'll kill you, and the girl will die as well."

The way Boaz handled the gun, it was clear he hadn't acquired much skill in it's use. I might have been able to run. There was more than a good chance his bullet would miss. But Mehrukenah's knife would not miss Renae. The old man had planned this affair so flawlessly. It was a shame I couldn't reward such stratagem with the return of the sword.

I kept walking toward my apartment, climbing onto the sidewalk and heading around the front of my building. Reaching the door, I could hear the television blaring within. Opening it, Benny and his girlfriend, Allison, were seated close together on the couch, watching a horror video. Lars was in the front room, too, perched on the arm of the easy chair. I could also see Andrew in his bedroom, studying at his desk.

Entering the apartment, they all turned to note my arrival, even doing a double-take when they saw I had company, but then they turned back to the movie, which was nearing its climax.

"You got a phone call, Jim," remembered Benny, keeping his eyes glued to the tube. "Long distance. A guy named Garth Plimpton. He said he'd call back later."

I didn't respond, but Benny thought nothing of it. As I moved toward my bedroom, Allison turned her head to give us a smile, but on the whole, everyone was completely oblivious to what was going on. Boaz remained silent and kept behind me. Opening my bedroom door, I switched on the light. My computer was still on from my attempts to complete a report for "American Heritage" the night before, but the monitor light was off. As I stepped past it, directing my attention toward my closet to pretend the sword was on the upper shelf, I discreetly flipped on the monitor. It always took several seconds for the light to come on. During that time, I reached toward the closet shelf and wrapped my fingers around the bronze statue of a cavalry scout on a horse—a gift from a sculptor I'd baptized in Portland.

When the monitor light ignited, it was accompanied by a faithful hiss of static. Boaz glanced away from the closet to see what had caused the sound, and his eyes were momentarily captivated by the bright blue screen. That was all the time I needed to introduce the bronze cavalry scout to the back of Boaz's head. Grunting once, the Gadianton collapsed onto my bedroom floor, dropping the gun. I picked up his weapon and bolted back into the living room.

Everyone had heard the statue strike and the body fall.

"What happened?" Benny exclaimed, then he saw the gun in my hand.

"I need some duct tape! Where do we keep the duct tape?" I demanded, throwing open every drawer in the kitchen.

Andrew arose from his studies to peer into my bedroom. The others were rushing over to do likewise. Andrew gasped at the body on the floor.

"Did you kill him?" he asked.

The duct tape was in the drawer next to the silverware. I pulled it out and fought through the crowd to get back into my bedroom. Everyone in the apartment watched as I hoisted Boaz's arms behind his back and proceeded to wrap them in tape.

"Who is this guy?" asked Benny, "What has he done?"

There was no time to concentrate on answering their questions, which would have only inspired dozens more. Boaz was starting to awaken as I finished multiple wraps around his hands and began working on his feet.

Groggily, with his face to the floor, he uttered, "I'll kill you, Jimawkins! For this you will die!"

I picked up the gun again and left him there on my bedroom floor. Then, reemerging into the living room, I looked at Andrew.

"Call the police," I told him.

"Not until you tell us what he's done," Andrew replied.

Could you believe this guy? I barely resisted my temptation to clobber Andrew with the same bronze statue. Instead I slammed the arrogant Californian against the bathroom door. The expression on my face was so intense I actually saw dread in Andrew's eyes.

Through gritted teeth, I hissed, "If you don't call the police, I'll break every bone in your body!"

This wasn't like me. I'd never seriously threatened anyone with bodily harm before in my life. Benny came to his rescue.

"I'll call the police," he promised and went toward the phone.

I ran to the door, the gun firm in my grip. Before I rushed out, I turned back and begged everyone, "Please don't follow me! Whatever you do, *don't leave this apartment!*"

I was sweating profusely. The night air had grown much colder and it gave my face an icy sting. Starting down the sidewalk, I tried to think rationally. What could I do? If Mehrukenah saw me coming around the corner with Boaz's gun, he wouldn't hesitate to slit Renae's throat then and there. I certainly wasn't a good enough shot to hide in the bushes and pick him off through the rear window. Everything still seemed so hopeless.

And then, beyond my wildest dreams, a figure came running toward me down the sidewalk. It was Renae!—dishevelled and crying. Upon seeing me, she hastened her pace, calling out my name. The two of us embraced. She was shaking out of control, unable to curb the flow of tears.

"What happened!?" I shrieked. "How did you escape?"

Through her panting and sobbing I could barely make out what she said: "It was Muleki. It was all so fast. He pulled open the door. I pushed away. The man with the knife was yanked out of the car. They were fighting. I got out and ran."

This had to have occurred less than sixty seconds ago. I released Renae and scrambled toward the parking lot. Stepping onto the icy asphalt, the area was empty of life—nothing except a few snow covered cars. The Honda Prelude was still sitting where I'd parked it, but no one was inside, and the back doors were ajar.

Then I saw my sister, Jenny, kneeling behind the Prelude. Striding toward her, around the other side of the Prelude, I noticed her Mazda was parked down the street about a hundred yards. They'd done it! They'd found the hidden key and guessed correctly the first place to look!

As I approached Jenny, I saw she was holding someone. Muleki was lying quietly in my sister's arms. Reaching them there on the ground, Jenny looked up at me with tears streaming down her face. There was blood on the ice. Though the wizened Gadianton named Mehrukenah was nowhere in sight, he'd left his sleek obsidian blade embedded beneath Muleki's ribs.

CHAPTER 10

I wanted to be there when Muleki opened his eyes. That didn't happen until mid-afternoon on Sunday. It took some fancy talking to convince the hospital staff at Utah Valley to let me stay by his bedside since I wasn't a member of his immediate family, or even a distant relative. Noting my determination, they sighed and shrugged their shoulders.

His wound was pretty bad. The doctor told me the blade had damaged several organs—even piercing his appendix. During any other century, Muleki would have suffered a long and agonizing death. Even in this age, the Nephite was pretty lucky. Mehrukenah knew all the best places to stab a man. It was hard to believe such a decrepit, saturnine figure as Mehrukenah could maintain such agility. Muleki was not an incapable opponent—I'd seen him in action. Yet in spite of that, the old wraith had struck his wound. Still, it couldn't be denied, Muleki's surprise attack had saved Renae's life.

On Friday, the night of the attack, I told Provo Police that the whole thing began as a mugging and soon evolved into a kidnapping. When they brought Boaz out of my apartment, now in handcuffs instead of duct tape, I further revealed that Boaz had admitted to me his involvement in the police station hold-up in Cody, Wyoming. From the back seat of the patrol car, Boaz shouted a plethora of threats and obscenities in my direction. I was sure when they started questioning him, he would say many things accredited to an insane man. Things about being a citizen of Zarahemla and coming up to this land through a cavernous volcano. Things which would insure his permanent incarceration in an iron-barred asylum.

Now there were only two Gadiantons left.

When they took Muleki to the hospital, I'd wanted to ride in the ambulance with him, but the head paramedic decided to be a hardnose. Instead, Jenny, Renae, and I were taken to Provo's police headquarters where homicide detectives drilled us with questions for two and half hours. After the three of us detailed all the events of the evening, I spelled out a description of Mehrukenah, Shurr, and Mr. Clarke. Finally, I told them I knew nothing of Muleki's background, adding that, from what I understood, he *had* no immediate family.

During the entire interview, I would glance over at Renae and find her carefully watching me. She knew, based on what she'd heard Mehrukenah say, there was much I was not telling the police. Yet Renae remained silent, uncommonly trusting and loyal—though I could tell she expected a full explanation before the night was over.

She got it about three a.m., as we sat in Utah Valley Hospital, impatiently awaiting word on Muleki's condition. Jenny was the only other person in the waiting area with Renae and me. Unable to keep the sleep out of her eyes, she curled up in an armchair across the room and drifted off.

Renae had heard Mehrukenah claim he'd known me when I was younger, so I had to start at the beginning. I told her about the stone mural Garth and I had discovered along the Shoshoni River and how it hinted the existence of a mysterious 'rainbow room' deep inside the caverns on Cedar Mountain. I told her how the underground river had sucked us into a dark tunnel and how we had awakened to find ourselves back in the days of the Book of Mormon. I told her about our adventures among the Nephites and how we had prevented Mehrukenah and the kingmen of Zarahemla from assassinating Captain Moroni and others. I put it in a way that admitted I wasn't sure if it had occurred in reality—or at least the reality we were familiar with. Maybe it was a kind of vision, a gift from the Almighty designed to help a back-sliding youth return to the fold. But whatever the case, that same parallel reality had invaded *our* day. I told her the organization Mehrukenah represented. I told her who Muleki was, and used his uncanny ability to understand languages as proof. Then I told her why they had come and what they were seeking.

Shortly after I'd finished, the doctor found us and reported that Muleki had been admitted to intensive care and that his prognosis was excellent. However, since the chance of infection and other complications were very high, he would need to remain in the hospital for a couple of weeks, though even after he was released, full recuperation would still require an additional thirty to sixty days.

We thanked him for taking the time to tell us, then Renae's uncle arrived to take her home. I couldn't read her heart as she climbed into her relatives' car and drove away. Did she believe my story? Perhaps she thought I was as nuts as Mehrukenah! Maybe she decided, even if my story *were* true, it was clearly too dangerous to go on with our relationship. Apparently she needed time to sort it all out in her mind. I feared she would opt for a normal life with me out of the picture. Could I blame her? How I wished *I* could return to such a life! But I was in too deep now. It was because of me that the Captain of the Guard in the Palace of the Chief Judge of Zarahemla lay unconscious in ICU, with an oxygen mask over his face, an I.V. in his arm, and a heart monitor verifying his life pulse.

Jenny was with me Sunday afternoon when Muleki awakened. His first muzzy words were, "I'm so thirsty."

I placed a straw leading to a cup of ice water into his mouth. He'd never used a straw before, but it only took a moment to catch on. He sucked dry the entire cup and started to reach over to his bedside table for more, causing him to wince in pain. "Don't move," Jenny commanded.

"Where am I?" he asked.

"You're in a hospital," I explained. "It's a big building with lots of doctors and fancy equipment that—"

Jenny interrupted, "He's not delirious, Jim. He certainly remembers what a hospital is."

"But the wound was fatal," said Muleki. "I should be dead."

"With an attitude like that, it's a miracle that you're not," chided Jenny.

"They'll take good care of you here," I promised. "Do what they tell you."

Shortly thereafter, Muleki dropped off to sleep again. Jenny and I left Utah Valley Hospital and returned to our apartments.

The rest of the afternoon, I received many visits from a concerned bishopric and home teachers and from unconcerned ward gossips. Then, toward late evening, I was completely alone. My Nephite bodyguard was gone. I'd had to take the gun I'd disarmed from Boaz and turn it over to the police for evidence. But the first gun they'd given me in the parking lot at *Steck's*—the one they'd hoped I'd use to kill Muleki—was still under the mat in the trunk of Jenny's car, next to the tire jack, with four bullets still in the chamber. I retrieved it and determined I'd carry it with me wherever I went.

Fortunately it was winter, and I could conceal such an object in my jacket. But what if I were forced to use it? Could I actually pull the trigger? Could I kill someone? What if I had to kill *several* people? How long would the authorities buy a plea of self-defense when bodies were piling up around me? My thoughts caused me to shudder, and I couldn't sleep that night.

Finishing out the semester seemed out of the question. Finals were about as far from my mind as another galaxy. I attended my classes on Monday, but I don't remember a word that was said. I was just following the routine in hopes of postponing a nervous breakdown.

I began to think every stranger was watching me, especially the ones alone on street corners. I found myself taking out-of-the-way routes to school and back to my apartment, and I made sure I got home well before dark.

Late Monday afternoon, Renae called. She wanted to

know how I was doing and she wanted to see me that night. Closing my eyes tightly, I thanked her. I needed a friend so badly.

Things had gotten back to normal in my apartment. Friday night's events had been the primary topic of conversation all of Sunday. But by Monday evening, Benny and Lars were again excited about the prospect of attending the Bernardian meeting in Provo that night.

"Why don't you come?" Benny urged. "It'll get your mind off things for a while."

"You might even discover some solutions to your stress," added Lars.

"No thanks," I declined. "I got a date."

"So bring her," said Lars. "Tonight's a big night. Mr. West will be there. He's the new president of the whole organization. Incredible man."

"Mr. West?" I repeated. "What's his first name?"

"Tim, Todd, Tom—something like that. I can't remember."

My heart starting racing like a jackhammer. *Todd West was Todd Finlay's pseudonym!*

I came to my feet. "What does he look like?"

"I don' know. Kinda thin, mid-thirties, wears glasses. You heard of him?" asked Lars.

I couldn't believe it! Could he actually be the person we were seeking? If he were, how did he come to be involved in a UFO club? Lars had said the organization had been around for some time, though it had only begun attracting widespread attention over the last few months. This was too bizarre! It had to be a different guy. And yet . . . .

"Yes, I want to go to your meeting," I proclaimed.

Returning to my room, I slipped into my jacket—first verifying its weight to be sure the gun was still in the pocket. In the kitchen I heard the phone ring again.

Andrew shouted through my door that the call was for me. As I took the receiver from him he added, "It's collect."

"Hello?"

"Collect call from Katie Workman. Will you accept the charges?" droned the operator.

"Yes, of course" I replied.

"Mr. Hawkins?" began the voice on the other end. "This is Katie Workman at the West Valley *Smith's* store. I'm at home now. I couldn't call you from work. I don't think the manager would much appreciate knowing I was helping you anyway."

"That's fine," I replied. "Have you seen him again?"

"Mr. West came in this morning," she admitted. "He bought two more money orders—to pay some bills, I think. He was in quite a hurry. I don't think he much appreciated it when I asked him to write an address in lieu of having no phone. Nevertheless, he scribbled it down quickly and left. There at the end I had a feeling he suspected something. It wouldn't surprise me if he does his shopping at *Albertson's* from now on."

"Did you save the address?" I asked, unsuccessful at masking my impatience.

"Uh, yes. You got a pen?"

"Got it."

"1480 South 2344 West. I'm afraid I can't help you anymore. If my boss found out I might lose my job."

"I don't think you'll have to," I replied. "You've given me more than I thought I could hope for already."

Renae had decided to stay with her aunt and uncle a few days rather than sleep at her apartment in King's Court Arms. As I drove over to Cherry Lane, and as I walked up to her door, my hand inside my jacket caressing the pistol's handle for security, I committed in my mind to end our relationship, despite my selfish needs for a friend. I had to tell her I didn't feel anything for her anymore—it was for her own protection. If only she knew it was going to break *my* heart far worse than her own.

When Renae answered the door, already bundled up in her suede jacket and ready to go, she looked out at me on the front porch and seemed to sense what I was about to say.

Speaking first, she confessed, "I believe what you told me, Jim. I want to help, if I can."

"Renae, you don't know what you're saying—"

"Of course I do. I was there Friday night, remember? I understand the danger. That's why I want to be with you most of all. Because somebody has to look out for you. Because—"

She cut herself off.

"Because why?"

She whispered it very quietly, "Because I love you."

For a girl who'd shied away from me a month back because I was coming on too strongly, this seemed to be a dramatic change of policy. I knew I was experiencing the same depth of feeling. I'd known I was in love with Renae Fenimore since our very first date, but tonight just wasn't the right time to admit it. If I were any kind of man, I'd tell her such feelings didn't matter, turn around, climb into my car, and speed away.

Opening my mouth to say exactly that, my tongue slid into the back of my throat again. Before I could loosen it, Renae had stepped past me down the front walk. I turned around and watched her open my passenger's side door. Before climbing inside, she turned back around. I was still standing on her front porch, my mouth hanging open to catch a few winter flies.

"Oh, I forgot to mention," she called back. "You don't have a choice in this matter."

CHAPTER 11

Renae was a little surprised when I announced the evening's agenda. I think she was expecting a peaceful drive to Utah Lake and around the Provo Temple in nostalgic remembrance of our first date. Fortunately, she trusted me when I said my presence at tonight's Bernardian meeting was crucial.

It was being held in the conference room of the city power building on 200 West. As we drove the Mazda across town by way of darkened side streets, Renae insisted on more details.

"I'm hoping to meet up with an old acquaintance of mine," I explained. "He's supposedly the Bernardians' principle speaker."

"And who are the Bernardians? What do they represent?"

"They're a UFO Club," I explained. "They think aliens from the second planet of Bernard's Star are visiting earth to usher in the next stage of its evolution. Lars and Benny define that as meaning the Millennium. I know the whole thing sounds out in 'la la land,' but it's becoming quite popular."

"I have to tell you, Jim," confessed Renae, "I don't feel good about it. Even as you were explaining it I . . . "

"Well, I don't think it's anything *dangerous*," I defended. "They don't seem to be teaching anything that contradicts the gospel."

"According to *whom*?" challenged Renae.

Her challenge brought things into perspective. She was right. My fanatical roommates might have twisted things any way they wanted to convince themselves nothing was wrong.

There was no parking near the building. The nearest space we found was over a block away. We walked in just before the meeting started and found the room utterly packed—standing room only. Many people were content just to listen out in the hallway. Renae and I were lucky enough to weave into a spot along the back wall which gave us a porthole view of the podium. I could see Lars and Benny up near the front. They'd gotten here early enough to take one of the seats.

Most of the people in the room appeared quite young: high school kids—the rebellious sort with outrageous hairstyles and clothing. Some kids looked conservative enough—football jocks and computer eggheads. A few older people were sprinkled among them, housewives and laborers. I even saw a couple of yuppie-types with their three-piece suits and day planners. A photographer and a reporter had situated themselves close to the podium. Apparently the Bernardian furor had attracted the local press.

Smoking was not allowed in the conference room, but Renae and I were sandwiched between several people who reeked of tobacco, enough to nauseate us. Nevertheless, there were other things which made us even more uncomfortable—particularly the conversations around us. Lars may have insisted the Bernardians were uplifting, but they attracted a crowd which was into everything from Astrology to *I Ching* divination. A threesome of junior high girls behind us were actually attempting to read the minds of several boy friends along the wall. Another couple to our right was discussing how Buddha, Confucius, Christ and Mohammed were great teachers, but they had all failed to take advantage of the 'full potential' of nature—whatever that meant. Three persons were seated behind the podium, two men and one woman, neatly dressed, casual, nothing threatening. Not a one of them resembled Todd Finlay, even in the cleverest of disguises. I began to think I'd misled myself, that I should take Renae by the hand and make an exit. I stayed because one of the chairs up front was empty, as if a member of the panel had not yet arrived. And I couldn't deny it, I was strangely curious to see what was going to happen—what these people had to say.

The first person, a 'Steven Spielberg-looking' gentleman with a beard and thick glasses, arose to take his place behind the podium causing the audience to commence whistling and applauding. With a 'ringmaster' smile on his face, the man raised his hands to stop the clamor.

He began by saying calmly and methodically, "What a great crowd we have tonight. We feared Utah County wouldn't have an ear for us. It's been a pleasant surprise for us all over Utah, Southern California and Arizona to discover that the human mind is not closed. That the ancient drive to seek truth and understanding has not diminished. Nevertheless, you who came tonight are among the minority—and I should make it clear, ladies and gentlemen—you will always be in the minority.

"Tonight you will experience phenomenon beyond your greatest imaginations. You will witness powers of the mind which learned men throughout the world are only beginning to accept, and none to understand. Some of you may stomp out of here angry and upset, perhaps before we've even finished our presentation. Others will go home debating amongst themselves, some skeptical, others disclaiming. And some of you will come away with a precious seed of conviction and a determination to devote your lives to tapping into every glorious faculty your brain has to offer. If nothing else, tonight you will know that we are not alone in this great universe."

His delivery was magical. The crowd melted in the palm of his hand. For the next several minutes he expounded the theme and purpose of the Bernardians, which was basically to add new insights to the way people thought without diminishing their present beliefs one iota. In fact he declared that the things we learned tonight would *prove* the Bible was inspired, would *prove* the Book of Mormon was no delusion—would *prove* the Koran, the Vedas, the *Popol Vuh*—and a score of other theological volumes. He said the

Christian, the Jew and the atheist would all find tonight's teachings in harmony with their own. Then he introduced the next speaker, and a second gentleman arose and took his place behind the podium.

This new man had an executive manner, with a flare for the dramatic, like a TV evangelist. He began by telling us a little about his life, how he had once been overweight and unhappy, unlucky in love and failing in his career. He said that one night he learned a wonderful secret, and that secret had changed him into that man he was today.

Though I found his presentation hard to follow, rather deep and abstract, the people around us were enthusiastically nodding their understanding. He talked about how the human soul had progressed though various stages before we were born, and how it would continue to progress in the life to come until we achieved perfect balance and harmony with the universe.

This was not at all what I'd expected from a UFO club. I thought I'd hear testimonies from people who'd seen flying saucers or who'd been abducted to other planets. Instead, the meeting exuded a peculiarly mystical and religious spirit. Then things started to get really weird.

The second man testified to having received his knowledge from a race of beings whose influence on the earth was as old as time itself. He told how ancient peoples and cultures had sung praises to them and built monuments in their name from the earliest of days. He said the time was soon at hand in the history of the world for these "beings" to show themselves in a way they had never done before. The goal of this club was to prepare the planet for the coming of these beings—"with fire and sword if necessary"—or else the very fabric of creation would be disrupted and the race who called themselves 'human beings' would cease to exist.

I chuckled out loud. I couldn't believe anyone was buying this! A few people scowled at me. Embarrassed, I turned my attention back to the front.

The second man now introduced the lady to us by saying she had a very special power—the power to communicate with these beings through a sophisticated field of mental telepathy initiated by the aliens themselves. She was quite mousy looking, with straight hair and little make-up. Her words were shy and brief, telling us she didn't know why she'd been chosen, but that it was an honor beyond any she'd ever received.

A video projector was turned on and we were shown a taped interview with this lady in an alien-induced trance. The voice emanating from her was credited with being that of an inhabitant of the second planet of Bernard's Star. It was a low, masculine drone, quite different from her natural voice.

The words and thoughts were expressed in an odd pattern, as if this alien presence was struggling to translate its thoughts into tangible concepts. The alien voice seemed unaccustomed to communicating with language and explained that the process was 'archaic' in its own culture since its kind were now entirely able to communicate through thoughts and emotions.

An interviewer asked the alien several questions, which were answered via the lady. "Why was it communicating with us at this time?" "How did it travel from place to place?" "How was it influencing the universe as we knew it?" "What was the destiny of mankind?" "How did the great prophets and philosophers of the earth fit into the vast scheme of things?" "Were such prophets and philosophers indeed inspired by alien beings such as itself?"

The answers were so abstract and esoteric that I felt myself straining to understand. The voice kept talking about the fabric of nature and the truth inherent in all things, the soul of the earth and the destiny of mind and matter. The entire discourse gave the impression of being breathtakingly profound, but I couldn't help cocking my eyebrow and wondering if it was all a mishmash of mystical hogwash, made to appear profound by the theatrics of language, when in reality, it was nothing more than meaningless platitudes.

There was an overwhelming air of vain pride around me. The audience put itself upon a kind of pedestal, convinced they were witnessing something extraordinary—something no one else in the world was privy to.

I suppose on a semantic kind of plane, there was no direct contradiction to the gospel—even the thing about souls progressing from dimension to dimension. Latter-day Saints had always taught that men progressed: from an intelligence, to a spirit, to a temporal body, to a celestial body. It had just never been described in quite the same detail.

It was the next thing she said which tripped the little red 'trouble' light inside me.

The interviewer asked the lady if it was more proper to pray to the "powers of the universe" or to "God." The lady, in her alien voice, said that it was not proper to pray *at all*, that prayer was an improper form of begging and did not appropriately exemplify a correct relationship between man and his maker. It was much better to meditate, become one with the environment, and allow the wisdom of the universe to flow, unhindered, into the depths of the human psyche. A scripture in 2nd Nephi began repeating in my mind: *"The evil spirit teaches man that he must not pray . . .The evil spirit teaches man that he must not pray . . . ."*

"Let's get out of here," I said to Renae. She was in full agreement, relieved that I had taken the initiative. I felt frustrated to have subjected us to such a spirit while utterly failing to accomplish my goal. As we fought through the crowd, the discussion turned toward dream stages and astral projection.

After breaking free into the hallway, we heaved a sigh of relief, as if there'd been no oxygen inside, though it was plentiful here. Continuing to hold Renae's hand, I led the way toward the front of the building. There were two sets of glass doors leading out. The bitter cold awaiting us outside would be a welcome sensation compared to the unbearable heat in that conference room. Pushing our way out, somebody else was pushing their way in. This gentleman was in such a hurry, we almost collided.

Keeping his eyes toward the ground, he apologized, "Excuse me. I'm a bit late."

The man tried to slip by, but suspecting him I grabbed his shoulder and spun him around so I could see his face clearly.

"Todd Finlay!" I exclaimed.

For an instant, the man's eyes widened with horror.

I knew he recognized me, yet he replied, "I'm afraid you've made a mistake. My name is West. Now if you'll excuse me, I'm scheduled to speak in two minutes. If you'll follow me, we can all join the meeting."

He tried to pull away, but my hold was firm.

"I've heard enough," I proclaimed. "I want to know where the sword is, Todd—the one I gave to you at the scene of the accident near Colter's Hell last summer."

He began to rave furiously, "I don't know what you're talking about, young man, and I advise you to take your hands off me voluntarily or I'll call someone who'll do it with force!"

He freed himself and pushed his way quickly through the inner door, disappearing down the hallway. I was tempted to pursue him, to knock his block off if I had to. Renae grabbed my arm.

"It's useless, Jim," she pleaded. "If you go after him they'll have you thrown out."

"That sword was Muleki's reason for coming," I reminded her. "I have to get it back!"

"Bullying him won't accomplish anything," Renae declared. "He obviously isn't carrying it with him."

As I stood there collecting my thoughts, an eruption of vigorous applause echoed down the hall. Mr. 'West' had made his entrance.

"I know what we gotta do," I told Renae. "We have to go to Salt Lake, and we have to go *now*—before this conference is over."

The drive to Salt Lake City took less than forty-five minutes. Renae chewed her fingernails most of the way.

"Don't worry about a thing," I reassured her. "We'll find his address, take the sword, drive back to Provo, and it will all be over."

This was, of course, assuming the sword was even there. It was also assuming he hadn't left a security guard, or a doberman behind to protect it.

Upon reaching Salt Lake, we exited the interstate at 13th South, then continued west in search of the address obtained by Katie Workman. As we approached the specified area, the neighborhood became more and more industrial. Soon we discovered that the corresponding streets were non-existent. The closest point we found to 1480 South 2344 West was a trucking company and a field with warehouses. Todd Finlay had scribbled for Katie a line of bogus numbers.

I pulled over to the side of the road to mourn. If it wasn't one brick wall, it was another! Even if Todd went back to the West Valley *Smith's*, which Katie suspected was unlikely, I no longer had anyone to keep an eye out for him.

"Well?" I turned to Renae. "Any ideas?"

"What if you turned it around," she suggested.

"Turned what around?"

"The address. What if we tried 2344 *South* instead of 2344 *West*."

I almost scoffed at her suggestion, and then I thought about it. Maybe she had something there. Turning the numbers around would put the location much closer to Smith's, which seemed to make more sense. Todd may not have wanted to write his honest address, but in his rush, he may not have had time to invent anything more creative.

We turned north on Redwood Road and took a right at a 7-11 store on 2320 South. Entering a quiet residential neighborhood teeming with duplexes and tiny brick homes, my confidence in Renae's theory was rising. Only a single block later, we'd reached a street marked 1480 West.

There were very few street lamps to help illuminate the house numbers, and most residents either didn't have porch lights or simply forgot to turn them on. I decided to park in the street and search for the address on foot. Before climbing out of the car, I grabbed a flashlight from the glove box and handed it to Renae. I knew there was a brighter flashlight in the trunk. Opening it, I retrieved this one for myself.

After discretely crossing several lawns, we found 2344 South—exactly as Renae had suggested. It was the left side of a red and white duplex. To our relief, neither driveway had a car, and there were no lights emitting from any windows. Best of all, when I knocked on the doors, I wasn't greeted by the bark of a vicious canine. There was no answer on either side.

Overall, the building appeared quite dilapidated. Worn siding, cracked windows and duct-tape repairs. The sidewalk and driveway were unshoveled, though frozen footprints to and from the door publicized the presence of a tenant. This seemed like a rather humble dwelling for the president of one of the fastest growing organizations in Utah. I began to wonder if I was about to make a terrible mistake, trespassing into the home of innocent people. If I was wrong, I'd send the address some anonymous cash to over-compensate for any damage I might cause.

Renae and I sank into the darkened corridor along the side of the house where a high wooden fence shielded us from the view of neighbors. There was a window there, at eye level. I pried off the screen and apprehensively tried to push it open. It slid quite easily. The tenant had carelessly left the window unlatched.

Before climbing through, I looked back at Renae. She was shivering and I could hear her chattering teeth. I'm sure it wasn't just because of the cold. From my coat pocket, I brought out the .357 Magnum and placed it in her slender hand.

She looked at me queerly, "What am I supposed to do with this?"

"Just in case," I replied.

She tried to hand it back, "I can't use this—"

Refusing its return, I told her, "Just hold onto it for me. It's too heavy to lug around anyway." I hoisted my shoulders through the window and fell inside.

No furniture obstructed my fall, but I found my leg tangled up in an electric cord and I yanked an alarm clock off a bedside table. Of course, it started buzzing out of control and sent me into several unnerving moments of panic while I tried to hit the off-button. Carefully, I placed the clock, now silent, back onto the table.

As Renae handed me my flashlight, I instructed her that if anyone came, she should signal me with her own by flicking it on and off. The house was refreshingly warm. I closed the window so the current resident wouldn't find his room ten degrees colder than when he left.

Flipping the on-switch on my flashlight, I proceeded to search for the sword. The place was filthy. I don't mean *cluttered* filthy; I mean *filthy* filthy. The rugs hadn't been vacuumed for months. In the bedroom were bowls of half-eaten food burgeoning with mold. Piles of dirty clothing decorated every corner—much more, it seemed, than would normally be owned by one man. He either had roommates, or frequently bought new clothes to avoid the hassle of washing the old ones.

I won't even mention how many dishes were in the sink, and I certainly won't mention the smell. If this was where Todd Finlay lived, I couldn't imagine it was where he slept. My nose could barely stand to walk through the place!

The mess made it difficult to search for the sword. I looked in every closet and cabinet, under the furniture and between the mattresses on the bed. I dug through every shred of clothing and even checked in the refrigerator. It just wasn't here. Maybe he sold it, I started to speculate. Maybe that's how he got the financing to build up the reputation of the fledgling UFO club he'd joined late last summer.

I was beginning to conclude we may have infiltrated the wrong house altogether when I turned to see Renae's flashlight shining on and off in desperation on the hallway wall just outside the bedroom. I had no idea how long she might have been signaling me since I'd spent the last several minutes searching through storage debris in the back bedroom.

Before I could respond to her signal, I heard a key turning in the lock on the front door. Somebody was already stepping inside. I froze. What could I do? Whoever it was, they wasted no time crossing the front room. Footsteps were already creaking across the floor of the kitchen.

The hallway light above my head flashed on.

CHAPTER 12

The switch to the hall light above my head was just around the corner. My legs, having decided they could no longer wait for instructions from my brain, slipped into the master bedroom in what must have been a split-second before whoever had entered the house, turned into the hallway. But the footsteps were still coming, as if this person was following me by a sense of smell. I glimpsed at Renae's face out the window. After sending her a quick gesture to get down, I flipped off my flashlight and slipped into the closet. The clothing heaped up within muffled any sound I might have made. Reaching the deepest corner, I became deathly still as the bedroom light switched on.

I didn't even breathe. Did it matter? All this person had to do was peek inside. There were a few hanging shirts which may have hidden my torso, but my legs were entirely conspicuous. A shadow blocked the light which crept into the other end of the closet. After the shadow passed, I heard the box springs on the bed creak as the person collapsed on the mattress.

There was silence for several moments, so long that I thought whoever it was had left the room. Then I heard a sigh, long and tortured, followed by a moan.

"I can do better," said the male voice. I recognized it immediately as belonging to Todd Finlay.

But who was he talking to? Was he praying? Was there a phone in the room? It was hard to believe I wouldn't have heard it ringing or the tones of dialing.

Then he repeated himself, this time emphasizing the first word, "*I* can do better."

Several seconds later he said the same thing, this time emphasizing the second word, "I *can* do better."

He said it twice more, emphasizing the third and then the fourth words, as if rehearsing a speech, or his only line in a community play.

Again, there was silence—several minutes worth. Finally, another long sigh, and then Todd rolled off the bed and came to his feet. His shadow fell heavily across the open half of the closet again. Todd was coming in. Dropping the flashlight in the clothes, I braced myself to vault forward and attempt an escape, but only his arm entered the closet—his arm, and something else which he leaned against the back wall. Then he slid the closet door closed and turned off the light.

There it was. The silver-plated sword I'd once held in my hands over Colter's Hell, west of Cody. The jewels in the hilt were like eyes peering back at me with the eyeshine of a cat. We stared at each other, and I couldn't help but shake my head. How could such an article, as sleek and ancient as it may be, stir up so much excitement?

Yet somehow I felt as though I were not alone in this closet. There were two of us secretly hiding: me from Todd, and it from anyone Todd might have thought would take it away.

I heard Todd undressing, and the boxsprings on his bed creaked again as he climbed under the covers and attempted to sleep. The hall light was left on. Todd wanted it on, apparently insecure in total darkness.

So the sword had been with 'Mr. West' all along. Perhaps some other Bernardian had kept it safe and returned it to him at the convention. I doubted that. Most likely the object had been hidden in the car which he'd driven to Provo. This whole trip to Salt Lake, the predicament I was in now, might have all been avoided if only I'd seen where he'd parked his vehicle. I resisted an urge to touch it, to feel the weight of it in my hand. The very thought was ludicrous. Certainly such movement would make a sound and alert Todd. Yet what was I going to do—stay here the entire night? Renae was probably still shivering outside the window, close to panic.

I could grab the sword and make a break for the front door as soon as Todd fell asleep. Renae and I might have time to jump in the Mazda and speed away before Todd, in his groggy state, could figure out what was happening. My only fear was the likelihood that Todd kept a firearm near his bedside. He'd once been a policeman, so it was certain his aim was fairly accurate. I should have let Renae return the Magnum to me. I had much greater need of it right now than she did. I was left with no alternative but to attempt a sudden lunge for the door. My mind was in process of rehearsing just such an action, when the doorbell rang.

Todd bolted up in his bed. "Who the—!"

Oh, how I hoped that wasn't Renae. Didn't she remember he'd seen her with me at the convention? She'd never get away with it!

Todd didn't appear convinced he should answer it. The boxsprings creaked again as he settled back into his covers. Then the doorbell rang a second time. Finally, cursing, Todd rolled out of bed and pulled on his pants. I heard his footsteps pass the closet and enter the hallway.

Just in case this was indeed Renae's attempt to spring me, I felt compelled to follow through with her intent. Leaving my flashlight behind, I crawled to the other end of the closet and hefted the sword into my arms. The moment I touched it, adrenaline seemed to surge anew in my bloodstream. I slipped open the closet door and took two strides toward the window. Sliding it open, I dropped the silver sword into the shallow snow and swung one leg out into the cold.

Todd's silhouette suddenly appeared in the bedroom doorway. He stood transfixed, momentarily dumbfounded as to how I might have gotten inside so fast. Then he screamed at the top of his lungs, "Noooo!" and vaulted toward me. I fell out the window, grunting as I crashed onto the frozen earth. Digging my fingers into the snow, I found the hilt of the sword and hurled myself toward the street. Todd literally dove through the window's tiny opening, tumbled as he landed, and rose quickly to his feet.

Rushing across the front lawn, I expected to feel the piercing sting of a bullet entering my back. The bulky sword, slowing me down, gave Todd plenty of time to take aim. When I reached the sidewalk the sword actually slipped out of my hand. Picking it up again, the blade seemed heavier than before, almost as if it were desperate to remain where it was.

Renae was already positioned in the passenger's seat of the Mazda. She'd merely rang Finlay's doorbell and ran. If only I'd given her the car keys. She could have had the Mazda running by now and served as a getaway driver. As it was, she reached over and opened the driver's side door to facilitate my entrance.

If Todd still owned a firearm, in all the confusion, he'd forgotten to bring it with him. As it was, he was bounding after me through the snow wearing no shoes and no shirt.

Reaching the car, I tossed the sword onto the back seat.

"Lock your door!" I cried to Renae as I took my place behind the wheel, plugging the key into the ignition.

The Mazda was just starting to lurch forward when Todd Finlay threw himself onto the hood, his face contorted with rage. I threw the gear shift into reverse, and he tumbled off onto the pavement. Continuing in reverse all the way to end of the block, I soon met the adjoining street. Todd was running after the vehicle as fast as his bare feet would carry him. As I maneuvered the car into a forward position and shifted into first, Todd caught us again, grabbing the back door—the one I'd forgotten to lock! As it began to open, the tires squealed. Todd fell again to the asphalt, rolling once, then rising to continue his barefoot pursuit, tears streaming down his cheeks. Renae reached back to close the doors as he faded into the background. I achieved fifty miles an hour in a twenty-five zone and at last reached Redwood Road, directing my headlights back toward Interstate 15.

"So that's the cause of all the commotion?" wondered Renae as she gazed upon the sword lying peacefully across the center of my back seat.

"That's it," I confirmed. "Hard to believe, isn't it?"

She continued staring at it for several moments, entranced by the highway lights reflecting on its silver plating. Facing forward again, she stared blankly ahead down the interstate.

"I don't like it," she blurted.

I looked over at her, not quite sure how to interpret her words. Was she referring to an acquired taste in swords or was it something else?

"It's only a hunk of metal," I assured her.

She declared, "Whatever we have to do, Jim, wherever we have to go, know that I'm with you one hundred percent. I'll help you in every way I can, but you must promise me something: Never ask me to touch it. *Never.*"

I watched her curiously for another moment, and then I agreed to her terms. Melodramatic reactions like hers caused me much more anxiety than anything I'd ever perceived about the sword. Psychology taught me these reactions could all be explained by phenomena of the mind. If people believe a thing possesses unusual powers, they begin attributing their behavior to the influence of that thing, when in reality, the power is all in their imagination. Such a simple solution—how I hoped it was applicable here!

We pulled up in front of Renae's house just after 11 p.m. She made me promise to get in touch with her the next day, then we embraced and I thanked her for all she'd done.

"I couldn't have made it without you," I said. "Physically *or* emotionally."

She smiled warmly, then she waited a moment more. I think she wanted me to reciprocate the words she'd spoken to me earlier that evening. I decided not to. When I told her I loved her I didn't want it to be out of obligation. She pretended to understand and turned around to go into her house.

Driving away I felt terribly selfish. The fact was, I *did* love her. Maybe she needed to hear me say it more than I needed to wait for the right moment. Mehrukenah and the others were undoubtably still stalking me. What if I never lived to find a right moment? Renae might always question how deep my feelings actually were.

I decided not to return to my apartment that night. Something inside whispered that an ambush was awaiting me there. Instead, I drove to campus and parked my car in front of the Harris Fine Arts Center. Retrieving the sword off the back seat, I carried it under my coat all the way to the Wilkinson Center. The building was still unlocked due to a late showing at the Varsity Theatre. I sneaked into the study area west of the front doors and found a private corner, hidden from the view of anyone who might have walked through in search of loiterers. Removing my coat, I rolled it up into a pillow. Then I curled up on the floor with the hilt of the sword snuggled under my arm.

Here in the dim after-hours light of the Wilkinson Center, with the blade only inches away from my nose, I studied the sword until my eyes grew heavy with sleep. Aside from its antiquity, there seemed to be nothing unusual about it. The surface glaze was dulled by numerous fingerprints—doubtlessly Todd Finlay's. There were a few more chips in the silver plating and tiny gouges along the blade, making the oxidized copper underneath more apparent. Staring at it, no darkened vibes imbued my mind. If anything, I felt pity. What a shame such a priceless artifact should be the object of so much prejudice and hatred. In a way, I felt sorry for the sword.

This was silly. I was endowing a chunk of metal with human emotions! Before long I'd be talking to it! Reciting nonsensical gibberish in the privacy of my bedroom, like Todd Finlay. After sharing a laugh with myself, my eyes fell shut, and I dropped off to asleep.

I was standing in the mist again, only the mist was aflame. The jungled hill was a conflagration of billowing black smoke and dying voices. The summit was discernible, but the cluster of trees, the lightning-scarred trunk, the beckoning old man—all were gone, consumed by the igneous rage.

Yet in the midst of the holocaust, something else was soundlessly watching me—a presence, hiding in the fire as easily as a shadow hides in the dark. It spoke, and the voice resonated like low mountain thunder.

I've missed you, Jim. Serve me faithfully, for in the previous existence, we knew each other well. Welcome to my noble ranks. Welcome home. You have . . .

". . . to go home!"

"What?" I groggily responded.

"Home! You shouldn't be here. You have to go home!"

A student janitor was standing over me, shouting at me. His face was pocked with acne and his hair was in serious need of a shower. In his hand was a small carpet-sweeper.

"What time is it?" I asked.

"Almost 6:00 a.m. Have you been here all night?"

"Guess I fell asleep studying," I replied.

He seemed to buy my story because he didn't notify his supervisor. I picked up the sword and quickly left the building. The morning was crisp and new, obscurely light—providing me just enough confidence to return to King's Court Arms. I felt certain the Gadiantons were not yet desperate enough to strike in daylight, though I didn't know how long that policy might persist.

Entering my apartment, I opened the door very slowly in hopes of muffling the squeak in the hinges. It was still an hour before the first of my roommates came to life so the place was ghostly still—only the ambience of the refrigerator and the light on the microwave clock. Stealthily, I crossed the kitchen. The last thing I wanted to do was awaken a roommate and reply to his baiting suspicions about where I'd been all night. Approaching the door to my room, I suddenly hesitated. It was a well established habit of mine to always close my door until I heard the click of the doorknob, yet at this moment, it was two inches ajar, allowing me to peer into the inner dimness.

I reached into my pocket and found the butt of my pistol. Simultaneously, I felt another inspiration. The sword was just as formidable a weapon, and perhaps more appropriate. Following my second inclination, I tightly gripped the hilt and held the blade firmly aloft. After two deep breaths, I kicked open the door, filling our silent apartment with a boisterous crash as it slammed against the wall.

Charging inside, I flipped on the light. The blankets on my bed flew in every direction as the intruder reacted to my entrance. He'd been asleep! This must have been one of the more ill-chosen of the Gadiantons' modern recruits.

I lunged forward with the sword, more prepared to strike than I'd ever thought myself able. Then I saw the intruder's face, his fire-red hair, and the freckles on his cheeks. He was backed against the far corner wall. Upon recognizing me, he heaved a sigh of relief.

"You could have killed me, Jim! Is this the way you always greet your old friends?"

I heard my roommates stirring in the other room, aroused by the ruckus. As I stood there gaping, still trying to recover, the intruder couldn't help but smile. There was no mistaking that smile. It was the kind, wise smile of my comrade-for-life, Garth Plimpton.

CHAPTER 13

After my startled and grumbling roommates had wandered back into their bedrooms, Garth and I embraced. His arrival was the answer to a prayer I thought too far-fetched to even utter.

Garth's boyish features had subsided a bit, replaced by the wisdom of years. He was still an inch or so taller than me, but his skinny build might have caused people to perceive it the other way around. Covering his body and freckled arms was a sweatshirt with a picture of the earth and the slogan, *A Planet is a Terrible Thing to Waste.*

"I got your letter Friday afternoon," Garth announced. "It began on the wrong premise—the premise that I'd forgotten our days among the Nephites. The Prophet Helaman told us the only way we'd lose the memories was if we told them. I never told."

"I still can't get over it," I rejoiced. "You're actually here!"

"Didn't your roommates tell you I called?"

I remembered something vaguely Friday night as Boaz held a gun in my back, but in all the excitement the message never got through.

Garth continued, "When I didn't hear from you by yesterday, I snatched up my savings and took the next flight to Salt Lake City at 8:45 last night. I tried to call you two other times—first from Boston and then from Chicago, but both times you were out. You must have had a busy evening."

"You could say that," I replied. "How did you get here from the airport?"

"Taxi. Cost me an arm and a leg. I woke up one of your roommates around midnight and he said I could wait in your bedroom. I fell asleep around two deciding if you weren't home by eight this morning, I was calling the police."

"But what about Harvard and finals?"

"At Harvard finals don't start until mid-January. All I did was finish a few assignments early and take an extra week off for Christmas. I shouldn't get too far behind. I can't always fly to Utah and meet a Nephite and an old friend. So where is this 'Son of Teancum' you mentioned?"

"In the hospital," I answered.

Garth's face reflected the gravity of my reply. Sitting him down in the swivel chair beside my computer, I proceeded to update him on all the events which had occurred since I'd written the letter. I told him about our confrontation with Mehrukenah and Muleki's subsequent injury. Then I told him about Todd Finlay and the Bernardian meeting which Renae and I had attended the night before.

"The sword you mentioned in your letter—" Garth wondered, "is that the same instrument you almost used a few minutes ago to chop my head off?"

I nodded, "We got it back last night. By the skin of our teeth, I might add."

Garth arose and wandered over to get a closer view of the object, now sitting at the end of my bed.

"Like I told you in the letter, Muleki believes it was forged by the Jaredites using black magic," I said. "It was then passed down from wicked king to wicked king. Muleki thinks it inspires evil wherever it goes."

I sincerely hoped Garth would put an end to such bunk here and now. Instead, after musing over the concept a moment, he replied, "The Nephites had the same kind of traditions, only with articles they considered sacred. The Liahona, the Urim and Thummim, the Sword of Laban— they passed down these relics from generation to generation until the time of Moroni, and even into the hands of

Joseph Smith. King Benjamin was still wielding the Sword of Laban in battle five hundred years after Nephi brought it across the ocean. It's a firm policy of Satan, whenever the Lord establishes something good, he'll mock it by establishing a wicked imitation. I think what Muleki believes should at least be respected."

That wasn't what I wanted to hear. Oddly, Garth seemed to feel the same aversion toward touching the object that Renae did.

"Now that you have the sword, what are you going to do with it?" asked Garth.

That was an easy question.

"*Get rid of it!*" I responded.

We took a shower and changed our clothes to get ready to drive down to Utah Valley Hospital to return the sword to its rightful bearer. Garth showered first. When I finally stepped out, Andrew marched past me, whining about the amount of hot water we'd used, and slammed the door.

Benny and Lars were already up and dressed. They were both sitting at the breakfast table with Garth. From my bedroom where I dressed and shaved, I couldn't help but overhear snippets of their conversation. They were telling Garth all about last night's Bernardian meeting while he politely listened to every word.

As soon as I emerged from my bedroom, Benny asked me what I thought of the talk given by Mr. West.

"I didn't stay that long," I replied.

"Really? How could you miss the best part?" Lars asked.

I couldn't let them continue basking in Todd Finlay's deception. The Bernardians had to be exposed; better now than after it was too late—especially for Benny.

"Todd West isn't his real name," I announced. "It's Todd Finlay. He's a former police officer from Wyoming, suspended for insubordination and suspected of dealing drugs."

Benny and Lars glared at me open-mouthed.

"I'm sure those are lies," Lars declared.

"I knew him in Cody," I continued. "I personally met the wife and daughter he abandoned."

"More lies!" Lars threw his hands on the table, then turning to Benny he said, "They concocted the same kind of lies about Joseph Smith!"

"Do you put this man in the same category as Joseph Smith?" asked Garth.

"In the area of understanding which he's chosen to pursue, yes!" Lars replied.

Never until this moment was I aware of how abberent the thinking of Lars had become. I'd always considered his explorations into the preternatural to be innocent speculations—and maybe in the beginning they were—but somewhere along the line his love for the "twilight zone" exceeded his love for the truths God had already liberally given.

"Lars, what motive would I have to lie to you about this?" I wondered.

"Because of the self-righteous brainwashing you've had all your life which tells you if somebody thinks differently from you, they need to be dragged back into the fold," Lars responded.

"That's not true," I insisted. "I'm only telling you who 'Mr. West' really is."

Garth added, "If what you've told me about the Bernardians over the last ten minutes is accurate, it sounds like an organization bordering on the occult."

"The occult? Satanism? Don't be ridiculous!" scoffed Lars. "Nobody is performing blood sacrifices or conjuring up demons."

"That's not the way Satan works in the beginning," Garth explained. "First he determines where we're most vulnerable, usually an area of vanity—like a self-aggrandizing passion for uncommon knowledge or power—then he lures us in with something which seems perfectly harmless. Bit by bit, we find ourselves in the vortex of out-and-out witchcraft. Do you follow what I'm saying?"

Lars wouldn't respond, but Benny admitted, "Not entirely."

"Put it this way," said Garth. "Satan's church is like a bicycle wheel. There's a whole variety of spokes which can bring you to the center. One spoke might be Astrology, another might be drugs, and another might be bizarre psychic powers, or Ouija Boards. Ultimately, Satan's goal is to use one of those spokes to bring you as close to the center of the wheel as possible. He's always on the lookout for better disguised methods and means."

Lars laughed, "Are you saying just because a guy reads his horoscope in the paper he's one step away from becoming a devil worshipper?"

"No," Garth replied. "But if his horoscope starts coming true day after day, and if he starts following its counsel, how much more likely is he to turn to astrology in a time of crisis, than to prayer and fasting? That's the danger."

"It's people like you," Lars accused, "who create the kind of prejudice and fear of knowledge which ends up inspiring people to burn each other at the stake!"

"I desperately hope not," said Garth. "The Lord commands us to learn and discover all we can in this life. There's nothing wrong with wanting to know the mysteries of outer space or the latent powers of the mind. The problem comes when we desire to use that knowledge for our own gratification, rather than to build the kingdom of God."

"I should have learned by now," Lars scolded, "if someone insists on ignorance, there's nothing I can do or say."

Lars made a hasty exit into his bedroom.

Benny continued to sit across the breakfast table staring at his soggy bowl of raisin bran. He shook his head back and forth, "I don't know which end is up anymore. All the lines seem so thin."

"What lines?" I asked.

"The lines between truth and error. It doesn't seem like I can depend on anything anymore. Not even the Church. Not after the stuff Andrew brought up last week."

"What stuff was that?" Garth inquired.

I told Garth about Andrew's discourse on doctrinal controversies, particularly the contradiction on plural marriage found in Jacob 2:24 and D&C 132:38.

Garth smiled. He spoke to Benny in a compassionate, uncondescending tone. It was moments like this that reminded me why Garth Plimpton was one of my heroes.

"Benny, I promise you, the Lord is the same yesterday, today and forever. Those two scriptures no more contradict each other than the Law of Moses and the higher Law of Christ. They were teachings given to different men under different circumstances and in different times. If a parent commands a little child not to play with matches, and then commands a teenager to light the campfire, is this a contradiction? It's only a question of preparedness—one is ready and one is not. If you read Jacob 2 closer, you'll notice in verse 30, right after Jacob calls plural marriage a sin, he suggests the rule may have exceptions."

Benny nodded. He accepted Garth's explanation, but it failed to raise his spirits. "How many more questions am I going to have to struggle with? How many more controversies are there?"

"The closer we get to the Second Coming, the more confusing it may all become," Garth replied. "Our only real hope is to cling tenaciously to the Spirit and follow the prophets' admonition to stay in the mainstream of the Church."

"But I still don't understand." Benny complained. "Why was I so easily deceived by the Bernardians in the first place? I don't have a 'self-aggrandizing passion for knowledge and power.' I could care less about being smarter than everybody else!" Garth felt inclined to respond, but I saw him hesitate, perhaps to be sure his words were carefully chosen.

"The only thing I can suggest," he said, "is that something in your life is driving away the Spirit. But only you can know what that is."

At that moment, the doorbell rang, and in barged Benny's girlfriend, Allison, as usual, without waiting for anyone to answer.

"Surprise, surprise!" she called over to Benny. "I decided to drive *you* to school today. Ready to go?"

Benny was awe-struck by the coincidence which had caused Allison to make an entrance at this particular moment. Without anybody needing to say a word, it became clear what might have been amiss in Benny's life. In all the months that Benny seemed to be spending more and more time with his girlfriend, I wouldn't allow myself to suspect anything negative about their relationship. I didn't want to know. I decided it wasn't any of my business. As Benny turned back to see our reactions, Garth and I were both watching him. He looked away, then fidgeted a moment more before deciding to stand. Allison was now frowning as well, intuitively uneasy about what might have been said before she made her appearance.

"Is everything okay?" she wondered.

"Sure," Benny replied, and without looking at her face, he retrieved his coat from the closet. Then the door closed behind them, and Benny and Allison were gone.

Garth and I ate breakfast quickly, then we returned to my bedroom to get the sword. I didn't feel comfortable carrying it out in the open. I had to find some way of disguising it.

Sitting in my closet was the guitar I'd purchased shortly after my mission. My intention had been to master the instrument by this Christmas, but I only ended up completing about a lesson and a half. It had been gathering dust ever since. I decided it was time my investment fulfilled a practical purpose—at least the case part. I tossed my guitar on the bed and was pleasantly pleased to discover the sword was just the right length to fit into the case.

As we were preparing to leave the apartment, the phone rang. Garth stood behind me as I picked up the receiver and set the guitar case on the floor.

"Hello?"

"I want to speak with Jim Hawkins," wheezed a voice on the other end of the line. It was Todd Finlay.

"This is Jim," I confirmed.

"Jim!" he exclaimed. It sounded as though he were trying to control a flow of tears. "We need to get together this morning. I need to talk to you. We need to talk in person."

"I'm not able to do that," I replied.

There was silence on the other end for several seconds.

"I want the sword, Jim. I have to have it back. Please. You don't understand what it means to me. I'll do anything if you'll agree to hand it over without any trouble."

"I can't do that, Todd."

He grew angry suddenly, "What is it to you? It means nothing to you!"

Todd sounded on the brink of mental collapse. Like a junkie desperate for another hit, he seemed dependent upon the sword for his very well-being. How serious was this addiction? Would he die without it? The impression I had that he was literally suffocating was quite convincing.

"Todd," I said, my voice sympathetic, "you've become mixed up in something beyond your control. Something I fear the sword has inspired. I've given you a chance to get out, and get out fast—"

"Fifty thousand dollars!" he cried. "It's everything I have. It's all yours if you'll just give it back to me."

Fifty thousand dollars? Was he serious? It's not that I was tempted. It was just that . . . .

"I can't," I insisted.

His voice became shrill and harsh, no less than insane. "You're a dead man, Jim Hawkins! I'll kill you if you don't give it back! You AND your girlfriend! I'll kill you all!"

I hung up the phone. Todd's voice was loud enough that Garth had heard the death threat quite clearly.

I turned to him, smiled and shrugged my shoulders.

"Typical of my life these days," I said.

CHAPTER 14

Garth and I arrived at Utah Valley Hospital shortly before 9:00 a.m. I carried the guitar case with its ancient cargo all the way to ICU. Muleki was awake when we walked into his room. His breakfast tray was sitting in front of him and he was busy enjoying a hospital danish.

"Jim!" he called out enthusiastically. "I've missed you."

Upon seeing Garth enter behind me, his face brightened even further.

"The spotted boy!" he exclaimed. "I remember you. You're Garthplimpton!"

Garth stepped over to Muleki's bed.

"And you're Muleki, son of Teancum. You know the first thing you said to me when we met years ago was that if you looked as pale as I did, you'd cake your face in mud and wash it off over and over again until your face was brown."

Muleki blushed. "I was an outspoken child."

Dropping the guitar case at the foot of Muleki's bed, I unlatched the buckles and lifted the lid, displaying its contents to the Nephite. Muleki looked down at the silver-plated sword, and then he looked up at me open-mouthed, shaking his head, refusing to believe it could be true.

I nodded.

The Nephite was so ecstatic he nearly tore his stitches trying to sit up. "It can't be! How? How did you do it?"

I told him all the events of the previous night. I told him how I'd slept on campus because of my fear of an ambush waiting at my apartment.

"It's important to follow such instincts," Muleki commended. "But remember, the longer you possess the sword, the harder you have to concentrate if you're to be sure the inspiration comes from the correct source."

"I don't *want* to possess it any longer," I said. "I'm turning it over to you."

Muleki became very tense, "You can't leave it with me! Not here! Not while I'm like this!"

"What else am I supposed to do?" I asked. "If *I* hold on to it, it's just a matter of time before Todd Finlay or the Gadiantons spot a moment of vulnerability and steal it back, leaving me in some back alley with my throat cut."

"You're right," Muleki agreed. "If you fooled them last night, I fear not even daylight or crowds may stop them now."

"I could hide it," I suggested. "Someplace where no one would look."

"No," Muleki objected. "They may be watching you, even if you're certain you're alone. But even if you *could* hide it, there's no safe place. The sword has a way of attracting an owner for itself—always the wrong kind of owner."

I could see where this conversation was leading and I didn't like it at all.

"Muleki, I came here to get rid of this," I declared. "I'm sorry for what happened to you. To make up for what I've done, I've gotten your sword back and laid it at your feet. I can't do anymore than that."

"You *must* do more," Muleki insisted. "Because of my wounds, I can't carry it back to my land. You're the only one I would trust to complete the mission."

"The mission can wait sixty days!" I cried.

"Two moons is a long time," said Muleki. "Too much evil can occur. We can't take the chance. Not even *I* would want to possess the sword more than a few days."

"So what are you saying?" I asked. "Are you suggesting I go back to the year fifty B.C.?"

"No," said Muleki, and I felt a wave of relief. "You must not go through the caverns. The way will be heavily guarded by the men of Gadianton by now."

My relief was quite short-lived because he clarified the situation by adding, "You must go to the Hill Ramah as it stands in this day and time. Find the coffer at the highest summit point and place the Sword of Coriantumr within it."

"And what's that supposed to accomplish?"

"The Jaredites cursed many swords with evil ritual, though none were as powerful as the one wielded by Coriantumr. After the last battle ended, Ether walked among the dead gathering all the accursed swords together and buried them in a spot of ground which he'd blessed. Here the curses were lifted and the swords returned to the dust. The only sword Ether was unable to find was Coriantumr's. The king kept it with him until the day he died among my ancestors, the people of Zarahemla. Petty sorcerers kept it hidden for generations, unable to grasp its full potential. Then Gadianton discovered it. It must not fall back into his hands."

"Let me get this straight," I said. "You're asking me to go to the last battleground of the Jaredites—a place I'm not even sure exists in our day—and climb to the top of a hill to find a sword-filled box that's about twenty-five hundred years old? What makes you think the box is even there anymore? Who *knows* how far earthquakes and erosions have carried it. We might have to dig up an area the size of a football field. You're asking too much, Muleki!"

"Please, Jim. I'm begging you. Without you, the mission will fail. All the efforts of Judge Helaman, all the years I've spent trying to destroy it, will have been in vain."

I couldn't believe what I was hearing! The doctors must have done something to Muleki's brain. Did he know who he was talking to? This was a job for heroes and prophets. I felt about as far from both those stations as an ant does from the surface of the moon.

"One thing is for sure, Jim," Garth declared. "You can't stay in Provo. Based on what I've heard, it would be suicide. The only way to end this affair once and for all might be to do exactly what Muleki suggests. You won't be alone, Jim. I'll be with you every step of the way."

"But we don't have any money," I tried as a last resort. "If we're going to travel, we need money. I only have about two-hundred and twenty dollars until the end of the semester."

"I've got another hundred and fifty," said Garth.

Muleki directed us to the closet where his clothes were hanging.

"Reach into my coat pocket," he said.

Garth did as he requested and retrieved the pouch I'd seen on Thanksgiving—the one which had contained the gold nugget he gave to my brother. Garth dumped the contents into his hand. There were two nuggets left. I had no more excuses.

"*All right*," I sighed. "I'll go."

I saw tears well up in Muleki's eyes. But he was still gravely concerned by my lack of commitment.

"If you are lukewarm about this quest, Jim, you will surely fail," he stressed.

"I'm fine," I assured him. Then less confidently, I mumbled, "I'll be perfectly fine."

Muleki added another warning, "The power of the sword will grow more and more intense as it nears the land of its creation. This will make the going harder for you, but it will make it easier for your enemies."

"Great," I said sarcastically. "It's not as if the wolves aren't crashing through the windows already."

Muleki's pleadings had made him extremely weary, though he insisted on using the last of his energy to grip my right hand in both of his. Looking into my eyes, he offered one final word of advice.

"Stay close to God, Jimawkins." He looked at Garth and then repeated, "Hold as tight to His principles as ever in your life, or the sword will destroy you as mercilessly as it did Shiz under Coriantumr's hand."

"We will," I agreed. "I promise."

The force of his admonition made me very uncomfortable. This was crazy! What had I gotten myself into? I wanted

Muleki to let me go, but he held on for a moment longer. Finally, his weariness caused him to release my hand. The nurse came in to remove Muleki's breakfast tray. Upon seeing his weakened condition, she shooed us out immediately, and scolded us for having forced him to exert himself.

"The sword," muttered Muleki as we were walking out of the room.

I'd left it on his bed. My determination to get rid of it had sunk into my brain to the point that I almost left it behind. As I shut the guitar case and lifted it into my arms, Muleki smiled peacefully.

"God be with you," he whispered, and then Garth and I left the son of Teancum alone once again.

"This is like old times," Garth said. "You and me fighting against overwhelming odds."

I nodded, my depression showing no signs of lifting. Garth knew me better than any friend ever had. He used to depend on me to make him laugh. Not finding my sense of humor cocked and ready concerned him a great deal. It didn't seem natural. I'd *always* found something to laugh about, no matter how serious the situation. In the past I was convinced it made life's pains infinitely more bearable.

After Friday's events I'd begun to question my whole outlook on life. It was my levity which had gotten me into the most trouble in my life. It was my levity which led me to step off campus when I'd been warned of the danger. Because of it, Renae's life had been threatened and Muleki lay recovering in Intensive Care. Because of it the mantle of Muleki's burdensome quest had been laid upon my head.

Arriving back at King's Court Arms, I parked in the south parking lot hoping that since I'd never parked there before, it might go unnoticed by anyone who might have been watching.

Slowly, I vacated my car with one hand on the butt of the Magnum. My paranoia was infectious. Garth also found himself looking for sudden movements around the corners of buildings and turning quickly to pinpoint the source of every sound.

Entering my apartment, Garth recited a checklist of duties to be accomplished before leaving Provo. First we would pack, then we'd try to reach as many of my professors as possible to let them know I was leaving town on an emergency. Then we'd find a local pawn shop or refining company to buy Muleki's gold. If all went smoothly, we'd be out of town by sundown.

Andrew was the only one home for lunch. He listened curiously to our conversation and devoured some leftovers. "Where is it you're going?" he wondered.

"New York," I answered him. "Palmyra, New York—"

Garth interrupted, "I don't think so, Jim."

"Huh?" I responded. "We're going to the Jaredite battleground, right? I always understood the Hill Ramah and the Hill Cumorah were the same hill."

"Yes," Garth confirmed, "but that doesn't mean that the hill in New York where Moroni gave Joseph Smith the gold plates, is the same hill where the last battles took place."

"Doesn't the Book of Mormon say that?" I asked.

"On the contrary," explained Garth, "Mormon 6:6 states that Mormon went to Cumorah and hid up all the records *except* the gold plates, which he gave to his son, Moroni. Mormons have always *assumed* that Moroni hid them up in the same location, but the Book of Mormon never states that."

This was a monkey wrench I hadn't anticipated. "So what are you suggesting?"

"I'm suggesting if we want to find Ether's coffer we need to go to the place where the last battles took place, not the place where Joseph found the plates."

"How come the hill in New York is called Cumorah if it's not the same Cumorah as in the Book of Mormon?" I demanded.

Garth went on, "Most people believe Oliver Cowdery named it that. The Angel Moroni never called it Cumorah, nor did he say it was the same hill where his people fought their last battle. Joseph Smith never said it was the ancient Nephite or Jaredite battleground either."

"The 'Two-Cumorah' theory, eh?" chimed in Andrew.

"You should know, folks have been shooting down that one since the 1960's."

"Not much any more," said Garth. "You may still find a few die-hards, but most people who study the matter feel certain the hill in New York can't be same hill mentioned in the Book of Mormon. In fact most don't believe Nephites ever set one foot in New York, or even in the United States for that matter."

"Such are the speculations of men," Andrew decided. "If you want to 'hold to the rod' you better stick with what the Lord had to say."

"The Lord has never spoken on this matter," Garth charged. "Joseph Smith, himself, was left to speculate. In Nauvoo's *Times and Seasons*, he suggested Zarahemla might be in Central America."

"But he also said that Manti was in Missouri," Andrew countered, "and that Zelph, a skeleton found in Illinois during the Zion's Camp march, was a white Lamanite who fought during the last great struggle of the Nephites and Lamanites. That sounds like Nephites in the United States to me."

"Neither of those statements can be clearly attributed to Joseph Smith," Garth replied, then he stopped himself and offered a keen observation, "But I have a feeling you already know that as well as I do."

"Maybe I do," he admitted.

"Be careful," Garth warned. "It's an unwise habit to use knowledge to further personal ends. Truth should never be used as a means to make us prisoners. It was meant to make us free."

Andrew frowned. Garth's assessment seemed to strike a tender chord. Ever since I'd met Andrew, I'd wanted to see him grapple with Garth Plimpton, but today it was making me quite impatient.

"How come I've always been taught differently about this?" I demanded.

"Tradition," Garth replied. "Sometimes traditions are hard to break. I think the biggest single piece of evidence that the Book of Mormon never took place in New York is the fact that never once in the entire scripture does it mention snow, cold weather, ice, or any other kind of drastic seasonal change that you'd expect from an ancient New Yorker."

I thought of a solution, "Maybe the majority of it took place in Central America, and then, at the end, the Lamanites drove the Nephites to New York?"

"That's over three thousand miles!" Garth exclaimed. "We're talking about a battle involving a quarter million Nephites—and who knows how many Lamanites! Why would anybody want to travel that far, crossing hundreds of rivers and encountering other tribes of potentially hostile people, just to fight a battle? The Book of Mormon gives us a clear account of an expedition traveling all the way from the Land Southward, through the narrow neck, and discovering the last battleground of the Jaredites—and all in a matter of weeks! If we assume the Limhi expedition went all the way to New York in search of Zarahemla, it would have taken years—if not their entire lives!"

"Then tell me this," I requested. "How did the gold plates get to New York?"

"There's a gap of more than three decades from the time of the last battle until Moroni enscribed his final entry," said Garth. "It's not implausible to suggest Moroni spent those final years traveling in strange lands, preaching the gospel to various peoples, and finally depositing the plates right where Joseph Smith unearthed them. He may have even hidden them in New York as a resurrected being. To me, it really doesn't matter."

"So where *is* Cumorah?" I finally asked.

"Good luck with that one," Andrew scoffed. "Folks have proposed more sites than Brigham Young had wives."

Garth was much more encouraging, "Well let's look at the facts: It has to be a prominent landmark—much more prominent than the tiny hill in New York. It has to be within a day's journey from a large and ill-defined body of water which Ether called the Waters of Ripliancum and which Mormon called 'many waters, rivers and fountains.' It has to be small enough for an injured man of eighty years, Mormon, to climb to the top and enjoy one last night with his son and twenty-two other Nephite survivors of the first day of battle. Yet it also has to be high enough for Mormon to view hundreds of thousands of bodies on the plains and hillsides below. It must be near the eastern seashore, near the narrow neck, and in the midst of a volcano and earthquake zone. In the many volumes I've read, the only place which seems to fit all the criteria is a hill north of the Isthmus of Tehuantepec and south of the Papaloapan water basin in the state of Veracruz, Mexico called *El Cerro Vigia*.

"Mexico!" I exclaimed. "Are you suggesting we take a plane to Mexico?"

"No, I don't think that would be a good idea," said Garth. "A silver sword would never get past an airport's metal detector. If what Muleki says about its potential for being stolen is true, there's no way I'd leave it in the hands of Mexican baggage handlers either."

"So how are we supposed to get there?"

"We drive," Garth confirmed.

"*Drive*?! How far is this place?"

"I'm not sure. At least 2,500 miles."

"*In Jenny's Mazda*?!" I cried. "Garth, I wouldn't trust that wreck too many more times to get me to Salt Lake and back! It's got over 90,000 miles on it, and the tires are nearly bald."

"Do you have a friend with a better car?" he asked."Not that would let me drive it for 5000 miles!" I proclaimed.

"I'd talk my Mom in Rock Springs into letting us use her Chevette," Garth said, "but it's in a lot worse shape than your Mazda. Unless you can think of a better idea in the next couple of hours, I'm afraid we'll just have to risk driving Jenny's Mazda—and pray the Lord is behind us."

CHAPTER 15

Since there was far less chance of Garth being recognized, I gave him the pistol and sent him out alone to complete the last minute shopping. On his list was motor oil, coolant, enough junk food for two days, and enough maps to get us as far as El Paso, Texas. While he was gone I rolled and tied the sleeping bags, packed my duffle bag, and contacted my professors. Explaining that I had a personal but tragic family crisis, they compassionately agreed to let me take incompletes for grades and contact them when I returned for word on how to make up finals. The only bugger was my stats professor, wanting more of an explanation than I was able to give. He agreed to my terms only if I took the final by the first week in January.

Still, it was hard to believe I was actually going through with this. You just don't wake up one day in Provo, Utah and decide before lunch that you'll be driving practically to the Yucatan Peninsula.

After he'd returned safely from shopping, I asked Garth, "Have you been to this hill before?"

"No, but I've seen pictures of it," he replied. "It's just above a small town called Santiago Tuxtla."

"Do you know how to get there?" I asked.

"Not really. But I'm sure we can buy a detailed map of Mexico at the border."

My confidence was starting to wane.

"Have you ever even *been* to Mexico?"

"No, I haven't," Garth confessed. "Don't worry. We'll be fine. I still speak Spanish quite fluently from my mission in Guatemala. If worse comes to worse, we can always ask someone for directions."

Personally, I'd never been out of the continental United States. My impression of Mexico was formulated strictly by old western movies and postcards from Acapulco. I imagined the Mexican frontier to be a wasteland of cactus, gila monsters, and roving bandits.

"Are there any special laws we need to know?" I asked. "What are we going to do if Jenny's car breaks down?"

"Take it to a garage, I suppose," Garth answered.

"But the car is Japanese," I pointed out. "Will they have Japanese parts?"

"I don't know."

"And what if we get into trouble? Do you know anybody down there we could call?"

"Not a soul," admitted Garth. "But remember, Mexico has one of fastest growing Latter-day Saint populations in the world. It shouldn't be too hard to find Church members."

"Oh, Garth," I groaned. "This trip may be the most ludicrous thing I've ever done—and that's sayin' something. I hope we know what we're doing. I can just see myself rotting in some Mexican prison until I'm eighty years old. My parents, my family—nobody will know where to find me."

Garth scoffed, "It's not like we're going to Mars. Retired folks drive their motor homes around Mexico for months on end."

"That's old people though," I pointed out. "They're not gonna bother *them*. It's the young people they need to work the salt mines."

Garth laughed. "Don't sweat it. Sure, it would be better if we took along a person who knew Mexico, but I don't see how we could find someone on such short notice."

I did know of one person. Renae had said she'd been to Mexico as an exchange student. I wasn't about to ask her to go with us, but it seemed wise to call her and see if she had any advantageous information, or to see if maybe she could give us the names and phone numbers of people who might come to our rescue. Calling both her uncle's house and her King's Court Arms apartment, I couldn't locate her. I left the same message in both places: *Leaving today for Veracruz, Mexico. Wanted to know if you could give us helpful hints. Call as soon as possible.*

Afterwards, I called Jen. Somebody in my family had to know where I was. But for the first minute after she answered the phone, I couldn't get a word in edgewise. She was terribly frightened.

"Jim, there are people following me. I can't leave my apartment. Even looking out my kitchen window right now, there's a man standing under the tree across the street. He's been there ever since I came home from class."

"Have you called the police?"

"What would I tell them? They haven't done anything yet. I don't even know how many there are. Two different people followed me home from the Jesse Knight Building."

"You mean they were on campus?"

"Yes," she confirmed.

This news was quite disturbing. Somehow I was under the impression BYU campus was an impregnable safety zone. It occurred to me, the Gadianton's modern-day converts might not feel the same discomfort on dedicated ground. I doubted many of them were acting with the same knowledge and accountability as someone like Mehrukenah. Jenny could be abducted any moment—whether on or off campus.

"You've got to get out of Provo," I told Jenny. "They'll use you to get at me. I'm leaving town tonight. I have something they want desperately."

"Where are you going?"

"Mexico."

"Mexico? Not in *my* car you're not!"

"What are you talking about? *I* pay the insurance! *I* buy all the gas!" I quelled my temper. "Jenny, *please*. It's not by choice. My *life* is in danger!"

"Why Mexico?"

"It's a long story. I'll tell you when we get back."

"You'll tell me *today*," she demanded. "Because if you're taking my car, I'm going with you."

"You can't," I told her. "It's too dangerous."

"And it's less dangerous here?" she cried.

I closed my eyes tightly. Her point was indisputable. How could I have placed the people I cared for the most in this world in such precarious circumstances? The stress would have been so much more endurable if it had been only my neck on the line.

"Call your professors, pack your bags for two weeks, and sit tight," I told my sister. "We'll be over to get you in fifteen minutes."

It was actually in less than fifteen minutes after tossing the guitar case, sleeping bags,and luggage into the trunk that we screeched into the parking lot beside Jenny's apartment. Immediately, I saw the man she'd mentioned, leaning against a tree, standing shin deep in snow. He watched us knock on Jenny's back door, looking concerned as we were allowed inside.

Jenny had actually finished packing—an amazing feat for any woman in that length of time. Her clothes, make-up, shampoo—all of it was piled into one suitcase.

She was ecstatic upon seeing Garth and left some lipstick on his cheek. The gesture turned Garth's face instantly flush. As Jen went to her bedroom for her coat, he turned to me and remarked, "She's *really* grown up, hasn't she?"

It occurred to me, this was quite a noteworthy reunion. Almost ten years before, the three of us had stood together upon an ancient land. Though Jenny was the only one with no memory of it, she still felt an odd nostalgia about the occasion. But greetings were short lived. Before we could hit the road, we still had to sell Muleki's gold.

As we emerged from Jenny's apartment, the man under the tree was quick to notice. He signaled to someone unseen and began approaching our vehicle. To my surprise, another man came out from around the corner of the building. I drew the Magnum out of my jacket.

"Keep back!" I warned.

They both stopped sharply. Jenny climbed into the back seat and Garth hurriedly looked for a place in the trunk to stuff her suitcase.

"You got a problem?" called the second man, pretending to find my gesture offensive.

They were both wearing heavy coats. In them they could have concealed their own firearms just as easily. But if they had weapons, they were too intimidated by my weapon to draw them. I kept the muzzle of my pistol on them all the while I climbed into the driver's seat and started the engine. Our trunk had been so badly organized, Garth was forced to toss the guitar case behind the front seat to allow room for Jenny's suitcase. The strangers watched our tires kick up the icy slush as the Mazda pulled back onto 900 East.

We drove toward South Provo, where an assayer in a local pawn shop had promised to look at our gold and make an offer.

"Why are you bringing your guitar?" asked Jenny.

"There's no guitar in it," I admitted. "It contains an ancient sword. That's what these people want to take from me."

"What are you doing with such a thing?" she asked, hoisting the guitar case onto the seat and proceeding to open it.

"The sword has been cursed," Garth explained. "We're traveling to Mexico to destroy it."

"You've got to be kidding me." said Jennifer. "Cursed? Destroy? Sounds like something out of *Lord of the Rings.*"

Jenny opened the case. Her gaze was transfixed by the glittering jewels and glossy silver for several moments. In the rearview mirror, I saw her hand reach out to touch the cold surface. Recalling Garth and Renae's repulsion, I thought of shouting out against the action, but I'd have felt ridiculous. After all, I'd hefted the object at least a half dozen times, and felt no differently for having done so.

Jenny's fingers closed around the hilt. She gripped it for a good ten seconds and then she released it with a gasp, looking up at Garth and me with widened eyes, as if it was the first time she'd ever seen us.

"What's the matter?" I asked.

"Pull over!" she cried.

Quickly responding, I pulled into the gutter a half block from University Avenue.

Turning around, I demanded, "Are you all right?"

She was smiling, looking at Garth, and then back at me with eerie wonderment.

"I'm fine," she proclaimed.

Reaching back, I shut the guitar case and replaced it in the foot space behind the seat.

"You shouldn't mess with this," I told her.

"But I remember it all now!" Jenny announced. "I remember the cave, the 'rainbow room,' the underground river." Her eyes darted around, as if she were seeing the images in her mind as clearly as sights outside the car. "I remember the jungles, the people, the Lamanites—all as if it were yesterday! *It really happened!*"

Garth and I considered her carefully. Not even my memory had been restored so instantly. It had filtered in slowly, over the course of a night and a day.

"Did the sword tell you all this?" I asked.

"I don't know," said Jen, "It just rushed into my head, like a gust of wind—like a geyser."

A second later Jenny looked dizzy. She sat back and touched her palm to her forehead. "I feel a little . . ."

"You okay?" I demanded.

"Yeah. Just a little nauseous."

Clearly, if the sword could give, it could also take. Why hadn't anything like this ever happened to me? I'd handled the hilt for much longer periods and never felt so much as a chill. Maybe I was immune to its supposed power.

"Go ahead and drive," Jenny instructed, closing her eyes and breathing deeply.

Pulling the car back onto the street, I told her, "I don't want you touching it anymore."

"I think you don't have to worry," Jenny said. "I won't."

At the assayer's shop my sister still felt a little lightheaded. Garth asked for a chair behind the counter and sat her down while we waited for the nuggets to be priced and weighed. I waited by the window, watching for predators.

Finally, the assayer came forward and offered us three hundred dollars for our nuggets, reporting that they just weren't of a high enough grade to pay much more. I almost objected, knowing pawn shops weren't famous for their generosity, but time was running short. We couldn't waste a day shopping around.

So our total finances to reach Veracruz, Mexico, including the seventy-five dollars Jenny had in her purse, were seven-hundred and thirty-three dollars and twenty-five cents.

Back in the car, Jenny asked if we could see Muleki before we left.

"I'm sorry," I replied. "We just don't have time."

Garth noted Jenny's disappointment. It was clear to him she harbored some tender feelings for the Nephite. I got the impression he found her affections disturbing. Turning away, Garth shook his head, seemingly scolding himself for imagining what it might be like for a girl like Jenny to feel something for him. All our growing lives, I'd never suspect-ed that Garth had safeguarded any feelings for my sister beyond simple friendship. Garth was too wrapped up in his studies for women. I'd always supposed Garth wouldn't get married until he was thirty or forty. Even then, the girl would have to make it blindingly clear she was in head-over-heels before he'd be willing to make a move.

Garth may not have been the gawky, no-shouldered kid I remembered from grade school—in fact, I'm sure many girls would have found him quite attractive—but it was obvious that when it came to women, he still viewed him-self as the same nerdy misfit he'd been growing up.

We neared the University Avenue on-ramp for Interstate 15. Just as we were about to make a clean escape from Provo, Garth blurted, "Hold it, Jim. Did you bring your birth certificate?"

"You never said I needed it!" I whined.

"Well, I got mine," said Jenny.

"How is it *you* were so inspired?" I asked her.

"I wasn't inspired," replied Jen. "Everybody knows you can't get into Mexico without a birth certificate or passport."

Groaning, I turned the car around and headed back toward King's Court Arms. This was exactly what I didn't want to do. The light was fading fast. I even considered swimming the Rio Grande like a wetback and meeting the others on the opposite side. Pulling into the south parking lot one last time, I handed Garth my pistol again and told him to stay with Jen and watch the sword. After carefully studying the shadowy corners of all the buildings, I made a mad dash into the complex.

As I burst through the doorway of my apartment, I was alarmed by the presence of Renae Fenimore, seated in a chair at the counter, bundled up in a warm sweatshirt. a pair of jeans and her black suede jacket. She heaved a sigh of relief and came to her feet.

"Thank goodness you're still here!" she cried. "I was beginning to panic."

Her suitcase was sitting on the floor beside her.

"What are you doing?" I demanded.

"My uncle dropped me off and Lars let me in to wait. Your message said you were headed for Mexico tonight. You're going because of the sword, am I right?"

"That's right—but I wasn't asking you to go with us!"

"I didn't figure you were. That was my own decision."

"Don't be absurd," I scoffed, and went into my bedroom to grab my birth certificate from my top dresser drawer.

She was waiting at my bedroom door as I emerged. "Jim, it's okay. My professors are all being cooperative. My uncle's not too keen on the whole thing, but he knew there was nothing he could say—"

"Well I have a say," I retorted as I picked up her luggage and started back out the door. "And I say we're getting in the car and I'm taking you home."

She followed me outside, pleading, "Jim, I was an exchange student in a town called Poza Rica. It's only about six hours from Veracruz. I know that area especially well. I have friends there who can help us. It would be stupid for you to go without me. You don't even speak Spanish."

"An old friend of mine is coming with us. He speaks it just fine."

"Does he know Mexico?"

Stopping, I turned to face her. I couldn't let her succeed.

No matter how much I may have wanted her company, I wouldn't allow her to talk me into it.

"Renae, I've already endangered your life twice in the last week. The odds are running against the two of us. I couldn't live with myself if anything happened to you."

"Jim, I've told you how I feel about you. Don't you understand how much greater the horror would be not knowing where you were, compared with anything we might face together?"

"But I need you to be here when I come back. I need to know you're safe, to know you're protected."

"Then your only hope is to let me come along." Then Renae revealed, "They know where I'm staying, Jim. My aunt saw a man watching the house this afternoon."

If Jenny was in danger, certainly Renae was in the same predicament. She was right. I had no choice but to bring her. She was correct in assessing that Garth, Jenny and I alone stood a good chance of getting completely lost in Mexico without a guide. Her knowledge might save us an infinite amount of time, as well as saving our lives.

So there would be four members in this expedition. As I thought about it, if this journey had even half the hazards Muleki had warned of—if this was to be a struggle more dangerous than any I had ever faced—there was no mortal fellowship from whom I could have gained greater strength and endurance than the one which was with me now: My kid sister, my best friend, and the girl I loved.

Call it the "Fellowship of the Sword." Indeed, as Jenny suggested, I felt a strange kinship to Frodo, the humble hobbit from Tolkein's trilogy. Like him, it was my quest to carry the One Ring to the eternal fires of Mordor. And all the while, the evil, penetrating eye of Sauron would be watching my every move, eagerly awaiting the moment when he could crush me in the grip of his terrible hand.

CHAPTER 16

Arriving back at the Mazda, Garth reported that several cars had driven past the parking lot very slowly while we were gone. I introduced Renae and Garth as quickly as I could and pulled our vehicle back into the street.

No sooner had we reached the first stoplight when two automobiles seemed to deliberately pull into the lane behind us. One was a blue Suburban with silver trim, and the other was a grey Cavalier. As it was now twilight, I couldn't make out the passenger's faces, but the silhouettes told me there were four in each vehicle. They followed us all the way to Center Street, keeping a modest distance of fifty or so yards. At the intersection with University Avenue, the one that was closest pulled into the other lane to hide behind a pickup full of high school girls. The attempt to remain unseen was almost laughable. All of us were perfectly aware of their intentions.

Making our way toward the interstate, I did some fancy swerving in and out of the traffic. By the time we hit the on-ramp, I was confident I'd shaken off the Cavalier, but I couldn't be certain if I'd lost the blue Suburban. The sky had darkened to the point that all I could see in the rearview mirror were headlights.

The fuel gauge read less than a quarter tank. I'd planned to fill up before leaving town, but now the risk was too great. Gadianton patience had certainly been worn to the breaking point. The first time we stopped for any length of time—even if only for a few minutes—they would assuredly move in. How far could I get on a quarter tank? Hopefully we could fill up when I turned off the interstate at Spanish Fork, only ten minutes up the road. It was the last fuel stop I knew of before Price, Utah—over a hundred miles away.

We also had to find a way of organizing the trunk to fit in Renae's luggage and the guitar case. For now, the case was sitting upright in the middle of the back seat with Garth fighting at every turn to keep it from falling on Renae's head.

As we took the exit, a vehicle followed right behind us. Passing near a streetlight, it was clearly the blue Suburban.

"We have to find a way to shake him," I told everyone. "I don't believe we have enough gas to reach Price."

"Duck into the city," Garth suggested.

The municipal center of Spanish Fork was west of the highway. I executed Garth's suggestion, driving through residential neighborhoods at dangerous speeds and knocking my passengers about as I screeched around the corners. Though I'd have never thought a bulky Suburban could imitate such moves, it remained on my tail. You'd think such a crazy chase through city streets would attract the police, but despite forcing two other cars off the road, no one came to our assistance. Where was a cop when you needed one? Upon returning to the highway, I still hadn't shaken the mystery car, and now the news on my fuel gauge was even worse. Climbing into Spanish Fork Canyon, the headlights of the Suburban continued beaming through our back window.

I floored the gas pedal, but the Mazda was just too gutless on this terrain. I couldn't get it to exceed seventy miles an hour for any stretch of time. Just as the road would give us a downhill run, an upward slope would impair our acceleration. Jenny leaned over to see the gas gauge again and paid me a concerned glance. It was now sitting just above empty. "Don't worry," I told her, "We've still got at least fifty miles in the tank."

My words gave everyone hope, but to be honest, with the gas pedal as floored as it was, I couldn't believe there was much more than twenty-five miles remaining. It would have been so much better if we'd just taken our chances and filled up with gas in Provo or Spanish Fork. Maybe my instincts were wrong. Maybe they *wouldn't* have tried anything in a public gas station. But surely they wouldn't hesitate to attack a stalled vehicle on the side of the road. I'd made a terrible mistake.

The landscape began to broaden and I was able to increase the speed to ninety. The Suburban did likewise, and together we left every other vehicle in our wake. Soon the gas gauge was reading *below* empty. It was just a matter of minutes, I thought. Contemplating the pistol in my jacket, I again began to wonder if I could ever force myself to use such a thing. Soon I was going to have to answer that question once and for all. The car choked once and then regained power—the first symptom of a dying engine.

Coming over a short rise, we passed a darkened car on the side of the road. Instantly, its flashing red and blue lights burst into action. Never in my life had I imagined a police siren could sound so wonderful—and our luck didn't end there. Before it could pull onto the highway, the Suburban passed it as well. The officer decided that ticketing the larger car would be equally justified.

My passengers erupted into applause and hoots of joy as we watched the Suburban pull over and the highway patrolman park behind him. They were fading well into the background as our car again choked for want of gas.

Lights appeared up ahead—not a moment too soon. Driving off the road on our last pocket of fumes, we rolled up to the gas pump of a place called Cedar Haven. I was confident the inspiration of some crazy entrepreneur to build a place of business in such a remote locale was for no other reason than to save our lives this night. My gratitude was such that I only complained once that the gas was ten cents a gallon higher than it was everywhere else.

After filling the tank, we secluded the Mazda behind the building and rearranged everything in the trunk. Gratefully, we found a place for both Renae's bag and the guitar case. Garth returned from his lookout post at the corner of the building about ten minutes later to report that the Suburban had not passed by on the highway.

"I don't understand. All I can think is that they turned around and went back to Provo," he concluded.

We decided it was safe to leave and began climbing back into the car.

As we continued down the highway past Price and on toward Green River, Garth sat in the front with the map. There was no further evidence of being followed. The only regrettable fact was that they'd seen us leave in the first place. Surely they must have rushed back to Provo to try to find out where we were going, rather than searching blindly for us in the dark. The only people who knew the answer to that question were my roommates and Renae's aunt and uncle. I began to wonder if either of them might be in danger. The Gadiantons, and perhaps even Todd Finlay, would certainly try to interrogate them. I decided to find a gas station in Green River to call and warn them.

In the neighboring phone booth, Renae's watch read 10:35 p.m. when Benny accepted the charges on my collect call.

"Where the heck are you?" he asked.

"I better not tell you any specifics," I said. "I wanted to warn you that people will be coming to the house, asking where we've gone."

"Somebody already came," said Benny.

"Who?"

"One of your classmates."

I couldn't imagine why any of my classmates would be looking for me.

"What did he want?"

"Just what you said. He wanted to know where you were. He appeared completely dumfounded, saying you and he had planned to do a class project together this evening. Andrew told him not to expect you. That you'd gone all the way to Mexico to a hill called—Now how did he pronounce that?—*El Cerro Vigia.*"

Just great! He couldn't get much more specific than that.

"Another one called for you," added Benny. "I don't know what he wanted. Lars spoke to him."

"Is Lars there?" I asked, hoping for more details.

"Not at the moment," Benny replied. "When are you coming back?"

"Hopefully in a week to ten days."

"You should know," Benny continued, "the Bernardians cancelled all their meetings for the rest of the month. It's as if all the head honchos packed up and left. Lars is still pretty upset about what you and your friend said this morning. I wanted to thank you. I was getting pretty messed up. I know it's kind of personal to tell you, but Allison and I saw the Bishop tonight. Everything's gonna be okay. I love you, man."

"You take it easy, Benny," I said. "I'll see you later."

Renae got off the other phone the same time as I hung up.

"Nobody's been by," she said. "I told my uncle not to talk to any strangers at all until I come back."

"The news wasn't so good on my end," I admitted. "Andrew, told them everything. Still, I think even in the worst scenario we're at least a couple of hours ahead of anyone who tries to follow by car. We've just got to keep moving."

The tiny stretch of desert beyond Green River was the only time we'd see interstate until reaching Gallup, New Mexico. Garth predicted we'd cross the Mexican border sometime the next afternoon. Around Moab, I was finally having trouble keeping my eyes open. Garth took over the wheel and steered us on toward Cortez, Colorado.

Driving south, the snow on the shoulders of the highway grew ever thinner. It was a shame to be driving through such beautiful country in the dark, but our forebodings of what lay ahead would have shadowed our appreciation of it anyway. I think I got about twenty minutes of sleep the whole night. Being in the front seat didn't help matters, but the worst sleep deterrent was listening to Jenny in the back and that endless snore which would one day drive a husband crazy. She was the only person I knew who could make a snore sound effeminate—a crisp, clipped little mew. I wondered how Renae got any sleep at all.

Upon reaching Cortez, Colorado at about 2:00 a.m., we turned south and traveled through the Navaho Indian

Reservation with its ghostly silhouettes of towering mesas brooding over us like primeval gods. I knew this was an area rife with legends of Indian mysticism and black magic. It was a grateful moment when we reached Gallup, New Mexico at 3:50 a.m. Merging with a new interstate, we proceeded on toward Albuquerque.

"You doin' all right?" I asked Garth.

"I was drifting off pretty badly about an hour back," he admitted. "But I seem to be okay now."

"Don't take any chances," I told him. "We can't afford to stop and sleep, but we *especially* can't afford to wreck."

The New Mexican sun was just beginning to rise in the east when the road signs announced our arrival at Albuquerque. At this moment, the only sound worse than Jenny's snoring was my stomach growling. Spotting the great golden arches, we pulled off the highway and stuffed ourselves with hot breakfast biscuits from McDonald's.

When we were finished, I told Jenny it was her turn to drive. She sternly objected.

"I can't drive *here*—not on an interstate! Semi-trucks like to crowd out little cars like mine just for amusement. Let me drive when we get back on a normal road."

"That won't be until we reach Mexico," I said.

"And believe me," added Renae, "if you hate crazy drivers, you'll want to drive in Mexico as little as possible."

"This is a long trip, Sis," I concluded. "You gotta pull your weight."

Diffidently, Jenny took her place behind the wheel. Garth sat beside her and I was the lucky stiff who would finally find a couple hours of sleep in Renae's lap—or so I hoped.

Not ten minutes after we'd changed interstates and continued our southward route toward El Paso, Texas, I was jolted abruptly as the car lost power and began slowing down.

I sat up. "What's the matter?"

"I don't know!" cried Jenny. "The engine just shut itself off. Didn't I tell you? This always happens to me! It's a curse!"

The Mazda rolled onto the shoulder and came to a stop. Jenny tried the ignition several more times. I asked her to move aside and give me a shot at it, but my efforts didn't help. The car wouldn't even attempt to turn over. Popping the hood, Garth and I climbed out to investigate—not because either of us knew anything about engines, just because it was an appropriate macho-type thing to do.

The two of us glowered at the engine, still humming from the sound of churning steam in the radiator. Of course we couldn't make heads or tails of anything. I tried grabbing this or that to see if it appeared loose. If I'd have judged this tired ole' automobile by that criteria, the whole thing would have hit the junk pile years ago. About all I got for my efforts was a greasy hand.

"Well," I said to Garth. "This might be the end of the line."

"Don't give up the ship 'til it's sunk," he replied.

Leaving the girls with the car, Garth and I marched across the interstate and set our sights on a construction warehouse about a quarter mile in the distance which we hoped had a phone for us to call a tow truck.

While holding apart a barb-wire fence between us and the warehouse so Garth could crawl through it, I added to my pessimism by saying, "Even if it can be fixed, it might exhaust all our finances."

"Have more faith, Jim-buddy," was Garth's response.

That was a hard thing for me to muster at the moment. I felt like if God were truly behind what we were doing, we wouldn't have experienced this trouble in the first place.

Upon reaching the warehouse, the gentleman in the front office was nice enough to let us call the nearest tow company. He even got on the line to give the switchboard lady directions to our locale. She promised a truck would be by to rescue us in about forty minutes.

We thanked the gentleman in the warehouse and made our way back across the fields and fences to return to our dead Mazda 626. Climbing the rise to the asphalt surface of the northbound side of the interstate, and looking across the way, I saw what I thought had been impossible.

Our lead time hadn't mattered. Parked behind our Mazda was a bright blue Suburban with silver trim.

CHAPTER 17

In spite of an oncoming barrage of northbound traffic, including two or three semi-trucks, I bolted across the road to reach our Mazda and the Suburban. I can only vaguely remember the sounds of brakes screeching and cars honking as vehicles tried to swerve into neighboring lanes to keep from running me over. Even more vague is the sound of Garth's voice calling something from behind which sounded like, "False alarm!"

All I knew was that I had to reach our car—I had to maneuver a rescue for Jenny and Renae. How could I have been so thoughtless, leaving them alone on the highway? I hoped one of them saw me place the pistol in the glove box last night and was presently utilizing it to coax the Suburban's passengers back into their own vehicle.

As I drew nearer, it was clear that was not the case. The hood of our Mazda was still sitting open. My sister and one of the men from the Suburban were looking over the engine. He was an older man—perhaps Mehrukenah in a cowboy hat. There were others still sitting within the Suburban, but I didn't take the time to count.

"What's going on?" I shouted across the highway.

Jenny looked up at me, alarmed by the tension in my voice. The man in the cowboy hat perked up as well. Crossing the southbound side of the interstate, again causing a few tires to skid and horns to honk, I realized this man was not a Gadianton. He must have merely been a proselyte to their evil cause.

"Get away from there!" I growled upon reaching my car.

The man in the cowboy hat threw up his arms and backed away from the engine.

"Just seein' if I could help," he defended. "Pardon my neighborliness."

"What's the matter with you?" Jenny asked me angrily.

The man seemed sincerely offended. As he stomped back to the blue Suburban, I noticed that his other passengers were a mother and a flock of youngsters.

"See if I ever help anybody on the highway again," the man called back.

He climbed into the Suburban and drove away. I noticed the license plate was from Texas, not Utah.

"I thought it was the same car which followed us last night," I meekly confessed.

"Don't be stupid," scolded Jenny. "The one last night was *dark* blue and it didn't have any luggage racks on the roof."

I heard Renae laughing in the back seat. Sensing my overwhelming embarrassment, she climbed out of the car and decided I needed a hug. Garth now arrived and scolded me further for almost getting flattened by traffic.

"Didn't you hear me call to you?" he asked. "I could tell from way over there it wasn't the same Suburban."

"Well, *I* couldn't tell," I replied angrily.

I don't know why I was angry. I guess it was a combination of my heart still racing, the laughter which persisted until the tow truck arrived, and the fact that nobody seemed to appreciate my noble effort. A half-hour later, as I thought about that poor offended Samaritan and how he'd stomped off in the cloud of steam which came out of his ears, I was finally able to laugh at myself as much as everybody else. It was a much needed release of tension.

We told the tow truck to take us to the nearest garage. His bill of $45.00 obliterated a full quarter of everything I had left in my personal account. The tow truck dropped us off at one of those generic garages where the owner spits chew and the mechanics have worn the same overalls for five years without a cleaning. They did a quick inspection of the problem and announced that the fuel injector belt had snapped and needed to be replaced.

"How much is that gonna cost?" I asked.

"The part itself's only about twenty dollars," the owner replied. "But the labor's gonna run you at least another seventy-five. See they gotta dig quite a bit to get to it."

"Fine," I regretfully agreed. "When will it be done?"

"Well, it's a dealer part so we'll have to run up town to get it. I got all these other cars ahead of you. I'm afraid we're not gonna be able to start on it until tomorrow morning."

I moaned a little more to try and rush things along, but to no avail. We were stuck in Albuquerque, New Mexico, for the night in a neighborhood where the mayor was clearly not a resident.

The good news, if you could call it that, was that a dive called the *Sandia Motel* was only a half-block away. Each room was thirty bucks a night—another five if we wanted to view the current triple X feature. It was five bucks we didn't have much trouble reaching a unanimous decision to save. I suggested we only get one room and insure privacy by hanging a blanket between the beds, but the girls were adamantly against it.

After toting our luggage down the block and across the street under the watchful eye of least a dozen street urchins, we entered our motel rooms and did an inventory of our remaining finances. Renae had added another $90.00 to the pool. After paying the repair bill, we'd have approximately $530.00 left to make it to Veracruz, Mexico and back.

The day passed slowly and boredom reigned. About five o'clock we all went out to eat at a *Skipper's Fish and Chips*. When we got back, one of the street urchins we'd seen earlier in the day was standing near the side of the motel. He seemed to be serving as a lookout and upon seeing us returning, signaled to someone else. The two of them made a hasty retreat.

Garth and I discovered they'd tried to break into our motel room. Though the effort was unsuccessful, I made a vow to never leave the sword unattended again. Muleki's warning that the sword had a way of attracting new owners seemed to be accurate.

That night, Jenny and Garth ventured out again to do some window shopping. Renae and I watched the networks' selection of sitcoms in my room until they returned. I admit, it felt a little awkward being alone in a motel room with a girl—not that I didn't trust myself, it's just that, well, maybe I was afraid my bishop was about to burst in and I wouldn't have an acceptable explanation.

When Garth and Jenny came back, my sister announced she had a present for me.

"There's a little antique shop a couple blocks from here. I thought you might find a use for this."

She brought her gift out of a paper sack and thrust it forward. It appeared to be some kind of leather scabbard and belt.

"It was only fifteen dollars," said Jenny. "The lady said it was Asian, though I don't think she believed it was very old. I figured it might make the sword easier to tote around."

"If you have to, you could keep it on your person at all times," added Garth.

"But I'd look ridiculous," I said.

"No," countered Renae. "You'd be in Mexico. Mexicans *expect* Americans to look ridiculous."

I took the silver-plated sword out of the guitar case and carefully slipped it into the scabbard. Then I strapped the belt around my waist. "What do you think?" I asked.

"You look like a Samurai warrior," said Renae.

I felt a rush of pride. Now I understood why Genghis Khan felt invincible—enough so to conquer all the lands between the Pacific Ocean and the Black Sea. I could do the same. In fact I could go much further . . . .

These thoughts couldn't be good. I felt conspicuous and placed the sword and scabbard back into the guitar case.

"Thanks," I told Jenny while I was still fighting some weird feelings swirling in my head, "It could come in quite handy."

After the girls retired to their own room, I suggested to

Garth that maybe *he* should be responsible for the sword.

"I don't know if my spirituality is quite up to par," I explained.

"Even if that's true, I don't have your stamina," Garth replied. "I think I can best serve this expedition by acting as its conscience." He put his hand on my shoulder. "Don't worry, Jim. Like Muleki said, the most important thing for us is to stay as close to God as possible. If the powers of that sword are as real as I suspect, our only defense is going to be righteousness. We need to truly understand what it means to strive for perfection—in every way—our thoughts, our words, our actions."

I lay awake for quite some time, long after Garth had fallen fast asleep. I couldn't get over how attached I was getting to the sword. It frightened me a little. Somehow the ancient weapon gave me a sense of security. I was grateful Garth had declined my offer. In reality, I didn't want anybody else to touch it. The sword was mine.

I shook off my feelings. At least I had the presence of mind to know the feelings were wrong. But as sleepiness took control of my thoughts, and I drifted into a dream about Roman legions on the field of battle, I wondered if I'd always be able to shake them off so easily.

The good ole' boys at the repair shop didn't declare our car "good as new" until after 1:00 o'clock the next day. Besides that, their bill was ten dollars higher than they'd estimated. Albuquerque inflation, I'm sure.

Twenty-nine hours after our breakdown, the Mazda was again carrying the four of us toward Mexico and the Hill Cumorah. Renae had commented on how lucky we were that our automobile broke down in the United States. She said our Mazda would probably be the only one on the Mexican highway.

"All cars in Mexico are Fords, Chevys, Volkswagens and Datsuns," she recalled.

I didn't feel lucky when I heard that fact at all. Who knew what part would wear out next? It seemed destiny that we should find ourselves stranded in some podunk

Mexican town waiting two months for a Mexican mechanic to get a three dollar factory-made bolt in the mail.

Also, if our Mazda was destined to stick out like a sore thumb, it wouldn't be hard for the enemy to spot either. If my hunch was right, and Mehrukenah's gang was indeed following us to Mexico, our delay in Albuquerque had given them plenty of time to set up look-out posts all along the way to report our arrival. We continued down the interstate toward El Paso, Texas. It was about the time we passed by a New Mexican town named "Truth Or Consequences," that Garth decided to go a bit overboard with the principles of his speech in the motel.

"You're going eighty miles an hour," he notified me.

"We're fine," I explained. "These are long stretches. If there was a highway patrolman anywhere, I'd spot him a mile away."

"That's not the point," said Garth. "We're striving for perfection, remember?"

"Garth," I said, "I think the Lord would approve of me trying to make up for lost time."

"I don't believe that," Garth declared. "I think the Lord would have you obey the law of the land."

"Are you serious?"

"As a heart attack," he replied. "If we're going to be as righteous as possible, we can't make up our own rules along the way. Latter-day Saints tend to be guilty of that a lot. Pornography and profanity are wrong, unless we find them in good movies and music. Stealing is wrong, except when pirating computer disks or videotapes. Cheating is wrong, except with income taxes. Gambling is wrong, unless it's a state supported lottery—"

"You're straining at gnats," I accused. "That was the downfall of the Jews."

"If you've been speeding all your life, it becomes a pretty big gnat. You believe murder and suicide are wrong, don't you? Then how can you continue to speed knowing statistics have been compiled for decades proving excessive speeds can cause either?"

"You're saying if I speed, I'm a potential murderer? Give

me a break, Garth! You're getting *way* out of line," I scoffed.

"God can't look upon sin with the least degree of allowance, Jim," Garth proclaimed. "Do you really understand what that statement means? If we want to keep God's Spirit as close to us throughout this trip as possible, we can't indulge in things we know are wrong."

"He's right, Jim," agreed Renae.

Great, I thought, now he's got the women on his side.

"All right!" I grudgingly agreed. "I'm dropping down to sixty-five."

"Please don't do it grudgingly," Garth pleaded. "How many people find themselves forced to strive for utter perfection and know how it feels—even if it's just for a week?"

"But no one can be perfect," I said.

"Maybe we can't be as perfect as Christ. But if eventual perfection wasn't an achievable goal, why have the Atonement or repentance in the first place? We can do it for a week, Jim. Even if we can't, we have to try harder than ever before in our lives. Our success depends on it. Look at this like it's a great blessing!"

I'd never felt a blessing could be so much of a curse. Not only did we have to putt down the highway at a turtle's pace, we couldn't play the radio for fear a song would come on with questionable lyrics. I'd heckled every anti-rock and roll talk I'd ever been forced to listen to. It was just music!

If people were afraid of being influenced by somebody else's sins, maybe they shouldn't read the paper or watch the news or read Shakespeare—or even *live life*! The only argument which even came *close* to influencing me, was one by my favorite mission companion, Elder Bigler. He admitted we couldn't escape the influence of sin in the world, but did we have to pay money to see and hear it firsthand?

But even that argument didn't hold water after a while. I was always of the opinion that knowledge was power. Seeing life in all its shades of black and white could only make me a stronger person in the end. Maybe that outlook wasn't true for everyone, but I felt certain it was true for me.

"If I don't hear some kind of music," I shouted, "I'm going to go *nuts!*"

Garth's prescription came in the form of a cassette tape of *Saturday's Warrior*. His choice almost made me lose my breakfast. I'd always prided myself on having never seen a Mormon musical. The clips I'd heard left no doubt that trite inanity had made its mark upon the world.

"No way!" I barked. "I *won't* have that garbage in my tape player! If we can't listen to *real* music, why should I have to suffer through this cornball nonsense?"

Unfortunately, I was in the minority. Into the tape player went the Flinders family and Elders Kessler and Green. As I was rolling my eyes and shaking my head throughout the program, I couldn't help but notice Renae in the back, looking disappointed in me.

It was somewhere around Las Cruces, New Mexico, Elders Kessler and Green were singing *"We are not the ordinary, fearlessly extraordinary . . ."* for the second time through, when my spirit started to break down a little. I couldn't admit it to anyone, but I was actually enjoying the tape. I recognized the efforts behind it and the beauty of the message it was meant to present. I began to wonder what arrogance within me had caused my outburst. What was it about me which made it so necessary to tear down something which had given so many people so much pleasure?

The feeling didn't stop there. It spread deeper. I began to wonder why I did so many similar things in other circumstances. Why did I spend so much energy justifying my weaknesses rather than admitting them and finding a solution? It seemed such a hopeless part of my personality. Did the sickness have a cure?

As the character of Tod began singing *"What is that sound rising up from the world . . ."* the spirit took the time to whisper a few words to my soul. I was given the tiniest inkling of understanding for the destiny of God's plan and my potential within it. I began to comprehend why 'lukewarm' had no place in the Kingdom of God. The feeling I was granted passed quickly, but it left a tear in my eye. Nobody saw the tear. The girls were napping in the back and Garth had aimed his attention down the highway. Discreetly, I wiped the tear away, and when I felt my composure had been regained, I spoke my first words to Garth since my temper had flared.

"You know," I began, "when I was a little kid, I thought everything was entirely black and white. I remember being so hurt, so disappointed, when I realized everything was grey. As I've grown older, it seems I've been just as disappointed, and struggled just as hard against the awareness that everything is really as black and white as I always thought it was."

"You're right," Garth agreed. "There are only two forces at work in this world—black and white. Only people are grey."

CHAPTER 18

Driving the interstate into El Paso, Texas I got my first up-close view of a foreign country. The highway ran parallel to the Rio Grande for a short span. On the American side of the river, industry was booming with high-tech factories and mirror-polished office buildings. On the Mexican side, the hillside was crested with dilapidated adobe dwellings and bedrock roads. The contrast was quite disturbing.

"Since we're going to take the car in, we should get Mexican car insurance," Renae suggested.

"I think we're gonna have to risk it," I said. "Money's a little tight."

"That's not a smart thing to do," counselled Renae. "An accident in Mexico is considered a criminal as well as a civil offense. Even running into a fence, you could go to jail."

My phobia for Mexican prisons resurfaced.

"Lead the way," I conceded.

We took the next exit and drove around the downtown streets of El Paso until we found a sign signifying *Palm's Mexican Insurance*. Inside we purchased seven days of insurance, expending our resources another fifty dollars. In return, I was handed a lime-green sticker and advised to put it in my window. If I didn't, I ran the risk of having a Mexican driver deliberately ram into me in hopes of receiving a pay-off. Already, Mexico was sounding like a really charming place.

We also bought a three-dollar tourist map, and upon returning to the car, Garth and I took a moment to locate Veracruz. It was a big oil port on the Gulf of Mexico, way down where the country's landmass makes its eastward bend toward the Yucatan Peninsula. My finger pinpointed our final destination. Santiago Tuxtla looked to be a blink-and-miss town about a hundred miles south of Veracruz, near a big lake called Catemaco, maybe thirty miles inland from the ocean. We still faced two thousand grueling Mexican miles. According to Renae, there was no such thing as an interstate in Mexico. The going would likely be very slow.

"We should exchange our money over there." Renae pointed down the block at a sign which read, *Exchange Rate: 2875 Pesos.* "You'll always get a better rate on this side of the border."

I traded four hundred dollars, and received in return over a million pesos.

"I'm a Mexican millionaire!" I raved.

Foreign money was a whole new experience for me. The bills were multi-colored and the coins were fat. I knew there were other monetary systems in the world, but I guess I didn't *really know* it. This was gonna take some getting used to. My whole perception of the value of things was severely distorted.

I handed Garth half the Mexican pesos they gave me and provided Renae with the remainder of our American green, about one-hundred and thirteen dollars. Garth stuffed the greater portion of his money into the bottom of his shoe.

"Of course, you know," I teased, "the odor you're giving that cash will make it very difficult to spend."

Renae also advised us to enjoy one last American meal, so upon spying a nearby *Pizza Hut*, we accordingly gorged ourselves.

"Two things we must remember while we're down there to avoid Montezuma's Revenge," Garth instructed, lapping up a string of pizza cheese off his chin. "First, remember to ask if the water is *purificada*. A lot of places won't purify it, so be prepared to drink a lot of soda pop."

"And second," continued Renae, "don't eat anything that grows in, or on, the ground—carrots, potatoes—that kind of stuff. Mexican farmers sometimes use human excrement to fertilize the soil."

Such conversation served to make our dinner all the more palatable.

After dinner, we hopped back on the interstate and soon found ourselves in the midst of a spaghetti-twisted panorama of on-ramps and off-ramps. One of the off-ramps was preceeded with a sign saying: *Mexico, Cuidad de Juarez.* After crossing the Rio Grande, we took our place behind a fast-moving line of cars passing through what appeared to be a line of toll booths. Looking over to the left, I was grateful I wasn't *leaving* Mexico. The line of cars to get out of this place went on for a mile.

"Everybody take out your birth certificates and passports." Garth warned.

But upon reaching the border guard, he took one look inside our Mazda and waved us on, failing to care if we had any evidence of citizenship or not.

I glared at Garth. "Looks like I didn't need it after all."

Garth shrugged his shoulders, "Well, you'll need it to get out."

We drove on through. I was officially, for the first time in my life, inside a foreign country.

We'd watched the climate grow warmer and dryer every inch southward. Here there was absolutely no evidence that winter ever touched the ground. It felt rather peculiar to be sweating in December.

The first thing which struck me was how old the cars were. In America, maybe one out of ten automobiles on the road was older than twenty years, but here it was every other car. Some of these scrap-heaps were literally held together with nothing more than tape and twine. I don't think I've ever seen so many Volkswagen Bugs in one place in my life.

Every tree in a nearby park was painted white about four feet up the trunk. I thought maybe it was to ward off a kind of insect.

"What's the matter with the trees?" I asked Renae.

"It's decorative," said Renae.

"Painting a tree is decorative?" I scorned.

"They do the same thing in Guatemala," added Garth.

A moment later, we found ourselves floundering in the bustling streets of Juarez, Mexico. This place was a circus! Bumper stickers telling other cars that they were driving too close was a sadly missed commodity.

"We need to find the Pan American Highway," said Renae. "You're gonna have to ask somebody for directions."

About then we hit a stoplight. A bony-looking man on a bicycle rode up to my window.

"You look for souvenir?" he asked. "Eh, souvenir?"

Then he leaned down and grinned in at me wryly, flinching his eyebrows. "You look for young girls? Pretty girls?"

Noticing Jenny and Renae in the back he added, "Maybe hotel, eh?"

His inferences were highly offensive to Jenny and Renae.

"Drive on," Renae insisted.

"We're looking for the Pan American Highway," I told the man.

"Souvenir?" the man repeated.

"No," I said. Then slowly I repeated, "We're-looking-for-the-Pan-American-highway."

The man gave no indication of understanding a word I was saying. Garth leaned over to translate my question for him, but the man had already pedaled away from the car and was riding on ahead saying, "You follow! You follow!"

"Don't follow," said Renae, as the light turned green. "He only knows enough English to con the tourists. All he wants is for you to follow him so you'll be obligated to pay him some money. If anything, he'll probably get us more lost than we already are. Then, if you don't pay him what he wants, he might smash a dent in your hood and ride away."

"Well, who *can* we ask then?" I cried. I wasn't expecting frustration and culture shock to set in for at least a few days. Not in five minutes.

"Pull over here," said Garth.

Stopping at the curb, Garth opened his window and

spoke in Spanish to a couple walking down the sidewalk. The only word I recognized was *Panoamericana*.

Cordially, the man and his girl began replying in Spanish and pointing toward the east.

Garth waved his thanks to them, *"Gracias."*

Then Garth turned to me, "Take a left—not at this street, but the next one. You'll know it because it's a one-way."

The filth and poverty I saw over the next few blocks left me speechless for several minutes. There was garbage everywhere—the kind that's years old and decomposed into slime. Hadn't street cleaners been invented yet in this country? Cars were parallel parked on both sides of the avenue, making the way chokingly thin. There didn't seem to be a stainless, sturdy building in sight. Bright orange and blue paint just didn't look right on stucco and adobe.

My sheltered existence in the western United States was grossly apparent. I hadn't known what a real slum looked like before this. There were a few bad places in Portland, but nothing I'd ever seen in my life even approached what I was seeing now.

In spite of the poverty, the people appeared clean, and for the most part, wore remarkably clean clothing—especially the girls. Pants on a woman seemed to be outlawed. I never saw a girl in anything but a dress, and the school children were always in uniform.

Advertising was posted everywhere!—on telephone poles, fences, buildings, sidewalks, trees—you name it. Most of the time the posters were faded or torn, having hung in the same spot for a decade. And just like in America, massive billboards along the Pan-American Highway shouted at us all the way to the city limits. It seemed like half of the billboards were hailing the slogan *"¡Solidaridad!"* which Renae translated as "Solidarity!" She defined it as an effort by the current Mexican government to unify all the states of Mexico into a solid national unit.

"Why? Are they on the verge of revolution or something?" I asked.

"Not necessarily, but that *is* a continual threat in most Latin American countries," explained Renae. "Mexico, though, is one of the more stable."

American industry was alive and well south of the border. Everywhere I turned were businesses touting American-made products from *Coca-Cola* to *Kinney Shoes*.

We pulled in for gas at a Pemex Station. Actually *all* the gas stations were Pemex—short for Petroleum Mexico.

When we stopped our car, it was surrounded. Two eager boys took a tin can filled with soapy water and sent a wave across my windshield, afterwards vigorously wiping with towels. Few places in the U.S. gave you this kind of service anymore.

Salesman approached all four windows, peddling various kinds of jewelry and food. Jen couldn't resist the charm of a five-year-old girl outside her window distributing tiny packages of Chicklet's Gum. She bought four of them for an American quarter. The guy at my window displayed a plate stacked with skinless, dripping fruit—a kind I'd never seen before—brilliantly colored in red and yellow and green.

"What's this stuff?" I asked.

"It's called *tuna* or *atun*—the fruit of the cactus flower. If you want one ask him 'How much?': '*¿Cuanto Cuesta?*'"

The man said five hundred pesos. Wincing, I replied 'no way!' and shooed him off. He was persistent, but the gas tank was full, so I payed the attendant thirty-thousand pesos and prepared to drive away.

"What about the boys who did your windows?" Renae asked me.

"I have to pay them too? I thought they were just being nice."

"Nobody in this country is just being nice," said Renae. "This is how they feed their families."

I handed one of the boys a fifty-peso coin. He looked very disappointed.

"What more does he want?" I wondered.

"Jim, fifty pesos is less than two cents," informed Renae.

Renae handed the boy a one-thousand peso coin. He looked significantly happier and went on to the next windshield.

"Are we gonna have to pay everybody who so much as waves 'hello?'" I asked.

"As many as we can," said Renae, "or you'll make enemies real fast."

Continuing down the Pan-American Highway, my eyes were darting from place to place with such wonderment, Garth almost insisted he do the driving. This was indeed a different world. A world I'd intentionally kept in the back of my mind. My attitude made me feel a certain degree of shame. It seemed whenever I'd met foreigners, whether at BYU or elsewhere, they always had a keen interest in lifestyles outside their own country in a way most Americans couldn't comprehend. We were sometimes too wrapped up in our own culture and lifestyle to care.

Passing the Juarez Airport or 'Aeropuerto,' we set our navigational sights on the city of Chihuahua, two hundred and fifty miles into the Mexican interior. The sun was dropping into the Mexican desert, providing the sky with a bright and friendly blanket of red, and making me finally feel relaxed and welcome for the first time.

But the feeling only lasted another ten miles. A little further into the desert, in what I'd have termed the middle of nowhere, there was another inspection post. A line of a half-dozen cars was moving through it a lot slower than the one we'd been through already.

"Maybe this is where birth certificates and passports come in handy," I concluded.

As we neared the front of the line, I noticed a station wagon parked about a hundred yards up the road which didn't appear to have any connection with the official vehicles or personnel who talked with the drivers. There was a man leaning on its hood, wearing dark sunglasses, and studying all the cars which drove by. As our Mazda reached the inspection official, I noticed the sunglasses man take special interest in us, unfold his arms and step toward us a few paces for a closer look.

The official, through a heavy Mexican accent, asked me for my tourist card.

"My what?"

Renae spoke to him in Spanish for a moment. It was determined we had to go all the way back through the border and show my birth certificate and car registration in order to get a tourist card. Such was the required ticket if we wanted to get any further into the country.

The sunglasses man was still watching as we turned the Mazda around and aimed it back toward Juarez. Nobody else seemed to notice the man or care. Looking across the desert, this appeared to be the only road leading into the Mexican interior for hundreds of miles in either direction.

If the Gadiantons had successfully deciphered Andrew's information and determined our destination, there were only four or five major border crossings they had to be concerned with. If I were them, and if I had enough manpower, I'd position lookouts at key locations inside each of those borders. I started to wonder how foolish it may have been to come into the country the way we'd come. Maybe we should have crossed over at some totally obscure location like Del Rio, Texas or Nogales, Arizona. For that matter, maybe my earlier idea of swimming the river like a wetback wasn't so absurd.

I decided to shrug him off. The man in sunglasses could have been standing there for any one of a thousand reasons. Besides, if he were the enemy, why wasn't he following us back into Juarez?

It was disturbing enough to drive all twenty miles back to the border. I was never too patient with bureaucracy anyway—even in America—but in Mexico I had no idea who to complain to.

Renae apologized. "I've never driven a car into Mexico, so how could I have known?"

We waited in the line of cars a full hour to get back through to the American side of the border.

"This is it for your firearm," Garth said. "If they search our car and find it, we can kiss this trip goodbye."

"What if I took my birth certificate and registration and hiked up to the border post by myself, without having to drive through?" I wondered.

"I think it's too late," said Renae.

She was right. We were in the far right lane of a six-lane line of cars. This conveyor belt was moving no direction but forward, and there was no way to turn around.

"What do you suggest?" I asked.

"Toss it into the river," Garth replied.

Sighing, I stuck the .357 Magnum in an old McDonald's sack and threw it into the shallow, grey waters of the Rio Grande before we reached the booth.

It was another twenty minutes in a standing line before we were able to present my birth certificate and Jenny's car registration. All I got in return was a tiny slip of paper. What a waste to have driven all the way back here just for that! Nevertheless, when we reached the interior inspection post again, I was able to show them that slip of paper and drive right on through.

The station wagon and sunglasses man were no longer waiting a hundred yards beyond the inspection area. My suspicions about him being a Gadianton spy were obviously a mistake.

The drive to Chihuahua would have to be executed under a darkened sky. Earlier in the day, Renae had expressed some concerns about driving in Mexico at night. Her reasons were soon dramatically clear. The highway was comfortably divided for the next few miles, but then it combined into a single two-lane road. Not only were the lanes cardboard thin, there was no shoulder if we wanted to stop. The asphalt seemed to have been laid across the desert without any consideration for making it level with the surrounding ground. Thence, there was a six to eight inch cliff on either side of the road. One false move would send an automobile hurling into the desert like a tumbleweed. To make matters worse, there were no reflectors or guidelines to remind you where this cliff began. Since a greater portion of the road was in disrepair, there was often no center line either. None of these obstacles seemed to slow down the Mexican traffic though, and at night that consisted of mostly semi-trucks and buses.

In short, it was a total nightmare! My muscles constricted every time headlights drew nearer and whizzed past. Our average speed was about forty miles an hour. I learned quickly that the term *peligre* meant dangerous, because signs used the word to define highway conditions at almost every turn. Needless to say, nobody slept for the first two and a half hours.

About half-way to Chihuahua, I stopped the car in a one-horse town named El Sueco to catch my breath. Parking in front of the white picket fence of a small church, I got out of the car and walked around a bit, taking in the soothing sound of Spanish music coming from someone's radio nearby. Everyone else got out to stretch as well.

"Do you want me to drive?" asked Garth.

"No," I quickly replied.

My nerves were frazzled enough by my own driving. I didn't need them to frazzle worse trying to 'back-seat drive' somebody else.

Renae noted a sign on the roadside reading, 'Neuva Casas Grandes' with an arrow indicating a right turn at the next intersection, about fifty yards ahead.

"The Mormon colonies are off in that direction," she said. "I've never been there but I . . ."

I didn't hear the rest of what she said. I was too busy watching a certain station wagon make a restless approach, spot us, and then ease on the brake to be sure we were who the driver thought we were. I assumed the man in sun-glasses was still its pilot, though it was too dark to tell. The station wagon stopped between our car and the next inter-section and idled for several seconds. I was about to step up to the driver and ask him what he wanted, but he abruptly pulled back onto the road and sped away. Garth had been watching this phenomenon as well.

"Who was that?" he asked.

"I don't know," I replied.

So the station wagon *was* following us. Nevertheless, I decided it was best to not yet concern the others. Something compelled me to open the trunk. I just wanted to make sure the sword was still in the guitar case. It was, along with the scabbard Jenny had bought me in Albuquerque. I decided it best to keep the sword up front with me the rest of the journey. I don't know why the idea made me feel more secure. It just did. Tucking the sword inside its scabbard, I tied it securely about my waist and climbed into the front seat.

"A bit bulky, isn't it?" asked Garth.

The sword fit perfectly under the dashboard. I didn't feel like it was in the way at all, but even if it had been, I'm certain I'd have endured the awkwardness.

Leaving El Sueco, I realized I wasn't feeling the same tension as during the first half of our drive to Chihuahua. The road had not improved, but somehow I was able to navigate the obstacles with much more deftness and precision. A good portion of the highway still lacked a center line, but I could almost sense a natural barrier which kept me from crossing over it, or from going off the edge. My speed increased to sixty-five miles per hour.

"The sign says 70 kph," Garth remarked.

"But that's only forty-five miles per hour!" I grumbled.

"Perfection. Remember?"

I slowed down to 70 kph, and sometime between now and the end of the Millennium we arrived at the city limits of Chihuahua.

CHAPTER 19

It was midnight, and everyone was of the opinion that nothing in this world could feel as glorious right now as a soft, cool bed in a sweet, clean hotel. Renae had led us to believe hotel prices in Mexico were quite inexpensive, but from our initial investigation, her assumption was sadly inaccurate. You see, Renae's experience in Mexico was limited to an area much further south, where touring gringos were few and far between. Chihuahua was still reasonably close to the border, and hotel owners were all too aware of the liberality of American spending. Room costs were about the same as in the United States—if anything they were a little higher.

The highway was divided the last few miles into Chihuahua, as well as along the main strip through town, giving us a wide-angle view of all the hotel's signs. As we began checking each of them out, we understood how they got away with such inflated prices. It was simply a matter of supply and demand. We couldn't find a single vacancy anywhere in the city—to say nothing of our hopes of finding two adjacent rooms. The experience was almost worse than seeking lodging in Las Vegas on a weekend.

After checking a dozen places on the main strip, we decided to plot a course for the older part of the city. After coming up empty at two more prospective inns, and after facing the embarrassment of having to back up twice on one-way streets, we spotted the flickering white neon sign of the *Hotel Apolo*.

The lobby should have been our first clue of the hotel's condition. The couch's covering was worn to paleness and the springs had collapsed until the only possible seat was in the very middle. The manager was a squalid-looking geezer with nose hair comprising most of his moustache. For a room with two double-beds, he quoted us a price of 98,000 pesos (thirty-five bucks). Our exhaustion bound us to his offer.

I paid the man and signed my name and address to the register. The manager took his pen back and added the number ten under my name, handing us the corresponding key. After climbing a flight of creaking stairs, we braved the dim and peeling hallway in search of a door with a number matching that on our key. The decal on the door had long since been torn away and the number '10' was drawn in with a pencil. Turning the knob, Jenny entered first, and not two seconds later, she shrieked and reeled backwards, being caught by Garth. There was a cockroach with the wingspan of a sparrow crawling up the rust-stained porcelain sink.

"Look," I told Garth, "the National Bird!"

The insect began scaling the wall above the sink. I did a karate-style kick, adding the appropriate yell, and crushed the beast under the weight of my shoe. It's carcass stuck there a moment, then dropped conveniently into the drain. Putting my hand on the hilt of my sword, I did an oriental bow for Renae and then for Jenny. When I went to wash its remains down the pipes, no water came out of the faucet.

Garth came back from investigating the shower and reported, "The water doesn't work in here either."

"These beds are disgusting," winced Renae. "I don't think I can sleep on this blanket." She leaned down to smell it. "I take that back. I *know* I can't sleep on this blanket."

"Let's get our money back," Jenny insisted.

The four of us marched down to the manager with our eyes ablazing, but he didn't seem influenced by them a bit. In Spanish, Garth announced our opinion of the situation. The manager responded and shook his head.

Garth turned to me, "He says he can't give us all our money back. He can only give us half."

I stomped around the lobby. "I can't believe this! Of all the dishonest—!" I turned back to Garth, "Tell him we'll take it out of his hide!"

"Let's just take half the money and go," suggested Renae.

The manager began speaking again.

Garth interpreted, "He says he has two other rooms which might be a little newer—though they *are* quite small. He says they adjoin. We can have them for 'only' fifty thousand pesos more."

"Do they have running water?" asked Jenny.

Garth asked the question and the manager replied.

This time Renae translated. "He says the city shuts off the water supply during certain hours of the night. It should be fine in the morning."

"Let's see these other rooms," I grumbled.

The manager dropped a different pair of keys into my palm and we headed back up the stairs. The newer rooms were at the very end of the same hallway as room ten. They weren't much larger than rabbit hutches—one single bed apiece, but they did have a newer appearance. At least the blankets looked fresh. With our revulsion only slightly tempered, we agreed to endure the night. Renae was able to haggle the price down twenty-five thousand pesos.

"Next time," Garth said, "we need to insist upon seeing the room *before* we hand over any money." As Garth and I went down to retrieve our luggage, we decided it might be best to park the car a few blocks away, where the neighborhood looked a bit more private and secluded. Garth took up the bags while I went to park the car.

Though it was past one in the morning, the town hadn't seemed to slow down much. A good deal of traffic was still honking in the streets and the sidewalks were fairly crowded. As Renae promised, people sent me some pretty strange glances upon seeing the sword and scabbard around my waist. I started to worry that carrying such a weapon unconcealed might not only look ridiculous, it might be illegal. I decided while out in public it might be best if I cloaked it somewhat under a towel or sweater.

I noticed a few Christmas decorations here and there—a string of tinsel and colored lights in a couple of windows.

Actually, my walk back to the hotel was quite refreshing. I even stopped a moment in front of the neighboring bar to listen to Phil Collin's "Land of Confusion," playing on the stereo inside.

The lyrics were tame enough. I didn't feel I was violating Garth's appeal for perfection. It made me feel comforted, like I wasn't as far from home as I might have imagined.

Returning to my room, Garth was asleep in my sleeping bag on the floor, his Spanish edition of the Book of Mormon—the same one he'd dragged with him every-where he went since his mission to Guatemala—sitting open under his hand. Grateful for his noble generosity which left me with the bed, I dropped down on the mat-tress, the cold steel of the sword still in its scabbard tucked under my arm. I could still hear rock music seeping up through the floor boards. For all I know it could have gone on another few hours, but I was so tired I could have slept through BYU's half-time marching band.

I must have awakened sometime around seven. Jenny's chirping snore, audible even through the thin walls of the neighboring room, was the only sound I could hear.

I had cottonmouth and I couldn't seem to work up enough spit to wet it down. Upon recalling a purified water dispenser down the hall at the top of the stairway, I got up and went out the door of our room, but not before tying the sword and scabbard around my waist. Keeping the sword with me at all times seemed to have become an entrenched habit in a matter of one day. As I proceeded down the hallway in my bare feet, grateful that someone had vacuumed at least the strip of faded carpet which ran down the center, I passed by the infamous room ten and was surprised to see that the door was open. I was certain we'd locked it when we went back down to complain to the manager. Maybe he'd found another sucker.

Looking into the room, my eyes widened. The place was a shambles. Furniture had been overturned; the mattresses had been flung off the beds; someone had even tried to rip the sink out of the wall—either that or my karate kick had a delayed reaction. Though our room was five doors away, I couldn't believe we hadn't heard anything. The four of us must have been awfully tired, or maybe all the ruckus from the bar downstairs led our subconscious to think nothing of it.

Not quite sure how to interpret this situation, I continued walking to the end of the hallway and got my drink from the dispenser. Maybe the manager had taken our complaints to heart and decided to start remodeling early this morning.

I felt an urge to run downstairs and see if the manager was still awake. As I rounded the corner and approached the front desk, nobody was there. The registry was setting open on the counter. The last page—the one I had signed my name to—had been torn from the book. I looked around. I considered calling out; maybe the manager would emerge from a back room.

Then I noticed the streak of dried blood on the carpet behind the counter. I heard a noise. Glass fell and broke in the back room. The noise was followed by a groan.

Removing my sword from it's sheath, I moved carefully behind the counter. Taking a breath, I charged into the back room with my conscience fully prepared to assault whatever I might find. The room was empty, except for the manager. He was lying hog-tied in the middle of the floor, his hair still damp with blood from a blow to the head. The sound I'd heard was a lamp he'd knocked over. Pieces of smashed bulb lay strewn across the floor.

He mumbled something to me in Spanish, but of course I didn't understand. I proceeded to untie his knots, and the moment he was free, he got to his feet and stumbled forward into the lobby to get at the phone on his front desk, all the while pressing his palm to his forehead in an effort to sooth what I'm sure was a terrible headache.

As I followed him out, Garth was standing on the other side of the counter, greatly concerned.

"What's happened?" he asked.

"The manager was attacked last night. I don't know what time."

Garth started asking the manager questions. He answered until somebody came on the other end of the phone line.

"What did he say?" I demanded.

"He said five men attacked him. He thinks it was around four a.m. He doesn't know what they wanted."

"Did you see our old room upstairs?"

"Yes, I did," Garth admitted.

"They were trying to find us," I revealed. "They know we were here."

I grabbed the registry off the counter and showed Garth the torn page.

"The only reason we're still alive is because we changed rooms," I concluded. "The manager didn't make the correction on the registry. They must have clobbered him before he could notify them of the switch."

Garth examined the book. "But how could they have followed us? How did they know to check this hotel?"

I couldn't even begin to answer Garth's questions. The only clue I had was the man in the station wagon. They would have had to check the registries of almost every hotel in Chihuahua to find us.

The manager was talking into the phone a mile a minute, still pressing his palm to his head.

"Is he calling the police?" I asked Garth.

"I think he's calling a relative," Garth replied. "Maybe the owner of the hotel."

"Wake up the girls and let's get out of here."

The manager didn't seem to connect us with the attack, so he said nothing while we made efforts to vacate the hotel as quickly as possible. The girls were told they had about three minutes to pack and wash up—not welcome instructions for waking women. Then Garth and I rushed to bring the car up to the front of the hotel. The fact that the Gadiantons hadn't found our Mazda parked anywhere nearby might have been our saving grace. They must have concluded we'd left, and thus, there was no reason to search every room.

Our car was still sitting untouched in its quiet corner a few blocks away. How I wished I knew enough about the back roads of Chihuahua to find an obscure route connecting us with the Pan-American Highway far beyond the city limits—

but perhaps even that would have been futile. Who knew how many people Mehrukenah and Shurr had working for them now? There could be spies setting up ambushes all the way into Mexico City—maybe even all the way to the Hill Vigia!

As we pulled up in front of the hotel, the girls had taken the trouble of bringing all our luggage into the lobby. As Renae climbed in the front seat, I told her she looked great without make-up. I'm not sure why, but she gave me a look intended to turn me into stone. Either my timing or my wording was seriously off. Who could figure with women?

We found the Pan American highway again and proceeded through the rest of the city. A large hill with the road cutting through it seemed to mark the city's southern boundary. It was just beyond this point where the first car, a grey Cavalier with Utah plates, was patiently waiting. It pulled into the lane behind us. I didn't recognize the driver. He had long black hair, a thin beard, and like the man I'd seen yesterday, his eyes were concealed behind a pair of sunglasses.

Giving this situation the benefit of the doubt, I pressed on the gas pedal. Sure enough, the Cavalier matched our speed. But I still felt confident. The highway beyond Chihuahua appeared divided and relatively clear of traffic, giving us an empty speedway across the hilly plains. But it wasn't a half-mile later when two other cars pulled in behind the Cavalier. Among them was the station wagon.

"I think we're in for a chase," I announced.

My passengers gripped any and all handles in the car. I increased my speed to ninety-five miles an hour. The other automobiles had no trouble keeping up. Now I noted four cars behind us.

A gold-colored Camero led the pursuit and sped up beside me in the other lane. The burley driver glanced over and smiled as he passed, his speed exceeding 110 mph. As the Camero pulled into the lane in front of me, the Cavalier veered into the other lane and accelerated, attempting to follow the same course as the Camero. The station wagon then sped up to tighten the gap from behind.

Their intentions were obvious. I was about to be locked into a deadly vise-grip on three sides, allowing the other cars to carefully decelerate and force my Mazda to slow down with them. How could I prevent this? I couldn't lose them by going any faster. I slammed my fist on the dashboard yelling, "You gutless piece of garbage!"

The Cavalier was in position at my side. As I'd predicted, the Camero began to slow down. My passengers were breathless with fear. There seemed to be no escape. The moment we stopped, the other drivers would climb out of their cars and surround the Mazda. Upon seeing the sword at my side, grins would form under their sunglasses. They would have no reason not to slit our throats. Who would stop them in the middle of the Mexican desert?

I thought about the sword and the way it had given me a kind of power surge the night before as I tried to navigate the hazardous highway. For some reason it was not inspiring me at this moment. But why? Did it know who surrounded our car? Did it *want* me to be defeated? I had a feeling that was not the case. It didn't seem to care who its owner was, as long as that owner was devoted. I would not be inspired unless I *asked* for the inspiration. No longer would its services be freely given. I had to *request* them. Where were these thoughts coming from? It was as if the sword were speaking to me. But that was insane! Nevertheless, in the next instant, I found myself wrapping my fingers around the cool metal hilt, while my other hand remained glued to the wheel. Because of this gesture, my mind began flowing with confidence and my limbs were surging with energy.

As our vehicle continued to slow, the Cavalier misread the rate of deceleration and slipped past us several yards. With flawless precision, I grabbed that space behind the Cavalier and escaped the vise.

Two more enemy cars had joined in the chase. That made six altogether. Where were all these vehicles coming from? They were adjusting to my escape by closing in the gap from behind again, this time with the object of pinning me into the *left* lane.

Ahead, I saw a turn-around space between the divided highway. Upon reaching it, I veered the Mazda sharply to the left and found myself separated from the enemy vehicles entirely, though I was now facing oncoming traffic. A Mexican farmer with a pickup full of cabbage was the first one threatening a head-on collision. I saw the farmer's eyes widen in horror as he gripped his steering wheel and swerved into the other lane at the last second. A head of cabbage hit the hood of our car and rolled over the top. Jenny shrieked.

I looked over at the enemy vehicles still speeding beside me on the southbound side of the divided highway. The Cavalier had unintentionally taken the lead, blocking the Camero, and allowing me to pull a few yards ahead of them.

As the Mazda came up over a rise, I was startled by the blasting horn of an oncoming semi-truck passing a Volkswagen Bug. "Watch out!" Garth hollered and shrunk in his seat.

I made a split-second decision to play chicken with the Bug instead of the semi and switched lanes. The Volkswagen's driver hit the brakes, allowing the semi to pass him. Just in time, he veered into the inside lane, unable to stop before his vehicle dove into the brush growing in the median.

Up ahead, the road combined into a single two-lane highway again. I dodged another Mexican farmer and found myself back on the same roadway with the enemy cars. They were about ten yards to the rear, and the Camero was closing in fast to get into position for another forced deceleration. As the Camero tried to pass, I swerved into the center, forcing him to stay where he was and continue eating my dust.

Where could this end? My gas gauge was back to its familiar quarter tank. At these speeds I could only keep going for another fifty miles. Something would have to happen well before then, if we had any hope of escape.

Just then we rounded a corner and saw a seventh vehicle waiting just off the highway. As our convoy approached, with me leading the way, it pulled forward into the road, blocking both lanes of traffic. It was a dark blue Suburban with silver trim and this time there was no mistaking its identity.

CHAPTER 20

Our hopes for deliverance appeared grim. With six vehicles in hot pursuit and the blue Suburban—whose occupants were certainly Mehrukenah, Shurr, and Mr. Clarke—blocking the road ahead, what options did we have?

My fingers still gripping Coriantumr's sword, I found myself reaching inside it, reaching beyond the silver-plating and into the copper fibers themselves. My right hand seemed welded to the metal—indeed, the two had become one—and my left hand turned the steering wheel sharply to the right.

Our tires kicked up a cloud of dust as we turned into the driveway of some sort of ranch with rusty tin warehouses and fencelines of wood and stone. A Mazda 626 was not built for this kind of treatment. Two of its wheels lifted off the ground—so high I thought the car would flip, but my passengers shifted their weight and somehow the treads gripped the roadway. After fish-tailing a time or two, and regaining our balance, I guided the car down a dirt road beside the warehouses. The Camero was nipping at the Mazda's bumper, along with four other vehicles close behind it.

Mexican boys sitting on the fence watched the chase with intense excitement. There was a gate up ahead. Ranch hands were in the process of closing it, but upon seeing our stampede of automobiles, they abandoned their aim and leaped free of the road.

I hit the unlatched gate and sent it sprawling backwards, opening the way for everybody else and leaving a hefty dent in my hood. One of the enemy vehicles tried to go between the gate while driving collateral with the station wagon and smashed into the right post—a log the width of a telephone pole—and buckled up like an accordion.

Veering left, the remaining vehicles pursued us down a roadway which was little more than two tire tracks beside a ditch. We were in the middle of a pasture where several massive brahman cattle watched intently, chewing the cud, not concerned enough to get out of the way. The station wagon made an error in judgement while dodging a bull and high-centered into the ditch, knocking itself out of commission. The only cars still after us were the Cavalier and the Camero.

Fifty yards further, I could see that this humble excuse of a road connected again with the highway. A second gate obstructed the way, but I figured one good dent deserved another. Crashing through, the thin and rotting cross-posts snapped like popsicle sticks and did little more to our car than add scratches to the paint.

Nevertheless, the explosion of wood served to greatly frighten the driver of a top-heavy semi-truck with an open roof, its wooden sides bulging with the weight of a full load of scrap metal. It coughed a cloud of black exhaust like a barrelling locomotive while the driver hit his brakes and attempted to dodge the flying debris and oncoming cars. We heard a horrible screech—like the death-cry of a great hulking monster—as the truck began to tilt, overturning on its side, and sending a thunderous wave of twisted metal across the asphalt. I thought we were going to be crushed, but when the dust had cleared, it revealed a highway completely cut off to traffic, and the only vehicle south of the debris was our Mazda.

There was no way for the Gadiantons to get around. The strewn metal and a strip of rocky terrain blocked any passage around the right; a muddy riverbed blocked any passage around the left. This sparsely populated region wasn't like America where a vehicle could backtrack a few miles and find an optional roadway. Unless the Gadiantons wanted to go hundreds of miles out of the way, they'd have to wait several hours for the mess to be cleared.

The driver of the truck hoisted himself out his skyward door. Waving his hands, he began assaulting the Gadiantons and their modern minions with an arsenal of Spanish obscenities while they vacated their own vehicles to climb around the mess and ascertain our position.

We sped away, stopping only after the highway climbed to the top of a hill which rose a good half mile above the accident. Looking back toward the roadblock, there was a man standing in the middle of the highway on the south side of the over-turned truck. It was almost certainly Mehrukenah. His fists were clenched and, though it was too far away to tell, I'm sure his teeth were grinding. Once again we'd slipped out of his sinister grip.

"I think I was safer back in Provo," Jenny decided.

Renae had taken over as driver, with a hell-bent desire to get as far away from Chihuahua as possible.

Exhausted, I gazed out across the Mexican frontier, hilly and forestless, yet abounding in brilliant green grasses and pricking at the sky with shrubbery similar to Joshua trees. There were many small houses and farms, some so meager it was unbelievable that people lived there. Stone fences crawled all the way up the mountainsides, no matter how steep, and appeared as tiny lines scissioning the prairie. Stacking all those rocks must have taken decades.

The other passenger's temperaments remained on edge for quite some time. Garth, behind me, seemed especially tense. For the next twenty miles, no one spoke, and when I turned back to see Garth again, his expression hadn't changed.

"You all right?" I finally inquired.

"No, I'm *not* all right," he snapped, his tone unusually threatening.

I had no reason to think his animosity was directed at me, but I thought I'd better make sure.

"You're not mad at *me*, are you?"

"There's something wrong, Jim. Something horribly wrong."

"Not anymore," I contended. "Even if the Gadiantons finally get through, there are so many trails and highways between here and Veracruz, it would be virtually impossible for them to track us—unless they have a hundred more lookouts we don't know about—"

"It's not the Gadiantons I'm worried about anymore," Garth interrupted. "It's you, Jim."

My jaw dropped. "What are you talking about?"

I looked over at Renae and back at Jenny to see if Garth's animosity was infectious. Fortunately, they were both staring at Garth with the same bewilderment, though I suspected Renae was waiting for Garth to confirm something she already feared.

"What happened back there wasn't natural, Jim. You're not a Hollywood stunt driver—not unless there's a part of your life I don't know about. How were you able to maneuver like that?"

"Why do I have to be a Hollywood stunt driver to execute a few simple moves?"

"You grabbed the hilt of the sword, Jim. Why?" Garth demanded.

"I don't know. It gave me confidence, mostly."

"Did you make a conscious decision to ask for its help?"

I laughed nervously. "Garth, what are you accusing me of? You're treating me as if I were a criminal! As if I'd committed some kind of cardinal sin!"

"Then I'm right? You asked for its help?"

"Not in so many words," I admitted. "I just knew it could help me drive better. I can't explain why—I'm sure it's psychological."

"After all you know about the sword—after all you've seen and everything Muleki has told you—you think its *psychological*?!"

"Maybe," I contended. "Isn't everything psychological? If we *believe* something gives us power, can't we sometimes gain real power from it?"

"Yes!" Garth clamored. "It's called faith. All the power in

the universe is controlled by it, and the blessing hand is either God . . . or it's not God. You exerted your faith toward something which was not God!"

"Now, don't point all hellfire and damnation at me," I huffed. "If the sword has power, I've just proved it can be used for good instead of evil, right?"

"Wrong!" Garth thundered. "It wasn't ordained to that end. It was ordained for evil. To use it any other way goes against its very nature. If I were wrong, there'd be no harm in experimenting with witchcraft or black magic. Many people are fooled into thinking those powers can be used for good, but it can't be done."

"The fact is," I contended, "if I *hadn't* used it, we'd all be dead right now!"

"Maybe you're right," Garth agreed. "Maybe we would be. But when death is staring you in the face, the source to look to for help is not an inanimate object, it's our Heavenly Father."

"Joseph Smith used seer stones, didn't he? Correct me if I'm wrong, but those are inanimate objects, are they not? What's the difference between that and what I did?"

"The difference is that Joseph Smith always knew the power through which the stones operated. They were tools to help his faith in God, and eventually he didn't need them anymore. Like the Liahona in the Book of Mormon— it's power was entirely predicated upon faith in God. Like the Priesthood itself! If one attributes its powers to himself, or to anything other than God—amen to that power. The sword was the sole object of your faith, Jim—not God."

"But we're alive!" I reminded him. "Our survival was a *good thing*! Are you saying our survival was evil?"

"If by it, the sword has gained your unyielding devotions, then Jim, the answer is yes," Garth replied.

They were all staring at me, their eyes burning holes in me from every angle as they awaited my response to Garth's accusation.

"Yes! Okay! Fine! No problem!" I angrily exclaimed. "I won't ask for its help anymore! Will that make you happy? Is that what you want?"

Indignation was boiling inside me; I felt caustic bitterness toward every person in this car. They were all against me! I'd saved their lives and what was my reward? To be pronounced a cheater! A person possessed! How could their consciences not feel the painful heat of such seething ingratitude?

I looked over at Renae, gripping the steering wheel as intensely as if it were a Catholic rosary, struggling to keep her attention fixed on the highway, but failing to stop a tear from burning a path down her cheek.

"What's the matter with you?" I barked.

She turned to me and glowered. Jenny put her hand on my shoulder.

"This is not you, Jim. You're not acting like yourself," she said.

"Of course I am! You think because I'm angry, I'm a demon?"

Garth sat forward and asked the most sobering query of all. "Jim, can you give me the sword?"

A variety of sensations erupted within me. How can I describe them? Every inch of my flesh was pulsating. I shivered. I felt cold, and yet my palms were sweating. It was so important that I didn't hesitate, so important that I fooled them.

That I fooled them? Why had I thought that? Who was I trying to fool? What was the matter with me?

I began untying the scabbard from my waist. Then I held one end of the sword in each hand and thrust it toward Garth. My old comrade was looking into my eyes, not at the weapon.

"Well? Are you going to take it?"

"No," Garth replied. "Keep it. I just had to know if you could do it."

A few minutes later, it was *my* conscience that burned. Profusely, I begged forgiveness from everyone in the car telling them how sorry I was for having acted like such an idiot and how I had no idea what had come over me. Once again I tried to hand Garth the sword, only this time I did it with sincere contrition. Again, he refused.

"I would take it in a minute if I felt it were the right thing to do, Jim. I feel it's not. It was meant to be *your* burden. I believe when Muleki singled you out in the hospital as the only one he fully trusted to complete this mission, he did it deliberately. I can't tell you why, I just know his choice was right."

I laid the sword in the space between my seat and the passenger's side door. Looking at Renae, I noticed her right hand was free of the steering wheel, so I took it in my own hand and held it gently. She continued to look ahead, but smiled, compressing my palm with equal tenderness. I leaned back and closed my eyes, wondering about what Garth had said. Why *had* Muleki chosen me? Garth was certainly more spiritual. Maybe he wouldn't have chosen me at all if he'd known Jenny and Renae were coming—they weren't fooled for a second by the source of wrong voices. I couldn't think of a single advantage I had over any one of them.

Maybe it had something to do with the way righteousness was channeled. Garth placed much of his faith in his *knowledge*—in his personal power of reasoning. In a way, that was *his* seer stone. It would be so until he could one day tune his instrument more perfectly to receive the pure intelligence of God unbounded, as had Joseph Smith. As for Renae and Jenny, their seer stones were intuition and emotion and by exercising them in righteousness, they could one day partake of the same promise.

And me? I guess I was somewhere in the middle—and constantly plagued by questions. Maybe that was *my* seer stone. Skepticism forced me to gain a testimony in areas others took for granted. It made the going a little slower, but at least the road was perfectly paved.

One thing for sure, I still had many skepticisms about the sword. I couldn't bring myself to fully liberate the notion that it was all in my mind. Maybe in this instance, my doubts were a gift which made it subtly more frustrating for the sword to tie an enduring knot. I certainly didn't feel the same fear toward it that everyone else did. Could my nonchalance in this instance be a strength? I couldn't decide.

Passing through a town named Delicias reminded us of the void in our stomachs. Unfortunately, this part of Mexico didn't appear to have invented drive-thru restaurants yet, making it difficult to eat on the run. We found a tiny eatery off the road called the *Caballo Locho* where I ordered pancakes. Though they lacked maple syrup, the corn syrup they offered was unexpectedly good.

Garth sat beside Jennifer translating every item she pointed at on the menu. She enjoyed his attention, but seemed to be fighting any feelings which might be developing. Now and then she'd remind herself of her devotions by mentioning Muleki's name and I would watch Garth's face lose its exuberance. I started to wonder if my old comrade had secretly harbored a crush on my sister for years.

Garth and Jenny ordered *heuvos rancheros*—basically eggs and salsa—and Renae had *heuvos queso norteno*, a sensuous smelling cheese, egg, and tortilla dish which made me regret having played it safe with pancakes.

Outside, a kindly old gentleman squeezed us some oranges with a manual juicer. The oranges were green instead of orange and not as sweet as the ones from Florida, but it felt stylish to be drinking fresh-squeezed juice off the street. Each of our meals, including the juice, were less than two dollars. At last we were getting far enough from the tourist sites to enjoy true Mexican prices.

Just beyond Delicias, there was a monument in the middle of the road—a smashed car on a pedestal. It might have been a Volkswagen Rabbit—the chasis was so twisted it was quite hard to tell.

"Mexicans make statues out of wrecked cars?" I asked.

"Only the worst ones," Renae revealed. "They believe it encourages drivers to be more careful. You'll see those kind of monuments all over Mexico. Also, whenever you see a grave site or a wreath of flowers along the road, an accident occurred there in which somebody was killed."

"How gloomy," I decided.

"The family members consider the memorial as sacred as a grave site in a cemetery," said Renae.

Filling up with gas again at the local Pemex, we paid some boys another thousand pesos for washing our windshield, and continued on toward Jimenez and Torreon. The road remained in fairly good condition, though once we had to slow down to traverse a short stretch which was six inches under water.

Garth spent much of the afternoon talking our ear off about the ancient ruins of Mexico—Palenque, Monte Alban, Chichen Itza, and perhaps the greatest of all, Teotihuacan with its massive Pyramid of the Sun. He told us that prominent LDS scholars felt they had about eighty percent of the Book of Mormon's sites locked down. I was anxious to see how time would bear them out.

Near every Mexican municipality there were roadside stands selling everything from fruit, to pistachio nuts, to wood carvings. I finally tasted the cactus fruit they called *tuna*. It's sweet juices were tasty, but I had to spit out so many seeds that it just wasn't worth the effort.

The poverty we saw got me down at times. Most people offered some kind of menial service to earn a few pesos, even if it was just shining your tennis shoes, but a good number of people appeared resigned to begging. They'd trained themselves to spot Americans from a mile away and sometimes their open palms were thrust in our windows the moment a town's speed bumps forced us to slow down. Each time we refused one, I suffered guilt pangs, like maybe I wasn't as good a Christian as I'd hoped, but if we'd given to everyone who asked, we'd have been penniless by evening. We were always generous to cripples—the blind and the lame. Renae claimed that handicapped people in Mexico received little if any government compensation. Since they couldn't work, they got no social security when they grew old. What they earned by begging was generally all the money they ever saw.

It wasn't so much that Mexicans were illiterate and unlearned. Renae insisted that Mexico was quite educated compared with most third world countries. A college education was not uncommon, but neither was seeing an attorney plowing a field, or an engineer driving a cattle truck.

There just weren't enough jobs to support the professional working force.

Nearly every community boasted a magnificent Catholic cathedral, rising out from the shantiness of a town like an oasis from the desert. In the poorest places one could find tall statues of Mexican heroes and fiery white effigies of the *Cristos* looming down from the tops of the highest hills.

Despite the conditions, the people appeared happy and humble—making the best of life in spite of the package it came in. What a contrast from America's poor, who so often seemed angry for one reason or another.

I felt blessed for having been born in a wealthy and healthy nation. But at the same time, the humility of an old woman I saw standing in the mud selling rugs and necklaces day after day in the endless struggle to feed her family, made me wonder if her chances of reaching the celestial kingdom might be greater than my own. I had a temper which was prone to flare if my steak were cooked medium-well instead of medium-rare. In the eternal scheme of things, was my station a blessing or a curse? I found some comfort in knowing I still had the power to decide.

CHAPTER 21

The sky was just starting to dim as we passed through the town of Fresnillo. We'd come so far south now that the days were a few hours longer. Upon reaching Zacatecas we discovered our first fast food restaurant—*El Pollo Chicken*. I couldn't help but wonder if it was the same franchise as the one I'd seen in Salt Lake City. Our dinner thusly consisted of barbecued bird and french fries—and of course, a stack of corn tortillas, just to stay true to the culture.

Though my experience with roads into Chihuahua had made me leery of driving at night, the roads here seemed considerably better so we opted to go a little further into the darkness before seeking a hotel. An hour and a half later we found ourselves navigating the thin cobblestone streets of San Luis Potosi.

San Luis Potosi was a magnificent place—even at night. As one of the oldest colonial cities in Mexico, it's architecture boasted a grand heritage of arching colonnades and "Romeo and Juliet" balconies. Had this town been in the United States, the government would have spent millions repainting every corner and replastering every crack. Somehow such restoration would have dissipated some of its charm. I was glad it was in Mexico where available financing may have forced restorations to be more practical in nature.

The first hotel we discovered was the *Hotel Filher*. Entering its lobby I imagined I could hear all the ghosts of its first hundred years singing hearty songs of welcome. We stared up in awe at its lofty ceiling and the filagreed walls of its various levels further dignified by expansive murals of old Mexico—the Conquistadores and Catholic friars, the Aztec cities and glorious revolutions. The handrails of the upper floors were burgeoning with tropical plants whose weeping vines dropped down to the floor below. The wide staircase was divided into two walkways spiraling inward as it climbed, finally joining at a platform between the floors and then dividing again for the final ascent.

At the risk of sounding like a travelogue, I'll add that the price was surprisingly affordable—thirty thousand pesos less than the cockroach-infested dive we'd tenanted in Chihuahua with rooms five times as nice. Also, the water worked, which was a pleasant variation.

The clerk was a perfectly-trimmed gentleman with a cheerful smile. He spoke good English and told us the *Filher* was actually a three star hotel. The reason it wasn't four star, and remained inexpensive, was because they hadn't added all the possible modernizations—carpeting, new paint, and the like. For that I was grateful. It was the colonial authenticity which made it enchanting.

I advised Garth it might be best if we signed a pseudonym to the registry. For our room he signed Eduardo Ramirez. For Jenny and Renae's room he signed Louisa Ortega. It was just a precaution. I actually didn't expect to see Gadiantons again until we reached the Hill Vigia. If we were very lucky, perhaps we'd beat them there as well. We left a wake-up call for six a.m. to try to maintain our lead. The only way they could pass us now was if they drove all night. Certainly even Gadiantons needed sleep—and on something less bumpy than a Mexican highway. I parallel parked our car in a small gap between a new Ford Fiesta and an older Scirocco about a block west of the hotel. There was a plaza there with stone benches and massive trees projecting so many branches I'm sure I'd have deliberately lost myself in them as a kid. San Luis Potosi was the first Mexican town I'd seen which made a serious effort to put up Christmas decorations. The park was aglow with lights. I won't say it looked like Christmas at Temple Square but it was impressive in its own right. The lights were arranged to create shapes and figures—the Virgin Mary, the Christ Child, a donkey. Yet somehow it all seemed out of place. Maybe it was the humidity. I just couldn't put the Christmas season and ninety degree weather in the same scenario.

We carried the luggage up to our rooms. In spite of our weariness, Jenny and Renae were determined to enjoy an ice cream soda, or whatever was the Mexican equivalent, in the hotel's restaurant before retiring. I was agreeable. Our muscles were so stiff from driving, and we sorely needed a moment of recreation. What a waste of Mexico to only see it from the highway. The girls insisted they needed twenty minutes beforehand to take a shower and do whatever it is girls do. As we waited for them in our own room, I lay back on the soft twin bed and let my face absorb the coolness of the breeze blowing through the curtains above our balcony doorway. All these nights of lost sleep were catching up with me. I certainly would have passed out entirely if I hadn't found it so amusing to watch Garth try and get ready for his date.

He gave himself a towel bath and washed his hair in the sink. Then he carefully shaved every stubby hair on his chin and combed every crimson lock on his scalp, all the while whistling and humming the theme "I'm Gettin' Married in the Mornin'" from *My Fair Lady*.

Once he turned to me and asked, "Do you have any . . . um . . ."

"After shave?" I guessed.

He looked embarrassed, as if he's asked a female store clerk about the location of underwear.

"Yeah," he replied.

"In the end pocket of my duffel bag," I told him.

As he began slapping the stuff on his face in front of the mirror, he became aware that I'd been smiling at him from my bed the whole time.

"It's obvious, isn't it?" he asked.

"Yes, it's obvious," I declared.

"Is that okay?" he wondered, as if I were Jenny's overlord.

"Hey, I wish you the best of luck in the world."

Garth sat on the end of my bed.

"What does she see in Muleki anyway?" he asked. "Doesn't she know he could never be happy here? And I *know* she could never be happy there—not living as a Nephite. There's just no way!"

"I think you're right," I concurred. "But I gotta warn ya, she's not an easy catch. Many a noble knight has died of broken heart trying to slay hers."

"Maybe they haven't used the right weapon."

"Maybe not. What's yours?"

"I was hoping you could give me some ideas."

"The only one I don't think anyone has used is fortitude."

"Fortitude?"

"Yep. If Jenny lets you get your foot in the doorway, don't leave. I've seen her use some pretty harsh pesticides to get rid of boyfriends. I think the guy who wins Jen is going to be the bug that keeps coming back for more."

Garth thought about that, nodded hesitantly a time or two to let it sink in, then pursed his lips and repeated, "Fortitude."

Of course the girls took twice as long as they'd promised, so I had plenty of time to change my own clothes and throw on a little aftershave myself. I also covered the sword a bit by tucking the end of a sweater in the hip of my jeans, and letting it hang, preppy-style. When the girls finally knocked on our door, and we met in the hallway, neither of us doubted it had been worth the wait. It's amazing what a shower, a dab of make-up and a touch of perfume can do for a girl. Renae looked outstanding, easily the most beautiful creature I'd ever seen.

Both girls held out their elbows to be formally escorted down the stairs. Garth was so busy gawking at Jenny that he nearly missed his cue. We guided our princesses gracefully down either side of the staircase and into the dining room. There was no ice cream, but the hostess highly recommended a fruit bowl which included mango, papaya, pineapple, watermelon, walnuts, raisins, coconut and a special whipped topping. The dessert was celestial, but it nearly did me in. Any other date would have thought me very rude as I struggled to keep my eyes open. Renae just put her arm around my shoulder and kissed my cheek.

The hostess suggested we see the colonial church before we left. Though we were all a bit reluctant, she went on to describe its grandeur saying the carvings were some of the finest in Mexico and the ceiling in the rotunda was ornamented with pure gold. It was built in the late sixteenth century. I couldn't imagine anything that old in the new world. The pilgrims hadn't even landed yet. The church was only a couple of blocks from the hotel.

Enraptured by the description, Jenny and Renae begged for an additional fifteen minute reprieve from the day's anxiety to take a glance at the edifice. In spite of my interest, I was just too tired. Garth sighed and agreed to be their escort. I climbed the stairway back to my room, this time with Renae doing the guiding. Outside my door, I embraced her and whispered goodnight. I think she'd have let me kiss her as well, but half asleep as I was, my subconscious took the liberty of deciding our first kiss had to be something I fully remembered.

For Garth's sake, I gave her my room key and told her to make sure everyone was back at the hotel and in bed in half an hour or less. Then I shut the door, turned off the light, unbuckled the scabbard and sword, dropped it to the floor, and fainted onto my bed.

The ancient man behind the lightning-scarred trunk was beckoning more fervently than ever before, his face deathly white with terror. The sword was in my hand. I tried to climb through the jungle to reach him, but the sword became so heavy I could go no further. Then suddenly the sword took on a will of its own. Still gripped in my fingers, it lifted itself high overhead, and an instant later, swished through my neck with the ease of a guillotine.

I sat up abruptly in my bed, gasping for breath, my fingers entwined around my throat. It took a few seconds for the realization to sink in that it was only a dream and that the dream was over. When it finally did, I sighed deeply and closed my eyes. Opening them again, my eyes focused on Coriantumr's sword, still in its sheath right where I'd dropped it, the jewels in the hilt continuing to watch me. Maybe it was laughing at me. I don't know what made me think that.

I noticed it was faintly light outside. Throwing off the covers, I set my feet onto the cold stone floor. Facing the other end of the room, I could no longer fail to notice that Garth's bed was empty.

Stretching my lids to make sure I was interpreting things correctly, I confirmed that the covers were unruffled. It hadn't been slept in at all. Trying desperately to quell the panic rising within me, I actually stood to make sure he hadn't fallen off and was sleeping along the wall on the other side. The phone rang. It had to be Garth, apologizing that he'd stayed up the whole night talking with my sister in the hotel lobby. Not such a terrible thing. I'd committed similar crimes. But reaching for the receiver, I decided to punish him with a good tongue lashing anyway.

"Hello?" I responded.

"Front desk," said the heavily accented voice on the other end of the line. "You request six o'clock wake-up?"

"Yes," I replied, "Thank you."

I opened my mouth to ask him if Garth was in the lobby, but he hung up too quickly. Still dressed in yesterday's clothes, I rushed into the hallway, continuing to tell myself there was yet no reason to panic. Passing the girls' door, I pounded several times—a little louder than may have been necessary. The door was locked or I might have stormed in. Instead I continued down the staircase, fully expecting to see Garth and Jenny asleep in the lobby's loveseat, nestled in one another's arms. The lobby was empty, except for the young desk clerk who stared at me with obvious consternation.

"Have you seen my friends?" I asked.

"Your friends?" he repeated, making sure he'd understood the words correctly. "No, I not see."

I leaped back up the staircase, five at a time, and found Jenny and Renae's doorway again. After knocking even louder, I called out both their names. There was no answer.

I ran downstairs again and demanded a key to their room. Entering, I could easily see that their beds hadn't been slept in either. Now I felt my panic was justified.

Returning to my own room one final time, I found the sword on the floor and without bothering to shroud it, restrapped it around my waist. I rushed back down to the lobby for the third time. The desk clerk was still quite attentive to my behavior.

"Where is the church?" I demanded.

He didn't understand.

"The church!" I cried. "The Catholic Church!"

"Ah, Catholic!" he repeated. Then he pointed out the door and to the left.

With no time to thank him, I charged out the doorway and bounded down the skinny cobblestone street. At this hour there was very little traffic, except for an early-bird cabdriver in a Volkswagen Bug. He offered me a ride. I ignored him and ran toward the end of the block.

The spires of the four-hundred-year-old sanctuary loomed above me, silhouetted against the new morning sky. A flock of pigeons parted as I ran into the courtyard. Though I'm sure it was disrespectful, I darted from one statue or fountain to the other in hopes that my companions might be hiding behind them, perhaps hurt or afraid. Reaching the church's towering doors, I found them chained and padlocked.

I left the courtyard and ran back toward the *Hotel Filher*. I began pacing wildly back and forth in the street before it. What else could I do? Where else could I look? The cab driver had decided not to bother me further, deciding it best to leave a loco gringo with a sword to himself.

The car! It was my last hope. I hurried up the street toward the plaza where I'd seen the Christmas lights. As I rounded the corner, I saw the Mazda was still parked in the street, wedged between the same Fiesta and Scirocco. But even from a distance I could see its open trunk, and broken glass in the street.

The triangular window behind the rear door on the driver's side had been smashed. All the maps and other papers from the glove box were strewn about. The trunk had either been picked or pried open. The jack, spare tire, and the carpet which covered them were lying on the plaza lawn.

Had the circumstances been different, I might have interpreted this as the work of local vandals, but the note left propped upon my steering wheel removed all doubt as to who was responsible. The front door was open a crack so I reached in and grabbed it, reading the words with horrified apprehension.

> *Found your friends. Sorry you weren't with them. Had to kill one to set an example. Other two are safe for now, but will not be so after six o'clock tonight. At that hour we will trade their lives for the sword. We are waiting at the Pyramid of the Sun in the place you call Teotihuacan. I'm told the park gates close precisely at six. If you are not there, we will add their blood to the hundreds of gallons already spilt in sacrifice upon its steps.*
>
> *I look forward to seeing you again, my quetzal feather.*
>
> *Mehrukenah*

CHAPTER 22

I sat on the ground, with my back to the Mazda's hub-cap, for what must have been fifteen minutes, drinking in the devastation. The note containing Mehrukenah's words, though certainly not his handwriting—perhaps it was Mr. Clarke's—was crushed in my fist. I was in too much shock to cry, too embittered to mourn. What had made me think it was safe for them to go sight-seeing? Did we think we were tourists?

Now one of the people I cared for most in this world was dead. In a gesture of added torture, Mehrukenah hadn't told me who it was. The horror of guessing the answer was indescribable. I shared something precious and irreplaceable with each. My sister Jenny—I couldn't bear it if it were her. And Garth—the best friend I'd ever had or ever *would* have. Renae, my love—the only person I could see in the role of my eternal companion. I was shaking all over and I couldn't stop. How could a soul like Mehrukenah have found himself among our Heavenly Father's two-thirds in the pre-existence? How could such a spirit have been allowed to receive a tabernacle of flesh? I was soothed by my bitter hatred. Revenge would feel so good.

I realized my hand was gripping the hilt of the sword, and I removed it as if from a hot stove. The moment I did, my emotions were released. Tears pricked at my eyes, trickling down my face. Around me the residents of San Luis Potosi were coming to life. The street vendors were setting up their wares; the laborers were making their way to work. Nothing in their day had changed. All their goals and aspirations were the same. Whatever pains they may be experiencing in their individual lives—whatever loneliness, or heartache, or bitterness—they still had to make a living. They still had to endure to the end. Determination swelled up within me and I felt strong enough to stand. Breathing deeply a time or two, I started back to the hotel to get everyone's luggage. There was much to do this day. I couldn't let my emotions distract me. I wasn't sure how far it was to the Pyramid of the Sun. Garth had mentioned that Teotihuacan was near Mexico City. Mexico City was six or seven hours away.

But what would I do when I got there? Would I simply hand over the sword, expect them to automatically make good on their promise to release Garth and Jenny, or Garth and Renae, or Renae and Jenny? A Gadianton's promise was very thin. If I showed up at the ruins after the park had closed, it would be an easy matter to kill us all on the temple steps like one of the thousands of Aztec sacrifices from centuries past. If I were a true soldier, I'd ignore my loved-one's plight entirely and go on to Cumorah without them, knowing our cause justified the losses. But I was not a true soldier. I couldn't lose them all. I just couldn't lose them all.

What did it matter to the twenty-first century world if the world of fifty B.C. experienced a little more pain through the return of the sword? I could live with that, couldn't I? After all, they'd been dead for two thousand years already! Their pains were part of history. I would never know the anguish, or see the turmoil. Nothing in my world would change.

Or would it?

I thought about Muleki. Though he was still healing in a Utah hospital, he soon expected to return to his people as if past and future were one and the same. I knew in my heart, if I gave them the sword, I *would* be accountable.

There had to be another solution. But for now, my concern was to reach Teotihuacan within the next eleven hours. After loading our luggage, I shut the trunk tightly, grateful it still locked after all the tampering. Then I started the car and drove through the cobble streets of San Luis Potosi until I again connected with Highway 57 which would take me through Queretaro and on into Mexico City. The traffic became gradually more congested, and the population density became thicker and thicker. Beyond Queretaro the road was permanently divided, which made the going considerably faster.

It was about one o'clock when I reached the toll gate of Mexico City. Getting through it cost twelve thousand pesos! Stopping a ways further, at a roadside stand, I bought a bag of Mexican potato chips and an apple soda. For now, this would have to suffice as both breakfast and lunch.

In need of gas, I pulled up to a pump marked "Extra" at the first Pemex I could find. While waiting for the tank to fill, the attendant stepped up to my window and began speaking in Spanish. Though I kept repeating "*No hablo Espanol, no hablo Español,*" he kept right on yakking, seemingly determined that I follow him around to the back of my car. He led me around to the license plate, and began pointing at it frantically and waving his arms. I knew he was trying to tell me something was wrong, but I had no way of knowing what it was. After a few more shakes of my head, the attendant finally threw up his hands and walked away. What had it been? Was I parked incorrectly? Was the car somehow damaged? Had I run over somebody's foot? I felt so desperately alone.

Before pulling back onto the highway, I found Teotihuacan on the map. It was about thirty miles north of Mexico City. There was probably a shorter way to get there—some way I could have avoided Mexico City center altogether—but I was too afraid of making a wrong turn. This was one of the largest cities in the world—almost twice the size of anything in the United States. Though some of the hillsides were as steep as "Y" mountain behind BYU, they were terraced all the way to the top with housing. I felt if I didn't stick to the major highways, I'd lose myself among these twenty-five million residents and never find a way out.

Mexican drivers were absolutely insane in this place. All five or six lanes of traffic insisted on traveling seventy miles an hour despite being almost literally bumper to bumper. If a car wanted to cut in front of me, he did so without hesitation, giving me two choices—either let him in or crash.

It was two hours before I realized my mistake. The tourist map was so confusing. One page had a blown up schematic of the streets of Mexico City, but it didn't give the streets any names! I knew I had to cut across at one particular point to reach Highway 80 and then Highway 130 to Teotihuacan, but I had no way of knowing what the crossover highway was called, or where I needed to exit Highway 57. If only I could find someone who spoke English!

I wandered aimlessly through downtown Mexico City, discovering many buildings as old and colonial as the ones in San Luis Potosi. Finally I found another major highway. Jumping on without knowing what it was or where it led, I soon found myself headed southeast toward Puebla. Pulling over to the side of the road again, I studied the map further. I had only three hours left to figure this maze out, and reach the ruins.

My face was still buried in the tourist map when I heard a rapping on my window. A Mexican policeman was standing outside, looking in. He was fat and wearing sunglasses. If not for his Latin features, he'd have perfectly fit the stereotype of a backwoods southern sheriff. Turning around, the lights on his patrol car were flashing, and his partner was waiting behind the wheel. I'd been so preoccupied, I hadn't even noticed them pull up!

I rolled down my window and the policeman began speaking to me in Spanish. Shaking my head, I told him I didn't understand. He paused for a moment, then spoke to me again in Spanish. Couldn't these people get a clue?

"I don't understand you!" I cried. "*¡No hablo Español!*"

The officer nodded and stepped back to the patrol car. Fearing for the sword, I tried to stealthily cover it over with a dingy towel off the floor. The officer's partner, even more overweight and also wearing sunglasses, emerged and came forward. This one had learned to speak English.

"You are driving illegally," he said.

"I am?"

"Your license plate ends in six. Today is Saturday. Fives and sixes may not drive."

"I don't get it," I replied.

"It is law of Mexico City. Pollution control. Autos which end in certain numbers may not drive on certain days."

Now I knew what that guy at the Pemex was trying to tell me. "I'm sorry," I said. "I wasn't aware—"

"You cannot drive today. There will be a fine. Your car will be impounded until morning."

"What?! You can't!" I pleaded. "I have to be somewhere at six o'clock! It's desperate!"

"The fine is three hundred thousand pesos," he said, unfazed by my pleadings. "You must follow us."

He looked in at me another moment to be sure I'd comprehended.

"*Please*! How can a foreigner be expected to know your driving laws? You don't know what you're doing!"

"Follow," he repeated, and stepped back to his vehicle.

I sat there nonplussed while the patrol car rolled ahead of my Mazda and waited. I hesitated, then did as I was directed. They couldn't get away with this. Was there no justice at all in this country? During any moment of this trip, I never missed America more than I missed it now.

The patrol car pulled onto a new street and started heading in the opposite direction. I decided I'd have to make a break for it. At the next intersection I would twist the steering wheel to the right and attempt an escape. It didn't matter that I might go to jail. Nor did it matter that I might be shot. But before we reached the intersection, the patrol car pulled off the road again, and waved me to do the same.

The English-speaking officer came back to my car and directed me to step out and join him. I unbuckled my scabbard and left it covered on the passenger's seat, greatly dreading if they noticed the sword they would impound it as well. The officer was carrying some paperwork written in Spanish. He spread it out on the trunk of his patrol car.

"Here is where the law is written," he pointed. "This is

where it says the law includes foreign cars."

This seemed rather stupid. Did he think I had any way of reading what he was pointing out?

"I believed you the first time," I said.

The officer continued glaring at me, as if there was something I was supposed to do. Finally, he looked back at his partner and shook his head, as if to say, "This gringo is not very bright."At that moment the reality of his intentions popped on in my head like a light bulb.

"Can I . . . give you some money?" I inquired.

The officer looked relieved, shouting in his mind, "Finally!" Nevertheless, he continued playing out his part.

Shrugging his shoulders, he replied, "Well, I don't know. How much do you have?"

I thought hard for a moment. What would be the least amount I could offer without insulting his intelligence? Since the official fine was three hundred thousand pesos, I figured one third of that amount should suffice.

"One hundred thousand pesos?" I meekly suggested

The officer seemed pleased. Clearly I had proposed much more than he expected, but there was no way to retract my offer now. Reaching into my wallet, careful not to let him see how much there actually was, I pulled out two fifty-thousand peso bills.

He took them quickly and stuffed them in his pocket.

"Can you tell me how to get to Highway 130?" I asked.

"You still may not drive today," he said. "But we will not impound your car. If you try to drive, the police will stop you again. We will follow you to the nearest hotel."

These guys were operating one heck of a racket. I wondered if the government ever saw a dime of collected fines. Bribery seemed a way of life. Who could you trust in a country if not a patrolman? No wonder the injured manager in Chihuahua called the hotel owner before he called the police. I now had first hand understanding why Mexicans avoided entanglements with cops at almost any cost.

I started my engine and headed back toward the heart of Mexico City. About a mile later, I saw a sign indicating Highway 80, which I knew connected with the highway leading into Teotihuacan. When I looked in the rearview mirror, the patrol car was no longer following. A few blocks back, it must have decided to not bother with me anymore and turned off. My only fear now was that another patrol car would spot my license plate and do exactly the same thing. Finances had been chiseled desperately thin as it was! Merging with the traffic on Highway 80, I was careful to avoid any vehicles which might be official. Now I knew what it had felt like for someone behind the Iron Curtain to try and escape to the west.

Upon reaching the toll booth at the city's boundary, I was fear-stricken that someone would stop me again. It was five o'clock now. I had only sixty minutes to reach the ancient ruins. Passing through the toll booth without any problems, I heaved a sigh of relief.

The city began to give way to open country and agriculture. Only a short distance later, I reached a sign displaying the emblem of a pyramid. Teotihuacan was only seven miles away.

A half mile further, I found a secluded spot off the road and parked. If I was going to come up with a plan, it had to be now. Looking over at the sword on the passenger's seat, the temptation to hold it in my hands and ask for its inspiration was very strong. I could almost hear a voice within the metal calling out my name.

Instead, I bowed my head and said a prayer to my God.

At one point near the ruins the road divided. I had the choice of going to the *Pyramidae del Luna* or the *Pyramidae del Sol*. The similarity to the words lunar and solar were recognized easily enough. I knew which road would take me to the Pyramid of the Sun. Nevertheless, I took the road to the Pyramid of the Moon.

The pyramids loomed above the trees long before I reached the parking lot. It was hard to believe an ancient people, using nothing but backbone and sweat, could have constructed something so massive. The people in the distance climbing the pyramids' steps in their variegated clothing looked like candy sprinkles on a sundae.

Even as I pulled into the parking lot, it appeared the majority of cars were pulling out. In a few minutes, the park would be closing. Finding an empty stall, I cautiously climbed out of the Mazda and surveyed the area. As one would expect at any tourist attraction, there was a row of vending booths along the walkway to the ruins. A man leaning on the side of one of the booths met my gaze and then ran down the flight of stone steps and into the wide roadway which ran from one end of the park to the other called the Avenue of the Dead. I'm sure his intention was to reach the Pyramid of the Sun to the south and warn the Gadiantons of my arrival.

Stepping around to the back of my car, I opened the trunk. I'd wrapped Mehrukenah's elongated package in two towels and bound it with string. Lifting it under my right arm, I proceeded to descend the same stone staircase and enter the Avenue of the Dead, ignoring the pleas of vendors to have me look at their wares.

The ruins of Teotihuacan covered about eight square miles of ground—a city area larger than ancient Athens or Rome. All around me were the remains of great palace walls and platforms flanked by lesser pyramids and temples. High stone pillars projected from the earth in many places, having once supported a mighty roof. The great Pyramid of the Moon was behind me now and the Pyramid of the Sun, the mightiest edifice of them all, was about a half-mile ahead, it's facing of volcanic rock towering over two hundred feet toward the clouds.

Peculiar feelings filled my breast. This seemed both a place of great righteousness and a place of great evil, perhaps each phase flourishing centuries apart from one another. Garth had said Teotihuacan meant "City of the Gods" or "The Place Where Men Become Gods." Perhaps that title once had the proper implication. Perhaps this site was once a great center of spiritual learning. But later that purpose seemed to have been callously perverted and thousands of lives were sacrificed for rulers who thought to make it a center for proclaiming themselves gods on earth.

A uniformed gentleman who was the equivalent of park ranger passed by me and announced—in Spanish and in English—to everyone in the hearing of his voice that the ruins were closing. The merchants who'd set up their jewelry and ornaments on blankets in the middle of the park were busily gathering their wares into baskets and suitcases, pausing only to attempt one final sale of the day to camera-toting tourists. Since there was also a parking lot just south of the Pyramid of the Sun, it was only natural the rangers would assume that was where I was headed.

Still toting my towel-wrapped package, I started down another flight of steps which brought me into the ancient city's central plaza, positioned directly before the staircase of the great pyramid. I could see about a half-dozen figures standing at the summit. Except for them, the surface the pyramid was now entirely void of tourists. As I proceeded to climb, I noticed there was a ranger standing on the ground near the southwest corner, watching me, but making no effort to remind me the park was closing. Obviously he'd been well paid to allow this rendezvous to occur without interference.

Continuing to climb the pyramid's narrow steps, I soon found myself panting. Making my ascent one step at a time, I refused to stop and rest. The landscape began to stretch out in all directions and the vastness of all the various ruins of Teotihuacan became apparent.

Nearing the top, I began to recognize the faces which were awaiting me. Mehrukenah and Shurr were among them, as well as three of their minions—including one who appeared to be Mexican. Indeed, the Gadiantons seemed to find friends wherever they turned.

There were two others, seated about ten yards away, at the edge of the pyramid's eastern face. There was no staircase on that side. It would certainly result in a fatal fall if the thug nearby happened to give them a shove. Their hands were bound behind their backs and a gunny sack had been draped over their heads. By their slender builds, I had to conclude I was looking at Jenny and Renae.

"Welcome!" greeted Mehrukenah. "I'm so glad that you

could make it. I trust you had a pleasant journey?"

"Jenny? Renae?" I called to the figures under the gunny sacks.

"Perhaps we can relieve you now of that sword." Mehrukenah reached out his hand to take it from me.

Though I was sure he had a dagger under his vest—and that everyone else up here was armed as well—I nevertheless demanded, "Release them first. I want to see their faces."

Mehrukenah feigned offense, then he grinned. He was quite confident of his victory and saw no harm in playing along with my request.

"Of course," he said. "I wouldn't want you to feel we were dishonest in our end of the bargain."

He directed the thug to remove the gunny sacks. As he did so, Shurr and the others had a difficult time suppressing a fit of laughter. When the gunny sacks were lifted, the faces of Jenny and Renae were not revealed. Instead, the faces of two very frightened Mexican girls were unveiled, surely abducted for this very charade.

"Then again," laughed Mehrukenah, "honesty in bargains was never one of my stronger traits."

"Well, it's almost always been one of mine," I replied, "but today I thought I needed a change of pace."

Pulling back the corner of one of the towels, I exposed the leafy stub of a three-foot branch.

CHAPTER 23

The taunting cachinations of the Gadiantons ended. Mehrukenah's smile changed abruptly to a scowl upon realizing his precious sword was not in my hand. The double-crosser was not accustomed to being double-crossed. He stepped forward and yanked the towel-wrapped branch out from under my arm. Unexpectedly, he swung it at me and clobbered me on the side of my head, under the ear. The old man packed quite a wallop. I fell onto the jagged stone of the pyramid's summit and shook off the disorientation, my hand massaging the bruise. Mehrukenah then flung the branch away with a cry of anguish. It flew out over the edge and toppled end over end, striking a stony shelf about a hundred feet below. Then Mehrukenah came at me with his corroding teeth agrinding and his eyes full of fury. He thrust his palm in front of my face, its tendons rigid.

"I could raise this hand over my head and the throats of your sister and lady-friend would be slit from ear to ear," he seethed.

I glanced down to the valley floor, where Mehrukenah's signal would be received. South of us was the lot I would have parked in had I not followed the road around to the Pyramid of the Moon. If I'd done that, I might not have made it this far. Thugs might have grabbed the towel-wrapped package and killed me before discovering my ruse. The blue Suburban was there, along with nine or ten other vehicles, many of which I recognized from yesterday's chase. These were the only vehicles still in the parking lot. The drivers stood around, looking up at us, awaiting the very signal which Mehrukenah was threatening. Most likely, Jenny and Renae were imprisoned in the Suburban.

"But you won't," I replied to Mehrukenah. "Not now. If you did, I promise you would never see the sword again."

"Then I'll kill your lady friend! Perhaps bargaining for the sole survivor will make you a little more humble."

"You've already murdered Garth. If *that* didn't humble me into bringing the sword, what makes you think killing another will?"

I struggled to appear unconquerably fierce, but inside my emotions were near collapse—my heart felt as though it might burst. I knew full well if I'd brought the sword, sending that signal would have been exactly what Mehrukenah would have done. Immediately thereafter, the old wraith would have used the blade to slaughter the two Mexican girls, and lastly, he would have killed me. Why else would he have chosen Teotihuacan for this rendezvous if his intention were not to pay homage by letting the weapon taste it's first blood in many years on one of the most notorious edifices for evil ritual ever constructed in the history of the world?

"Where is it?!" he thundered.

"It is safe," I replied. "Before I arrived, I hid it in a place where no one would find it for a thousand years."

Mehrukenah pulled a dagger from a sheath strapped under his shirt and matted it against my throat.

"If you don't take us there immediately," he roared, "I will kill you without waiting another moment."

I smirked at Mehrukenah. "You're ranting, old man. Don't act like a fool. I know full well the only thing in this world you'd love more than killing me, is to feel the weight of Akish's creation in your fist."

Mehrukenah studied my face a little longer, then his expression relaxed, and the wizened Gadianton chuckled. He turned around and continued to feign amusement, glancing back at me and shaking his head. Stopping sharply, he presented another idea.

"I could torture you," he realized. "It's an art form which I've mastered well. You would retain no secrets."

"Maybe," I concurred. "But maybe my stamina is a little greater than the weak-minded souls you've dealt with in the past."

I was bluffing of course. Just the thought of enduring a torture session made my skin crawl.

"Why waste the time?" I continued. "It's really not necessary. I'm perfectly willing to turn over the sword, as long as I can be assured you'll complete your end of the bargain. You have to allow the three of us to depart in peace. I've already lost my best friend. I won't lose anyone else. The sword isn't worth it to me. I can't stomach being around it a moment longer."

Mehrukenah was pacing, never entirely taking his eyes from mine, trying to read them. He glanced at Shurr, his partner in intrigue. Gadianton's brother was clearly resigned to my view of the matter. Their passion for my death, and the scheduled ceremony of bloodshed atop this pyramid, were trifles compared to finally obtaining the sword. With a nod, Shurr communicated his opinion to Mehrukenah. Mehrukenah turned back to me.

"What do you propose we do about this, Jimawkins?" he requested, slanting his vision.

"Somehow we must find a way to deliver the sword into your hands while, at the same time, guaranteeing our deliverance to freedom. Our trust for one another runs thin, so it would have to be on terms we both agreed to."

Mehrukenah didn't like this arrangement at all. The muscles in his neck were pulsating. He'd never tasted compromise, and he didn't like its flavor.

"I'm listening, " he stated.

"First, let the señoritas go," I insisted. "Without the sword, you have no need of them."

Mehrukenah ordered their bonds to be cut. This was an easy concession. Such hors d'oeuvres for his sacrificial appetite could be recaptured at the snap of the finger. The girls were apprehensive about what to do with their sudden freedom. They looked about, cowering.

"¡*Vaya Te!*" the thug beside them commanded.

The *señoritas* scurried down the pyramid's steps. The highway was quite visible from here, with its many buses running back and forth to Mexico City. Shortly, they would be aboard one of those buses, safely returning to anxious families.

Though this forfeiture was trivial, Mehrukenah treated it as though I'd requested him to chop off a limb.

"We will make no further concessions," he growled.

"If it means getting the sword, you will make as many as I choose," I stated. "Now I will return to my car. Bring Jenny and Renae to the fork where the road into the park divides. Bring only one vehicle."

"And then?"

"We'll discuss it at that time."

I turned around and began descending the Pyramid of the Sun. They made no effort to stop me. Even *I* had underestimated their cooperative spirit. Though they'd surely never touched it, lust for the sword was consuming their minds. As my feet touched the ground of the Avenue of the Dead, and made their way northward, I could feel myself hyperventilating in an effort to keep the tears from flowing. I wouldn't let my mind think about Garth. I couldn't let my focus stray. But the harder I tried, the more easily his face appeared, laughing, scolding, accepting, loving unconditionally. In spite of my efforts, the tears burst from my eyes. Why, Heavenly Father? Why couldn't it have been me? Garth had done nothing but spread knowledge and goodness all his life. How could I be expected to finish this without him? I need his strength, his force of will, his conscience to guide me.

Upon reaching the platform steps which took me to the north parking lot, I dropped to my knees. Shaking and gripping the bottom of my shirt in both my fists, I wiped my eyes dry, closing them while I inhaled a few hearty breaths. The air tasted so clean and life-giving. I arose and began climbing the final stone staircase.

I still faced the horrible chance I might be mourning three loved ones before this day was over. One of the reasons I'd told Mehrukenah we'd discuss what to do when we got there was because I still had to figure it out. I knew my final intention—to outwit the Gadiantons and free Jenny and Renae in one piece—I just wasn't quite sure how to execute the finer details. I also knew that Mehrukenah would try and sabotage my intention at the first opportunity.

The Mazda was the last automobile to depart the north parking lot, except for a few trucks belonging to merchants and grounds keepers. Still praying for inspiration, I drove down the road and exited the park. Upon reaching the designated intersection, I saw that the blue Suburban had already arrived. Just as I'd instructed, the vehicle was alone. I pulled onto the grassy shoulder about ten yards down beyond them. Mehrukenah and Shurr climbed out of the Suburban and met me half way. Mr. Clarke remained in the Suburban's back seat with Jenny and Renae.

"We're going to trade vehicles," I announced.

Mehrukenah was already shaking his head. "Do you think I'm a fool?"

"Hear me out. The three of you will transfer the girls to my car. I will drive the Suburban. Then you will follow me to the place where I've hidden the sword. When we get there, our cars will park a hundred yards from each other. You will then toss my car keys onto the seat, and I will watch you do it."

"Then what will happen?"

"All of you will walk away from my vehicle and return to the Suburban."

"Unacceptable," stated Shurr. "The prisoners will take the keys and escape. Since you value their lives more than your own, you will not fulfill your end of the bargain."

"Then keep the binds on their hands," I suggested. "That should keep them from driving away, don't you agree?"

"And what happens next?" asked Mehrukenah.

"I'll tell you where the sword is hidden, and then we'll depart."

"Again, unacceptable," parroted Shurr. "How are we to know the sword is hidden where you've said?"

"You'll have to take my word for it."

Mehrukenah laughed. "No, this arrangement will not work. Not unless *you* retrieve the sword."

"I'll agree to that," I replied, "but I won't hand it to you directly. I'll display it from a distance and drop it on the ground. Then you will allow me to return to my vehicle and drive away."

Mehrukenah was still quite wary. I could see the wheels spinning in his mind, trying to find the flaw in my plan. Something occurred to him. He seemed to be remembering the night he was attacked by Muleki. He'd been confident that the Nephite had no way of following us, yet follow us he did.

"These terms are acceptable on one condition," said Mehrukenah. "That we first be allowed to search you and your car."

"Certainly," I said. "Do you hope to find the sword?"

"No. A spare key."

Mehrukenah indicated the ignition key still in my hand. It was on the same ring with every key I owned—the one to my apartment, the one to my P.E. locker, and the one to my post office box.

"In case you attempt something stupid, I need to know that yours is the only key," he stated.

I pretended to be surprised by his request. "Be my guest."

I lifted my arms and they searched me thoroughly. Then they searched every inch of the car's interior, including under the floormats. The search took a good twenty minutes, with Jenny and Renae watching all the proceedings. Their windows were open so I'm sure they overheard most of the conversation.

Satisfied that no spare key existed, Mehrukenah coordinated the transfer of prisoners from one vehicle to the other. I was made to stand on the opposite side of the road while Mehrukenah and Shurr, each with a knife at one of the girl's throats, guided them, hands bound behind their backs, to the Mazda 626.

Jenny and Renae appeared grief-stricken and disheveled. As they were herded by, they looked into my eyes for assurance.

"Everything's going to be all right," I called to them.

The Gadiantons thrust the girls into the back seat, then Mr. Clarke approached me and requested my keys while at the same time handing me the ones to the Suburban. There were two or three keys on their key ring as well, but only one was for the ignition.

"Is this *your* only ignition key?" I asked him.

"You'll have to wonder," replied Mr. Clarke and turned around.

His coy reply didn't fool me. The Suburban had no spare.

I climbed into the driver's seat, put their key into the ignition and started the engine. Mr. Clarke did the same. Mehrukenah was seated with Jenny and Renae in the back seat, holding his knife where it was plainly visible for me to see, in hopes I'd be discouraged from any foolish notions. They waited for to me pull past them, and when I did so, they were quick to follow.

I took them down the road for several miles. At one point we turned off the main highway and followed a road with more potholes than pavement. Parallel to this road was a high-flowing canal, about eight feet wide. Though there were a few scattered neighborhoods of humble stucco homes, the scenery was still quite rural. We crossed a railroad track and continued another quarter mile until we reached an unused park and picnic area situated on the south side of the road, across the canal. This may have once been a thriving recreational retreat with a green and inviting lawn, but now the landscape was choked with weeds. The swing-set was a rusted skeleton without swings or chains. The picnic tables were good for nothing but slivers. Farther south was a wire fenceline which separated the picnic area from the remains of two buildings, roofless, with crumbling walls. Half-buried garbage was everywhere, along with planks of wood and rusty pipes. On either side of this dumping zone were acres of the tall cactus plants from which the *tuna* fruit was harvested.

The park was encircled by a two-tire, dirt road accessed by crossing cement bridges on the east and west ends. The east end of the park appeared quite muddy, as if the canal had an overflow point nearby. I stopped the Suburban just this side of the west-end bridge and waited for the Mazda to pull up beside me. Shurr's passenger side window was open.

"Park it here," I instructed, "But first turn it around to face back toward the highway."

They acted reluctant about it, knowing this positioning promoted an easy escape. I drove the Suburban on across the bridge, and around the muddy circle until I'd reached the other end of the park, a good hundred yards from where I'd instructed them to park my vehicle, then I opened the door and stepped outside.

I felt I'd chosen my location well. It was far enough off the main highway that their minions would have a hard time following us, and there were so many places to hide something it would have been foolish for the Gadiantons to hold the three of us at gunpoint and search for the sword themselves. Besides, they had no way of knowing if I was telling the truth or not. Maybe it wasn't here at all.

Mehrukenah, Shurr and Mr. Clarke were all standing outside the Mazda now, scrutinizing me. Jenny and Renae were still in the back seat. The driver's side door was open. Mr. Clarke was standing beside it.

I held their key ring over my head, so that they could see the keys dangling. Mr. Clarke did the same. I tossed their keys onto the front seat. Mr. Clarke conspicuously did the same. The sound of me shutting the Suburban's door was echoed by the shutting of the door on the Mazda. We walked toward one another, finally meeting under the rusty swing set.

"I won't bring it out of hiding, until I see all of you standing over by the Suburban," I told them.

Mehrukenah stepped up to me and glared into my eyes.

"I warn you, Jimawkins, if you attempt to betray us, I will have to assume you can *never* be trusted. I'll kill you and the others without hesitation—whether we have the sword or not."

I didn't believe he would kill us, yet he'd certainly exercise the torture idea—or worse, torture Renae and Jenny before my eyes to test my proclamation that Garth's murder made me numb to their demands—a test which I would most certainly fail.

The Gadiantons did as they were directed. I patiently waited until they had completely reached the Suburban before I went into action. There was a dry ditch running along the park on the west end. From the Gadianton's point of view, they would have seen me step into it, momentarily hidden by the high weeds, and emerge again with the guitar case I'd planted there an hour or so earlier firmly in my hands. They would have seen me open it, reach inside to grab something, and close it again. As I expected, they were not true to their word. The moment they saw the guitar case, they began stalking in my direction. Spies had undoubtedly reported to Mehrukenah that Garth had taken just such an odd case out of the trunk to put in the back seat the same day we picked up Jenny from her apartment. When I saw them approaching, I tossed the guitar case into the canal, and made a mad dash for our car, allowing the current to carry the package downstream, toward the Gadiantons. As the guitar case was thrown, and as it landed with a sizable splash, they should have heard a bulky object bouncing around inside. They also should have noticed that the guitar case floated low in the water, as if it contained something quite heavy. As I'd hoped, their pursuit faltered. Mehrukenah commanded Mr. Clarke to jump into the water after it.

Just as Mr. Clarke had seized the case and was trying to swim it back to the edge, I reached the Mazda and threw open the front door. There was no time to enjoy my reunion with Jenny and Renae or even untie them.

"We've got to get outa here!" I cried. "When they open that case, all they're gonna find is the tire jack."

"Then where's the sword?" asked Renae.

"Where the tire jack used to be," I replied. "Under the carpet in the trunk."

"You mean it was here all along?" shrieked Jenny.

Renae added, "So that's what Mehrukenah meant when he said he felt the sword was very near."

Fortunately, he hadn't known *how* near. I picked up the

key-ring off the seat. After a quick glance at its keys, I simpered and tossed the whole bunch of them aside.

"What's the matter?" asked Renae.

"Mehrukenah is too predictable," I declared. "The ignition key is missing from the ring."

In the rearview mirror, it was clear the Gadiantons had found the tire jack. We heard another splash as it and the guitar case were angrily tossed back into the canal. Now the Gadiantons were marching toward us with their guns and daggers drawn, a slavering Mehrukenah leading the way. Jenny and Renae looked back in terror.

"They promised to kill us if you betrayed them, Jim!" gasped Renae.

The girls were near hysteria when suddenly they heard the car's engine turn over as I twisted the spare key in the ignition. Mehrukenah screamed out a terrible curse and began charging us. The other Gadiantons were thinking much more practically and began running back toward the Suburban. As I hit the gas pedal, my wheels sent a spray of black Mexican mud onto Mehrukenah's clothing. The Mazda peeled away down the road, back toward the main highway.

"But I saw them search you," Jenny declared. "I saw them look under the floor mat. Where was it hidden?"

"In the guitar case," I revealed. "When we reach the main highway, I'll untie you."

"Never mind!" Renae insisted. "They'll be behind us any minute."

"I don't think so," I said.

"What are you talking about? Why not?"

"Because warped minds think alike," I replied, and to prove it, I held up the Suburban's ignition key.

CHAPTER 24

"Garth isn't dead," Jenny declared. "No matter what they've told you, I don't believe it."

"Explain to me everything that happened," I urged.

"After we visited that old Catholic church," Jenny began, "we wandered up to the plaza where we'd parked the car to look at the Christmas lights. That's where they attacked."

"They threatened Garth with death if he didn't tell them where you were," added Renae. "When Garth continued to resist, Mehrukenah told Shurr to take him somewhere quiet where no one would hear him scream. Shurr and some other men put him in one of the other cars and drove away."

"Where were they taking him?"

"I don't know," Jenny admitted. "But Shurr met us on the highway about two hours later. We watched them through the window. We couldn't hear what they were saying, but we could tell Mehrukenah was furious, as if Garth had escaped. They told us a few minutes later he was dead, but I didn't believe them."

I spoke sympathetically, "Jenny, I don't want to crush your hopes, but maybe he was angry because Garth refused to give in all the way to the end."

"*No!*" Jenny insisted. "I know he's okay. Even when they told us he'd been killed, I couldn't cry for him, because I knew it wasn't true."

It occurred to me that if Garth *had* escaped, the first place he'd go would be the *Hotel Filher* in San Luis Potosi to try and find me. We had to locate a phone.

Turning north on Highway 130, we found a tiny motel and parked where our car couldn't be seen from the highway, fearing the Gadianton converts might already be searching. The motel's desk clerk helped us make a long distance call to the *Filher*. Renae spoke with the *Filher's* manager, asking if Garth had returned—asking a half-dozen different ways to see if it might inspire a memory. Finally disheartened, she got off the phone and shook her head.

"I don't care!" Jenny cried. "He's alive! Call it intuition—call it anything you like!"

A psychologist might have called it denial. But despite our dread, it was Jenny's steadfast assurance which gave us all a sliver of hope.

"We should go back to San Luis Potosi and look for him," I suggested.

Jenny eagerly agreed, but Renae took it upon herself to be the voice of reason.

"If he did escape, he wouldn't have stayed in San Luis Potosi. He would have tried to follow you, Jim. Whether he's alive or not, he would have wanted you to continue on to Veracruz and complete your mission. You *know* he would."

Renae was right, but going back toward Mexico City to pick up the shortest route to Veracruz would doubtlessly put us in the middle of a desperate ambush. At Renae's urging, we continued north on Highway 130. Our destination was the city of Poza Rica, where Renae had once been an exchange student. She said we could stay with a family she knew there, maybe get some help, and rest up on the Sabbath. I almost objected to waiting a day, knowing the delay would allow the Gadiantons time to position themselves at the Hill Vigia, but the fact was, going to Poza Rica would give them an eight or ten hour advantage over us anyway. Besides, Garth would have approved of our resting on the Sabbath. It was dark by the time we reached a town called Tulancingo. Our anxiety over Garth kept anyone from feeling hunger, but to keep up our strength, I insisted we get something to eat. We found a place with a big sign reading *Hamburguesas*.

Before we'd even ordered, Renae announced she was feeling ill. For the last couple of hours, I'd felt sickness coming on as well, but I felt obliged not to tell anyone. Somebody had to get us over the winding mountain roads Renae said would dominate the rest of our journey into Poza Rica. Renae ate one bite of her hamburger, and asked to be excused. I forced my own meal down with another bottle of apple soda. After dinner, we found Renae curled up in a blanket in the back seat of the car, her face ghostly white.

"You gonna be okay?" I asked.

"Sometimes it doesn't matter how hard you try," she confessed, "you still get a touch of the 'revenge.' Don't worry. Normally it only lasts twenty-four hours."

Taking my place behind the wheel, we continued into the mountains. The perils of driving this stretch at night were many; nevertheless, I navigated without the help of the sword. Only an hour out of Tulancingo my nausea was overwhelming and tonight's meal ended up in a ditch along the side of the highway. "Jen," I moaned, "you're gonna have to take over."

"Here?!" she cried. "On these steep roads? I can't!"

"It's either that or we spend the night here in the mountains."

"When *my* curse kicks in, we'll spend the night in the mountains anyway—or at the bottom of a cliff."

"Please, Jenny," I begged. "Remember the cavern so many years ago? Remember how you were afraid to climb down into the pit? I saw a courage well up in you then—one I hadn't seen before. Please remember it. You have to try."

Only after I'd pleaded another minute would she give up her place in the passenger's seat. Fighting great trepidation, my sister pulled back onto the roadway. Renae handed me a couple of pills left over from her first trip to Mexico saying they'd keep us from having to stop at every other restroom.

The road seemed to become ever narrower and more dangerous. The curves were so sharp and obscure, there was little way of telling if another vehicle was approaching. The asphalt was even more broken and decayed than the road into Chihuahua, but to make matters worse, one false move, rather than sending us hurling into the desert, would send us tumbling into a chasm hundreds of feet deep.

Every time a pair of oncoming headlights appeared, Jenny would squint and slow down. Once the headlights were a semi-truck, barrelling down the slope at maximum speed. Jenny froze, remembering a terrible image from a highway of her past. She hit the brakes and brought the Mazda to a complete stop in the middle of the road. She covered her eyes, and the truck whizzed by, missing us by an inch. Maybe it was a foot. My illness had put me in too much of a delirium to say for sure.

We sat still in the Mexican night for what seemed several minutes, until a car came up from behind, honked its horn, and drove around us. At that moment I saw that familiar grit rise from Jenny's soul—the sternness of a sea captain. The Mazda lurched forward, soon even passing the car which had overtaken us.

Since leaving Teotihuacan, we'd seen three different kinds of terrain. Entering the mountains, the dry plateau became a coniferous forest. Shortly after our descent toward Poza Rica, we seemed to have entered a tropical jungle, about as thick as a jungle can get—the hillsides flourishing with vast plantations, bananas and coffee.

Ever since I was a little boy I dreamed of seeing a jungle. The only thing missing was that I was no longer a little boy, carefree and nestled in cheerful fantasies. Though the sword remained in the trunk, where I thought I was free from its influence, there were moments I swore it was whispering to me, insulting me, desperate to convince me that without it, I was nothing. Grossly ill, full of grief, and trying to solidify my convictions for righteousness, these weren't the whisperings I wanted to hear.

It was just past midnight when Jenny announced we'd arrived in Poza Rica. The streets were busy with traffic and pedestrians. Nobody seemed to sleep in this country. It was the Christmas season and every night was a time for *fiesta*.

Wearily, Renae sat up and instructed us to turn at the next intersection.

We entered a quiet and darkened neighborhood where the car high centered twice on the unlevel dirt road. A few blocks further, Renae directed us into the driveway of a small, but well-constructed home with a yard full of plants and fruit trees. There was an old, mud-splattered Chevy pickup in the driveway ahead of us.

A pair of curious faces still awake from the night's celebrations pressed against the screen on the front doorway. As we emerged from the car I heard the children shout "Renae!" and lunge forward to embrace her.

Renae mustered her remaining strength to wrap them in her arms and cry, "¡Rosalinda! ¡Nephi! ¡Como Te Has crecido!"

This was the Corral family—Latter-day Saints *extraordinaire*, right down to the poster of the Mexico City Temple on the front room wall and the five boys named, from oldest to youngest, Mormon, Helaman, Ammon, Moroni and Nephi. One of the girls was even named Sariah. The father, Guillermo Corral was a member of the bishopric. He and his wife Julia had been baptized as newlyweds and sealed two years later in the Salt Lake City Temple. Though the home was phoneless, with only throw rugs, Guillermo was actually one of the richer members of the community—considered upper-middle class. He operated a distribution business, supplying rubbing alcohol, aspirin and vitamins to many of the drug stores or *Farmacias* in the state of Veracruz.

There was a ninety-year-old grandmother living with them—her eyes sparkling like my Grandma Tucker's had in the years before she passed away. She took my hand in hers and said, "*Es Su Casa.* (Consider this your home.)"

Guillermo spoke decent English, thanks to Renae's former tutelage. We told him about our plight, omitting some of the more incomprehensible details. Fortunately, he trusted Renae and anyone associated with her. Though we couldn't fully explain why we had to reach Santiago Tuxtla and the Hill Vigia, he didn't push, and asked what he might do to help.

"We need a place to stay," Renae told him. "And we'd like to go to your sacrament meeting—if we can make it. Jim and I are a little 'under the weather.'"

"We'll be gone early Monday morning," I promised.

Truly, these people had stepped out of the pages of a fairytale. Though we said we'd already taken some medicine, it didn't keep the mother from concocting a bedtime recipe of her own. Though we told them we'd happily spread out our sleeping bag and blankets on the floor, the parents and two of the older children had already dragged in the blankets off their beds for themselves to sleep on the floor. Everyone showered us with love and attention. The fifteen-year-old daughter noticed the bruise from Mehrukenah's blow under my ear and created a poultice for it. I thought *my* family was accommodating.

That night, though I lay in my sleeping bag on a comfortable mattress, sleep came only with patience and effort. The walls were thin and I could hear Jenny sobbing in the next room. In daylight she was fully confident Garth was still alive, but it was dark now and her subconscious doubts were rising to the surface.

A canopy of shadowy clouds had floated in off the Gulf of Mexico. Through my bedroom window, I watched them move across the sky. When a hole appeared and the glimmer of a few Mexican stars broke though, I was finally able to fall asleep. Together, I felt Garth and I could travel to the ends of universe and back. As long as the universe was still up there, Garth had to be alive in it somewhere, looking up at those same stars.

The next morning Renae's health had returned. Though I was still in the last hours of recovery, I was at least well enough to attend church with the Corral family in their newly constructed stake center. Jenny and I sang "Now Let Us Rejoice," and "I Know That My Redeemer Lives" in English while everyone else sang it in Spanish.

The sacrament talks and Sunday School lesson were hard to follow since Renae couldn't interpret the words fast enough, and in priesthood meeting, I had to be content to sit there and smile. But it really didn't matter what they were saying. What mattered was that today I was among the Saints. I realized it made no difference where I was in the world, if there were Saints, I was home.

I hoped the Corral family didn't consider us rude, but after we'd eaten a hearty lunch with the children, the three of us were so exhausted from the trials of the previous days, we napped all afternoon. Jenny and Renae went right on napping into the evening.

I was unable to sleep much later than 7:00 on account of some very pressing and difficult matters on my mind. I approached Guillermo with a very serious request. The primary problem I faced in getting close enough to the Hill Vigia to fulfill my mission was Jenny's Mazda. The enemy had trained themselves to spot it. According to the map, there was only one highway into Santiago Tuxtla. With the enmity I'd inspired between myself and the Gadiantons, I was quite confident I'd never make it there if I drove the Mazda. So I asked Guillermo if I could borrow his mud-splattered Chevy.

He was hesitant at first. Guillermo depended upon his truck to operate his business. A car couldn't carry a dozen crates of rubbing alcohol. But the fact was, his truck was worth about five hundred dollars, and the Mazda might bring in a couple thousand. I told him if we returned his truck inoperable, he could sell the Mazda for a much worthier set of wheels. I was sure Jenny would agree. With a smile, Guillermo accepted my terms. His generosity made me ashamed to have to make one more request.

"I cannot take the girls," I told him. "Where I am going, I must go alone. Jenny and Renae would never hear of that. They would strap on the seatbelts and refuse to get out of the truck."

"Especially Renae," Guillermo chuckled.

"They believe we're leaving in the morning. Instead, I will leave tonight—right now. Please take care of them until I return—and whatever you do, don't let them follow me."

Guillermo saw the solemnity in my eyes, and knew how much pain it brought me to have to make such a decision.

"I will do this for you, Jim," he agreed.

I also persuaded their oldest boy, Mormon, to loan me his sunglasses and a visor cap with the slogan *"¡Que' Sabroso!"* stamped across the front to advertise a bottle of soda pop.

Retrieving my duffle bag from my bedroom, I quietly made my way past the rooms where Jenny and Renae were sleeping and back toward the front porch. The door to Renae's room was slightly ajar. Peering in, I watched her for a moment: the crimson light of the lowering sun was creeping in from her window, illuminating her face, and reflecting off the flowing locks of ebony-black hair which curled around her pillow.

"I love you," I whispered, unheard.

As I drove away, I was haunted by the regret of having never announced those words to her out loud. Would she ever hear them? I determined in my heart, if I were allowed to return to her embrace, they would be the first words out of my mouth.

This was the last leg of my journey. The sword was firmly set in its scabbard on the passenger's side of the seat. I turned onto Highway 180 and ascended into the tropical hills above the town, rife with sugar cane, banana and coffee. Within an hour the highway began to parallel the angry, sapphire seas of the Gulf of Mexico, its waves climbing high up the grassy beaches, trying to escape the storm swirling out in its skies. There was lightning out there too; the fiery white projectiles becoming more bright and menacing as the sun faded behind the inland mountains.

A few hours later, as I crossed the bridge at Santa Ana, I heard a voice, as distinct as if I'd been entertaining a passenger beside me, but the voice had not been created by sound.

I know where you're taking me . . .

I looked at the sword, still displaying an appearance as frozen and dead as the first time I saw it, yet somehow, tonight it was breathing. A burning began in my breast, spreading outward to my limbs, pulsating, trying to imitate God's confirmation of truth. Turning forward again, I tightened my grip on the wheel.

. . .but I don't think you understand.

Muleki was right. I'd sensed an increase of power in this object through every mile of our journey. I was now close enough to the land of its forging to feel the heat from its ancient smeltery upon my brow. Words continued coming into my head as if they were my own thoughts. Maybe they were.

This is not a land of death, Jim. It is a land of glory. Not the glory of cowards like yourself. The glory of heroes.

I couldn't believe this. A hunk of metal was calling me names! I laughed out loud. It didn't seem to appreciate my sense of humor.

You don't have to be a coward, Jim. I can make you anything you desire. Anything you're brave enough to dream.

Then I want to be left alone. I want my thoughts to be my own and I want to *know* that they're my own.

Do you think they're not? Do you think I can create such aspirations out of the blue? I cannot—not unless the thoughts were there to begin with. You've never been a man who bows down to mediocrity, Jim. There's a whole world out there. A world you've always dreamed could be yours. There's no greater pain than to have a passion for greatness with no certain means of obtaining it. Why be tortured by failure and shattered hopes? Why waste all that time and energy? Why, Jim?

Because it's *my* time, and it's *my* energy—not yours. And it never will be.

Never? Never is long time, Jim Hawkins.

This was oil country, and Veracruz was one of the largest ports for crude export in the world. I could see its lights glowing up into the night from twenty miles away, reminding me of the lights of Las Vegas from way off in the desert. I never saw its streets, only the lights. It was unnecessary to go through Veracruz. The highway bypassed it on the west and soon its glow faded well behind me.

Within a few miles the highway was paralleling the ocean again. There was a ten mile stretch where the grasses on either side of the road were especially tall. Dozens of white crabs could be seen dashing out of the grass and making their way across the road in an attempt to reach the ocean. Many had been smashed by the wheels of the previous car, their exoskeletons carpeting the highway. Even at this hour of the morning, local anglers patrolled like wolves along the shoulder with a ready bag.

I crossed many more bridges, and followed the highway further inland. All along the way, I expected to see familiar cars off to the side of the road, watching for my arrival in the Mazda. Curiously, I never noticed any—although darkened vehicles hiding in the shrubbery might have been easy to miss.

A few miles further, a sign announced I was entering the village of Santiago Tuxtla. Even in the pitch of night, with an overcast sky, the landscape was still slightly darker than the heavens. Rising above the village, not far to the southwest, loomed the silhouette of a mighty hill, barely too small to be called a mountain. This was doubtless the fortress locals had christened Vigia or "Lookout Hill." What I hoped beyond all hope was that it was also the place where a quarter-million Nephites had made their final stand—the hill which the ancient prophet Mormon had called Cumorah.

CHAPTER 25

As small as the community of Santiago Tuxtla was, it didn't take long to find the plaza square. I parked along its edge and turned off the headlights of Guillermo's Chevy. It was four a.m. now, still hours before the sun would make an appearance. It would be insane to begin my ascent of the jungled hill in the dark. The odds of losing my way in the light were bad enough. My body clock was all screwed up. In spite of yesterday's rest, I was struggling desperately to keep my eyelids up. I slapped myself. I couldn't allow myself to fall asleep—not here, out in the open and vulnerable. Who knew what faces might be sneering down through my window when I reopened my eyes. Looking at the distant profile of Vigia, it was certain the elevation would require an arduous two to three hour climb. In my weary state, the demands of such a hike filled my head with the most dismal imagery. I had to get some sleep, if only for a couple of hours.

Neon lights across the square were flashing, *Hotel Castellano*. The building was by far the tallest structure in the community—an eight-story circular edifice, not unlike the Leaning Tower of Piza, but on more stable ground. I wondered how such a large hotel in this small of a town could ever make any money.

Strapping the sword to my waist, I cautiously exited Guillermo Corral's rusty Chevy. The village square was graveyard calm, void of all but tropical plants. The humidity was so thick I thought I might have to cut my way through it with the sword. There was a gigantic boulder in the middle of the square, about seven or eight feet tall and wide. Someone had carved it to look like a massive head.

Only a few lights illuminated the neighborhood, the brightest being the ones shining from the hotel lobby. Inside, I found a boyish desk clerk with his nose buried in paperwork. My voice startled him when I requested a room. This was not a common time for him to receive new patrons. Though he spoke little English, we were able to determine I would stay until Tuesday morning. He wasn't entirely certain if I should be charged for one night or two, but in the end he chose the greedier route—the one I'm sure his boss would have approved—and I was too tired to argue with him. After forking out one-hundred and sixty-thousand pesos, he handed me a key to room 307. In my wallet there was only a little over one-hundred thousand pesos remaining, or about thirty five dollars—not even enough for the gas it would take to get back to the U.S. border. Renae told me the residue of our American money had been stolen by Mehrukenah's men. The rest of our finances had been with Garth. Even if he were still alive, would they have left his bankroll intact? It seemed entirely doubtful.

Sleepily, I signed my name to the register. It was almost too much energy to come up with a pseudonym. I spelled out 'George Bush' and gave myself an address in Washington D.C.

Even though my floor was only two flights up, I chose the laziest means of ascension. Approaching the elevator doors, I passed under the center circle of the hotel, hollow all the way to the ceiling—an architectural view even more dramatic than the one in the *Hotel Filher*, but without the weeping vines or nineteenth-century elegance.

All the rooms on the third floor, as on all the floors, were situated at the outermost ring of the circle. The elevator was built into a side hallway, or rather a gap in the outermost ring. The hallway led around to each room's door, meeting back where it started, and was contained by a solid, plaster handrail. Twenty feet and two flights below I could see the cushy furniture of the hotel lobby. My room was just around the corner and two doors to the right.

I wished I'd left my duffle bag in the truck, instead of adding to the tremendous burden of carrying the sword. It had become so inexplicably heavy. I was certain it was only an illusion, but illusion or not, when I unbuckled it from my waist and let it drop to the floor, I felt like I'd unloaded a granite-filled backpack.

I nestled myself onto the soft mattress of the double bed without removing my shoes or clothes. My intention was only to doze until it was barely light outside. It hadn't occurred to me I might not have the willpower to combat the desire to crash for a full eight hours.

My body met me half-way, and I slumbered for four hours. Nevertheless, when I awakened I narrowly avoided cursing. The sun was quite bright out my window—*too* bright. I'd hoped to begin my climb in the dimness of sunrise, when pedestrians were scarce and I could spot my enemies more readily. It was now almost nine and the skinny streets of Santiago Tuxtla would be bustling with natives.

Slapping sink water on my face, I washed away the travel dust. There were two bottles of mineral water on the nightstand between the beds. I guzzled them both, and wiped my mouth with the back of my hand. After re-strapping the cumbersome scabbard and sword about my waist, I cautiously opened the door and poked my head out into the hall.

The coast was clear, except for a maid's supply cart outside one of the open rooms across the circle. It was somewhat comforting to know that even if I'd failed to wake up when I did, the maid's knock would have alerted me in a few minutes anyway. I hailed the elevator and pressed the button which took me down to the lobby. The elevator was facing the hotel's front entrance.

Stepping into the street, I had to pause. The first daylight view I had of *El Cerro Vigia* held me breathless. Behind it, far to the west, were the remains of last night's overcast sky, giving the jungled hill, its base terraced with bright green pastures and crop-filled fields, a darkened backdrop which made it all the more menacing. A horseshoe of clouds hung around Vigia's summit, illustrating my destination like a circle on a map.

I hesitated no longer. The base of the hill was just beyond the borders of the village. As I climbed into Guillermo's truck again, I was being watched. Not by Gadiantons—at least I didn't think they were Gadiantons—but by the police. A patrol car was parked at the north end of the plaza, its officers enjoying breakfast at one of the food stands. I wish I knew what they were thinking. Maybe they'd seen the unconcealed sword. Or maybe they thought it strange that a gringo should be climbing into a truck with a Mexican license plate. What proof did I have that I hadn't stolen it? Boy, all I needed was more trouble from the cops. Fortunately, as I started the engine and rolled past them around the square, they stayed in their places and continued chewing their food.

Making my way through the village's muddy cobble streets, I dodged more burros than cars. It didn't take long to find the street which brought me closest to the hill. All roads seemed to converge into it, but before long, the pathway became so narrow and ill-defined, traversing it with a vehicle was quite impossible.

After parking on a grassy patch along the edge of a grove of orange trees, I donned the cap and sunglasses Guillermo's son had given me in Poza Rica. It was a miserably meager disguise. The fact was, even if I was wearing 'Freddy Kruger' make-up, the sword made me identifiable in a cast of thousands. As a final solution, I reached into the pickup bed and grabbed a plastic tarp which Guillermo undoubtedly used on rainy days to cover his stock. I wrapped the sword inside it and bundled it all together with an accompanying strip of cord. Over my shoulder, it looked like a bedroll of sorts. The very end of the sword's hilt stuck out of the bundle, making it easy enough to draw, should the situation require it. I knew this get-up would only deflect attention for a few seconds, but maybe that few seconds would be all I needed.

Abandoning the pickup, I continued up the narrow and muddy road. It led me down a final declivity, bypassing a last row of shabby homes as well as gawking housewives, children and farm animals. A maroon-spotted pig, at least twice my weight, seemed to know I didn't belong here. He snorted at me and kicked his heel. Gratefully, the thick rope which kept him yardbound had plenty of knots.

At the bottom of the hollow, there was a bridge of wooden planks crossing a stream of the clearest water I'd yet seen in Mexico, gushing no doubt from a fountain somewhere amidst Vigia's slopes. Lizards darted from stone to stone. One was a good fifteen inches long, counting the tail, with a fin on its head like a dinosaur. It escaped across the water on two legs which were spinning so rapidly the creature didn't sink.

The path was cobbled now and still very muddy, despite the fact that this was Mexico's dry season. The way became steep, and I was left to conclude I'd officially begun my ascent of the hill. Several Mexicans passed me coming down. They smiled and nodded, finding my presence curious but not something to stop the presses. They'd seen American tourists before, many of whom I'm sure were Latter-day Saints.

I was dripping so much sweat you'd have thought I'd stepped out of the shower. Oddly, the Mexicans' pores hadn't leaked a single drop, even though heavy loads of stick bundles and coconuts were strapped to their backs. They were usually barefoot, with mud drying all the way up to their knees. The mud was just as high up my jeans.

The jungle grew thicker, and the number of huts off to the side of the trail seemed to be tapering. It wasn't long before I found myself panting and turning back to check my altitude. Either the village of Santiago Tuxtla was sinking or I'd made a considerable amount of progress. I could see the hotel where I'd slept and the highway which had brought me here. The landscape was enchanting, it's rolling hills burgeoning with life and sustenance—but I couldn't allow myself to get caught up in the scenery. My regard for the task at hand had to be unwavering. The weight of the sword already seemed to have doubled since beginning the climb. And there was so much farther to go.

I was surprised by the approach of a man with a machete. He was older and his hair had a heavy touch of grey. Though he didn't seem to be attacking, he was yelling at me frantically, half in Spanish and half in English.

"*¡No seadelante! ¡Mala gente los espera en El Cerro Vigia!* Bad people on mountain! *¡Les esperamos y ya llegaron!* They are here! You stop and go back!"

"Why?" I demanded. "I don't understand. Who is on the mountain?"

"The Gadiantons," announced a familiar voice behind me.

I turned abruptly, in time to see Garth Plimpton emerging from the trees.

This was likely the closest I would come to understanding the joy felt by onlookers who saw Lazarus rise from the dead. My soul was doing somersaults as we embraced and held each other's shoulders. Garth's first concerns were for Jenny and Renae.

"They're fine!" I reported. "Mehrukenah tried to use them as bait for the sword, but I outwitted him. They're staying with an LDS family in Poza Rica, about six hours north."

Garth looked relieved. "I've been hiding here since Saturday night, watching for them and for you. I knew you'd come this way. It's the only trail on this side of the hill. Antonio here has been helping me. He's an Indian. That's his house over there. I trust him."

"Garth, how did you get here?"

"By bus," he explained. "Mexico has buses to every corner of this country. Actually, Santiago Tuxtla is a major stop from Veracruz. It's the main highway to the resort area of Lake Catemaco."

"Then Mehrukenah and the rest are here?" I asked.

"They arrived yesterday afternoon. About twenty of them climbed this trail. I don't think Mehrukenah and Shurr left a single man behind to watch for us. I get the feeling they seem to be keeping everyone in fairly close proximity for fear that one of them will get hold of the sword before them and steal it for themselves. They're up there waiting for us now. We've got to go another way. Antonio gave me directions to a road he says leads to the very top by a completely different route. He helped build it many years ago to get equipment for an electrical relay station up there. It's a long jungle road, crossing a score of other hills before it reaches Vigia, and there might be a few places washed out by last season's rain, but according to him, it's the only other way."

"You go now. Get back before dark," said Antonio.

Garth took off his shoe and reached in to grab some ten-thousand peso bills. Stuffing the money under his foot hadn't been such a silly idea after all. He handed the bills to Antonio saying, "*Muchas gracias por todo su ayuda.*"

Antonio took the money gratefully. I'm sure it was more than he made in a week.

Before we left, Antonio pointed back up the hill and asked, "Those men, they thieves or witches?"

Garth considered his question. "A little of both, I reckon."

"Thieves, we have no use for," Antonio said. "I get neighbors, we fight. But witches . . ." His tone grew somber. "We no mess with witches."

Walking back down the hill, Garth told me how he'd escaped from Shurr, and the two other thugs brought along to witness his execution.

"I was in the back seat with Shurr as we drove out into the country—looking for some place private and secluded to conduct their 'interrogation.' The knots on my hands gave a little. I'd discreetly slipped my left wrist free just as the car slowed down to avoid barrelling through a large fiesta crowd outside a country church. A fat man—I'd swear he was drunk—started banging on the car's hood and then on Shurr's window. Seeing Shurr distracted, I instantly threw open the door and splashed into the crowd. I'm sure they pursued me, but I ran across the countryside for an hour without looking back."

"Why didn't you go back to the hotel?" I asked.

"I did," Garth insisted. "But by then it was nine o'clock. You'd already left."

"You should have left a message. Jenny and Renae were told you were dead!"

"Can we call them?"

I shook my head. "The people they're staying with have no phone."

"I'm sorry," Garth sighed. "All I could think about was finding a bus to Veracruz and then to here. I knew my only hope of ever meeting up with you again was to arrive first."

"Well, then let's get this sword to the top and get out of this country," I prescribed. "How long is the drive up this road?"

"Antonio said a couple of hours—about the same length of time it would take to climb."

"And you think we'll be unopposed?"

"I hope so," Garth stated. "Antonio says not many outsiders know about the road. The fact is, either route takes us to the same summit. If they're waiting for us at the very top, I'm fresh out of ideas."

We reached the stream and bridge. A minute later we were climbing back into Guillermo's Chevy. Desperate to get something to eat before our trek, we returned briefly to the hotel. Upon reaching the city square, I asked Garth if he was still convinced we'd found the right hill. Garth pointed out the ancient stone head in the middle of the plaza.

"Antonio says the villagers found that head on Vigia many years ago. It had been up there three thousand years, carved by a people Archeologists call Olmec. The Olmecs are considered to be the oldest civilization in the New World. LDS scholars believe the dates of the rise and fall of the Olmecs correspond so closely to the rise and fall of the Jaredites that, for all practical purposes, Olmecs *were* Jaredites."

We climbed out of the truck. As Garth continued to speak, I kept my eye on the policeman visiting with local merchants along the south street of the plaza. Either they hadn't seen us return, or they'd lost interest.

"What's even more fascinating," added Garth, "Antonio says the villagers are taught that the Olmecs fought a great battle here."

Entering the hotel lobby, I told Garth my room number and left him in the restaurant to order us some lunch while I went upstairs to change into some unmuddy pants and sneakers. As I carried the tarp-bundled sword into the elevator, the mud on my shoes left some ugly tracks. I felt bad for the poor maid who'd just mopped it.

Closing my room door behind me, I proceeded to change into another pair of jeans. I'd also brought an extra pair of 'high tops'—not as comfortable as the first, but at least they weren't crusted with mud. As I was tying the last shoelace, there was a knock on the door.

I hesitated, then asked, "Is that you, Garth?"

"Maid service," said a heavily accented female voice on the other side.

I looked around the room. The wrinkled covers on my bed had been pulled taut. There was a new towel hanging above the sink, and there were two new bottles of mineral water on the nightstand.

"You've already cleaned in here!" I called out.

There was no reply. I waited another moment. Apparently she'd recognized her mistake and decided not to bother me further. I felt very nervous all of a sudden. Would a maid who cleaned this building every day have made such a mistake? It occurred to me she might have seen the mud tracks up to the door. It would have been easy enough to find the culprit—just follow the trail. Then it occurred to me—anyone who'd seen me enter the hotel would have located me just as easily.

Lifting the sword and bundle back over my shoulder, I carefully approached the door, trying to keep the floor from creaking. Before opening it, I listened.

I called out again, "Hello? Are you still there?"

Again, there was no reply.

Had it been a mistake to come back here? Had Garth been mistaken about all of Mehrukenah's men climbing the mountain? Why hadn't I acquired an instinct for these things? I felt angry inside, as if the Lord should be doing more to keep me out of these situations.

Slowly, I opened the door, ready to slam it shut again if

someone tried to force their way in. Peeking out into the hallway, not a patron or maid was in sight. I had to conclude she'd disappeared into the elevator or stairwell. Slowly, I moved into the hallway and made my way around the circle. Half way to the elevator, I had that peculiar feeling of being watched. I glanced over the handrail and down at the lobby two floors below, thinking someone might be looking up.

My guess was exactly wrong. Behind me the door to room 306 was tossed open with a crash. A female voice shrieked. Standing in the room's doorway was Todd Finlay, gripping a handgun aimed at my belly. His other arm held the maid around the throat. Having no further need of her, Todd pushed the girl back into Room 306 and slammed the door crying, "Come out and I'll kill you!"

Then he turned his maniacal grin back on me.

"I wish you had listened. I always liked you, Jim. I don't know why you turned against me."

"Todd," I pleaded, "can't you see what the sword has done to you?"

"You're wasting my time! The sword and I have a mission—a *great* mission. Hand it over."

Carefully, I let the tarp bundle slide off my shoulder and drop to the ground. It seemed so tragic to have come so far, our goal only a stone's throw away. How could I give up the sword now? Its shining hilt was right beside my hand. It would slide out of the bundle so easily.

I can protect you, if you let me.

A split second later I found myself hoisting the sword out from between the layers of tarp. I held it aloft, prepared to follow an impulse to strike.

I heard the elevator arrive.

Todd was raising the nose of his gun, aiming it at my heart. He pulled the trigger. For a moment my mind blacked out. No—I was conscious—but I no longer had control. The blade of the sword adjusted but I don't believe it was my muscle which moved it. Yet who else's muscle could it have been?

The explosion from the chamber of Todd's pistol was nearly simultaneous with the chink of metal-on-metal, like a rod against a tuning fork. But the note ended bluntly, drowned out by Todd Finlay's scream as a spark created by the bullet's ricochet flashed on the muzzle of his pistol. He released the weapon as if it had shocked him, letting it fall to the floor.

Peripherally, I saw Garth emerge from the elevator, dropping our sandwiches. But I had no time to consider him. My next action seemed so obvious, so clear. Todd Finlay had to die.

But *I* couldn't do the killing! Such wasn't in my nature! Yet if that were true, why were my arms hefting the sword overhead? Why was I stepping toward him? Surely my actions were involuntary, and yet they *weren't* involuntary at all. Though I was fully aware of what I was doing, it just didn't matter. The hatred was so overflowing—so all-consuming. Did any man deserve this wrath? There was something horrid within me, something I never knew existed— never wanted to know! And yet at this moment, I actually liked it.

"Nooooo!" Garth screamed.

Todd was cowering on the ground, writhing like a mealworm. Destroying him was good. Nothing could be so righteous. The blade was falling. But before it could strike, Garth's shoulder hit my chest like a freight train.

The impact forced me to blow every ounce of oxygen from my lungs. My waist hit the railing—and I was still tripping backwards. Garth had sent us both plummeting over the handrail! We were doomed to fall all twenty feet to the stone-tile floor of the hotel lobby! Had Garth gone nuts? My best friend had just succeeded in killing us both! We flipped once in mid-air—the ceiling, the second-floor handrail, the lobby—all of them were rotating in my vision. Garth was now positioned beneath me for impact—and impact we did, but not on the stony floor. Garth's back collided with one of the couches, but it was not a bullseye. The back of the couch split from the bench and I heard the crack of Garth's upper leg against an armrest. The sword bounced from my grip when we hit, leaving a gouge mark in the tiles and ending up near the front desk.

I bounced off Garth and onto the floor, rolling onto my back, shocked and disoriented, my elbow and ribs throbbing with pain. My eyesight was blurry; the desk clerk's voice was echoing. The moment my vision normalized, and I could see that Garth was alive and moving, I yelled, "Are you crazy?!"

"You would have killed him, Jim," he mumbled, wincing at the pain in his leg. "You would have become one of them."

I hobbled to my feet, walking in a circle, trying to reorient my mind. Where was the all-consuming hatred? Had I really been a fraction of a second away from slaughtering a defenseless man? It seemed so long ago—so incomprehensible now! I felt nothing anymore, nothing other than an instinctive fear of a predator still lurking.

My head quickly turned as I heard the elevator doors open. Todd was emerging, the pistol back in his grip.

"¡Alto!" a stern voice commanded.

The police officers from the square were standing in the entranceway of the hotel, their weapons aiming at Todd, cocked and ready to fire.

"¡Pistola al suelo imediatamente—o te mato!"

I could tell it was a difficult decision for Todd to drop his weapon; nevertheless, Todd's survival instincts prevailed. He set down the gun and raised his hands in the air.

It was Todd Finlay who would live out my nightmare of incarceration in a Mexican prison.

CHAPTER 26

A moment later the Mexican police had Todd in hand-cuffs. As they began to escort him to the patrol car across the square, Todd turned and looked at me. His expression wasn't the threat of vengeance I expected. Instead, I saw bitter sadness—not remorse, but regret—and a lostness. He shook his head as if to say, 'Why couldn't you have just given it back to me?'

One of the officers called back to us, "*¡Que den se!*" and gestured with his hand that we stay put.

Many of the hotel and restaurant staff had gathered around; villagers on the sidewalk were peering in. The desk clerk was strangely drawn to the fallen sword, and had picked it up to admire its workmanship. I stepped over and stripped it from his hands. My sternness startled him, and he looked deeply embarrassed and apologetic. Turning back to Garth, still lying on the displaced cushions of the broken couch, I put my arm around his neck asking, "Can you stand?"

He made a feeble attempt and replied, "I'm afraid not. Don't try to move me. And don't wait here, Jim."

"But the policeman told us—"

"I'll handle the police," Garth insisted. "I'll tell them Todd attacked *me*, not you. If they find out the sword inspired all this, I fear they'll take it away. If they do, its almost certain we'll never see it again. Everything we've sacrificed will have been wasted. Find Antonio, Jim. Persuade him to take you to the summit. Give him anything he wants."

"But I can't leave you—"

"I'll be okay. Find me later—after you've destroyed it. And Jim—" His eyes became desperately pleading. "Promise me you won't . . . promise me that . . ."

I knew what he was trying to say. He'd seen me succumb to the sword again, and as a result, he was witness to the moment I nearly lost my soul. Was it useless for him to hope I could resist it now?

"I'll make it," I promised. "We're so close. I don't have much further to go."

I took the sword, now without a scabbard, and made my way out the back door of the *Hotel Castellano*, around the leaf-strewn surface of the swimming pool and through the gate of the rear parking lot. Creeping around to approach my pickup, I could still see the patrol car across the square, Todd Finlay in the back. One officer had remained with the prisoner. The other had made good on his promise to return and question us. Hopefully Garth was successfully covering my tracks—convincing him my involvement was accidental. The trees and shrubbery of the plaza square obscured the view between Guillermo's Chevy and the patrol car. I made a discreet escape, attracting no further attention. Since Garth hadn't had time to give me directions to where the road began which led to the top of Vigia, I followed his advice to seek out Antonio. Parking again beside the orange grove at the end of the road, I hastened down the path, crossed the stream, and climbed into Vigia's foothills. My last pair of shoes became mud-caked, but this time I would endure the discomfort. Indeed, I should have endured it before. Garth and I might have been halfway to the summit by now.

I found Antonio just off the trail, working in the forest. His legs were bowed around the base of a palm tree, making his descent after having severed five or six coconuts from under its leafy hood with his machete. Upon seeing me, his expression was a mixture of pleasure and concern.

"Where is Garth?" he asked, the accent almost incomprehensible.

"He has broken his leg," I said, using my hand and illustrating by swiping it against my calf.

"Broke?" he repeated.

"Yes, broke. I need you to help me, Antonio. I need to get to the top of the hill."

Antonio crinkled his brow. He turned to look up toward the summit. It was now hidden entirely inside a bank of clouds, like a dreary fog around an evil castle. The Indian turned back to me.

"Garth say men were thieves and *witches!*" he cried.

I couldn't lie to Antonio. What Garth had told him was true enough.

"I'll pay you fifty-thousand pesos," I offered.

Antonio's brow perked up, but not enough.

"All right, I'll give you everything in my wallet." I opened it for him. "One-hundred thousand pesos."

His superstitions seemed to melt at the prospect of money. Nevertheless, it still wasn't quite enough.

"Everything in wallet . . . and *wallet.*"

My wallet had been a present from my Uncle Spencer shortly after I returned home from my mission, and had cost him about thirty dollars. It was hand-crafted, a picture of the Salt Lake Temple with the Angel Moroni pressed into the leather. Still, I agreed to the old man's terms, taking out my license, BYU I.D., and temple recommend. I also began removing the pictures of four or five previous girlfriends, but he stopped me.

"Leave girls," he said.

This guy was a tough negotiator. I wished Renae were here to witness this. It was solid evidence of my overwhelming love. I gave him the wallet—girls and all—but half the money I stuffed into my pocket telling him he would get the rest when the deed was accomplished.

Antonio retrieved his straw hat from off the ground and said "We go quickly. Get back before dark."

Antonio's confidence had not been wholly inspired by the reward. He knew the men he'd seen were not local. To an old Indian acquainted with the subtleties of this jungle, no outsider was too mighty a threat, whatever his other powers might be.

Antonio brought his machete. When we got back to the pickup, I asked him to place it in the bed. I'd gone through too much to allow myself to fully trust a man I'd only met this morning.

Antonio directed us down a street which proved to be a shorter route to the highway. Then we turned left, back in the direction of Veracruz. About five miles later, Antonio pointed out a one-lane cobble road ascending into the jungle left of the highway. It seemed so obscurely placed, so indistinguishable from the other field roads and driveways, I was almost certain Garth and I would have backtracked a half dozen times before we'd found it.

We turned down the road and the sound beneath our wheels changed from the smooth glide of pavement to the disquieting rumble of crumbled stone. Steadily, the road ascended into the hills. In the distance we could see Vigia, the summit still veiled in clouds. It seemed so far away, so hard to believe that this, or any road, could reach it. The jungle grew thicker, the earth breathing only when an outcropping of volcanic rock forced the foliage to separate, or when a field had been cleared for coffee or corn. Even here, people lived. Deep in the jungle I could see the humble native huts, whose occupants for the most part might never see the world beyond the view of these slopes. As we passed several men riding burros or carrying bundles, Antonio would smile and call out to them, and they would wave and call back.

"Do you know *all* these people?" I asked.

"*Sí.* Many," he replied.

A quarter mile later, we passed a man herding a dozen cattle across the road with a whip.

"Bad year for cattle," Antonio commented.

"Oh, yeah? Why's that?"

"Thieves. Steal cattle and eat. Man I know lose eighty cattle."

"Can't you catch the thieves?"

Antonio shook his head. "We try. Only steal at night. That why we must get back before dark. They steal truck—steal all we own. Maybe kill us."

I turned to him, "Are you talking about the men you and Garth saw yesterday, or other men?"

"Other men," he confirmed.

This seemed to be a bad neighborhood all together—like an inner city street in New York. It was interesting to realize that in Mexico, people were much more fearful of the country than the city. Cities were places of refuge. Criminals were thought to mostly reside in the mountains. The attitude seemed exactly opposite from that of an American.

Antonio also revealed that witchcraft was very common in these hills. Lake Catemaco, which was only twenty miles away, was considered the Mexican equivalent of Salem, Massachusetts. He said *El Cerro Vigia* was a kind of mecca for witches—American witches. Every second week in March they would gather near Antonio's home and light candles, following the trail to the top for ceremonies he'd never witnessed.

This kind of neighborhood atmosphere only made sense. If it was truly Ramah/Cumorah, and two civilizations had been wiped out on these slopes, tradition would not make it a sacred place, but a place of evil.

But in spite of that, Antonio was convinced the cattle thieves were not witches, only scoundrels, and he hoped soon they would be caught. What he had in mind for them sounded a little like Judge Roy Bean-style frontier justice.

"Where did you learn English?" I asked, trying to lighten the conversation.

"Naycha-list from United States," he said.

"You mean a naturalist? A scientist?"

"*Sí*. He study animals, bugs, plants. I work his assistant for two years. This many years ago."

"How many children do you have?"

Antonio took a moment to recall the number in English. "Twenty-six."

My eyes bugged out. "How can anyone have twenty-six kids? How many times have you been married?"

"Three."

"Did you outlive them all?"

"No."

"You divorced the first two?"

"No."

"You have *three wives*? And they're all still alive?"

He laughed, amused by my surprise. "*Sí*. Yes."

"Do they all get along?"

"No," he smiled. "They no like each other—jealous. They live separate houses."

He told me he got his second wife by paying the government a fee. The third one was not really an 'official' wife, though she'd been the one who'd given birth to most of his kids. Though Antonio would have welcomed it, I decided not to dig further into his family life. All I knew was, when the Lord restored polygamy, it would be a principle eagerly supported by a certain Indian named Antonio—though clearly not so much by his wives.

The truck continued to climb, sometimes spinning its wheels to escape the mud or traverse a steep corner. The houses grew fewer and fewer, though evidences of civilization were never entirely absent. Antonio got out of the car to open and close several gates. There always seemed to be a field growing somewhere nearby, no matter how steep or inaccessible the hillside.

"Are there jaguars around here?" I wondered.

"No," Antonio confirmed. "Once many. Now only further south. But in river near my home there many crocodiles."

The jungle leaves on either edge of the road were bigger than umbrellas; Antonio revealed that many times umbrellas were exactly what they were used for. We soon found ourselves inside the cloudbank which hid Vigia's summit. Visibility was now only about a quarter of a mile. I felt certain the top of the hill, and the power relay station Garth had mentioned, would come into view any moment. It seemed to me if the Gadiantons were still on the hill, they wouldn't go near the very summit, where an on-duty operator might think their presence suspicious. They would wait for me somewhere below, along the trail.

I stopped for another gate. As usual, Antonio got out to open it, but this time he seemed to sense something different in the air. He paused before unlatching the wire loop from around the fence post and listened.

My window was open. I called out, "Is something the matter?"

"No," he responded. Yet his attitude continued to be quite cautious all the while he pulled back the gate and waited for me to drive through. As he climbed back into the truck, I asked him again if something was wrong, but he assured me by saying, "I imagine things sometimes. Happens when old like me."

A short distance later, as the road ran parallel to the fenceline, Antonio pointed out another gateway off to the side, only this one was meant for pedestrians. There was a muddy path coming up from the steep slope below and leading through it.

"That where trail lead down to my home," said Antonio.

My heart started racing. It took a moment for me to put together why I found Antonio's statement so frightening, then I realized—he was saying from here on out the road and the trail were connected!

"I thought the road and the trail were completely separate routes all the way to the top."

"No," Antonio confirmed. "From here they are one."

This meant, if my suspicion about Mehrukenah placing his men somewhere along the trail below the summit was correct, we were driving along the very section of trail where such a positioning would take place. I slammed on the brakes.

"Is there another way to the top?" I demanded.

Antonio shook his head. "I know of no other way. The jungle here very steep."

"Can you drive?" I asked.

"Sí. Of course."

"Then let's switch places," I said. "I'm going to lie low on the floorspace the rest of the way."

Antonio cocked his eyebrow, finding this change of policy quite curious.

"Okay," he agreed. Then looking forward, he suggested, "First drive through gate."

About ten yards ahead, another gate blocked the road.

"Tell you what," I said, "you open the gate and then come back and drive through. From here on out, I want to remain unseen. Onlookers should think you're up here alone."

Antonio nodded, still confused and somewhat alarmed by my actions. I guess the thought that we might be out-and-out attacked in broad daylight had not occurred to him.

After he'd stepped out of the pickup, I scooted over to his side of the truck and slipped uncomfortably into the floorspace, with my knees in my chest and my neck bent out from under the glove box. On the seat and under my left hand I continued to hold the sword. When Antonio returned and opened the driver's side door, the news was not good.

"There is chain and lock on gate," he said.

"Is that normal?" I wondered.

"No. Not normal," claimed Antonio. "Never lock on gate. Something very wrong."

"Turn back," I insisted. "Get us out of here. We have to find another way to the summit."

"Maybe trail other side of hill," thought Antonio. "Don't know for sure. Never had reason to go up that way."

"Well, we've got to look. Please turn the truck around—*quickly!*"

Turning around was not an easy task. As Antonio pulled forward, the hood of the pickup pushed back the foliage. He then turned the wheels sharply, backed up and broke a few more branches, turned the wheels again, pulled forward . . . After three or four more maneuvers, the truck was facing downhill.

I was biting my nails—something I hadn't done in years. If we could just get beyond the next gate, I would feel so much better. Suddenly Antonio accelerated the speed—but why?

He'd seen something in the jungle. I lifted my head enough to look. They were everywhere, shadows weaving through the foggy forest and vines, following with the truck. Remaining on the floor was useless—an idea instigated too late. I'd already been seen. Climbing back up on the seat, I prepared to jump out and throw open the next gate. It was just now coming into view.

Antonio stopped the truck. I leaped out and rushed up to the fence. As I began lifting the wire hook, I saw the chain. In the last few minutes, this gate had been padlocked as well. We were trapped.

The posts on either side of the gate appeared quite sturdy. I doubted we could smash through, but we had no other choice but to try. Jumping back into the cab, I suggested my idea to Antonio. He nodded and backed up the truck about fifteen yards. Behind us, men were emerging from the woods and rushing toward the pickup. Some I recognized from earlier encounters, some I'd never seen before. Antonio made a Catholic cross across his chest, and punched the gas pedal.

We rammed the fence. The two side posts snapped at the base. The gate sticks and barbed-wire stretched across the hood. The barrier was a shambles—but it was not broken. Antonio fought desperately with the steering and lost control of the pickup. The right tires slipped off the road and the vehicle came to a stop, stones grinding underneath the frame. The left tires continued to spin and rip into the gravel, but the effort caused the tail of the truck to slide off the road as well. Now only one wheel was on the cobblestone. We were hopelessly stuck and the Gadianton minions were closing in—and cheering.

"We go on foot, through jungle!" Antonio suggested. "You follow!"

Antonio pushed open the driver's side door and leaped out. I tried to open my side, but the door was obstructed by barbed-wire. Nevertheless, I pried it open enough to slip out, dragging the sword behind me. Antonio didn't wait. He vaulted over the fence, losing his straw hat, and disappeared into the jungle. I'd escaped the car, but it was another matter to escape the nest of barbed-wire and fence posts which our smash-up had created. I tried to step through, but my pant leg was caught and the barbs were biting my flesh. The enemy was arriving. Among them I recognized Shurr. There also seemed to be a number of local men with big machetes. Perhaps these were some of the thieves Antonio had mentioned—now Gadianton proselytes. In a panic, I tried to tear myself free, but my efforts only worsened the tangle and the barbs began biting my arm. I fell, dropping the sword. The fence had become a net and I was the fish. I could no longer move—the barbs would only dig in deeper.

The minions had gathered around me. They were laughing hysterically at my predicament. Shurr was cackling as well. He was standing over me now. His hand reached through the coils and found the hilt of the sword. Carefully, he lifted it out and brought it close to his breast. With his other hand, he stroked the silver-plated blade and sighed long and deep.

Then he held it aloft to the gawking crowd and announced, "Coriantumr's Sword is ours again!"

They cheered and I fainted, from the pain—and from the crushing blow of failure.

CHAPTER 27

I know I wasn't unconscious long, because I felt the barbs further tear my clothes and scratch my skin as they dragged me out of the nest. A noose of the wire was coiled about my neck, fortunately not where a barb dug into the skin unless I moved about. The other end of the wire was tossed over a tree limb and secured to a branch around the other side. They propped me against the trunk, as high up the bark as they could without suspending my feet. My hands were left free to try and relieve the pressure on my neck, but it was impossible to twist loose.

I remained in this unbearably awkward position for well over an hour while a runner went to fetch Mehrukenah who'd been lying in wait with Mr. Clarke and several other thugs at a point closer to the summit.

When they arrived and looked upon my miserable state, as I was coughing and bleeding, my fingers all that was saving me from choking to death, a grin formed on Mehrukenah's mug from ear to ear.

"Welcome to the Hill Ramah and the Land of Desolation, Jimawkins," he said. "We were beginning to think you'd never come."

I wouldn't reply. At this point speaking would only gratify his sadistic pleasures.

"This is my first visit as well," he announced, "either in your time or mine. I'm sure it's much more accommodating now, what with all the roads and people."

He stepped up close. "Have you nothing to say? I would love to hear your thoughts, even the rude ones."

I remained silent, though I couldn't fully hide my feelings. They were expressed loudly by my eyes and from them Mehrukenah received the gratification he was seeking.

Turning to Shurr, he requested, "Give me the sword."

Shurr was balancing himself on the hilt, with the point in the dirt. He gave Mehrukenah a queer look.

"You know I can't," he refused. "Gadianton's wish was that once it touched my hands, it would not touch another's. It was for that purpose which my brother sent me."

"Your brother is too distrusting," scoffed Mehrukenah. "I request only the honor of using it to spill the first blood. I'll then give it back, and you may keep it in your possession until the very moment it's presented to Gadianton."

Shurr hesitated, but only a moment. Mehrukenah's request seemed harmless enough. He presented the old wizened man with Coriantumr's Sword. Mehrukenah took it in his grasp and held it before him in awe. He tested its weight and swiped it against the air. Then he thrust it to the sky.

"Such glory!" he cried.

No doubt the sword was soothing him with the same promises it had given me. I was strangely jealous—resentful that the sword could be so fickle, telling the same lies to anyone it touched. That must have been how it had survived all these centuries since Akish. The sword played no favorites and therefore, among those who wielded it, the sword had no foes.

Mehrukenah glowered at me and shook his head. "How can a man so young become so misguided, Jimawkins? Couldn't you feel its power? Why would you want to destroy something so perfect?"

"Because it's *not* perfect," I replied. "It's the epitome of *imperfect*. If only you could see the state of your own soul, Mehrukenah. If only you understood the ultimate destiny of the being you worship—the founder of Gadianton's oaths and combinations—the founder of the power in that sword."

"Christians have always baffled me," said Mehrukenah. "You beg for blessings, sometimes receiving, most of the time not. If the traditions of our fathers are true, and I'm sure some of them are, I can only conclude your god is very weak. The power which binds our band, the power by which we live and breath, is the very power of the earth—ultimate and eternal. The formulas are as pure as spring water and with them one can soar as the eagles."

"But each time you follow those formulas," I said, "the eagle soars with one less feather. One day soon, Mehrukenah, you're going to plunge to the earth and be smashed."

"Speak for yourself. You're the one whose god appears to have left him shy of feathers. No wait, there's one feather remaining." Slowly, he moved the sword's tip forward and touched it against my throat. "This is the quetzal feather which I'll pluck for myself now."

He retracted the sword, placing the cold silver plating of the blade against his brow, then he closed his eyes and turned away, as if in concentration or prayer. The crowd around us watched in silence. Even Shurr lifted his chin and shut his eyes to reverence the moment of my execution.

I refused to close my eyes. Somehow I felt if I kept them open, I couldn't die. My soul was calling out to my Heavenly Father—but he didn't seem to be answering. Why wasn't he answering? Perhaps he no longer considered me a player on his team. Had the sword corrupted me beyond recovery? What would be the state of my soul in the life to come? There was a horrible dread churning inside me. How I wished I'd never touched it—never listened to its voice!

Everything from here seemed to move in slow motion. Mehrukenah began to scream. He brought the full weight of the sword to bear over his shoulder, and began twisting forward with a mighty swing. But his eyes and the sword swung right past me. I wondered if he was letting the sword's weight swing him in a full circle, to dramatize the strike as he came around a second time, but instead, his eyes fixed on Shurr, still standing in silence with his eyes closed. With all his might, Mehrukenah drove the blade into Shurr's belly. The brother of Gadianton opened his eyes and gazed at his comrade's face in horror. Mehrukenah kept the blade inserted until Shurr dropped to his knees. Then Mehrukenah put his foot against Shurr's chest and yanked the sword free. The eyes of Gadianton's brother rolled up into his head, and his lifeless body fell forward onto the dirt. All around Mehrukenah, the crowd was applauding. Mr. Clarke looked especially pleased. Apparently this conspiracy had been planned long before. Mehrukenah's motives were perfectly clear. Why return to 50 B.C. when he'd acquired a solid circle of followers here? Converts of this age and time would have no desire to return to the primitive world of Gadianton—not when there was so much more to be gained in the twenty-first century. Using the sword, Mehrukenah's knowledge of its potential could inspire a following greater than Todd Finlay could ever dream of.

The sword was still dripping the blood of it's previous victim when Mehrukenah stepped toward me again.

"Now where were we? Ah, yes." He turned around and made an announcement to the crowd. "Now witness the moment of death for the oldest enemy I have left in this world!"

He seemed to have forgotten Garth, who was just as responsible for thwarting his early evils as I. No, he hadn't forgotten. He simply wasn't aware that I knew Garth was still alive. Even as I drew my last breath, Mehrukenah would not comfort me by admitting his failure to kill him.

Turning back to me, Mehrukenah declared, "I'm sorry you'll never live to see the greatness of the kingdom I'll build in your day, Jimawkins."

He hoisted the sword overhead once again, this time skipping all elements of the ceremony, except for the scream. But the scream began in one pitch and ended in another as an arrow struck him in the shoulder, causing him to drop the sword before he could finish his swing.

The crowd began scrambling in confusion. The jungle was suddenly swarming with villagers, armed with machetes, clubs and—as was apparent from Mehrukenah's wound—at least one crossbow. They bolted out of the dense jungle foliage from all directions, causing Mehrukenah and his men to scatter. The villagers swung their weapons viciously. Though some of Mehrukenah's men had revolvers, few had time to bring them to bear. The villagers were thrice the enemy's number—maybe more. They pursued their prey in whatever direction they fled. I couldn't see all the action—the wire still kept me from turning my head—but I did see Mr. Clarke trying to escape down the road. The revolver in his hand had been fired twice at his attackers, but several more villagers sprang from the trees, and before he could empty another chamber, Mr. Clarke fell under a machete's blade.

From behind me, another machete swiped at the tree trunk above my head. After several more swipes, the wire snapped. I would have collapsed, except that someone caught me. When I looked up to see my benefactor, I was greeted by the beaming face of Antonio. He helped me stand and untwist the wire from around my neck, then he retrieved the crossbow he'd laid down behind the tree.

Returning, he said, "I could have bring more, but I no think there was time."

"Your timing was perfect, Antonio," I replied. "You saved my life."

"I think I save many cattle, too," he concluded. "Me think we have no more trouble with thieves, eh?"

"No," I replied. "I don't think you will."

Picking up the sword from off the ground where Mehrukenah had dropped it, I got out of the area as quickly as I could, fearing the villagers might consider me a straggler and come after me with their machetes as well.

Climbing up the road, I must have looked as though I'd been through the Battle of Waterloo. My clothes were in shreds, blood-stained from the wounds and cuts the barbs had inflicted on my skin. My neck was raw from the wire noose and my mouth felt bone-dry all the way down my throat. Add to all this a terrible nausea, as if my viscera were being twisted in a hurricane. At one point I dropped the sword and fell on my hands, ready to throw up, but there was nothing in my stomach to accommodate, so I only heaved and wretched in pain.

When I went to pick up the sword again, I swore it weighed no less than a ton. I nearly decided not to even try recovering it, except that as I did, the sword rose easily into my arms. It was no heavier than it had always been. The sword had overplayed its weight game. The illusion unwittingly provided me with strength. If I could lift a ton, I could certainly lift myself the rest of the way up this hill.

It was late afternoon. The fog was still very thick. I couldn't see any patterns of landscape in any direction, and I had no idea how much further it was to the summit. Maybe I should have waited for Antonio. He'd asked me to wait, and then he went off to help round up the rest of the villains. I knew by the time he was finished the sky would have darkened and his recommendation would have been to come back tomorrow. So I set off on my own, not knowing if tomorrow I'd even have the strength to lift a single finger.

Soon after traversing that final gate, the tower of the relay station began to emerge from the mist. There was only one more switchback, and I would be there.

What will it accomplish, Jim, if you destroy me? It will not change the course of the world. It will not put an end to the blood and horror.

Maybe not, but it may temper it some, and it may save a few souls.

It will save nothing! In fact, it may accelerate the damage. Haven't you learned anything since we became friends? I've saved your life at least twice. Together we can save many lives, and do much good.

No. Any good which you could ever inspire would be more than off-set as soon as you gained possession of my soul.

I am always subject to the will of him who bears me.

That's a lie.

But I love you, Jim. I love you more than anyone who has ever borne my weight. If you hurt me, it would be as if you'd murdered your own child.

You're incapable of love. Only hate and deception. If you loved me, you would have stayed Mehrukenah's hand. You wanted to see me destroyed even more than he did.

How can you say that? You're still alive, aren't you? Maybe you should think about that.

I'm alive because of Antonio—and God. No one else receives any credit.

You're being very ungrateful. If only you knew how much I would miss you. If you knew, you would not hurt me. You would trust me just a little longer, so I could prove my worth to you. What if I healed your wounds?

It would only be an illusion, like the illusion of your heaviness. The sickness would still be there, you would only cover it up.

You're wrong. Do you really think so little of my powers?

Yes. It's all an illusion—like any promise of Satan.

You have so much to learn. If only I could have time to teach you.

There was no fog blurring my view of the summit now. The road led right around to the top. There were two buildings comprising the power relay station, along with the basebox of the giant tower. The first building was directly in front of me now. It was guarded by a chain-link fence and appeared to be used for equipment storage. I could hear the hum of an electrical generator further up the road. I followed the sound, and found myself climbing the final bend to the top of the hill.

The jungle foliage was still quite dense on either side of the road. Just as the uppermost two-story structure of the relay station came into view, I saw something out of the corner of my eye lunging at me from the darkness of the foliage. Like a phantom flying through the air, Mehrukenah was charging.

Raise me, and I will save you. If you don't you will die.

The broken shaft of the arrow was still embedded in Mehrukenah's right shoulder. I did not raise the sword. I rejected its promise and let Mehrukenah barrel into my chest. As I fell against a rocky outcropping of soil at the side of the road, the sword dropped from my grip.

Mehrukenah wasted no time in retrieving it with his right hand and instantly the bleeding appendage received the strength it needed to hoist the weapon overhead. As the blade was coming down between my eyes, I rolled, and the sword split the stones which had been underneath me. Scrambling, I hoisted myself upward, my fingers clutching at the brittle branches of a bush for leverage. Mehrukenah continued yelling furiously and swinging at my legs. I was able to stand and plunge deeper into the foliage on the hillside between the upper and lower buildings of the power station. Though the undergrowth made it impossible to see where I should place my feet, I commenced running, my goal being to reach the upper station where I might receive help. If the operators had been able to hear Mehrukenah's screams they might have rushed out to rescue me already, but the nearby generator was so loud, it muffled the noise.

Mehrukenah was still pursuing, looking for his moment to strike. I thought I had a free run all the way across the hillside, but an instant later, I was face down on the ground, having tripped on something in the undergrowth. Looking down at my legs, I saw that I'd further unearthed a section of insulated cable extending from the generator to the upper station. Mehrukenah was standing over me now, panting. He smiled, showing the gaps in his teeth for me one final time.

"Goodbye, my quetzal feather."

As he raised the sword high overhead, I grabbed the power cable with my left hand and rolled onto my back. Mehrukenah shifted his body and fell to his knees. I unearthed the cable another few feet, and just as the sword was coming down, my right hand also found a grip. I thrust the cable upward, toward Mehrukenah, and the blade came down upon it, cutting through the insulation and into the copper core.

Releasing the cable, I rolled out from under the sword. There was a surge of noise from the generator as it tried to adjust for a loss of power. Looking back at Mehrukenah, his eyes were wide, and his hands, still gripping the metal hilt, were shaking. Over four hundred volts vibrated through his body for at least a quarter minute. Finally, the old wizened wraith fell forward into the undergrowth, convulsing once, and then lying still, his contorted expression frozen with the agony of his final moment.

As the sword touched the earth, its blade still wedged in the cable, the ground around me became fuzzy with an electric charge. Using a dead branch, I knocked the sword free from the cable with a single swing. The surge of power from the generator ceased, and the fuzziness in the ground dissipated.

The sword was hot now, as well as heavy, but the heat was no illusion, so I picked it up using the bottom of my shirt as padding. The smell immediately around Mehrukenah made my skin crawl. As hastily as I could, and with my free hand covering my mouth and nose to keep out the stench, I climbed back across the hillside and again found the road. Turning back to peer through the dense foliage, the two on-duty operators were coming around the other side of the hill, making their way down a trail leading to the generator in hopes of discovering what had caused the unusual loss and surge of power. It might be a while before they discovered Mehrukenah's body in the undergrowth. Because I had no time to answer questions, I remained out of sight, and followed the road around its final loop.

Do you believe me now? If I didn't love you, why would I kill Mehrukenah for you? Now it's three times I've saved your life, Jim Hawkins.

No, no. Again, this was the Lord's work. What killed Mehrukenah and what saved my life was a simple phenomenon called electricity. Again, you had nothing to do with it.

You're the liar, Jim, not giving credit where credit is due.

I was now standing upon the rocky soil directly before the two-story upper building of the relay station. The door was open since the operators were still around back. In thanks to my Father in Heaven, I submitted to the urge nearly forced upon me by weakness alone, and dropped to my knees onto the earth. This was it!—the destination I'd risked my life and the lives of those I loved most in this world to reach; the top of Cumorah—the final battleground of the Nephites and Lamanites and the summit of Ramah— where Coriantumr, with the very sword I now held in my hand, guided the Jaredite armies to their suicidal climax. Yet one mystery was still unsolved. Opening my eyes, I reassessed the ground upon which I knelt. Something was chillingly wrong. All my opposition had been crushed. Mehrukenah, himself, lay burnt and dead a short ways down the hill. Garth's leg had been broken. My own body was racked with wounds and sickness—and all for what? This building and the tower it supported, had been erected precisely upon the highest summit point of Vigia!

Ether's Coffer was gone! We were thirty years too late! The excavators, digging out the foundation of this station, had unearthed the stone box in the jaws of their Caterpillar, had crushed it into a pile of rubble and dust unrecognizable as ever having been fashioned by ancient hands. Ether's only means of destroying Coriantumr's sword had itself been destroyed by the progress of man.

The sword knew my mind, and it knew my heart, and it was laughing hysterically. How could I have come all this way only to let it defeat me?

I'm not laughing at you, Jim. I'm laughing with you. It's clear now that you can't get rid of me, and obviously you can't pass me on to anyone else whose convictions may not be as solid as yours. Therefore, your destiny is clear now, Jim. That destiny is with me! Now and for the rest of your life! Don't be disappointed. We have many great things yet to do together—righteous things— things which will advance the cause of happiness in the world.

I was certain it was fully aware of how taunting its words were—and yet it was right. I could never part with it now. It's curse was mine to bear—and I knew it *was* a curse—a punishment for ever letting myself be enticed away from my God—even for a moment.

My life as I knew it was over. I would never graduate from college. I would never marry Renae. I would never raise a single child. I had to steer clear of anything in life which might put another's salvation at risk. Only one course was before me—to be the Keeper of the Sword: to live with it, defend it from theft, listen daily to its haunting temptations, but never, *never* to give in—not even in the face of my own death, or the death of someone I loved. Now more than ever, I had to depend upon God for all my answers, all my decisions. I couldn't be irresolute about a single conviction. If ever I listened to the sword—or even to myself while under its influence—I was doomed.

Yet in spite of all this understanding, every fiber of reasoning within my soul told me this was impossible—I was not a perfect human being; I didn't even consider myself a runner-up for the crown. Sooner or later, the sword would secure its grip around my throat—just as it had every other soul who'd ever wielded it.

Garth was right. There were only two forces at work in this world. Lucifer had dragged down one third of all the children of our Heavenly Father and his goal for the other two-thirds was not necessarily to make them all sons of perdition. If a soul was aiming for the terrestrial kingdom, and Satan could drag him down to the telestial, his purposes had been successful. If a soul was aiming for the highest plane of celestial glory and he could drag him down to the level of a ministering angel, his vengeance had been met. To whatever rank of misery Satan could sentence mankind, that would be the rank he would shoot for.

Dropping my hands to the ground in anguish, I was certain the state of *my* soul was the most miserable of all. If any man ever needed God's mercy, I felt it was I. And then the thought entered my mind, as bright as sunlight so blinding it can't be escaped by closing the eyes, God had already extended that mercy in the boundless Atonement of His Only Begotten Son.

I felt an urge to raise my head, as if an unseen, but sacred hand was lifting my chin, and turned my gaze toward a grassy offshoot of the hill, southwest of where I knelt. It was a thin promontory of the main summit, protruding out about two hundred yards to a tiny cluster of trees. From where I knelt, it appeared to be perhaps a few feet higher than the spot of ground where the relay station had been erected.

Rising to my feet, the sword still firm in my grasp, I took several steps toward it. Then I stopped again. Somebody was waiting for me there. Squinting, I could see a man standing in the midst of that tiny cluster of trees. He was waving me toward him.

I passed by one of the steel supports to the tower, and climbed over one final crossing of barb-wire, continuing forward for the next hundred and fifty yards, forging through grasses as high as my elbows. Nearing the man who urged me onward, the only difference I noted from the way I'd envisioned him in my dreams, was his lack of ancient clothing. Instead, his garment, as well as his hair, seemed to flow like a river of brilliant white. As I drew nearer, his identity was revealed to me. It was Ether, the great prophet of the Jaredites and the compiler of their records—the man who'd witnessed the final Jaredite struggle from his vantage point in the cavity of a rock.

The clouds were no longer shrouding my view to the western plains—now glowing red with the setting sun— nor were they shrouding the waterways and swamps of the Papaloapan lagoon system in the distance. Nor were the clouds shrouding the hilly slopes of the western face of *El Cerro Vigia*. From here it would have been an easy matter for Mormon to look down and view the fallen Gidgiddonah and his ten thousand, the fallen Lamah and his ten thousand, the fallen Gilgal and his ten thousand— until he'd accounted for all two-hundred and twenty-thousand Nephite soldiers who died on that first day of battle, excepting the twenty-four weary and wounded stragglers who spent that final night with him and his son, Moroni— perhaps on this very promontory, huddled from the wind within a cluster of trees which were the seedling ancestors of the cluster I was now approaching. I drew close enough to see Ether's face and the beauty of his aquiline and eternal features, and to see his smile and the radiance of compassion glowing in his eyes—a compassion so deep, so indescribable—so doubtlessly acquired from his bi-millennial sojourn in the presence of the Father. And then the ancient prophet faded away. All that remained was the cluster of trees, and in the center of it all, an old stump, scarred black by a single fulminating stroke of lightning.

You're a coward, Jim Hawkins! A desperately misguided coward, turning on the spit of your own stupidity and blindness. Look at your life! The mediocrity, the failure, the loneliness, the misery, the weakness, the poverty! Don't you know I can change all that? Don't you believe it?!

Yes, I believe every word, and that's why I'm going to finish what Ether had wanted to do more than two thousand years ago.

With my free hand, I grabbed the blackened stump. It was hollow and deteriorated. Using my weight, and expending only a little exertion, I pushed the stump completely over on its side, and as it fell, a layer of soil at its base folded up. Underneath it was a rectangular stone, thick and unevenly cut. I knelt to brush away the soil and roots. Then I utilized the sword in accomplishing the only worthwhile task of its existence, as a lever, to pry open the lid of the coffer and push the stone aside.

Peering into the box, there was only a reddish dirt, and what appeared to be slivers of metal—copper and silver—the remains of weapons long since eaten away by rust and time. I held the sword in both my hands, directly over its grave.

I curse you, Jim! The rest of your days I curse you! Look to death as your only escape, your only relief! This is a promise I will fulfill!

I dropped the sword. It fell into the coffer causing the soil there to fluff as it landed. I stood a moment longer in the wind, gazing down at Akish's creation one final moment, when suddenly it deteriorated before my eyes; the silver-plating on the copper flaked away and the jeweled hilt turned to dust. Then the blade itself shattered and cracked until everything which had once been Coriantumr's sword blended perfectly with the rest of the reddish dirt and slivers of metal around it.

A welcome, peaceful silence settled around me.

There were no more voices.

CHAPTER 28

Antonio found me early the next morning, sleeping tranquilly on that grassy summit, within the tiny cluster of trees. With his help, and the help of a few of his neighbors, we pulled Guillermo's rusty old Chevy from the ditch. I tried to give Antonio the rest of the money I'd saved for him in my pocket, but he refused to take it.

"You keep. You help us stop thieves on Vigia. I should pay you."

To emphasize his point, he gave me back my wallet. Looking inside it, I smiled. He'd decided to keep the pictures of my old girlfriends.

I drove back down the skinny, winding road into the village of Santiago Tuxtla and found Garth Plimpton in a local clinic, a heavy plaster cast molded around his right leg. He was mulling over a selection of Mexican chocolates. I chuckled inside, remembering Garth's old opinion that chocolate was often the best medicine for any ailment. When our eyes met, his face ignited into the warm, compassionate smile which was his trademark. He knew I'd accomplished the mission. We said nothing for several moments, and then Garth, upon noting my tattered condition, offered me a chocolate and said, "It looks like you might need one of these more than I do, my friend."

That night, we drove to Poza Rica. I couldn't help but feel a little apprehensive as we turned onto the dirt avenue leading to the home of Guillermo Corral. Neither Renae nor Jenny were the type of women who liked to be left stranded, so I prepared myself for the tongue-lashing of my life.

Approaching the house, Renae was waiting at the end of the driveway, as if something had whispered to her that we'd soon be arriving. I did get a scolding, but it wasn't so bad. After a moment, Renae allowed me to rescue her from her tears with a heartfelt embrace. To be true to my promise, I told her I loved her and we enjoyed our first kiss. I was only vaguely aware of the Corral children giggling around us.

Once I may have thought this moment should be circumscribed by sunsets or waterfalls. Though there may have been no pyrotechnics, there was a unity of heart, and I discovered that such unity carries a spectacle of its own, much more beautiful in its blazonry.

Thanks to my parents, there was a two-hundred dollar money order waiting for us at the Western Union in Brownsville, Texas, to get us the rest of the way home. Crossing the border at Matamoros, Mexico, Garth handed all his leftover pesos, about thirty dollars worth, to a boy with no legs, ambling around in the middle of the traffic on his hands, which extended below his hips, actually using his torso as if it were now a third appendage. As an afterthought, Garth also gave the boy his Spanish Book of Mormon from his days in Guatemala, which he stuck in a vendor's pouch on his waist with a nod of gratitude. After parking our car in a border stall for the immigration officials to search, we looked back across the Rio Grande and saw this boy in the shade of a giant tree, take the Book of Mormon out of his pouch, and begin reading its pages. Somehow, I consider this the most glorious image I took back with me to Wyoming.

A week or so later, I did a little missionary work myself and sent the Elders to Antonio's hut in Santiago Tuxtla. But alas, the old Indian was just too set in his ways. The Elders did write me a letter though, and told me their visits had inspired him to hang a picture of the Mexico City Temple on his wall. I hoped seeing that image every day would at least bring his family—all twenty-nine of them—a little closer, and perhaps entice them toward a greater love of God.

It was the happiest Christmas I'd ever remembered. Though numbers around the tree were small since my brothers spent the holiday with their wives' families, the strings of bright and blinking lights nevertheless reflected on the faces of my mother and my father, my beloved sister, Jennifer, my old comrade, Garth Plimpton, and my favorite Nephite, Muleki. Finally, the Christmas lights glowed on the tender features of my fiance', Renae Fenimore, having accepted my proposal on Christmas Eve.

In fulfillment of my desire that the girl I married remove the ring with the shiny blue stone from my finger, Renae set out to accomplish the feat. It wasn't quite like Arthur removing the sword from the stone, requiring almost an hour and a tub of margarine, but she got it off. Her motivation might have been rejuvenated toward the end when I told her it had been given to me by another girl.

The next week, Jenny, Renae and I spent much of our time studying for finals. Our professors had agreed to let us take them the first week of January, before Winter semester officially began.

Somehow I'd gotten it in my head that since Muleki's doctor said he should take it easy for a few weeks, the Nephite would stick around until at least the first of February. It was kind of a shock for us on New Year's Day when he announced, just hours before our scheduled departure for Utah, that he wanted to be driven to the foot of Cedar Mountain.

I contested, "But the doctor said your wound wouldn't be fully healed until—"

"It's okay, Jim." he interrupted. "I feel strong, and my work here is finished, thanks to you and the others."

"What about the Gadiantons?" I warned. "You said they might be guarding the way."

"Don't worry. I know a few tunnels which they don't. Besides, it's not my time to meet God. There's still much to do in Zarahemla in preparation for the Savior's coming. I feel I have a future role in that, if only to protect the lives of my cousin's children, Lehi and Nephi. You've been a great friend, Jim, but it's time for me to return to my people."

I thought of chiding him further, accusing him of being as stubborn as his father, but I feared he would only take it as a compliment.

It was a cold day, with a temperature near zero, even with the sun high in a cloudless sky. I drove the five of us in Jenny's faithful Mazda down the West Cody Strip until we reached the snowy foot of Cedar Mountain. Scanning its slopes, I realized it would not be a difficult hike. Much easier, in fact, than the hike to the top of Vigia. The road, though buried under six inches of white, was still well-defined and would take the Nephite right to the mouth of Frost Cave.

We all got out of the car to watch Muleki depart, even Garth. He was still using his crutches and winced when he accidentally stuck his bare toes, which protruded from his cast, into the snow.

More tears were shed. One froze on Muleki's cheek as well. I embraced my ancient friend, and made the mistake of calling him a Nephite one last time.

"Jershonite," he corrected.

Muleki finished his goodbyes and turned away, climbing a few paces up the mountain before Jenny, shedding too many tears to freeze, cried out his name. Muleki turned back and Jenny rushed forward to give him one final hug. He kissed her cheek and, with his hand, brushed her face tenderly where he had kissed.

"I'll think of you often," he told her, "and the wonderful family you'll raise in the latter days."

Garth looked away, a bit uncomfortable with Jenny's intensity of emotion. He had hoped she'd gotten over Muleki, and that her affections toward himself had solidified.

"Fortitude," I whispered to him.

Garth turned to me and smiled, "Right."

Jenny returned to stand with the rest of us, and the Captain of the Guard in the Palace of Helaman, Chief Judge of Zarahemla, raised his hand and cried, "Farewell, my friends. Whether we meet again in this life or the next, I know the reunion will be glorious."

He choked a bit on that last word.

Wearing my old blue and white parka, faded Levi jeans, and a pair of hightop tennis shoes—clothing I'm sure would be quite the conversation pieces in Zarahemla—Teancum's youngest son left his footsteps in the snow as he ascended the roadway which led to the top of Cedar Mountain. We watched him until he turned around to wave for the last time, and then the Jershonite disappeared behind a switchback and a row of serried pine.

Garth didn't fare as badly as he might have thought. When we dropped him off at his home in Rock Springs, Jenny raised up on her toes and gave him the kind of kiss which leaves men stuttering. In fact, I doubt he was able to communicate in complete sentences again until long after we'd driven away.

In spite of the display, Jenny remained elusive to Garth's affections for another semester. But fortunately, my old comrade had taken my advice to heart. After he'd returned to Harvard, he got a part-time job, doubtlessly to support his long distance phone calls to Heritage Halls.

In the succeeding months, he proposed to Jenny no less than three times—once when he came to BYU during Harvard's spring break, once just after school let out and he came to see her in Cody, and once in early June when she went to Rock Springs to see him. Each time the poor guy was tragically rejected by a woman who seemed eternally unready for that kind of commitment.

It wasn't until my wedding on June 16th, when I was sealed to Renae for time and all eternity in the Tower Room at the top of the spiral staircase in the Manti Temple, with Garth as my Best Man, and Jenny as the Maid of Honor, that the heart of my little sister finally melted. Two days later she accepted Garth's fourth proposal. I'd swear we could hear his whoop of triumph all the way to the *Hotel Filher* in San Luis Potosi, Mexico, where Renae and I spent our honeymoon.

As the years passed, I used to feel sorrow that my destruction of Coriantumr's sword did not end poverty or pain in the world. It did not end bloodshed and crime, nor did it end misery and loneliness. I found some satisfaction in believing it may have slowed those things down some; maybe it prevented a few wars from being fought before their time, maybe it gave a few more people a chance to discover Christ and repent from their sins. But in the end, I came to realize, the primary soul which may have been saved that December, was my own.

I had a resurgence of hope that when the battle lines of the last days became more distinctly drawn, and those with lukewarm convictions found it increasingly more difficult to remain Latter-day Saints, that perhaps I might recognize the signs prophets said could fool the very elect, and be one of the survivors.

The memories of my adventures among the Nephites were not taken from me this time. I kept them sacred and did not abuse them, as I'm sure was the Prophet Helaman's fear when he'd told me the memories would only remain as long as I kept them hidden in my heart. When I was thirteen, his fears were certainly justified. I was grateful I'd reached an age and awareness to have the blessing of recalling them out loud sometimes, usually when Garth and Jenny got together with us for holidays and special occasions.

Often, Garth and I would contemplate returning to that cavern at the top of Cedar Mountain to see if there was still an ancient world at the end of the tunnels waiting to greet us.

And who knows? Maybe one day something will force us to follow through with our contemplations.

The thought seems reasonable enough. In fact, it almost seems inevitable. Because one thing a man fears more than growing old, is growing too old for adventure.